Blue Cathedral

Blue Cathedral

Contemporary Short Fiction

edited by Kate Gale and Mark E. Cull

Red Hen Press

2000

Blue Cathedral

Since this page cannot legibly accomodate all the acknowledgments, the following pages *(v & vi)* constitute an extension of the copyright page.

Special thanks to Peter Pryor for copy editing,
and to our last minute readers, Mike Boas and Joe Beltran.

Cover art "Spirit Sky" by Beverly Cassel

Book and cover design by Mark E. Cull

ISBN 1-888996-21-8

Library of Congress Catalog Card Number 99-68885

Published by Red Hen Press

First Edition

ACKNOWLEDGMENTS

"Something that Hasn't Happened Yet" by Aaron Balkan. Copyright ©1998 by Aaron Balkan.

"The Job" by Steven Barthelme. First published in *Latitude 30°18'*. Copyright © 1985 by Steven Barthelme.

"The World's Greatest Saxophone Player" by Mark Blickley. First published in *Stories Good 'N Short*. Copyright © 1994 by Mark Blickley.

"The Ninth, in E Minor" by Frederick Busch. First published in *The Georgia Review*. Copyright © 1997 by Frederick Busch.

"Little America" by Alan Cheuse. First published in *Gulf Coast, Summer 1992*. Copyright © 1992 by Alan Cheuse.

"Wherebouts Are We?" by Janice Daugharty. First published in *Flint River Review*. Copyright © 1994 by Janice Daugharty.

"Ant" by Stuart Dybek. First published in *Ploughshares, Winter 1997-1998*. Copyright © 1997 by Stuart Dybek.

"Suicide Notebook" by Lucinda Ebersole. First published in the *Marlboro Review*. Copyright © 1999 by Lucinda Ebersole.

"Tlaloc's Paradise" by Deborah Eisenberg First published in the *Voice Literary Supplement*. Copyright © 1997 by Deborah Eisenberg.

"Scarves, Beads, Sandals" by Mavis Gallant. First published in *The New Yorker*. Copyright © 1995 by Mavis Gallant.

"The Wrestler" by Michael Guista. First published in *The Crunge No. IV*. Copyright © 1996 by Michael Guista.

"Por Favor" by Ad Hudler. First published in *Wisconsin Review, Summer 1998*. Copyright © 1998 by Ad Hudler.

"The Watch" by Kyle Jarrard. First published in *North American Review*. Copyright © 1997 by Kyle Jarrard.

Contents

Preface

Don't ask for the true story;
why do you need it?

from "True Story"
—Margaret Atwood

WE BEGAN IN THE DARK, and from the dark, we created myths, stories, the children of Israel wandering in the wilderness, Odysseus returning home, Buddha sitting lotus quiet. We had a few good stories to sustain our wanderings.

Over several thousand years, the fire of myths began to burn out. Or we burned them out. We burned Troy, the prophets, and Joan of Arc, and finally, as one myth after another descended onto the pile of ashes, we found ourselves outside the church, the cathedral, the pyramid, the synagogue, with no path, and no journey. No Holy Grail to seek for, no reason to seek a grail. We pick up the skull of the storyteller, turn it over in our hands, fumbling for the eye sockets that used to see something. We don't know how to handle the skull, with what ritual to bury it, what song to sing for the dead or the living. The stories in this collection, address this place in which we've found ourselves, more aware of the dead than the living. The dead had their myths and their fire.

We have heat that comes from nowhere, and music that emerges full blown from boxes. We are in that place, under a blue cathedral, where we move through the ashes of Troy to find new myths. We've seen the possibilities: a myth shattering and blinding and able to vaporize the world. Once we believed that the edge of the world was a pit with monsters, and now we've found that we are the monsters destroying the world, piece by piece.

We want that blue ocean again. The rebirth of myths and legends. These stories are written from that place where new myths emerge, where anyone is possible. The stories in this collection collide with the end of the century. They set the pace for a new aesthetic: a jarring, crucially important, vivid re-envisioning of the political and social space we inhabit. More and more of the readers of literature are writers themselves, and would like to understand how language moves. Many of these stories work with language in new ways, re-working the ways that language profoundly shifts the space in which we live and the way we see the world around us.

At the beginning of the new century, we are still reading short fiction, and hopefully still will be at the end of the next millennium. Short fiction like this. Short fiction that readers experience like swirling color into a glass of water, watching the shapes change and shift, until nothing in that space is ever the same.

Blue Cathedral

Stuart Dybek

Ant

SHE WAS DOZING on a faded Navajo blanket with the filmy shade of a maple tree drawn like a veil across her skin. Her blouse was still opened to where he'd unbuttoned it down to the sky blue of the bra she'd brought back as a souvenir from Italy.

Martin was lying just beyond the edge of the shadows thrown by her eyelashes. He had removed his shirt and spread it beneath him on the grass. It was hot and lounging in her company seemed to intensify the light. Even the birds were drowsy. Only a single ant was working. It had him by the toe.

"Trying to tow me away," he would have called out to her but for the lassitude, and her aversion to puns. The Woman Who Hates Puns, she sometimes called herself.

With his eyes closed and the sun warm on his lids it seemed as if he and the ant were the only creatures on the planet still awake. At first, Martin was simply amused by its efforts, but after awhile he began to sense a nearly imperceptible movement across the grass. He squinted up into the high blue sky, not caring really where he was headed. It was a day for such an attitude, but then most any day spent with her could trigger a mood like that, could require it, in fact. Since he'd met her, Martin had increasingly spent his days in a trance for which he had no name. To describe this addicting state of mind he joked that he was living in Limbo.

This was Limbo: high, heavenly-looking clouds that threw no shadow and assumed no shapes. No wind, yet a faint hiss in the trees. Sunlight faintly weighted with perfume. In Limbo, where dream ruled, siestas were mandatory. The grass slid gently beneath him without leaving a stain along his spine. Grass blades combed his hair as he went by until his hair assumed the slant of grass.

So long as it was only a single ant Martin didn't mind. He wouldn't tolerate them marching up his body in black columns, swarming, entering his mouth, ears, nostrils, and eyes in a pulsing stream as if he were just another corpse to clean.

It was a morbid vision, not in keeping with such a lovely day.

Even here in Limbo, Martin thought, one apparently never recovers from having had *Leiningen Versus the Ants* read to him as a child.

He could still remember his anticipation—a mix of excitement and terror—on those Sunday afternoons in summer when his Uncle Wayne would arrive with a storybook under his arm. Uncle Wayne would come to babysit for little Martin while

Martin's parents went out to the backyard barbecues from which they would return "pickled," as his father called it—though they looked more as if they'd been boiled—smelling of Manhattans, and laughing too easily and loudly.

"Remember," his mother would caution conspiratorially before she left, "Don't ask Uncle Wayne about the war. He doesn't like to talk about it. And don't worry if he doesn't talk much at all."

As young as Martin was, it was clear to him that the babysitting was as much for Uncle Wayne's sake as it was for the sake of Martin's parents or himself.

Uncle Wayne usually didn't talk much when his parents were there. He seemed shy, embarrassed, almost ashamed. His face was pitted with acne which gave him the look of a teenager. Sometimes, Martin imagined that Uncle Wayne's face had been pitted by shrapnel.

"Do you like stories," his uncle had asked him during their first visit.

"Sure," Martin said.

"Good. Stories are what kept me sane," Uncle Wayne said, then laughed in the odd, stifled way of his as if at a private joke between them.

But reading aloud, his uncle lost his shyness. Uncle Wayne didn't simply read stories, he brought them to life. During "The Most Dangerous Game," Martin had to run from room to room while his uncle, reading aloud the entire time, stalked him, the story book in one hand, and in the other a bow made from a clotheshanger strung with a rubberband and armed with an arrow fashioned from a cardboard pant guard.

When they read "The Monkey's Paw," Martin hid behind his bedroom door while his uncle mounted the stairs with the heavy-footed ominous tread of someone dead who'd been summoned back from the grave. Nearly quaking with fear, Martin had tried to wish him back into his grave while his Uncle Wayne pounded on the door.

His uncle would open the book by Edgar Allen Poe and turn to his favorite story, "The Tell-tale Heart," and the boy would force himself to watch his uncle's face so as not to miss the instantaneous transformation when his uncle's eyes assumed a maniacal gleam and his mouth twisted into a malevolent smile as he read the opening words—"True!—nervous—very, very dreadfully nervous I had been and am! but why *will* you say that I am mad?"— then burst into a spit-flecked spasm of psychopathic laughter.

But of all the stories they read together it was "Leiningen Versus the Ants" that was the most frightening and memorable. How many Sunday afternoons, while other boys watched double headers or shot baskets at a hoop suspended above a carport, had Martin sat sweating and listening intently as Uncle Wayne read about Leiningen making his way through the jungle, evading the hordes of army ants?

The ants streamed past barriers of water and fire, relentlessly consuming everything in their path with their black grinding mandibles, mandibles that could strip a man down to his bones as neatly and savagely as a school of piranhas.

Martin ran from the ants through the house, pursued by his uncle, who was draped in a blanket that served as the amorphous shape of massing ants. Martin would race around the table with the ants gaining on him, knocking over chairs as they went. He'd gallop up the stairs with the ants at his heels, slam himself into his room, but the weight of the ants would force open the door. He'd jump on his bed with nowhere else to run or hide as the ants oozed over his feet and began to engulf him while flushed and wild he'd beat at them with a pillow, tussling, wrestling, and finally, overpowered, nearly smothered by them he'd have to scream, "Leiningen doesn't die! The ants don't get him! The ants don't win!"

Only then, reminded of the authority of the story, would his uncle sink back, his acne feverish, hands shaking, and silently they'd both return downstairs, which is where Martin's parents would find them, eating popsicles and watching the ballgame, when they'd return home.

Remembering his uncle, Martin had forgotten the ant. There was an obvious bad pun there at which the Woman Who Hates Puns would have groaned. But even had Martin said it aloud, she might not have heard him, for the ant had managed to work its way beneath Martin's back, and seizing his belt with its mandibles had succeeded in lifting him off the ground the merest fraction of a millimeter, balancing Martin so perfectly that neither his head nor heels dragged. And having succeeded in carrying Martin across the boundary of Limbo, back into the ordinary world, the ant now proceeded at a considerably more determined pace.

They went along like that, hurrying away from his slumbering Love, like a grain of rice from a wedding.

Deborah Eisenberg

Tlaloc's Paradise

THE YOUNG AMERICAN at the door was looking for a place to rent; Jean knew that as soon as she saw him. No, almost that soon, but in fact she was first seized, facing him there, by the violent and irrational certainty that he had come to tell her something—that he'd come down from the States to tell her something about Leo.

It was a moment before she began to thaw out and catch up with the boy's disorderly excuses. His name was Mark something, he was telling her; he'd been talking to a man in a cafe near the square. This man had said she and her husband were likely to know if there were a place available. He was sorry to just show up at her home like this, but he'd gone to the shop earlier and found it closed. He'd tried to phone, of course, but the phones just didn't seem to *work*, and since the man in the cafe had given him directions to the house . . . How did people manage, by the way, with these phones? Though that was part of the charm of the country, wasn't it?

He looked at her, and immediately began to apologize again: a cliché; it must be no-end irritating to hear this sort of thing constantly. And the fact was, he rarely found himself anyplace where phones did work. But sometimes one just opened one's mouth, and out came some —

"Of course," Jean said. "Well, and besides." He was large, and almost puffy, as though with fatigue, or some mild, chronic inflammation. "Anyhow, I don't think anyone would argue that malfunction and charm are related, at least here."

"Hmmm." The boy frowned. "'Related.' Right. *Complicated* . . ."

"I'm afraid I don't know of any places at the moment," she said. "Leo would, probably, but you'll have to come back. I'm sorry. I'm afraid he's up in the States right now."

"Ah," the boy said.

"I'm sorry," Jean said. "You just missed him. He only went up this morning."

"Well." The boy frowned again, nodding. "Thanks. Too bad. Oh—Should I come back sometime? Yes, you said that, didn't you."

"Some other time," Jean said. "Yes."

"So," he said. "I'll try again next week?"

"Fine," she said.

He was so big, just standing there.

He ducked his head. "Well," he said. "Thanks."

She sighed. "Would you like to come in?"

Inside, he seemed even larger, and more formless, as though her fatigue were allowing him to spread into the far reaches of the large room. "Did you take the bus?" she asked, attempting to anchor her attention to one spot.

He had. He was pleased to be asked, she saw; the ride was short—she and Leo were no more than twenty minutes from town—but it was confusing, and, for strangers, difficult to negotiate. Clearly the boy was a good traveler—he'd found her after only one day in town, though he'd been in the country, he seemed to be saying now, for several weeks.

As he talked, his shadowy bulk moved here and there, beyond the soft canopy of lamp and candlelight, vaguely inspecting her emissaries, as it amused Leo to call them—the tall figures she'd constructed over the years, of various materials. "The man in the cafe *mentioned* you were a sculptor," the boy said, as though it were astonishing that this should, in fact, be so. *Mark*, she reminded herself. They looked like they were loitering there, in the dim margins, or massing.

"Welded?" the boy said.

"That one, yes." Fine, something she could talk about almost automatically. "A number of the early ones are, but I haven't worked in metal for years."

He hovered near one of the figures, peering. "Interesting," he said.

His caution made Jean smile. "You don't have to . . . I have no great stake in their quality, as it turns out."

Each had represented—witnessed and represented—pressing matters; attitudes, preoccupations . . . Pressing at the time. But eventually each figure was merely subsumed into the slowly expanding crowd. "It's just something I enjoy."

"Mmm." Mark frowned. "Enjoy . . ."

It wasn't his size, exactly—it was his obstacle-like quality. Still, Jean reminded herself. New places. Things abruptly inflating with a puzzling significance, or, just as suddenly, draining of any significance at all. She remembered: Herself and Leo, sitting gingerly, like this boy, wary lest some chance phrase burst into flames . . . "There shouldn't be much of a problem with a house for you," she said. "You're off-season, and there are a few vacation places Leo's been looking after."

Actually, there were probably some things she should take care of herself—plants, lights to outwit the tireless thieves . . . Neither she nor Leo had given any of that a thought in all the chaos of booking his ticket, getting in touch with friends in San Antonio, getting him on the plane. "When Leo's back he'll . . ." She sighed.

"I'd hate to have . . . I mean, well—a *house*. I hadn't really been thinking of a whole—And I'd hate to have . . . your husband go to trouble if—"

"Leo likes it," Jean said. "Can you imagine? Well, who knows. Maybe that's the sort of thing you like, too. I can't stand it myself. Dealing with the propane, dealing with keys, dealing with cleaning girls. But I suppose it makes Leo feel . . ." She picked up a cushion near her on the sofa, looked at it, then let it drop. "Well, he likes it, that's all. That's all."

Mark took a deep breath. "Also, the price is something I'd . . . I mean, I don't have all that much—"

"Of course," Jean said. No, obviously this boy wouldn't have any money. "Well, that's something everyone down here . . . Anyhow, owners tend to want someone just to . . . Actually, you know, I've probably got all kinds of keys around here somewhere. Of course, even if I could find them I wouldn't know what key was what. Leo always says he's going to label, but you know how it is. *Years* go by . . ." Her head felt rubbery. She pushed her hair back; she'd forgotten to wash it in the morning.

The boy was watching her. "Oh, listen," she said. "Would you—How stupid I am tonight. Mark. Would you like something to drink?"

"Yes," he said. "Sure, great. Oh, but maybe you—God, it's late. I hadn't—"

"No," she said. "Believe me. I never sleep till two."

"Well, great, then," he said.

He kept his eyes lowered; he seemed almost afraid to look at her. But when he did, the intensity of his scrutiny was outrageous, practically comical. What did he suppose it was that licensed him to display such curiosity? The fact of his youth? His status as newcomer? There was nothing to prevent her from being annoyed, Jean thought, just as he blinked, and turned his gaze to the French doors.

She watched his large, moist eyes. "So," she said. "What's up?"

He shook his head and turned back to her, looking bewildered. "Lots of stars . . ."

"Oh, lots," Jean said. "Always. Very busy at night."

So busy. She'd never gotten over it—that sky, this room, dim and glossy with tiles and Mexican mirrors; all the faces amid the complex refractions—the faces of those figures of hers, of the pre-Columbian pieces and the masks she and Leo had scattered around; the brilliant Mexican night beyond the doors, with its festive, agitated stars and roses. Sometimes she and Leo stood here stricken, with all of that right around them, as though it were something that had eluded them . . . "Oh, heavens," she said. "Sorry. Usually I'm a bit more—Listen, all I can offer you is Canadian Club. Well, there's beer or tequila, but you'll get deeply sick of those if you're sticking around. We always used to have these great, sloshing reservoirs of alcohol, but I'm afraid we seem to be down to bedrock. The dreadful truth is, we're utterly at the mercy of whatever anyone grabs on the way through duty-free."

He'd picked up a small stone carving from the coffee table. "Actually, I don't really drink," he said, turning the figure over in his hand. "Do you have a Coke, or something like that? But really, I don't want to keep you up."

How often was she supposed to ask him to stay? "Pre-Columbian," she said. "Not a very good piece, and in terrible condition, but I like it."

"A big personality," he said.

"Oh, yes," she said. "That's Tlaloc. Very important—a harvest-cycle type. In charge of rain, also militia. He has this special little heaven you got to go to if you were a warrior, or died of drowning. A friend of ours brought it the last time he came through. He has great luck finding interesting ones. We have a little Olmec lady he brought us. And the one over there's Chac-Mool, the messenger, who carried the sun around—Corrigan brought us that, too. And in fact he's responsible for most of our masks."

She reached over for the figure Mark was holding. It lay in her palm as she looked at it. "Good lord, you're dying of thirst, aren't you. You'll have to—I was up at the most horrible—"

"I'm sorry," Mark said. "You must be—"

"Mark, you know, people don't get *tired* when they get older, they get *impatient*. Oh, look—" Right, hardly his fault that she—"Is Sprite okay? Didn't even know we had it."

"Perfect," he said unhappily. "Sprite."

"Sprite it is." It had been a long time now since Corrigan had last been through. He hadn't even been living in his Mixtec village then, just out in the desert by himself. And he'd seemed to be floating, ever so slightly away from them. She'd thought perhaps she was imagining it, but looking back she was sure. Of course eccentricities often began as choices, or tools, or positions. But they could take you captive . . . "You're not going to have some sort of religious crisis, Mark, are you, if I have a drink?"

"No—" He cleared his throat. "Oh, not at all. I mean, I used to drink, myself."

"You used to?" she said. "My God. How old are you?"

"Twenty-eight." He looked at her. "Is that—"

"Reasonable," she said. "I suppose. And neutral. Insofar as I'm concerned, at least."

"Strange," he said. "Isn't it? Such a narrow range. I mean, I can't tell at all how old you are. And then it just closes up behind you again, doesn't it. I mean, I can't tell if someone's seventeen or twenty-two."

"Seventeen or twenty-two," Jean said. "Ha. I can't tell if someone's seventeen or fifty. Jesus, you know, if the truth be told, I *loathe* CC. And you know what else? I can't even remember who the cheapskate was who . . . You see, at one time we used to have all sorts of . . . Ah, well. The fact is, people simply don't come down here the way they used to."

"No." He frowned. "I suppose not."

Twenty-eight. Yes, she could see it. He was boyish-looking, and easily unbalanced, but a backlog of worry seemed to slow, or blur, his movements. Although his features were unremarkable and blunt, his expression reflected with great purity the finest modulations of his embarrassment and confusion. Her filthy hair! Her undisguised rancor! Well, all something for him to contemplate, wasn't it; Jean noted dispassionately the thorny little tendrils of amusement uncurling within her at the consternation she was causing her guest.

"When is—when is your husband expected back?" he asked.

"It shouldn't be long," she said. "He's just up for tests."

"I'm sorry," he said. "Is that bad?"

She rubbed the bridge of her nose. Amazing, the tiny, tiny things you could do to make yourself feel better. Rubbing the bridge of your nose, your temples . . . There was some spot on her palm where Leo could rest his thumb, and the muscles of her back and neck would relax . . .

"I'm sorry," the boy said again.

"It's just tests," Jean said.

She propped her feet—nice feet, small feet, even in their funny sneakers—against the coffee table and leaned back, looking at the ceiling. Mark had gotten his hands into the middle of some futile gesture; from the corner of her eye she watched him trying to resolve it.

"Anyway, though, it still is interesting," he said. "Isn't it."

"Yes?" She lifted an eyebrow. "What is?"

"This place." He squirmed, but persevered. "This country. Even though people don't come here as much. It's still interesting."

"Ah," Jean said.

"The man in the cafe was interesting," he offered after a moment.

Jean meted out a glance of enquiry.

"The man who told me about you and Mr. Soyer."

"Ah, yes."

"He was German, I think. Well, I mean, he was."

"Plenty of Germans around," Jean said.

"This one was old—"

"Plenty of old Germans."

"A real character. He kept making these sort of . . . dark allusions. You know, he'd say, 'The *coffee* at this place is better than the *coffee* next door. Have you *tried theirs?*' It was as though he was a spy, and I was a spy, too, only no one had bothered to let me know."

Jean laughed abruptly. Beyond the seismic dislocation of her body she saw the boy peering at her with hope.

"And then for hours afterwards," he said, "everything seemed like that. As though everyone was telling me something else."

"Sounds like Schacht," Jean said.

"Actually, though, you know what?" Mark said. "Everything *is* like that, sort of, isn't it? I mean everyone *is* telling you . . . *is* telling you—Oh, and he had a kind of funny eye, I think, too."

"Yup," Jean said. "Schacht." Schacht sat at the cafes all day, a hairy disk of a spider, hors de combat. His legs dangled from his chair and one eye would drift enigmatically in and out of alignment while he waited for Mexican boys. A sufficient number were on hand, always, desperate for a meal—the price was no greater than an hour or two of boredom and the humorous remarks of one's friends.

"He was sort of nice, though, I think," Mark said. Jean looked at him, but his face had gone deceptively blank. "He seemed lonely."

"Lonely," Jean said. "Well, if you can't really talk about your life—I mean, people manage to believe all sorts of things about themselves, don't they. And it's very isolating to have an official view of your life with something else locked up somewhere."

"Do you—" A slightly gluttonous shine appeared in Mark's stare. "God. I've never actually met anyone from that—"

"Well, who knows, really," Jean said. She and Leo always referred to Schacht as "the Nazi," but his hand, as it clung to hers in greeting, was the hand of any old man—tremulous and age-spotted. "Actually, though, it's interesting—there's a place here, in town. Run by an Austrian family. And all the old Germans and Austrians in the area sit around shoveling down great slabs of swine and what-not, that's cooked and served by Mexicans. And they're all schmoozing away in German. Pretending, believe it or not, that they were born in Mexico, or that they were in this or that resistance. Oh, I mean there are bound to be a few old Jews, and a few old déclassé aristos from one side of the fence or the other, and maybe one or two of them really did hold a match to party headquarters at Berchtesgaden or whatever. But that was simply not the story with most of them, obviously—the place is swarming with fake passports and fake histories. But whoever those people were once, they're all sitting together now, missing the same real pastries, the same real streets . . ."

Mark nodded. "Oh, strangeness," he said. "Opacity."

As he and Jean raised their glasses to one another she saw a little heap—translucent, gelatinous, torn things. Memories, discarded by the barbed wire under a tiny, oil-colored sun. A little heap, growing on the icy soil as a shivering procession filed, naked and desperate as angels, past the guard post, where meaningless new memories were being issued. "Anyhow." Jean closed her eyes. "Pardon me, but another burning question—what's brought you down?"

"Oh, me." Mark shook his head. "Well, me. All right, let's—So who am I, what am I doing here, what—hmm. Okay, I was studying. Engineering, which is not such a ridiculous . . . But then I was finished, and I realized, my God, you know. This is my *life*, which I sort of hadn't grasped until then. And also at the same time, more or less, my father died. And I realized I hadn't known too much about him. And everything that I didn't know actually didn't *exist* any longer. And what did still exist was any little thing I did happen to know . . . And everything was just *flying* off the face of the earth, just flying *off* . . . But I didn't know how to . . . But anything less just seemed pointless. So I began to just sort of rush around, I guess. For a while I was catching salmon. For big companies off the coast of Alaska." He looked at her. "It's amazingly hard."

She nodded.

"And then I was working in the oil fields. Along the Amazon. Which isn't so easy either, in fact." He stared at the little stone carving on the table. "Anyhow, my Spanish isn't that bad. So." He looked out the doors again, voyaging.

"Where did you stay last night?" Jean asked quietly.

He sighed hugely, coming to rest. "Oh, I've put myself at El Parque. It's kind of a splurge. I mean, the room is fairly primitive—except for the bugs. Those bugs—wow, *advanced*. But I've got a view. I look right out onto the square, you know? So this morning I ran out to the market for oranges and bread, and then I came back and had breakfast on my balcony."

Jean leaned back and smiled.

"That square," he said. "It's really . . ."

"Hypnotizing," she said. "I know. And the incredible thing is, it simply never changes. It's absolutely eternal. Every day, decade after decade. The children, the old people, the band in the bandshell, the flowers, the fountains . . . Except that the children are always new children and the old people are always new old people and the flowers are always new flowers . . . The sun comes up, the sun goes down—all these years, and we've never gotten tired of it . . ."

"How many years?" Mark leaned forward. "Incidentally."

Jean regarded her glass—the answer seemed to be sleeping, deliciously, at the bottom of her drink. "Well," she said, slowly, "the fact is. We came down in the fifties."

"Mm," he said, with tact so inept that she laughed out loud.

"Yes, hundreds of—"

"Not at—"

"Anyhow," she said, "a lot of us came down then. Terrible things were going on in the States. Comparatively subtle, but nonetheless . . ."

"Oh, right," he said. "My mom and dad used to tell me. How everyone had to look exactly alike, and everyone had to be completely happy . . ."

"Yes . . ." she said. "Well, listen, Mark. You probably don't know much about it, but there were these sort of mild purges . . . You know, nobody was going around killing anybody, so it was all very vague and insidious. It was sort of a warning, really. Later everyone laughed about how absurd it all was, but I tell you, Mark, people just kept on being very, very careful. In their actions and in their thoughts, without actually remembering, or even knowing, exactly why."

He squinted at her, as though he could extract her meaning by looking. "Yes," he said. "Oh, actually, you know, I had a cousin, or something. No. My mom's uncle, Frank, she told me. She was still absolutely furious. The FBI came to the house, and Frank lost his job. But"—Mark looked at Jean with surprise, as though it were he who was hearing the story for the first time—"he wasn't a *Com*munist. He was an ichthyologist."

Jean looked at him. "Oh, yeah. Well. Anyhow, Mexico had a lot of glamour at that time. You know, that luster that moves around from place to place. Jesus, Mexico City—You can't—So jaunty. And pretty and chic. And the whole, strange, gorgeous country. The way those names sounded to us—Chiapas, Cuilapan, Patzcuaro, Tepotzlan, Ixtlan del Rio . . . Imagine how that felt—going where words like that were still alive! And all these fresh memories of bandit-saints and campesino intellectuals and painter-revolutionaries. And wild people from simply everywhere, those people who always go places to start things new . . . There was this one woman—a sort of Russian Gypsy Jew, truly stunning. She'd arrive on horseback. All this *red* hair. Men were simply shooting each other by the score . . ."

Mark nodded respectfully.

"Boring, boring," Jean said. "I know. Jesus Christ, we don't even get *movies* anymore. The currency's so fucking rotten they can't even import movies." She rested her fingertips against her eyes; if she could only keep herself from *talking*, maybe he'd . . .

"Mexico City—" But there was his voice again. Soft, relentless. "Mexico City's gotten pretty difficult, I guess."

"The thing is—" Jean looked at him. "She *died* a week or so ago. Someone happened to tell us. We only heard by chance. She drank. I mean, she was old—considerably older than, than we are—But, I mean, she fell. She fell down the fucking *stairs*."

Mark reddened. "Wow, that's—"

"Isn't it just," Jean said. "Anyhow, difficult, difficult. Yes, difficult, now, Mexico City. We all started off there, of course. Then most of our friends just went back up, but some stayed, and we came down here. For a long time we lived right in town. Our friend Corrigan—the mask guy?—lived right next door to us. Then he moved out here, long before we did. Now he lives way off in hell-and-gone by himself. Well, not by himself in his opinion—he's got one of those hateful little, those dogs. An esquintle, it's called."

"Oh, yes," Mark said. "One of those—"

"It's Aztec, he says, so he speaks to it in Nahuatl."

"Oh." Mark frowned. "That's funny."

"Funny," Jean agreed. "So, Mark. I'm having another of those delicious—How about you? More yum-yum Sprite?"

"Well. Don't mind if I—" He handed her his glass and wiggled his eyebrows elaborately.

"Such talent," she said. "It's actually been a couple of years, now, since we've seen him. I mean, I'm sure he's fine. Always up to his . . . In fact, we heard he was trying to generate his own electricity. Out of old socks, you may be sure, or something."

For a moment her voice split into harmonics, exposing a chord of other voices, crowding the room. Then a blinding sheet of desert light fell, and against its silence the tiny, distant figure of Corrigan was walking, walking . . . Jean closed her eyes. "The last time we saw him, he was teaching it Mixtec, too."

"Pardon?" Mark said.

Jean shook her head.

"Those stars. . ." He stood and went to the French doors.

There was no haze at all, Jean saw, or softness in the air. The stars snapped brilliantly against flat black, as if this were to be their final appearance.

"Strange," he said. "That people would get it into their heads that those things determined what went on down here."

"That anything determined what went on down here," Jean said.

He stood, looking out at the night. "Who are the women in red?" he asked.

Jean stood in alarm. "The women—"

"No, sorry," he said. "Not—"

"Oh—" She flopped back down.

"Not here. I meant the women in the square who wear those long red—"

"Yes, yes—" She'd known just who he meant. But for an instant she'd thought he was *seeing* them; that they'd come up here for some reason. For her.

"No, sorry, just—I watched them all day. The way they glide. Up and down in the square. I couldn't imagine who—"

"Yes," she said. "Indians. I mean, obviously."

"They look—They don't look—"

"No, not exactly real. A Tzotzil group, but I don't . . . they're not really from this area; they seem to be . . . well, 'displaced' is how people . . . God, Leo did the most marvelous paintings of them in the square at one time. I wonder—"

"I'd love to see them." Mark squinted eagerly past the fuzzy goldish mass of light in the center of the room.

"Ah, well," Jean said. "There aren't any here, in any case."

All this talk of hers, this evening; all this noise. And now she seemed to have implied this boy should come back. For more talk, more noise. "Actually, I think Leo probably threw all that stuff out when he gave up painting."

Mark started to speak, then stopped.

Jean shrugged. "He didn't think he would ever be good enough," she said clearly.

After a minute Mark spoke. "That's very courageous."

"Is it?" Jean said. "Oh, listen. Courageous, cowardly, who knows. It actually wasn't very painful for Leo to give it up. He just stopped, the same way I just continued. People have different ways of holding on to things. Our friend Corrigan, for example. In a sense he's the most acquisitive person I've ever met. If he sees something that interests him, an unusual mask, for example, or one of those pieces like that little thing on the table, he'll go to any lengths to get ahold of it. But then he just gives it away again as soon as he possibly can. The fact is, it makes Leo happy to give things up. It's a kind of exercise, I suppose. He's never so happy as when he's giving something up, or leaving something behind." The phrase sounded flat to Jean, as she heard herself saying it now, or sententious. Was it true, she wondered—Had it been true at some point? Or was it just something rather like the truth that she and Leo had settled on?

Mark was watching her intently. "Tell me something," he said. "Do you ever think of going back?"

"Back," she said. "And what would that mean, 'back'?"

Every day, how many species was it that disappeared, now, forever? There was some horrifying statistic—it used to be four hundred a year, she had read somewhere; now it was hundreds every day. And cadres of botanists, zoologists, anthropologists, God only knew what, swarming over the globe with instruments of every sort, praying to catch sight of one rare, precious organism or another as it died. "Oh, of course it's very nice to think—very seductive—that you have some sort of 'home' somewhere, that you could return to, that would make some kind of sense of your life. And Leo and I have always prided ourselves, I suppose, on resisting that. Because, a *place*—I mean, what is that? A place. What you leave, what you go to; here or there, 'home' or 'foreign'—Well, it's all based on, on the most fantastic misunderstanding, isn't it."

But was that true, either? Chiapas, Cuilapan, Patzcuaro, Tepotzlan, Ixtlan del Rio—ancient fragments irradiated by an ancient light. Yes, what she and Leo had left behind vanished with their departure, and what they'd wanted here had vanished, too. Vanished, not into the past, nor into some relinquished area of fantasy, but into the future. Into the future. Evidence of a continuity, of a fugitive precision would appear without notice—a swift concentration of the afternoon into heavy, golden shapes; a face like a key, glimpsed in the market; a perfect, trembling balance in the square as seen for an instant from a balcony . . . promises.

The nights here still smelled like honey. Jean could still be made happy by the braying of a neighbor's burro. Back when Mexico City had faded and they'd come out here, the nights always smelled of honey and woodsmoke, the days of chocolate and earth and peppers—rich anchos and poblanos in sacks at the market. How clean everything had been! The revolution had left the campesinos as penniless as ever, as clean as bones. They'd worn white; the coarse-loomed cloth showed up in the fields miles away. Roosters woke you, cacti bloomed in the churchyards. Toxins from new industry and traffic seeped into the earth, corroded the organs of the children. One murderous poverty replaced another. Refugees appeared, Indians, fleeing internment and slaughter in Guatemala and the secret wars up here, out in the muffled desert. Corrigan used to bring word of skirmishes. From time to time rumors would flicker through town. Alicia, who cooked for them, might let something slip, or Ramon, who brought the great jars of water. Once in a while, someone was said to disappear—someone's cousin, someone's son . . . The Tzotzil women moved back and forth across the square, in constantly changing configurations of blood red against the white walkways. They approached as you sat by the fountains, under the elegant palms. They stretched out their arms. You could hardly hear their voices. They looked past you, at something that happened in the distance. The tourists, dazzled by the beauty of their clothing and unearthly, famished faces, dropped small sums into their hands. Who were the women in red, they asked.

One shrugged: They were widows.

Often now—whispers of special forces deployed in the desert. Sometimes one would hear faint, high tones in the night, like bullets striking rock—"Was that the phone?" Jean said.

"No," Mark said.

"Ah," Jean said.

"Yes." He stood. "It's late. I'll leave you." His soft voice floated next to her ear. "Thank you, Mrs. Soyer, you've been—"

"Jean," she said. "Hardly." She closed her eyes, and the room blazed again with desert light. Why hadn't she gone up this morning? So long ago, that bright sun. The Tzotzil women would be dozing now, wrapped in lengths of red. Schacht, having a final tequila while he gazed out at the dark square. And up there—The suffocating imminence of drugged sleep? Rapid footsteps down the corridor? Whatever was happening in that white bed, she would wake up here in the mornings, she would go to the shop. She would come home and eat the food Alicia had prepared, have a drink, look at the stars . . . It had seemed ridiculous, in all that sunlight, to think of going along. Ridiculous, and imprudent, as though panic itself were malignant. All yesterday he had done his little tasks around the house, around the yard. Even this morning—He'd looked up at her from his gardening, shading his eyes against the sun, with the trowel still wedged in the earth—"So then." That soft voice. "Next week."

"Next week . . ." Jean repeated, but for moments she couldn't think what the boy was talking about.

Ad Hudler

Por Favor

I BET MY WHOLE SAVINGS of twenty-five dollars on some stupid horse with a promising name: Rosita's Rainbow. Pot of gold at the end, I thought, and Rosita sounds enough like my name, Rosa. It had to happen, but it didn't, and now I have nothing. Rosa has nada—again. Either I go back to work at El Sombrero or I do the sign thing out on the street again, and I m not sure about the sign thing because it's already July and the asphalt is starting to feel like that hot bread pudding I used to serve at Whittier's Pub.

I got fired at El Sombrero two weeks ago, but I think Marie would take me back. That was a bad day, *muy malo*. I was serving some couple who thought they could speak Spanish. After I took their order I was walking away from the table when the lady said, "Oh, y sin hielo, por favor."

"Sin hielo?" I asked. "Sin hielo? No ice? Lady, quit acting like you're on a trip to Mexico. This is St. Louis, they have chlorine in the water here."

I served them water with ice, and they got me fired. I should have looked at their car. Leticia always says you can tell a lot about gringos by their cars. They drove a Range Rover, silver with black stripes. Leticia says people in Range Rovers don't stop when they hit a dog.

Let me tell you how I got my twenty-five dollars, which really started as sixty-five but I spent forty for dinner at Red Lobster for me and my son, Willie. After Marie fired me, Leticia gave me the sign idea. Just stand out there on the corner, Rosa, over by Home Depot. Doesn't have to be anything great, just a piece of cardboard from a banana box, and you can get those behind the Albertson's. Most people will be too scared to hire you, she said, but they'll throw money in your can or hat or whatever. I borrowed a marker from Enrique in the deli: *Need job. Hard worker.* You wouldn't believe how many people throw you money, like burned-down cigarettes, out their windows when they drive by. A quarter here, dollar there, sometimes a five. Look for the Volvos and Chevy Suburbans, Leticia said. After a few days I got smart and moved to the Talbots on River Road. Good move, Rosa; I pulled in fifty-seven dollars one day. The more bags the ladies carry outside of Talbots, the more money they throw into my Folgers can. They never say nothing, and I don't think they look at me, but they almost always wear dark glasses so I don't know for sure. Leticia says be careful of dark glasses, because you can't see their eyes so you don't know what they're really thinking. Leticia's smart, big heart too; when I left Alberto she took me and Willie in. We met her at the Lotto machine at the Circle K on Manchester. She said, "I get Social Security, you can stay with me for awhile but you can't have any money from me." Willie is eleven. If I'm out working Leticia watches him when he gets out of school. He goes to Kennedy.

Anyway, one day a big blue Cadillac pulled up outside Talbots. The man inside, he wore more gold than a woman—gold necklace, gold bracelets, four or five rings. Leticia says people in Cadillacs like to spend money they don't have, so I opened the door and said, "Buenas tardes." I never let them know I speak fluent English, just a little. He turned down the jazz on the radio.

"I have some housekeeping I need done. Does six dollars an hour sound good?"

"Senor?"

"Housekeeping? Cleaning?" I just looked at him, pretending I didn't understand and then he said, "Hoover? Pledge? Spic 'n Span?"

"Oh, si, si!" As he talked, I looked around his car as fast as I could to see if he was some weirdo or something. There was a receipt from the ATM on the floor that I couldn't read and a takeout box from some place named Monty's or something like that. He reached over to move his briefcase off the seat and I saw that one of his bracelets had the diabetic sign on it—you know, that red star thing with the snake. I don't like snakes, but Leticia says diabetics can't get it hard, so I figured it was safe to go with this guy, and I got into the Cadillac. He smiled at me and turned the music back up. Real leather seats, nice. His car was real quiet, no leaky windows or rattles or shakes or anything. Being rich means you have a quiet car, I've learned that.

After about fifteen minutes, I was getting a little nervous, but then he turned off eighty, onto some exit called Parker Road. "Almost there," he said. I smiled and shook my head like a stupid Mexican is supposed to do.

Let me tell you about this house: Incredible. There were two cement lions on the porch just like the ones at Maximilian's castle in Chapultepec Park. Inside was this huge chandelier and white carpeting everywhere, wall to wall. We walked across a big rug that looked like a flower garden and went out to the swimming pool.

"Me work now?" I said, but I wondered what I was going to do because this house was already as clean as Ethan Allen, where I used to pack furniture. Mr. Cadillac brought me a feather duster, and then he disappeared. I noticed pictures sitting on the table in the TV room, so I started dusting there first. His wife was kind of fat, but beautiful and blond hair. Three kids, too, grownups now. Mr. Cadillac had their college pictures taken with those graduation hats that look like flat roofs. It made me think of a joke for Willie: Hey, Willie, you gotta go to college to get a roof over your head. Ha.

I was just doing my job when all of a sudden I turned around and there he stood—I swear to God—he stood there in some cocktail waitress outfit, with stockings and everything. Really fancy, lots of white lace. He wore gold earrings and pink lipstick and spike-heeled sandals. "Sweet Jesus," I whispered.

"Can I take your order?" he said to me. Can you believe it? I didn't want him to know I understood, so I shook my head and said, "No comprendo," and I stared because I had never seen such big feet in strappy sandals. They looked like heels of white bread stuck in the wire of a toaster. I thought, dear Jesus help this man.

"Can I take your order?" he asked me again, and he pulled a pencil and pad out of his pocket, just like the one I used at El Sombrero. I wondered if he knew I used to be a waitress, and if this was some kind of joke or putdown or something. I thought I'd better answer him.

"Si," I replied. "Tiene usted hamburgesas?" I was really hungry. The last time I ate was that morning, and it was only those little jars of jelly I took from the room service trays when I cleaned rooms at the Hyatt.

"Cerveza?" he asked.

"No, no, ham-bur-ge-sa," I told him again, and I held up a pretend hamburger and took a big bite, like this.

This man, God help him, he walked into the kitchen on those heels and brought me back a Budweiser and a bowl of Fritos. I really wasn't too worried, with him pretending to be a woman and everything. He seemed kind of sweet, so I sat back and let myself be waited on. Rosa, I said, you deserve this. It's your turn. I felt like I was playing a game with my son, Willie.

He brought more Fritos and then some ice cream. As I ate he kept wiping down the table and the other furniture, the kinds of things you have to do between the lunch and dinner rush. He brought me another beer, then another, and I started feeling a little like the water in the swimming pool.

"Can I bring you anything else?" Mr. Cadillac asked me.

"No, gracias." But let me tell you I was dying to ask him all kinds of things: Where's your wife? What's with the cocktail outfit? Where did you buy your shoes? But I always feel safer if people know I don't understand them. I try to be like a dog. Leticia says people kick dogs but they won't shoot them.

He lead me into the house. Some CD was playing, Patsy Cline. I know that because I'd heard it on the jukebox in the restaurant. The words went "crazy, I'm crazy for feeling so lonely," and I thought to myself, Rosa, you're crazy alright. What have you got yourself into?

Mr. Cadillac told me to sit in his leather chair and put my feet up on the stool. He took off my shoes and socks—that made me a little nervous—and he poured some oil on my toes that smelled like the peppermints at the cash register. Mr. Cadillac started—and this is all true, believe me—he started to massage my feet. I told Leticia I'd never felt anything so good in all my life. First he pushed his hands on the bottoms, like he was kneading dough, then he started to run his slick finger back and forth between my toes, which kind of excited me and made me a little nervous, so I jumped up and said, "Dance? Dance?" It was a slow song. I was a little taller than he was, maybe four inches, okay maybe five or six, and he laid his head down on my chest and closed his eyes.

We rocked back and forth, and after a few minutes he started to cry, kinda loud you know, sobbing, five minutes maybe. Then he stepped back and looked at me. The mascara gave him black eyes. He stumbled in his heels over to the kitchen table and pulled sixty-five dollars out of his wallet and I stuffed it in my bra. I could tell he needed another hug, some more crying, too, so I hugged him again. That's when I saw the clock over the refrigerator and it said three-thirty. Leticia told me to be back by four-thirty to get Willie because she had some errands to run. I hugged him once more, patted Mr. Cadillac's hairy back, and I wondered if the Belmont bus came out this far.

David Starkey

Rice

From: kreutzer1@indorice.com
To: rberryman@genetoplex.com
Subject: Arrival in Calcutta

Mr. Berryman,

This will follow-up on the several voice-mail messages I've left you over the past week or so. (The time difference makes it difficult to get in touch by phone.) I was FINALLY able to open an e-mail account at the IndoRice corporate headquarters in Calcutta. Telecommunications here, as you can imagine, are not what they are at home.

Let me apprise you of my progress. All the flights from New Delhi were booked. Evidently I should have offered some sort of "gratuity," or bribe to get on board, but I didn't know that. So I got a train, which took thirty hellish hours. I did get a chance to see some of the landscape of West Bengal through my filthy window: terraced paddy fields, thatched huts, coconut palms, children stripped to the waist staring at the train. Methods of cultivation are very primitive, but clearly labor costs are low as well.

At Howrah Station I was besieged. Women and children scrambled on board grabbing at everything unattended—plastic bags, newspapers, scraps of food, empty plastic water bottles. Porters snatched my luggage, though I gallantly tried to hang on. A boy of about ten tugged at my sleeve so persistently that I slapped his hand. I felt bad about that for a while, but the poor don't give you a moment's rest.

West Bengal, as you know, is one of the two communist states in India (Kerala, the other) and there are abundant signs of the Marxist government. Heavy traffic on Lenin Sarani is frequently slowed by protest marches—strikers from the university or hospitals or some union. Red hammers and sickles are stenciled on the bus windows.

Anyway, enough of the sight-seeing. I checked into the Oberoi Grand—fairly decent accommodations—and immediately set up a meeting with the staff of IndoRice. Most of them seem to be shocked by the news. They had no idea that Genetoplex had just purchased a 51% share of their stock. I got the usual questions about hirings and firings, etc., but—as instructed—I told them that at this time we intended to keep things pretty much on course, that we wouldn't be acquiring IndoRice if we didn't think it had vast earnings potential, blah blah blah. They seemed to swallow most of it and I've been busy with the paperwork ever since.

I'll keep you informed.

Sincerely,

Jeffrey Kreutzer

From: rberryman@genetoplex.com
To: kreutzer1@indorice.com
Subject: Well done

Kreutzer,

We knew this wasn't going to be easy, but you seem to have taken the bull by the horns. Be polite, but let them know who's boss.

Incidentally, everyone in the office enjoyed your little travelogue. Don't skimp on the local color. We get a kick out of it.

—RB

From: kreutzer1@indorice.com
To: rberryman@genetoplex.com
Subject: Working out snafus

Mr. Berryman,

We're slightly stalled in the matters of long-term research and development collaboration in the biotech department. They want more autonomy than I think we're willing to give. I'm trying to use a velvet hammer, but it can be difficult to pin

Indians down to specifics. Even when you think they've agreed, they haven't. And it turns out that when they shake their heads *No*, it really means *Yes*.

Anyway, I had a free afternoon today—two of their bigwigs had to attend a conference—so I took a walk around the city. It's incredibly hot here. (Reminds me of the time Genetoplex bought out Deveurex Inc. in Baton Rouge, and I had to spend the summer down there tying up loose ends.) I felt feverish in the overwhelming heat, but for the benefit of the folks back home, here are some of the things I saw. Packed trams. Whippet-thin rickshaw pullers hauling loads an elephant shouldn't be able to tow. A sprinkling of rain on the dusty neem trees. Men in dirty red turbans carrying twenty-foot lengths of pipe on their shoulders. Policemen in white uniforms with polished black boots. A very ambiguous sign on the back of a bus: "STOP GOOD LUCK."

The Indians are natural businesspeople, and the sidewalks are alive with commerce. A bare-chested man kneels to be shaved. Families cook over smoking braziers. Young men feed sugar cane into presses and sell the juice to a line of people who drink from the same stainless steel cup. As you walk along, you have to watch out for cow dung and sleeping people and dogs. The whole city sometimes smells like an outhouse, but on the whole I like it rather than otherwise. The people at IndoRice—especially the project manager, Paryag Chatterji—have been very nice. They think we're going to make them rich.

Sincerely,

Jeffrey Kreutzer

From: rberryman@genetoplex.com
To: kreutzer1@indorice.com
Subject: Keep your eye on the ball

In regard to the phone call you made to Whitman on Friday: You're right, engineering plants that tolerate current products may be cheaper than developing a new herbicide.

And don't forget to go the whole nine yards on the licensing revenues, Kreutzer. That's very important to us, and there may be a big bonus in it for you.

—RB

P.S. Good stuff about the city walk. Keep it coming. I forwarded your message home and my wife (who was an English major in college) loved it.

From: kreutzer1@indorice.com
To: rberryman@genetoplex.com
Subject: Cash tender offer from Stengel Industrie

Mr. Berryman,

As you know, rumors have been flying in the business pages of the Indian papers that we may be outflanked in our acquisition of Class A voting stock (as opposed to the Class B nonvoting shares that seem to have been dumped on us). The Germans have made a big impression with the Communist government here—don't ask me why. Please advise Corporate that significant steps to squelch any doubts about our authority need to be taken SOON. I'm only as strong as my home office, Mr. Berryman. I know you're aware of that.

In any case, I took another long walk this evening to clear my head. In Kumartali, the potters' colony, I rested on a stoop in the shade and watched a man sculpt the goddess Kali from clay. Four arms waved from her sides, her tongue stuck out, a necklace of human skulls hung around her neck. She's the goddess of death. Year-round the potters work making images for the Durga Puja, Calcutta's most important festival. In October, at the end of the three-day celebration, every single statue is dumped into the Hooghly where they mix with the rest of the silt already on the riverbed.

To spend all that time creating something you're going to destroy—I thought that was very profound. Very ironic, yet fitting somehow. After all, isn't life itself a kind of elaborate preparation for death? It makes you wonder, doesn't it?

Regards to Mrs. Berryman.

Yours truly,

Jeff Kreutzer

From: rberryman@genetoplex.com
To: kreutzer1@indorice.com
Subject: The cavalry saves the day again

Kreutzer,

I guess you will have heard via Whitman about the slight of hand we pulled on Stengel re. voting vs. total outstanding common stock. We are positioned to be the premier player in IndoRice's future, and no doubts about it now. It's up to you to nail down the issue of crop technology, then come on home.

By the way, Mrs. B. thinks you missed your calling: you should have been a poet.

—RB

From: kreutzer1@indorice.com
To: rberryman@genetoplex.com
Subject: The poetry of Rabindranath Tagore

Richard Berryman,

Per Whitman's fax of a couple of days ago, I went out to see some of IndoRice's experimental paddies in the country west of Calcutta.

How green everything is! A herd-boy was coaxing his cow in the river for a bath. The bamboo groves made a restful swishing noise when the wind blew. A cool moist fragrance rose up from the wet earth and the acacia flowers.

Paryag Chatterji and I were talking about estimated annual yield and insecticide-resistant strains, when I just sort of realized how lovely Bengal is. It was so quiet and peaceful then, I couldn't help but be reminded of part of a poem in a book Paryag gave me. This is the passage:

On the forest's thick canopy, shade is falling.
I find the sight of this country pleasing.
Nothing stirs or moves, neither water nor leaves,
Birds throughout the forest are sleeping.
All I can hear is bracelets on a jar

Down the empty path, sadly tinkling.
I find this gold-lit country pleasing.

Please let me know what your wife thinks of this poem.

Cordially,

Jeff Kreutzer

From: rberryman@genetoplex.com
To: kreutzer1@indorice.com
Subject: Stay on task

Kreutzer,

I have to tell you that my wife liked your last e-mail a lot more than I did. While I'm glad that you're enjoying nature, it's much more important that you keep up with business. Any gossip over there about Stengel's counter-offer? Does this Chatterji that you've mentioned suspect anything about what's really going on? Get your head out of the clouds, Kreutzer. You've got a job to do.

—RB

From: kreutzer1@indorice.com
To: rberryman@genetoplex.com
Subject: My resignation

Dear Rick,

At eleven o'clock on Thursday morning, I met Mother Teresa. I'd heard she sometimes greets foreigners, so I waited for three hours outside her office, and there she was. When I knelt before her, she took my greedy fingers between her soft old forgiving hands and said, "God bless you." It was wonderful!

Physically, she is not impressive. She's a tiny woman, not five-feet tall, wearing a white cotton sari and a habit trimmed with blue. Her nose is as big as Jimmy Durante's, one of her bare feet is deformed. "Thank you for coming," she told me. "I hope you are enjoying your stay in India." I nodded like a dumbfounded child. Finally, I was able to blurt out, "Mother, am I living my life as I should?" She looked at me, Rick, with these penetrating eyes. They seemed to see right through me. "My son," she said, "I think you already know the answer to that question."

My audience lasted no more than a minute or two, but I gave five hundred dollars to her Home for the Destitute. I just pulled out a traveler's check and signed it over to her. Where it said "Pay to the Order of," I wrote, "Mother Teresa, Saint." This hippie standing next to me said, "She's the most famous person I've ever touched," but that's not really the issue. She's the HOLIEST person I've ever touched, and immediately it made a difference in my life.

Mother has an orphanage just down the street, and I wandered over there. Fading posters of kittens and sunsets were taped to the wall. It was hot inside, but the fans were working and the facility was clean. In one crib a twenty-year-old man the size of a three-year-old lay fetal and uncomprehending, crippled by polio and a host of other diseases. A sign read, "Do Not Hug or Cuddle the Children for Health Reasons." Nevertheless, those who could walk or crawl were all over me, touching, imploring me to pick them up.

One four-year-old almost succeeded in lifting a hundred rupee note from my front pocket. Yesterday I would have called the police, or at least given the boy a furious scolding. But today, blessed by Mother, I just laughed. I didn't care anymore, but he gave the money back and smiled and kissed me on the cheek and went away.

As I was walking towards the river, I couldn't help but think, if the Indians caught us digging into their pockets, would we smile and give them back what we've stolen? I don't think so. And it's millions of dollars we're gypping them out of, not three and a half bucks.

Then a bus passed me with all but three of the seats full of truck tires; the three human passengers seemed to be oblivious of their seatmates. I realized that we at Genetoplex are oblivious to the harm we daily inflict, but which is all around us.

I can't do this, Rick. I just can't do. I've got to tell Paryag about our plans for IndoRice. And I think I'm going to stay on here. It feels like home to me.

Give my regards to your wife. She seems to have a beautiful soul.

—Jeff

From: rberryman@genetoplex.com
To: kreutzer1@indorice.com
Subject: Rick, My Ass

YOU ARE RELIEVED OF YOUR DUTIES IMMEDIATELY.

Kreutzer, goddamnit, don't breathe a word of anything to anybody. Either you have contracted malaria, or you are losing your mind. Whatever's wrong, you are obviously having a breakdown of some sort. We're talking about RICE here, for Chrissake, NOT THE MEANING OF LIFE!

Whitman is on his way over there right now to close the deal, and I want you on the next plane back to O'Hare.

Let me remind you of two things:

First, Mother Teresa is a scam artist, sort of an Indian version of Jim and Tammy Baker or one of those other televangelists. I read all about it in THE WALL STREET JOURNAL.

Second, here's what you're giving up: 1) a career that's not as promising as it once was but is still salvageable, 2) your BMW convertible, 3) your Gold Coast condo that all those Indians you love so much would probably kill for, 4) your girlfriend, (I've seen that picture on your desk and, believe me, she's a keeper), 5) your extensive CD collection (how do I know you have an extensive CD collection, Kreutzer? I know about it because EVERYONE your age has an extensive CD collection), 6) tap water you can drink and food you can eat without getting sick and medical care that will keep you alive past forty years of age. Am I leaving anything out, Kreutzer? Of course I am. Hundreds of things. And I'm sure that when you think of checking out of your air conditioned room in the Oberoi Grand and start considering where you'll be staying that you'll begin tallying up everything else you're forsaking.

Come home, Jeff. You've lost your bearings. Let cooler heads prevail.

—Richard Berryman

From: travelnet@igiairport.com
To: rberryman@genetoplex.com
Subject: My recent illness

Mr. Berryman,

I'm waiting for my connecting flight to Frankfurt at the New Delhi airport and was able to get on the Internet for a few minutes.

You're right, sir, I lost track of what was important to me. I think maybe that I had a case of dysentery. (Does that affect your brain?) Whatever it was, it made me lightheaded.

I never said anything to Chatterji. Just when I was about to spill the beans, he got this rapacious look in his eyes, and I knew that he was only in this for his own profit. We'd been conning each other. That's part of what changed my mind about staying.

The other part is I took a walk to a coffee shop near the university and I met a professor there. A die-hard communist, or so he said. But all he could talk about was American action movies. Stallone and Schwarzenegger were his favorite stars. And he wanted to go to America, he wanted me to pull some strings for him. I couldn't help but be cynical about the whole thing, and I really do love my Beamer and my apartment.

Like you said, It's just rice. So I decided to come home.

It's funny. though. For a couple of days there I felt like I was on the verge of seeing the world in a whole new way. God. I really I thought I knew what I was about.

Sincerely,

Jeffrey Kreutzer

Frederick Busch

The Ninth, in E Minor

THE MORNING AFTER I drove to his newest town, I met my father for breakfast. He was wearing hunter's camouflage clothing, and he looked as if he hadn't slept for a couple of nights. He reminded me of those militia clowns you see on television news shows, very watchful and radiating a kind of high seriousness about imminent execution by minions of the state.

I knew he had deeper worries than execution. And I was pleased for him that he wore trousers and T-shirt, a soft, wide-brimmed cap, and hip-length jacket that would help him disappear into the stony landscape of upstate New York. He *needs* the camouflage, I thought.

Although where we stood, in the lobby of the James Fenimore Cooper Inn, my father did seem a little out of place among the college kids and commercial travelers. The inn advertised itself as The Last of the Great Upstate Taverns. My father looked like The Last of the Great Upstate Guerilla Fighters. Still, I thought, He's got the gear, and one of these days he will blend right in.

"Hi, baby," he said. He tried to give me one of the old daddy-to-daughter penetrating stares, but his eyes bounced away from mine, and his glance slid down my nose to my chin, then down the front of my shirt to the oval silver belt buckle I had bought in Santa Fe.

"How are you, Daddy?"

He fired off another stare, but it ricocheted. "I have to tell you," he said, "half of the time I'm flat scared."

His shave was smooth, but he'd missed a couple of whiskers, which looked more gray than black. His face had gone all wrinkled and squinty. He looked like my father's older brother who was shaky and possibly ill and commuting from the farthest suburbs of central mental health.

He took his cap off—doffed it, you would have to say. His hair looked soft. You could see how someone would want to reach over and touch it.

"But I don't like to complain," he said.

I got hold of his arm and pulled my way along his brown-and-sand-and-olive-green sleeve until I had his hand, which I held in both of mine. He used enough muscle to keep his arm in that position, but the hand was loose and cool, a kid's.

I asked him, "Do you know what you're scared of?"

He shrugged, and, when he did, I saw a familiar expression inside his tired, frightened face. He made one of those French frowns that suggested not giving a good goddamn, and it pleased me so much, even as it disappeared into his newer face, that I brought his hand up and kissed the backs of his fingers.

"Aw," he said. I thought he was going to cry. I think he thought so too.

"Look," I said, letting go of his hand, "I saw Mommy in New York. That's where I drove up from. We had dinner two days ago. She asked me to remember her to you. She's fine."

He studied my words as if they had formed a complex thought. And then, as if I hadn't said what he was already considering, he asked, "How is she?"

"She's fine. I told you."

"And she asked to be remembered to me."

"Right."

"You're lying, Baby."

"Correct."

"She didn't mention me."

"Oh, she mentioned you."

"Not in a friendly way."

"No."

"She was hostile, then?"

"Hurt, I'd say."

He nodded. "I hate that."

I nodded back.

"Because I didn't want to hurt anybody," he said. "I just wanted to feel better."

"I know. Do you feel better?"

"Do I look it?"

"Well, with the outfit and all. . . ."

"This stuff's practical. You can wear it for weeks before you need to wash it. The rain runs off the coat. You don't need to carry a lot of clothing with you."

"Traveling light, then, is how you would describe yourself?"

"Yes," my father said. "I would say I'm traveling light. But you didn't answer me. How do I look?"

I walked past matching club chairs upholstered in maroon and aqua challis, and I looked out a window. A crew had taken down an old, broad maple tree. The sidewalk was buried under branches and bark, and a catwalk of plywood led from the street, around the downed tree, and into the inn. The tree was cut into round sections three or four feet deep, and a man in a sweated undershirt used a long-handled splitting maul to break up one of the sections. Behind him, another man, who wore a yellow hard hat and an orange shirt and a yellow fluorescent safety vest, stood, holding a long chain saw that shook as it idled, and he watched the other fellow split. A woman in a man's old-fashioned undervest who wore work gloves and battered boots watched them both. Occasionally, she directed the man with the splitting maul. Her hair beneath her yellow hard hat looked reddish-gold. The men sneaked stares at her shirt. She looked up and saw me. She looked at me through her safety goggles for a while and then she smiled. I couldn't help smiling back.

"You look fine," I said. "It's a beautiful spring morning. Let's eat."

In the Natty Bumppo Room, we were served our juice and coffee by a chunky woman with a happy red face. My father ordered waffles, and I remembered how, when I was in elementary school, he heated frozen waffles in the toaster for me and spread on margarine and syrup. I remembered how broad his hands had seemed. Now, they shook as he spread the margarine. One of his camouflage cuffs had picked up some syrup, and he dripped a little as he worked at his meal. I kept sipping the black coffee, which tasted like my conception of a broth made from long-simmered laundry.

"The hardest part," he said, "it drives me nuts. The thing with the checks."

"Sure," I said, watching the margarine and maple syrup coat his lips. "Mommy has to endorse your checks, then she has to deposit them, then she has to draw a bank check, and then she has to figure out where you are so she can send it along. It's complicated."

"I'm not making it that way on purpose," he said.

"No. But it's complicated." He looked like his son, sometimes, and then, suddenly, he looked more like his father. I understood that he might look like either, but that what I had thought of as my father, looking like himself, was no longer available. He was several new selves, and I would have to think of him that way.

"I'm just trying to get better," he said.

"Daddy, do you hear from her?"

He went still. He held himself that way and, in his camouflage outfit, he suggested a hunter waiting on something skittish, say wild turkey, said to be stupid and shy. "I don't see the point of this," he said. "Why not talk about you? That's what fathers want to hear. About their kids. Why not talk about you?"

"All right," I said. "Me. I went to Santa Fe. I had a show in a gallery in Taos, and then I drove down to Santa Fe and I hung out. I walked on the Santa Fe trail. It goes along the streets there. I ate too much with too much chili in it, and I bought too many pots. Most of the people in the restaurants are important unknown Hollywood celebrities from outside Hollywood."

"Did you sell any pictures?"

"Yes, I did."

"Did you make a lot of money?"

"Some. You want any?"

"Because of how long it takes for your mother to cash my check and send a new one."

"Are you *allowed* to not live at home and still get money from the state?"

"I think you're supposed to stay at home," he said.

"So she's being illegal along with you? To help you out?"

He chewed on the last of his waffle. He nodded.

"Pretty good," I said.

"She's excellent to me."

"Considering," I said. "So how much money could you use?"

"Given the complications of the transmission process," he said.

"Given that," I said. "They sit outside the state office building, the Indians off the pueblos. They hate the people who come, but they all sit there all day long, showing you the silver and the pots all arranged on these beautiful blankets. I bought too much. But I felt embarrassed. One woman with a fly swatter, she kept spanking at the jewelry she was selling. She'd made it. She kept hitting it, and the earrings jumped on the blanket. The rings scattered, and she kept hitting away, pretending she was swatting flies, but she wasn't. She was furious."

"Displacement," my father said.

"It's just a story, Daddy."

"But you told it."

"Yes, but it didn't have a message or anything."

"What did it have?"

"*In situ* Native American displacement, and hand-made jewelry. A tourist's usual guilt. Me, on the road, looking around. Me, on my way northeast."

"Did you drive?"

"I did."

"All by yourself?"

"Like you, Daddy."

"No," he said, fitting his mouth to the trembling cup. "We're both together here, so we aren't alone now."

"No." I heard the splitting maul, and I imagined the concussion up his fingers and along his forearm, up through the shoulder and into the top of the spine. It would make your brain shake, I thought.

"A hundred or so?" he said.

"What? Dollars?"

"Is that too much?"

"No," I said, "I have that."

"Thanks, Baby."

"But do you hear from her, Daddy?"

He slumped. He stared at the syrup on his plate. It looked like a pool of sewage where something had drowned.

He said, "Did I tell you I went to Maine?"

I shook my head and signalled for more coffee. When she brought it, I asked if I could smoke in the Natty Bumppo Room, and she said no. I lit a cigarette and when I was done, and had clicked the lighter shut, she took a deep breath of the smoke I exhaled and she grinned.

"What's in Maine?" I asked him.

"Cabins. Very cheap cabins in a place on the coast that nobody knows about. I met a man in New Hampshire—Portsmouth, New Hampshire? He was on the road, like me. He was a former dentist of some special kind. We were very similar. Taking medication, putting the pieces back together, et cetera. And he told me about these cabins. A little smelly with mildew, a little unglamorous, but cheap, and heated if you need, and near the sea. I really wanted to get to the sea."

"So you drove there, and what?"

"I slept for most of the week."

"You still need to sleep a lot."

"Always," he said. "Consciousness," he said, "is very hard work."

"So you slept. You ate lobster."

"A lot."

"And what did you do when you weren't sleeping or eating lobsters or driving?"

"I counted girls in Jeeps."

"There are that many?"

"All over New England," he said, raising a cup that shook. "They're blonde, most of them, and they seem very attractive, but I think that's because of the contrast—you know, the elegant, long-legged girl and the stubby, utilitarian vehicle. I found it quite exciting."

"Exciting. Jesus, Daddy, you sound so adolescent. Exciting. Blondes in Jeeps. Well, you're a single man, for the most part. What the hell. Why not. Did you date any?"

"Come on," he said.

"You're not ancient. You could have a date."

"I've had them," he said.

"That's who I was asking you about. Do you hear from her?"

"I'm telling you about the girls in their Jeeps on the coast of Maine, and you keep asking—"

"About the woman you had an affair with who caused you to divorce my mother. Yes."

"That's wrong," he said. "We separated. That's all that I did. I moved away. It was your *mother* who sued for divorce."

"I recollect. But you do understand how she felt. There you were, shacking up with a praying mantis from Fort Lee, New Jersey, and not living at home for the better part of two years."

"Do I have to talk about this?"

"Not to get *my* two hundred dollars, no. We're just having an on-the-road visit and I'm leaving soon enough, and probably you are too."

"I drift around. But that's a little unkind about the money. *And* about the praying mantis thing. Really, to just bring it up."

"Because all you want to do is feel better," I said, lighting another cigarette. By this time, there were several other diners in the Natty Bumppo Room, and one of them was looking over the tops of her gray-tinted lenses to indicate to me her impending death from secondary smoke. *Oh, I'm sorry!* I mouthed to her. I held the cigarette as if I were going to crush it onto my saucers, then I raised it to my mouth and sucked in smoke.

I blew it out as I said to him, "She's the one who led you into your nosedive. She's the reason you crashed in flames when she left you."

"This is not productive for me," he said.

"You're supposed to be productive for *me*," I said. I heard the echo of my voice and, speaking more calmly, I said, "Sorry. I didn't mean to shout. This still fucks me up, though."

"Don't use that kind of language," he said, wiping his eyes.

"No."

"I thought we were going to have a *visit*. A father-and-daughter reunion."

"Well, we are," I said.

"All right. Then tell me about yourself. Tell me what's become of you."

I was working hard to keep his face in focus. He kept looking like somebody else who was related to him, but he was not the him I had known. I was twenty-eight years old, of no fixed abode, and my father, also without his own address, was wearing camouflage clothing in an upstate town a long enough drive from the New York Thruway to be nothing more than the home of old, rotting trees, a campus in the state's junior college system, and the site of the James Fenimore Cooper Inn.

"What's become of me," I said. "All right. I have two galleries that represent me. One's in Philadelphia and one's in Columbia County, outside New York. I think the owner, who also runs what you would call a big-time gallery on Greene Street, in Manhattan, may be just around the corner from offering me a show in New York City. Which would be very good. I got some attention in Taos, and a lot of New York people were there, along with the usual Hollywood producer-manqué people, both has-beens and would-bes, and the editorial stars who hire agents to get their names in the gossip columns. It was very heady for me to be hit on by such upper-echelon minor leaguers."

"When you say 'hit on,'" he said, "what are you telling me?"

"Exactly what you think. A number of men fancied fucking me."

He let his head droop toward his plate. "That's a terrible way to live," he said. "I'm supposed to be protecting you from that."

"But why start now?"

"That's what you came for," he said. "I've been waiting, since you phoned me, to figure out why you would look me up *now*, when you might suspect I'm down on my luck and in unheroic circumstances."

"Unheroic," I said. "But you're wrong. I mean, as far as I *know*, you're wrong. I asked Mommy for your address because I hadn't seen you since I was in graduate school. And you're my father. And I guess I was missing you."

"And because you wanted to tell me the thing about men trying to—you know. Because it would hurt me. And you're angry with me."

"Well, you could say the way you left your wife was a little disappointing to me."

He'd been rubbing at his forehead with the stiffened fingers of his right hand. He stopped, and he looked around his hand, like a kid peeking through a fence, his expression merry and, suddenly, quite demented. Then the merriment left him, and then the craziness, and he looked like a man growing old very quickly. He said, "I have to tell you, the whole thing was disappointing for me as well."

"You mean, leaving your wife for the great adventure and then being dumped."

"And then being dumped," he said.

"Mommy said you were doing drugs when that happened."

"There was nothing we didn't do except heroin," he said. "If we could have bought it safely, I'd have stuffed it up my nose, shot it into my eyeballs, anything."

"Because of the sex?"

He looked right at me. "The best, the most astonishing. I haven't been able to acknowledge a physical sensation since then. Everything I've felt since then is, I don't know—as if it was *reported.* From a long way away."

"Jesus. *And* you loved her?"

"I've dealt with a therapist who says maybe I didn't. Maybe it was the danger. I seem to act self-destructively, from time to time. I seem to possibly not approve of myself. I seem to need to call it love whether that's what I feel or not. I seem to have conflated sex with love."

"A conflatable sex doll," I said. I snickered. He managed to look hurt. "I'm sorry."

"It doesn't matter much. I'm working on my health. It doesn't have to hurt to hear that kind of laughter. I suppose it's good for me. A kind of practice at coping with difficulties."

"No," I said, "I apologize. It just seemed like a very good damned pun, the conflatable sex doll. I am nobody's spokeswoman for reality. I apologize."

"Tell me how your mother is."

"She's fine. She's living a life. I'd feel uncomfortable if I gave you any details. I think she wants to keep that stuff to herself."

"So she's fine, and you've managed to endure the attentions of men with press agents."

"Mostly to evade them, as a matter of fact."

"Mostly?"

"Daddy, if anyone around here's fine, it's me. Nobody has to worry about men, nutrition, the upkeep of my car, or the management of my career. I do my own taxes, I wrote my own will, and I navigate my own cross-country trips."

"Why do you have a will? A legal last will and testament, you're saying? Why?"

"I'm not getting any younger," I said.

"Nonsense. You don't have a family to provide for."

"You know that, do you?"

"You *do*?"

I nodded. I found it difficult to say much.

"What, Baby?"

"A son. His name is Vaughan."

"Vaughan? As in the singer Vaughan Monroe?"

"As in Ralph Vaughan Williams. One of his symphonies was playing when, you know."

"I know nothing," he said. He was pale, and his lips trembled as his hands did, though in a few seconds his mouth calmed down. His fingers didn't.

"He's with Mommy."

"But he lives with you?"

"I'm thinking of living with someone downstate. We would stay together there."

"His father?"

"No. But a man I like. A photographer."

"Criminies," he whispered. "There are all those gaps, all those *facts* I don't know. This is like looking at the family picture album, but most of the pictures aren't in the book. Are you *happy* about this child?"

"Are you happy about me?"

"Sure," he said. "Of course, I am."

"Then I'm happy about my boy. Did you say *criminies*?"

He clasped his hands at the edge of the table, but they upset his breakfast plate. Syrup went into the air, and soggy crumbs, and his stained napkin. The waitress came over to sponge at the mess and remove our dishes. She came back with more coffee and the check.

"Criminies," my father said. "I haven't heard that word for years."

I was counting out money which I slid across the table to him. "I hope this helps," I said, "really."

"I regret needing to accept it," he said. "I regret not seeing you more. I regret your having to leave."

"That's the thing with those family albums, Daddy. People are always leaving them."

"Yes. But I'm a grandfather, right?"

"Yes, you are."

"Could I see him?"

"Ever get downstate?"

"Oh, sure," he said. "I get to plenty of places. I told you, I was all the way up in Maine just a few weeks ago."

"All those girls in Jeeps. I remember. So, sure. Yes. Of course. He's your grandson."

"Big and sloppy like me?"

"His father was a kind of fine-boned man. But he'll have my arms and legs."

"He'll look like a spider monkey."

"You haven't called me a spider monkey for an awfully long time."

"But that's what he looks like? I want to think of him with you."

"And very light brown hair, and a long, delicate neck. And great big paws, like a puppy."

"He'll be tall."

We sat, and maybe we were waiting to find some words. But then my father pulled on his camouflage cap, and tugged at the brim. He was ready, I suppose. I left the dining room and then the inn a couple of steps ahead of him. We stopped outside the front doors and watched the man, now shirtless, as he swung, working his way through a chunk of a hundred and fifty years. Splinters flew, and I heard him grunt as the wedge-shaped maul head landed. The woman in the cotton vest was watching it batter the wood.

I put my arms around his neck and hugged him. I kissed his cheek.

"Baby, when does everybody get together again?"

I hugged him again, and then I backed a couple of steps away. I could only shrug.

He said, "I was thinking roughly the same."

I heard the maul. I watched my father zip, then unzip his camouflage hunting coat.

He turned to the woman in the cotton vest and tipped his camouflage cap. She stared at him through her safety goggles.

He was giving a demonstration, I realized. With his helpless, implausible smile, he was showing me his lapsed world of women. He was broken, and he shook with medication, but he dreamed, it was clear, of one more splintered vial of amyl nitrate on the sweaty bedclothes of a praying mantis from Fort Lee, New Jersey. He had confected a ride with a leggy blonde in a black, convertible Jeep on U.S. 1 in Maine. And if she would talk to him before her tired and resentful men, he would chat up the lady foreman of the forestry crew and touch, as if by accident, the flesh of her sturdy, tanned arms.

That was why I backed another pace. That was why I turned and went along the duckwalk behind my father, leaving the wreckage of the maple tree and walking toward my car. I wanted to be driving away from him—locked inside with the windows shut—before he could tip his cap, and show me his ruined, innocent face, and steal what was left of my life.

Greg
Sanders

Motel Girl

BEHIND THE COUNTER of the motel office, a teenage girl was laboring with an antiquated adding machine, punching the numeric keys then cranking down a long handle causing the thing to cachink loudly and advance the tattered roll of paper. She glanced at me caustically, continued her bookkeeping, had pimples in neat rows on either side of her nose. Black heads, white heads, purple scars from attempts at eradication. But the subtle lines of her face, the sultry lips pursed in concentration, her high cheekbones, large flitting blue eyes (slightly glazed over), all indicated a beauty that was stark and undernourished. I couldn't help staring for a second. Once those pimples ran their course, I thought, she'd be in high demand, a real knockout.

"Passing through or stayin' for a while?" she asked, turning her blank gaze back to the narrow strip of paper feeding into the machine.

"Just one night. Thought I'd be able to drive straight on into the mountains. Front end alignment's off on the old beast though. Car pulls one way, you steer the other. You get tired fast driving like that."

"Sure," she said, keeping her energy focused on punching numbers into the machine. "It's $34.95 plus tax for the night."

I paid cash, got my key, left the girl to her torturous accounting.

The shower in my room had one of those heads that swirled or pulsed the water and could make skin with my relatively pallid hue the color of boiled ham. I put the thing on the coarsest setting and let it pulverize my back. I'd been hunched over all day, leaning forward in concentration, correcting the right-hand torsion of the steering wheel. After the shower, I wrapped myself in a towel and flopped onto the squeaky bed. Every time a car sped past the motel on the highway outside, a set of shadows from the headlights would crawl up the wall to the ceiling where they would stretch oblongly then crawl back down the other wall, as if the shadows were alive and had intent. I'd been seeing this pattern since I was a kid and was always comforted by it. These celestial creatures are cast upon our world, victims of light, angles, velocity. Suddenly the dance was broken by a huge, oblique shadow passing across the wall. A knock at the door followed. I opened it a crack and peeked out. It was the veiled beauty, the pimpled desk girl. "I need to change your bedding," she said. She seemed somewhat less dour this time. Now, at least, a small smile appeared, although it seemed accidental, and vanished immediately. I put my jeans on and opened the door. "Sorry about this. I shoulda done it this morning."

She got right down to business, tenaciously ripping off the old bedding, rolling it up and tossing it by the door and then just as energetically installing the new flat sheets and pillow cases. This all took a little while and I watched intently, fingering my navel with my pinkie like I do when I'm deviously amused. Despite the piteous state of her complexion, she was, by the most male and superficial of standards, a sexually enchanting girl.

"What about the comforter, are you going to change that too?" I asked.

"No need. Was only a couple a senior citizens in here before you. Doubt they could do damage."

"If possible, I'd like a clean one anyway. It seems a little mildewy."

"Why do you want a clean one when this one's clean? You mean you want a different clean one."

"It's a simple matter of sanitary conditions. I'm a little nuts about these things. Blame it on my mother; she ran a tight ship."

She mumbled something underneath her breath while violently whipping up the pillows.

"If you're talking to me," I said in my least confrontational tone of voice, "you can speak directly. It's better not to hold things back." She stopped pummeling the life out of the pillows.

"No offense, mister," she said, bending to one side like an MTV-taught homegirl, hands on hips, neck hinged forward doubly, "but I don't need a freakin' social worker type up here from New York City trying to guide me to a better way of life."

"I'm not a social worker," I said, a little offended at the remark. "It's just that if you're pissed off, don't worry about letting it out. It might make you feel better." This made perfect sense to me. She was young, trapped here under god knows what conditions, and probably, I assured myself, could use someone like me to teach her how to best release tension. If they're not careful, sweet things like her turn into angry obese housewives living with manic, unemployed, alcoholic husbands in trailer parks. They eventually get rich by burning the place down and suing the stove company, or the light bulb company, or any manufacturer that has product liability insurance. As an actuarial intern in college, I had catalogued some of these cases and was amazed at how good a living could be made out in the boonies by simply burning and suing. I'd been taught that when fatalities were involved, it was usually the real thing, in which case the settlement was always lower anyway.

I could see myself in the mirror over the headboard and I didn't like the expression on my face—amused condescension. And the amusement was at this: She seemed determined, by her behavior and expressions, to demonstrate how angry she was, but the attempt was so transparent and superficial—Look at me! See how very very angry I am?—that I had to laugh inwardly. I dared not try to determine with any certainty what was really going on with this young, confused nubile. My regret is that I didn't even try to look below this false surface. Had I, I might have sensed the darkness, the cold danger lurking beneath that blemished skin. All I knew was that I wanted a clean comforter, which at the time seemed not only reasonable, but necessary. Still, I was unable to keep my eyes off her slim body, virgin to cellulite, stray body hairs, and the inevitable post-adolescent spread. And that cute little body, I thought, would look even better in clothes that weren't ten years out of date. This thought—that her clothes were old, cheap, of the worst poly-nylon taste—elicited another self-righteous grin, which I hoped she hadn't noticed. I was a real jackass, that's for sure, but, for the time being, an amused one.

She held a corner of the comforter under her nose and gave it a quick whiff. She seemed satisfied. It did look perfectly clean, but you never know what kinds of microscopic monsters could be making a habitat—like herds of buffalo grazing the Indian plains—out of that comforter.

"You're not special, you know. I saw how you looked at me when you checked in. I see you lookin' me up and down now. You think I'm a hick; you think I'm a dumb teenager. What plans you got for me, anyway?"

What was this duplicity, I wondered, saying all this while measuring me up with a kind of seductive glare, tempting me to test my abilities on her? I hadn't seen a look like that since high school and it was a look I didn't particularly miss. It said that she knew of the power she possessed, feminine youth in full blossom, petals unfurling, sweet balm erupting. I said nothing in response to her question. At that moment I couldn't muster the moral armor I would need to strip a teenager of the last remnants of her childness. Yet I couldn't help wondering how she would behave under my guidance. My wonderings gave way to vivid conjurings of this straggly, glum girl lying supine beneath me, whispering softly, amorously groaning in my ear. An embarrassing state of arousal set in.

She turned to look out the window. I could see her face reflected off the glass, the way its expression took on a hardness when confronting its own image. Putting a hand on the window to shield against the glare, to cancel her reflection, she stared into the darkness. "It's begun to snow." Perhaps in a gesture of reconciliation, she directed me under her hand. Outside, tiny white flakes drifted down in a dense, windless current. "We're supposed to get a foot-and-a-half. Guess you didn't listen to the weather, huh."

She gathered up the old sheets and turned to me, hugging the large bundle to her chest. "You might be trapped here for a few days. Hope you got enough cash for the room." She opened the door to leave.

"Thanks for everything," I said.

"I'll be back later with a clean comforter."

The door clicked behind her and then all was dead silent, and even more so. I turned the lights off and watched the snow fall. At the far end of the motel parking lot fir trees rose, dark and shadow-like, towards the moon, around which a barely discernible corona of light broke through the haze of snow. With this burgeoning blizzard, the shadow-play on the walls ceased, and along with it the sense of motion I'd had, that it was the room itself gliding down the highway, passing stationary lights. Yet light was filtering in somehow, the bright eerie quality of which would make you think you were seeing in the dark by some special power. Sitting on the bed, I became very calm, feeling insulated by the storm, by the silence, and knowing that even in broad daylight my field of vision would be seriously limited. I thought: I cannot contemplate anything beyond the physical bounds of my sight. With my feet on the crummy floor and my back, still aching and unsprung, against the unwashed comforter, I dozed off.

There was a loud knocking on the door. Hazy-headed, I rose from bed and looked at my watch. It was one in the morning. The room was freezing. No heat rose from the radiator, no hiss of steam or creaking of electrical elements gave even the illusion of warmth. I opened the door and there stood the motel girl, a dusting of snow on her dirty blond hair. I turned the lights on. She stepped in, a blast of cold squeezing through with her.

She had changed her clothing, was wearing jeans, an olive green T-shirt with a low V. The clothing fit her snugly, revealing the intimate contours of her inner thighs and narrow ass, her nascent breasts, and the smooth bridge of her clavicles. In a year or two, I said to myself, her bodily presence would turn every head in any bar and cause most men to growl, blush, or grin helplessly, like adolescents. As if that weren't enough, she was shivering like a helpless and lost orphan, face flushed with cold—why hadn't she worn a jacket?—teeth chattering. Oh, I was bad. Her acne could be overlooked. It even added to the image of a dejected, do-anything teenage girl who has nothing to lose, not even her innocence. She held the neatly folded comforter, an ugly plaid flannel, at about the level of her breasts. "If you'd be kind enough to fold up the one on your bed, I'll lay this one out for you."

Doing as requested, I unruffled the old comforter and began to fold it. She leaned over me, watching my every movement. Her breath, warm and moist in the frigid air, lightly tickled the hairs on the back of my neck. I folded the comforter into precise halves, fourths, eighths, and sixteenths, continuing the equation in my head in order to distract myself from her presence: two to the nth power equals thirty-two when n equals five, sixty-four when n equals six, one-twenty-eight when n equals seven . . .

"I saw you lookin' at me just now and I bet I know what you were thinking. You were thinking 'I bet she's a good, tight, fuck.' Am I right?"

I sputtered some denial of the fact too quickly, confirming the truth contained in her statement. I tried to downplay my shock, the sudden and unwanted warmth that was infusing my body.

"Don't think I don't know that look," she continued, "I've seen it in half the truckers and salesmen who've passed through this damn place. You think I'm a naive thing for your taking, don't you?" She was wearing sparkly eye shadow, had made herself up for this.

I put the folded comforter on the floor. "I have no idea where you get your ideas but I think I've heard enough of them."

"Actually, I feel kinda sorry for guys like you. It must be hard at your age. All you wanna do is screw screw, screw anything that won't talk back: 'Oh you're the master, you're the king. No one does it like you!' Some little hick slut would be a lot of fun, wouldn't she? You'd feel good taking pity on her. 'Poor girl,' you'd say, 'miserable face.'"

I hesitated. Was this simply the manifestation of a hormonal imbalance? A reaction against overwhelming responsibility (after all, she seemed to be running the entire motel by herself)? "Listen to me, you are not ugly in the least. Saying that about yourself, that kind of self-effacement, is only going to make things more difficult. The truth is you're actually quite pretty." Pretty, I thought, that's not what she wants to hear. A girl is pretty, a woman is, what? "When that acne clears up you'll have the face of a model. And I mean a supermodel, as in one word, famous, paparazzi around every corner, focus of every guy's fantasies. Never a dull minute. I mean it all. Now why don't you leave me the comforter, then we can both get some sleep?"

She took a step towards me and stood like a pugilist, legs splayed slightly, jeans puckering mid-thigh. "I've had a hard time with guys like you. Maybe you're a little kinder than some of the others, but you still got that look that says you'll try to rape me in my sleep."

Suddenly I had the urge to comfort her, to run her tangled hair between my fingers, to lightly pass my lips over her pocked face. But what would she think I was doing? And all at once the urgency I'd felt to seduce her vanished. Had I been a young father, this girl could be my daughter. "Please let me alone to sleep," I said at last, now completely awake and suddenly a little sore about it. I held my arms out. "May I have the comforter?"

"Of course," she sighed, looking down at her feet. "I'm sorry for all this." I lifted the clean comforter from her outstretched arms and threw it on the bed. Beneath it she had been holding a pistol which she was now pointing at my chest. She was still, completely calm, and seemingly at peace.

"Do you know that it's physio—oh, what's the word? Yes, physiologically—do you know that it's physiologically impossible for a woman, or in my case, a girl," she added demurely, "to rape a man? If you don't want to be fucked by me, then you can't be fucked by me. Maybe if women could rape men, they'd be doing it all the time, same as you do to us." Though her voice had gone dead cold, there was a glimmer in her eyes which said that she was enjoying herself immensely, that she was getting off. "At least try to put a smile on your cute little face."

I stammered idiotically, trying but unable to stave off a nervous grin. After all, this couldn't really be happening. "What the hell are you doing? I don't need this."

"That's understandable. Now, come closer, my little growed up man." She giggled like a schoolgirl about to kiss a boy for the first time.

Outside, the wind had begun whipping little snow swirls against the windows, which were chuckling lightly in their frames. The gutters and vinyl siding of the place were beginning to whistle and rattle. I was waiting for the entire structure to disintegrate.

Hesitantly, I stepped forward, and could see sweat glistening around her lips, which, unlike the rest of her physiognomy, were fully formed and arced gracefully like the mantle of some exotic mollusk. Her neck and chest had turned crimson, as if from a sexual flush; her cheeks were pink beneath the flesh's lunar surface. For a girl, she was medium height, meaning she came eye to eye with me. She raised the shiny black pistol, a .45 caliber, to my face. The barrel was by no means small.

I tried to hang onto my pride but knew the panic was rising, could already see myself pathetically groveling at this girl's feet. The reality was that here, with this spindly, delicate girl—with this gun—only two inches from my self-loved lips, I was overcome by a warm paralysis.

"Open your mouth for my gun," she said impossibly, her voice throaty and lustful. "Come on Sweety, open your mouth."

"No. I won't."

"Do you want me to take you to where the lights don't shine?" She cocked the gun. "BOOM!" she shouted, then cackled demonically, holding the cold steel tip to my lips. Then I did open my mouth, but only a little. "C'mon, got to open wider if you don't want your teeth to get chipped. I don't plan on being so gentle. Yes! That's good. Boy, you've got such a nice pink tongue. Now don't fight me with it, keep it tucked away."

She slowly pushed the gun into my mouth then pulled it out, saw that it was dry, spat upon it, and thrust it in again. "Gosh, I wish this thing had nerves! Hah!" With one hand she held the pistol tightly, her trigger finger securely in its place, and with the other she held the back of my head. Using her arm she forcefully thrust the gun into my throat. I could taste blood drawn by the steel barrel; I could barely get air in and out through my nose. She moved her hand from the nape of my neck down to my pants, over my groin. "How sad," she said, tightening her grip. "Hope this doesn't become a condition for you. These things can last for years." I can still smell her pungent essence, rising up from between her legs, its sharp acrid brininess seeking not to excite, but to frighten, to repel.

Saliva and blood were dripping down my chin. My legs were weak and about to give way when the thrusting became so furious that I was sure, intentional, or not, this girl would shoot me dead. I managed to briefly escape the miserable confines of my body and float above an autumnal countryside, but she brought me back, saying that it was almost over. She was dripping with sweat, her huge black pupils emanating a calm animal savagery, immune to the way I must have looked—for I was suffocating and nearly unconscious. In the end there was the empty metallic click of the hammer. Her eyes fluttered, rolled back, and a few spasms shook her.

At last she removed the pistol from my mouth. "Shoot," she said, panting, regaining her composure, "I'm not gonna wash this gun for a while. It's good and sticky." Deliriously, I took a swing at her, but she blocked the lame punch easily, and then proceeded to pistol whip me. After that I was gone, utterly so, floating somewhere, a floating head, a pain-filled balloon, watching from above as she lifted my feet off the floor and rolled my limp body onto the bed.

For a few seconds, sitting up in my stiffened clothing, my breath rising in a cloud of frozen mist, I forgot where I was, what had occurred. In the cold, the pain was still sleeping, hadn't yet come into my physical consciousness. I rubbed the thin gloss of ice from the inside of the window, but snow had quaintly frosted the outside. I gave the glass a hard tap. It fell away from its frame, landing inaudibly in a small drift outside. Light and freezing air flooded in. The sky was a cloudless blue. In the parking lot a vortex of wind was sweeping snow, like dust, off the roof of the old AMC.

I made my way into the bathroom, my bones rattling with cold. In the flaking mirror over the sink, I saw that my lips were swollen and raw, but not torn up as badly as they were beginning to feel. Swallowing was excruciating. The wound issued by the butt of the pistol was about an inch in length and was raised in such a perfectly smooth and symmetrical fashion that it made my stomach turn. The hair surrounding it was matted with blood. I cleaned the sticky gash with a washcloth and some soapy water, put on an oxford, and collected my things.

As I was warming up the car, scraping ice off the windshield with shaky hands, I noticed that the motel looked worse than I had recalled. Much worse. I'd arrived in darkness so hadn't seen the broken windows nor the terribly faded vinyl siding, which, in some places, was hanging from the exterior in long strips. A few of the rooms were boarded up altogether, and over the entrance to one an old interstate sign was nailed, sealing it like a crypt. A large arrow, now half buried in snow, which for decades had probably guided a million drivers to some connecting capillary of a road, pointed downwards, the route number showing only a leading 3. I got into my car and revved the engine until the heat kicked on and began to defrost the windshield.

The tires spun wildly at first, but eventually they dug in through the snow to grip the asphalt of the parking lot. I made my way towards the motel office, slowly picking up speed. The old AMC, straight six straining at full throttle, tires singing in a glorious spray of icy froth, steering wheel pulling right, entered the motel office through the south-facing wall. There was a ferocious explosion of glass and particle board, cheap pine paneling, rotting studs. The front desk and various other furnishings were obliterated in a hail of splinters before the car came to a full stop. Glass crunched beneath my feet as I got out.

The place was empty, the motel girl nowhere to be seen. The ancient adding machine had been catapulted across the office and there had taken a fair bite out of the wall. Still caught in its steel teeth was the strip of paper on which the figures of her previous night's labors were indelibly etched. I pulled it out. It contained nonsense, random numbers in long strings. About twenty lines of them.

I went to each room in the motel, starting with the small one behind the office. With the exception of the one I had spent my night in, they all seemed to have been empty for years.

It was a beautiful morning, clear and brisk. I backed the car out of the demolished office and spit some blood into the snow. As I drove out of there I kept the windows open to let in the freezing air, which killed some of the pain. The sky was a Caribbean blue, that of a coral atoll giving way to the deep. I had to drive slowly in the snow as the tires on the old beast were not the greatest.

Dennis Must

Say Hello to Stanley

BUDDY HART HAULED the Hammond B-3 in a two-wheel trailer hitched to his father's Willys sedan. The family thought Uncle Stanley's talent as a barrel-house pianist had, by some mysterious route, passed down to Bud. And the miracle became even more fortuitous when Stanley lost two of his fingers in the cutting mill along with his gig.

The skaters loved Buddy's jazz-riff music. He'd imitate their gliding, pumping motion as they rounded the back wall of the Hi-Way Rollerdome smiling up at him in the open air booth that cantilevered the skate floor. The more venturesome rollers who executed the "Backslider," "Alice Goes to Market," or the "Janey Mae" he'd tease with several bars of *Salt Peanuts*. And Buddy sounded just like Chet Baker singing when he'd accompany himself on a ballad.

But on Saturday and Sunday night at the Bluebird Inn, no microphone banter accompanied his riffs. This playing was dead real. He dug into the organ's bed for inspiration, and when he got real hot, he'd grab a *D minor b5* chord in the upper register and sit on the damn thing for two unrelenting, screaming B-3 minutes. Buddy opened up Ohio's skies with a machete, for chrissake.

"Ain't he one mean dude!" a lady cried. "Sing, Buddy. Sing. Oh my God!"

The sweat rolling off Buddy's boy face, Chet Baker tears, dripping summery onto the Hammond B-3's keyboard.

What a white black musician he was. Uncle Stanley reserved a table every Saturday night to watch his nephew. Then Celia Hubbard, a twenty-three-year-old auburn-haired socialite, began showing up. Her presence added a certain *je ne sais quoi* to the bar, and at evening's close, she'd fold a fresh twenty-dollar bill in a glass Buddy kept on the organ. Celia drove a 1948 Nash Convertible, one of 750 ever manufactured in America.

"She walks in here like it were a salon," Peewee, the Bluebird's owner, said. "Do you watch all the women eyein' her, Buddy? I ain't ever seen a red snatch, have you?"

"She just digs the organ, man."

"I didn't mean no disrespect," Peewee nodded. "But she lights this place up like your music, Buddy. What you say her name was?"

"Celia Hubbard."

"Where's she from?"

"East Jesus."

"Don't shit me, man."

"Patterson."

"Uh huh." It made sense. Patterson, outside Warren, was an enclave for the rich. Homes on lots of several acres, many of them with their own barns and grazing horses.

"Her father invented the drinking fountain, Peewee."

"Jesus, yes? You see that damn car she's driving?"

"I been in it, Peewee. Cream leather seats, still smells new inside, too."

"Where'd you go, Buddy?"

"Over to the Glass Hat to catch Jolly's last set." Jolly Patchen was the local blues singer and guitarist many believed was better than John Lee Hooker, but who never made it out of Warren.

"She taking an eye to you, Buddy?" Peewee asked.

"Shit, I'm just a skate-wheel musician, man," he replied.

The day Buddy ceased playing for the Rollerdome all the regulars sat on the skate floor, the mirror ball chasing magenta, heliotrope, indigo and mustard-yellow lights circling the grand hanger in darkness, mechanical fireflies all on permanent tethers . . . It was the strangest melancholic night, almost masochistic for Buddy and the crowd. Some of the rollers had been attending regularly for the six years Buddy'd been playing. It wasn't the skating so much that kept them coming back as it was being shined on by his cherubic face, bathed by his boyish laughter and his Chet Baker's girl-voice ballads.

He was moving onto the big time now. No more sweat effluvium wafting up from the skate floor, the silly mechanical *pas de deux*, the skate-dancing charades, the maestros who only chose to dance alone. Forty-year-old women with hair freshly dyed and sculpted up like an Eiffel tower, their sequined skate costumes causing the colored lights to swirl on their derrieres like the mirror ball on the ceiling. Or the pompadour-hair men with cigarette packs—Lucky Strikes mostly—rolled up in their T-shirt sleeves, tight trousers held up by plastic belts, doing those leaps into the air to the beat of Buddy's sweet music, lost in their odeons, barbers and telephone clerks by day, stars in the Rollerdome orbit at night—Oh, God, he wouldn't miss them . . .

They wanted Buddy to sing to them. He had this "wish board" up in his booth that controlled every light on the floor, the speed of the mirror ball, the speaker system. Buddy Hart, the Master of the *mise en scène,* the Harlin County Artaud, the Rollerdome wizard. Tonight they wanted Chet Baker.

The giant mirror-faced moon he ratcheted down to a drug-induced revolution, the thousand shards of light-illuminated flies with mirror backs, all the colors of a dreamer's rainbow, and the B-3 began to drone, now in the lower register, a reedy vibrato. Buddy wasn't Jimmy Smith no more. Instead a lachrymose idol. Up there in the booth hovering over them. Long mournful *ommmmmms.*

As if he wanted to purge them with a colonic of sadness. The audience watched the flies circle the walls and the floor. Like some kind of star calliope jar they were inside, except lying on the floor looking up at the hangar steel-trussed heavens. Christ, it was strange out there on route I-27 on the outskirts of Niles, a dink copper-refinery town, its sulfureous odor hanging over the valley like a scrim. The skaters with their red-and-white yarn pom-poms on the toes of their skate-shoes parked forlorn alongside them.

And just when it became almost unbearable, Buddy began to sing *When Sonny Gets Blue* in his best Chet Baker voice . . . followed by *Nature Boy* and then—the surprise of the evening—*The Little White Cloud That Cried.* He was warbling like he was a damn skater, too; that he weren't any different than those folks down on the floor, surrendering to melancholy and nostalgia, ignorant of complicated chord changes, technique, and awesome Bud Powell lines . . . the stuff of the cognoscente. Surely if Peewee were in this audience of colorfully-laced skaters with pompoms on their shoes and Waveset in their hair, he'd stab the keyboardist out of his self-indulgent stupor.

"*Little Things Mean A Lot,* Buddy!" one sequined matron bellowed up from under his booth. Buddy smiled his oleaginous grin and began tapping the tune into the Hammond B-3. Several of the women yanked the pompons off their skates, tossing them up into Buddy's open box. The yarn balls rained on the organ, bouncing down to its pedals.

Christ, what if Celia came in, thought Buddy. A shiver went up his spine. "Lady's Choice!" he hollered, and beat out the *Beer Barrel Polka.* The mirror ball spun rapidly, its mechanical flies with mirror backs circling the skater's hall like traffic on a freeway. It took some time for the crowd to catch up. But resignedly they did. The crowd now circled the hangar like plastic fish in an arcade's Fish-Until-You-Catch-A-Winner trough. The calliope!

But the Harts lived on DeForest Road where the toilets, bathtubs, sinks, washing machines, all flushed into an open sewer. Barely a half dozen houses away alongside the railroad tracks sat one of the most notorious cathouses this side of Cleveland. (His mother worked as a nurses-aide on weekends, turning patients over in their beds like flapjacks.) What the hell was he doing messing around with this woman whose father invented the drinking fountain?

"I'll take away all your financial worries," Celia urged. "You can devote as much time as you wish to your music . . . what do you say?"

"Jesus, we hardly know each other."

"What's there to know?" she said. Then embarrassed him by asking, "Sex?"

He didn't respond.

"Say it, Mr. Hart. If it's sex you're wondering about, I got all that you want, too. Anything for you, Buddy."

Every poor man's dream come alive, a red-haired one no less with a magenta labial shrub. That and dollars, too, thousands of them. A sleek automobile instead of the old man's turtle of a Willys. Horses. What the hell was the catch?

When Buddy mentioned it to his father, Rupert said, "Fuck her if you want, but don't marry her, Son. You'll be worse off than your Uncle Stanley. When she's finished working you over, you'll sound like Johnny Ray. You like auburn cooz?"

"How do you know she got red hair, Pap?"

"Every man in Harlan County's got a wet dream off Celia Hubbard at one time or another. 'Cept you're the unfortunate one." Buddy's mother just shook her head. She walked over to the kitchen sink, opened the faucet, and began scrubbing her fingernails with a vegetable brush.

When the newlyweds returned from the Bahamas, an indigo-blue Chrysler station wagon convertible sat parked in Celia's driveway. Eustace Hubbard even suggested Buddy begin working in the corporate offices, and sent him off to his haberdasher for a fitting. Just like the movies. Buddy's kid sisters couldn't quite believe his good fortune. And within a year of the wedding the Hi-Way Rollerdome closed for lack of business. Peewee began politicking Buddy to gig at the Bluebird every night. But that venue become more irregular. The Hammond B-3 sat at the ready, covered over with a bed sheet on the back of the bandstand. Following one of the performances, Peewee asked why Stanley never showed anymore.

"No idea," Buddy said.

"Your old friends. They gone, too."

"It's botherin' you, Peewee?"

"She's watered you down, Buddy."

Buddy glowered.

"You dig, pal? Excuse the disrespect, but the cunt's dimmed your lights."

"Cut the shit, Peewee."

"Can't, brother. I known you too long. First a red-haired snatch. Then a yellow one. A magenta one. Puce. Goddamnit, the gash are gonna dry you up like the foreskin on a cadaver. Tonight, yeah, I could hear echoes of old Buddy Hart in there. But you just coastin' man. That rich shit is dragging you down. You ain't got the drive no more."

"You saying you don't want me playing the Bluebird no more, Peewee?"

"Buddy Hart's always welcome here."

"She's my wife." Buddy stood and headed for the doorway.

"Yeah, and her old man's that drinking fountain hanging on our shithouse wall, too! Come back to the tunes, man. *And say hello to STANLEY!*"

It's true, thought Buddy, traveling back to Patterson alone that night—no trailer on the hitch—having to pass the boarded-up Rollerdome with its mirror-ball heaven that once moved and bounced to his B-3. He hadn't seen Stanley. Or many of his other friends. But now he wasn't a shiny-ass piano man playing for a couple of dollars in bars reeking of disinfectant either.

So what if I'm Celia Hubbard's boy. Huh? Don't have to worry about nothing no more. Chet Baker, Johnny Ray, Jimmy Smith, Bud Powell . . . Christ, none of that shit bothers me. I fucking got it made. Fuck Stanley. Let him chop his index finger and thumb off, the ungrateful bastard. Celia and I offered to help. But the bastard's too poor . . . fucking jealous. One of us got lucky.

Just then the Chrysler came to a dead stop. He and Peewee had been drinking—that was new, too. But what the hell. He drank his shit. Screw the powder. He looked down at the dashboard and ground the starter several times, pumping on the accelerator. The engine wouldn't catch. The bitch's dry, he thought. Then Buddy saw a hot moon barreling straight for him. He fumbled with the window handle. It kept swinging on him, not catching like it should have.

"What the fuck's gone wrong!" he cried. "Open up, you cocksucker. Open up!" The locomotive caught the Chrysler's front end, dragging the car several hundred yards up the track, screeching to a halt. A screaming screech. *A* flat of the B-3, Buddy thought, lying on the floorboards. This is fucking scary. That never was.

Soon the engineer and several track men were pounding on the windshield: "Are you all right, mister? Speak to us. Can you hear us?" Once outside, Buddy watched the water spit through his radiator's chromium teeth, the automobile's remaining headlight still shone and the horn stuck.

"Christ, I'm fine," he sighed. "Ain't a goddamn thing wrong with me, boys. Thanks for stopping," he said, and let out a Chet Baker laugh.

The ride downhill went damn fast after that. "I don't like wearing suits all day," he told Eustace Hubbard one spring morning, who replied, "You either be one of us, boy, or none of us."

"I'll take the latter," Buddy says, and parked his and Celia's new car in Hubbard's driveway, then hiked back to their house in Patterson.

Now and then he'd get a call for a gig. But he'd show up for a set in the bag, forget the chord changes, and the rare club that did hire him kept back-up musicians—brass on the stage—who could take over when he slid.

Nobody saw Celia much anymore either. She looked weird, her hair unkempt and lips darker than they ever were. Almost black now. She'd rouge her sallow cheeks with a magenta color. Folks thought she resembled some kind of mythical bird—her shoulders stooped over like a carrion eater's—who glided in and out of town when she walked. Word had it that she began to drink as much as Buddy did. That the two of them would start in the morning and work through several bottles by day's end. At dusk they'd mount the horses stark naked.

The grocery delivery boy would buzz to be let in. Soiled dishes lay piled everywhere. He stopped putting milk or butter in the refrigerator, for food in there had rotted, causing an unbearable stench.

"Can you hear any music being played in the house, Cal?" Charley Tompkins, the owner of Patterson Market, asked the boy.

"Sounded like some adolescent kid, like me maybe, Charley, you know, unable to make the higher keys, a kind of voice like that coming from the bedroom and a sad trumpet sound."

Sure, thought Charley Tompkins.

Several months later that July, Rupert woke Myra over on DeForest Road one midnight. "Someone's down pounding our door."

"You're hearing things."

"Damnit, I ain't!" he barked, slipping on his pants. He shambled down the stairs and saw a form on the other side of the curtained oval. "Who is it?" he asked. "Whadaya want?"

"It's Celia," came the reply.

Rupert was stunned. "Just a minute," he says, fumbling with the key in the lock. Celia stood before him looking plumb frightened, weary and bundled in one of Buddy's camel hair overcoats. This flower has faded fast, he thought. Like one of those pretty things in his perennial garden that overnight becomes a shadow of its promise the day earlier, and three days later goes to seed. Fucking drinking fountain daughters. Same as copper smelt mill daughters and sons, fucking babies of the rich, all fair and shallot stocks for spines.

"Jesus, what is it, Celia? You look bad."

"Is Myra here?" she asked.

"Yes, what is it?"

"Tell her to come quick."

Rupert, seeing a woman's urgency—he'd been ordered about like this before—yelled up to Myra. "Mommy, get down here quick!"

Myra came running down the stairway with a nightgown covering her naked body like a sheer curtain, then, seeing Celia, drew it to her. "What it is, Honey? You sick?"

"I am, Myra. I'm sick as a dog."

"Where's Bud?"

"Don't know. Does anybody, for chrissake?"

Rupert understood. Buddy was probably out in some other woman's bed. What else? The money eatin' away at him like green cancer. Alexander Hamilton cancer.

Myra was solicitous. The young woman was in pain. No time to be thinking about any hurt or anger now.

Celia stared intensely at Myra, trying to answer her.

"Oh, shit. No, child!"

Celia nodded her head *yes*.

"Rupert, go put the kettle on for hot water quick! And get me some towels. They're down on the line. Grab every damn one of them. And hurry, Rupe, hurry!" Myra put her arm around Celia and rushed her up the stairs.

Rupert knew what this was about, too. What else could it be? No surprises in this life. Were there ever any? So the kid falls into a cesspool of greenbacks and gorges himself, fucks himself up and everything he touches . . . including this once beautiful breeze of a woman. Yeah, breeze, that's all she was. Fragile. Swept around the corner and cooled him off, smelling of magnolia and leather, Kentucky bluegrass, clean underwear and stockings every goddamn day, and food in the cupboards—the pitcher of milk, this auburn-haired breeze now shivering before Myra upstairs, vomiting her guts out in the toilet, her skin yellow as the shit carpet in our hallway, naked, the fluid dripping off her white breasts and rivuleting through her labial auburn forest with death. For that's surely what this night was going to be.

I can goddamn tell. Oh shit. A water death. Fuck you, Buddy . . .

Rupert screamed to nobody in the kitchen, and the tea kettle begin to scream, too, but unlike the engine that caught Buddy's lucky-ass Chrysler, or the *A* flat on the B-3—this one pierced like a bird of doom gone mad and flapping about on the kitchen ceiling trying to ascend, to escape this birth house of Buddy Hart on DeForest Road. Screaming Celia upstairs now echoing the tea kettle's noise, she's a bird up there, too. Rupert could hear a body slapping about on the tile floor of their bathroom. Like a fish pulled out of the water still alive. The screaming and her flapping her white legs and arms against the tile walls and linoleum bathroom floor. Screaming. Screaming the B-3. Only this got under Rupert's skin. And he turned cold.

"Goddamn it, hurry, Rupe! Hurry up here for chrissake!"

Rupert rushed up the stairs, teapot steaming in one hand, towels in the other, the bathroom door wide open and Celia now moaning, her legs wide open and Myra naked too, down on her knees on the floor dragging something out of Celia.

Oh yeah, Christ, he'd been there. Do I have to watch this, Jesus? he thought. Fuck Buddy. Fuck Bud Powell. Fuck Jimmy Smith. Oh Ray Charles, he cried. Ray Fucking Charles.

Then there was this loud UMMPH.

Like Myra had smashed a thick round pole into Celia's abdomen. But it wasn't that. There were two things lying on the bathroom floor, beating like hearts. They were wiggling, and kind of looked like something human, but maybe like fish, Rupert couldn't tell. He was down on his knees now, thinking he was going to faint. The teapot on the floor next to him. Steaming. Christ, he was going to pass out. Hold on to me, he kept saying to himself. Hold onto me. Jesus. What are those on the floor? Who are they, Myra? Jesus Christ. What's she brought home? Fuck you, Buddy. Fuck you.

Myra bit the cords, then turned on her haunches to see Rupert dumbly staring at her on his knees. Christ, he looks like a circus bear in shock, she thought. And slammed the bathroom door shut.

"Let me see 'em," moaned Celia.

"Ain't nothing there except water and blood, honey," Myra said soothingly. "It's all over, dear. Put your head back down. Close your eyes. Let me wash off your face with a cool rag."

Then Rupert heard nothing more till the toilet flushed. Twice.

"I saw Buddy a week ago," Stanley told Rupert. "He invited me over to hear his Dexter Gordon Paris recordings."

"He have anything to say?" Rupe and Myra hadn't heard from Celia or Buddy since that fateful evening.

"Everything's fine. Claims he's giging weekends in Cleveland again. They're thinking about having babies. He's bloated up like the Hindenburg. And full of shit. I can't blame it all on Celia, Rupe."

"I agree," Rupert said.

"Damn depressing. She took me into their *boudoir* to show off her new Louie the Fourteenth bedroom set. Seems like every six months she tosses the *old* furniture into the barn and goes shopping for new. This bed and dresser weren't ugly enough, Rupe. You know what she did?"

"What?"

"Painted it sapphire. The gallon of wall paint and brush scumming up in the hallway. Mother's-Day sapphire. You think it's going to smell like some old patootie's dusted bosom when you stand next to it. And 'round the mirror's frame—she painted that, too, slopping it over onto the glass like she smears lipstick onto her teeth."

"I said it was going to sour quick, didn't I?" Rupe said.

"We all kind of guessed it, but none of us wanted to believe it."

"Because all you bastards thought you were going to get rich, too! That old Eustace was going to come over here and drop a trailer-load of cash in your driveways. Well, he has. But it ain't cash, brother. Money's a plague, I tell you.

"Stanley, if there's just one goddamn quarter left in my trouser pockets on my death bed, I promise I'll swallow the fucker before I take my last breath. I ain't leaving anybody *shit*. They'll all be better off."

Stanley could only shake his head.

Buddy Hart got up early a Saturday morning that September to begin packing his belongings in a trunk he'd hauled up from the basement, one of the old metal-and-wood variety fashioned for journeys to Europe on ocean liners. Celia kept hers down the cellar to store toys.

She was still asleep, hung over from a session with Buddy the night before. At some point before dawn, it all became clear to him. None of this was fun anymore. In fact it was ugly. He missed the Bluebird Inn, even the old Hi-Way Rollerdome. And it was more than nostalgia. People were talking. Maybe he could turn his life around. A caricature of old Buddy Hart stared back at him in the mirror. Some men might choose to put a bullet through their heads, he mused. There were several rifles out in the barn. Eustace Hubbard had taken him clay-pigeon shooting. Now he at least knew how to load the gun and blow his head off. Didn't take much of a shot.

Yeah. And so what if Buddy Hart never made the lights outside Ohio? Jolly never did either. "Ain't fucking enough lights to go around, Hart," Jolly joked.

A lot of wisdom in that, too, Buddy agreed. I just got to get out of the nest. I don't need this booze shit. I liked things well enough before.

One gig. I'll get one gig. Clean my act up 'n' move onto the next.

And just as he was piling his sheet music into the trunk, Celia appeared in the hallway, naked, looking like a raven wraith.

Buddy broke into an ironic grin. Looking down at her stomach. Thinking how he and other men had dreamed about the auburn grove. It wasn't so pretty now. The day before she'd painted his baby grand piano—a wedding gift from Eustace—tomato red. Buddy cried when he saw it.

"Where do you think you're going?"

"Heading out, Celia."

"Oh, no," she said.

"We'll see each other," he soothed. "Why don't you work on the house here while I'm gone. Paint the kitchen cabinets. The floor, I don't give a good goddamn. I need air, Celia. The Hubbards are stealing my oxygen."

"You . . . Bunny Berigan?" she laughed. "You going to go back to DeForest-by-the-Open-Sewer? All the shit of man in the gully outside your house, Buddy? Nothing that ain't been flushed down there." She lifted a cigarette off the coffee table and collapsed into the sofa. Buddy emptied the top drawer of his bureau where he kept his cuff links, wristwatch, and money clips—all Hubbard gifts—into the trunk.

"You ain't leaving," she said.

Buddy turned to her. "I am, Celia. It's been goddamn interesting and in the beginning, fun."

Celia stood. She offered Buddy a cigarette and lifted a chromium Statue of Liberty lighter off the glass coffee table, lighting it for him. It was as if she suddenly changed moods. Commiserative, helpful, solicitous. It's how she was in the beginning. Nothing she wouldn't do for Buddy Hart.

"What you got in there, honey?" she said.

Christ, what's this about? he thought. She gonna let me go? Hot damn. And he bent over the trunk, grasping its edge at the metal rasp with his melody hand, and with the bass-driver, pointed towards the sheet music, when, without warning, Celia slammed the lid shut, causing to erupt from Buddy Hart, alias Chet Baker, alias Jimmy Smith, alias Johnny Ray, a big piercing Hammond B-3 vibrato—*A flat diminished seventh*. Along with the clothes, the spare change and the costume jewelry, now lay Buddy Hart's middle finger. The Hammond B-3 screaming one.

"*And say hello to Stanley,*" she crooned.

Joan Möbius

Bedbugs

THE BABY KEEPS CRYING, the toilet's backed up, and *he* says he has to work overtime. He must think I'm dumb as a box of rocks. I know where he's at—some bar, with his buddies. And here I am, alone with a newborn that won't stop crying.

"She's colicky," the nurse at the clinic tells me. "It's nobody's fault, some babies are just born that way. She has gas on her tummy, poor little thing."

So I walk with her in my arms, burping her and rocking her, the noise from the TV following me, at least somebody's talking to me, one room to the next: kitchen, living room, bedroom, back to the kitchen. It's a small house. All I can do is keep walking until she falls asleep. When I finally sit down, my leg muscles twitch.

She cries at night, too, I think she's teething. *He* says he doesn't give a shit why she cries, he just wants some peace and quiet. Like getting pregnant was my idea. Like I'm crazy about how his cum sticks to me afterwards, slippery, like the water I boil macaroni in except it smells. "I gotta go to work tomorrow!" he yells. "Keep a roof over our heads, put food on the table!" He grabs the paregoric and forces her mouth open and pours it over her gums. She splutters and shrieks.

I try to grab the bottle. "You'll choke her!"

He throws it to the floor so hard it breaks and slaps me across the face. "*Both* of you shut up!"

I do. She screams even louder.

He's sorry, he whines. He loves me—he didn't mean to hurt me. He just got a little crazy there for a minute, no sleep, the baby carrying on. Clumsily, he pats my ass.

I move away. Love? What does *he* know about it?

At least she sleeps through the night now, but days, nights—they're all the same. Unless he's home I wouldn't know Sunday from Labor Day. There's a taste in my mouth like dried blood and I can't get rid of it.

She's walking already, I have to keep my eye on her every second. I take her with me to the new supermarket. At the checkout lines, men in suits ask questions. If you answer right, they give you something: a pound of coffee, two steaks, three pounds of real butter. When it's my turn he asks how do I keep fruit from darkening after it's been cut. I don't know how I know this, but I tell him, "lemon juice." He gives me a whole bag of groceries.

Maybe there *are* tricks to being a wife and mother. If I learn them, maybe everything will be okay.

I start going to the library and checking out books on household tips. One day I'm dressing her for kindergarten and the zipper on her jacket sticks. "I know what to do," I say. I run and get a bar of soap from the shower. Kneeling next to her, I work it into the teeth and the zipper pulls free. She gives me a smile like I just pulled off a miracle.

I make toothpaste out of baking soda and salt and put it in the bathroom in a Mickey Mouse cup. He says it tastes like shit, he wants real toothpaste. When I tell him I'm trying to save money, he's always going on about how broke we are and I'm just trying to help, he says I'm turning into Mrs. Know-It-All. She says she likes it, but she wants it in a different cup. "I'm too old for Mickey Mouse, Mommy."

The first time I let her walk home from school by herself she comes running to me, trying not to cry, holding up her hand so I can see how swollen it is.

"I *told* you to stay away from that empty lot," I yell. "I don't care if it's a short cut! All the bums from the rail yard use it for a toilet and I don't want you anywhere near there!" Then she does cry and says she just wanted to pick the flowers, she didn't expect a bee in them. "Even flowers," I tell her. "Anything. Anything can get you!" I make a paste of boric acid and water to put on her hand to suck out the poison.

She's in junior high now and argues with me about everything. If I ask her to pick up her room, she tells me it's already clean. If I say any man who takes his daughter to the racetrack on her birthday is scum, she says she loves horses. All she thinks about is clothes. She wants a bigger allowance so she can buy her own—boots, jeans, leather vests—from stores that sell men's wear. She wants to look like all the other girls.

At least he doesn't slap me around anymore. He's getting fat; it's probably too much trouble.

I open her bedroom door and walk in. She's lying with her back to me, listening to music so loud the floorboards shimmy. The walls are plastered with pictures of rock stars with hair longer than hers. "What are you doing?" I ask.

She rolls over. "Listening to music. What does it look like I'm doing?"

"Let me smell your hands. What did you have for lunch?"

"*What*?"

"You heard me. And why were you lying that way?"

"I had a tuna sandwich for lunch and I was lying that way because I like lying that way! *Okay*?" She rolls back, away from me. "Now leave me alone!"

But who's going to teach her right from wrong if it's not me?

"You have very high blood pressure," the doctor at the clinic says. He's Chinese, Turkish, some brown color. "Cut out salt, take this medication daily, and avoid aggravation."

I catch her primping in the bathroom. "Where do you think *you're* going?" I ask. She won't look at me. She's meeting a boy at the 7-Eleven, she says, and maybe afterwards they'll catch a movie. "Be home by supper time," I say, "and if he tries anything, if he touches you, scream." But she's not listening. She wants to be touched.

He tells her—she still listens to him, sometimes—we can't afford a fancy wedding. She says if she gets married that's her business and maybe they don't *want* a wedding. He says to me, "The next time you want to know something, ask her yourself." He's wearing a Hawaiian shirt I've never seen before, and his hair looks different. I follow my daughter into her room to tell her that whoever this boy is, he's not worth throwing her life away for, but she slams the door in my face.

She decides to go to college; she wants to expand her intellectual horizons, meet new people. "People are the same everywhere," I tell her.

"You're right, mother. Whatever you say." Her voice is just this side of polite. "You know everything."

Halfway through her first semester, she elopes. That boy she was going with—I find out he's in the Marines, stationed near her college. She didn't want an education. She wanted free room and board for a while.

I spend Thanksgiving alone. I told him that if he wanted a big fancy dinner he could go to his ladyfriend's house.

My daughter calls to wish me a happy Thanksgiving. "Are you cooking a turkey?" I ask. "Be sure to take the giblets out before you put it in the oven."

She sounds relaxed, happy. "Yes, mother. Haven't I watched you in the kitchen all these years?" I tell her to shop the sales, buy meat on special and freeze it for later. When she answers that all she ever buys is hamburger, I tell her to use oatmeal as filler, or bread crumbs. I ask if she wants my recipe for home-made Bisquick but she tells me no thanks, she doesn't do much baking. She doesn't need any Bisquick.

I stay with her the first week after the baby is born. I sharpen all her knives for her—there's nothing worse than a dull knife—and poke a pencil into all the keyholes because I can hardly get my key to turn. When she comes home, she doesn't even notice. She's breast feeding, and her clothes smell like sour milk. Baking soda, I tell her. Even in the laundry hamper.

My granddaughter has a full head of fuzzy blond hair, like an angel with a halo. Every time I smile at her, she smiles back.

Her husband is transferred to a base out in the desert, I can hardly even find it on the map. One day I get a phone call from her and she's hysterical. "Clorox," I tell her. "Yes, even on babies. One part Clorox, five parts water. Splash it on her arms and legs, wherever they've bitten her, and rinse it off again with cool water. It stops the itching and the bites won't get infected." She hangs up without thanking me.

He files for divorce—he's had enough, he says. "Good riddance," I tell him. "I wish you'd done it years ago." I hire an attorney, a woman, but it's too late. He's been sly; there's nothing she can do, she says. After twenty-one years of marriage, all I get is half the savings. The house—his. The car—his. His health and retirement plans—all his. I move to the desert to be near my daughter. A second-floor apartment, small, easy to take care of.

She looks fat—I wonder if she's pregnant again—and her house is so dirty my nose won't stop running. "They make things so cheap these days. If you clean it, it breaks," she says, exhaling smoke through her nose. She never used to smoke. My granddaughter's crawling already, and the rug is so filthy her knees and hands are black. I get a washcloth. While I scrub the baby's hands I tell my daughter, "I'm going to buy you one of those vacuums, they look like that old carpet sweeper I used to have except you plug it in. And you should quit smoking. You know what they say about second-hand smoke."

My daughter grinds out her cigarette in a glass statue shaped like a swan. I gave her that. "I already *have* an electric broom. When are you going to stop telling me how to live?"

The apartment costs too much, so I move into a trailer park. Some park—it's crawling with roaches the size of field mice. Water bugs, the manager calls them. I call them cockroaches. I mix borax and brown sugar and pour it into jar lids and set them along the baseboards. I wonder if my daughter has trouble with roaches, but when I call, she hangs up before I can ask if it's a boy or a girl.

A letter arrives. Her father died, she thought I might like to know that, since I was the one who drove him away. I go to the funeral, hoping to see her, but she doesn't come. There's a wreath from her at the head of the casket: *I'll Always Love You, Daddy. Rest in Peace.*

There's dirt everywhere, where does it all come from? To keep the chrome in the kitchen shiny I use diluted white vinegar. To clean the aluminum sliding door, I make a paste of cream of tartar and water. To get the grease off the walls I wash them down with ammonia and liquid detergent and hot water. One day I read in the paper that if you want to remove old bloodstains, make a paste of unseasoned meat tenderizer and water. But I tried that a long time ago. They never really come out.

I'm driving to the store for bleach when a speck the size of a whitefly darts across the windshield. I wave it aside but all of a sudden it merges with dozens of others, zigzagging back and forth so fast my blood runs cold. They aren't whiteflies. They're ice-colored, like holes cut out of space, and I pull off to the side of the road because I'm dizzy and my heart is pounding and I don't know anything anymore, especially about love. If I knew how to love, why am I so afraid of dying?

Lore
Segal

The Talk in Eliza's Kitchen

ALFRED STONE SAID, "Winterneet couldn't make it. He's off in Copenhagen."

"Oh, never mind Winterneet," said Ilka, and looked gladly around the room, which was full of her new friends and colleagues at the Concordance Institute. Here were her hosts, Alfred and Alpha Stone, and there were the Ayes and the Zees and the Cones and the Bernstines. How could Ilka's back tell the difference between empty air and a body, male? Director Leslie Shakespere was standing behind Ilka, listening to his wife, Eliza, making Yvette Gordot laugh. "Your wife is terrific," Ilka said to him.

"Yes, she is," said director Shakespere, and he and Ilka stood and listened together.

"That was before I stopped Leslie from doing all the things he likes to do," said Eliza Shakespere. She was a Canadian, built nobly and on a grand scale. Ilka admired the width of her shoulders, the length of thigh. Her hair was so very fine and so electrically charged that it attached itself to her cheeks and temples. She kept palming it away.

Alpha called everyone into the dining room. Ilka was seated between Professor Zee and Leslie Shakespere, at the furthest remove from Eliza Shakespere. Eliza was entertaining her end of the table with a highly colored anecdote about a groom who had inadvertently locked Leslie in the stables and made him miss the equestrian tryouts for the Olympics. Ilka glanced at Leslie's great head, which was brooding over his soup. "Did he really lock you in?" she asked him.

"No," said Leslie.

"Are you really an equestrian?"

"I was," said Leslie.

"No, you weren't," said Ilka, "and I can prove it."

Leslie looked at Ilka.

Ilka said, "People I sit next to at dinner are not equestrians, and I'm sitting next to you."

Leslie smiled.

Ilka said, "I can prove you never tried out for the Olympics."

Leslie laughed.

"People I know are as likely to try out for the Olympics as they are to climb Mt. Everest."

Leslie blushed.

"You climbed Mt. Everest!" Ilka said, so loudly that Eliza said, "Before I stopped him."

"Did Eliza stop you?" asked Ilka.

"As a matter of fact, she did."

At the far end of the table Eliza was embarked on a tale about the Sherpa who carried Leslie's tent out into the blinding white expanse and disappeared. "Nothing as far as the eye could see except his abominable snow prints."

Ilka felt silly asking Leslie over and over what, in Eliza's stories, was the truth. She kept looking sideways at him. He said, "It was a preliminary expedition to test new equipment and methods."

Eliza said, "And Leslie tested a new type of nylon rope by falling off a mountain and hanging upside down, spinning, and yo-yoing, at one and the same time."

Here Leslie said, "Dear, did you ask Alpha if Mrs. Beeton has a recipe for gooseberry fool? Our real-estate man showed us two gooseberry bushes in our back garden." Leslie persevered. "Did you know that growing gooseberries is forbidden in several states of the union?" And having got the left side of the table discussing "Mrs. Beeton's Cookery" and the right side listing obsolete laws that continued on the books, Leslie returned to his soup.

Ilka had looked apprehensively down the table at Eliza, who had been stopped mid-story. Eliza's head was bent low over her plate, and her eyes were hidden.

Ilka did not drive, and the Shakesperes offered to drop her off at home. She walked down the dark path with Eliza, behind Alfred Stone, who was walking the director to his car. Eliza said, "It wasn't the gooseberries out back—it was the tiny tomatoes in the front that made Leslie buy the house."

Ilka sat beside Leslie. Eliza, in the back seat, said, "Doesn't Alfred Stone look like something out of 'Steve Canyon'? The iron jaw, the jutting forelock."

Ilka said, "Alfred says Winterneet is in Copenhagen. Are we sure there really is a Winterneet?"

"There used to be, before he got his Nobel Prize," Eliza said.

Leslie said, "The State Department sends him on tours."

"But you affirm, categorically, that Winterneet exists?" asked Ilka. "I cried when I had to leave New York and come to live in Connecticut. All my friends said, 'But Winterneet lives in Concordance.' My friend Jules said he knew a fellow whose accountant used to play golf with Winterneet's lawyer. At my interview, Zack told me Winterneet gave a series of lectures at the institute the year of his Nobel Prize; Jenny drove me by his house; Mary promised to have him for dinner, but he got a cold. At the Bernstines' reception, he was on the Coast. Martin Moses asked me to a party given for the express purpose of not being stood up by Winterneet, who wasn't invited."

"Well, we knew Winterneet before he was Winterneet," said Eliza. "Winnie was our lodger. That was before the baby."

"That's my house at the corner," said Ilka. "I rent it from some people called Rasmussen. They're off on their sabbatical."

"Leslie, aren't you going to be a gentleman, like Alfred, and walk Ilka up the path to her front door?"

"Ilka, do you need to be walked to your front door?"

"Absolutely not," said Ilka stoutly, and Leslie invited Ilka to come to a late breakfast Sunday.

Eliza said, "Leslie means brunch, which is a word his British mouth is unable to articulate."

Ilka walked up her path in a state of happiness she had not experienced since before she left her old friends behind in New York.

Leslie called on Sunday morning. "I have chores in town. Eliza thought you might like me to pick you up on the way home."

Ilka was so pleased that she kept inventing hardships from which Leslie's kindness was going to save her, well past the point at which she perfectly understood Leslie's desire to get off the telephone.

"Is eleven a good time?"

Eleven was the perfect time; by then Ilka would have finished grading the compositions of her class in Intermediate English. "This really is amazingly good of you."

"Oh, you bet," said Leslie.

Ilka felt the intense pleasantness of sitting beside Leslie Shakespere. Also, it made her nervous. She felt obliged to entertain Leslie's silence with speech, which she hoped was interesting without being *tiresomely* interesting. "Do you know that delicious moment when you have finished grading your last paper, and the whole week, before you have to grade your next class, is perfectly intact in front of you?"

Leslie seemed to be thinking this over.

Ilka said, "Like the second before a holiday has had the first minute bitten out of it?"

Now Leslie had two things to think over.

Ilka said, "Like that moment in the theatre when the curtain starts going up?"

Leslie said, "I do know that moment."

Ilka decided it was up to Leslie to think of the next thing to say, but he was turning in to his driveway.

Leslie took Ilka into the kitchen to say hello to Eliza.

"Can I help?" Ilka asked her.

"Christ, no!" said Eliza. "Leslie will make Bloody Marys."

Leslie and Ilka carried their drinks into the living room. Ilka said, "I don't know how you do it, but you and Eliza make me talk. You never ask me any questions, but I tell you everything."

"That *is* odd," said Leslie. When Ilka's glass was empty he carried it out to the kitchen, and Ilka heard him say, "Ilka says we never ask her questions, but she tells us everything. She asks how do we do it?" Ilka imagined Eliza standing with her back to Leslie. She couldn't hear Eliza's answer and got up and stood in the doorway and listened, and, hearing Leslie's returning footsteps, quickly sat down.

Leslie said, "Eliza says we ask questions in the form of suppositions."

Ilka said, "The truth of the matter is that you and Eliza are accomplished listeners. You don't have my compulsion to interject something analogous from my own autobiography into the other person's story. I mean to be expressing my sympathetic understanding, but all that does is take the conversation away from the other speaker. What you do is make these little sounds like *'mm'* or *'mf'* so that one feels you listening. Do you know what you do when somebody says something you don't like?"

"What?" asked Leslie.

"You uncross your right leg from over your left knee and cross your left leg over your right knee."

"I'll be damned," said Leslie.

"If I see you making some abrupt movement, like suddenly picking up or putting down your glass, I know I've got some common fact dead wrong."

Leslie said again that he would be damned, excused himself, and walked out into the kitchen to tell Eliza what Ilka had said. He came back and said, "Eliza says we should bring our drinks, and talk in the kitchen, where she can hear us."

Eliza once more refused Ilka's offer of help. Ilka and Leslie sat at the table while Eliza sliced and chopped and grated. The kitchen was a large room. Two snapshots, one of a little baby with a large bib, and one of an apple tree in full fruit, were stuck into the window frame.

Ilka said, "The Rasmussens' kitchen is the color of egg yolk, and full of doodads. When I moved in, I hid them all in the back of the cupboards and went shopping. I bought this beautiful Danish chopping board made of blocks of different kinds of wood."

"Did you?" said Eliza. "I fished *this* chopping board," and she pointed to a little square of oak with a cracked corner, "out of Lake Michigan in 1959."

Leslie said, "Ilka, tell Eliza what you said about the way I listen."

Ilka repeated to Eliza what she had said, and Eliza said, "How do I listen?"

Ilka said, "You look pleased when you hear some half-truth or nonsense—you get a satisfied look, as if the world were bearing out the opinion you privately held of it." Ilka was excited to feel them listening to what she was saying; she hoped she would stop talking. She said, "In the months I've known you I've told you all my stories, but I know very little about *you*," and she asked what Eliza had meant about asking questions in the form of suppositions.

Eliza said, "If you asked me point-blank how I lost my thirteen-month-old baby"—here Leslie got out of his chair and walked to the sink and stood beside Eliza—"I'd say what my rotten little American cousins used to say to me, like 'Mind your own beeswax' or 'That's for me to know and for you to find out.' But if you said, 'It was in April, wasn't it?' I might say, 'April 15, and one of those lovely-looking days.'" Eliza walked to the refrigerator. Leslie stayed beside her. "It *looked* warm, or maybe I *wanted* the Chicago winter to be over. When we got outside it was good and chilly." Leslie walked to the stove with Eliza. "I put the brakes on the stroller and ran inside, and got the baby's blanket, which I had already washed and put away. A box of mothballs fell out, and I ran and got the broom and dustpan, and I will drive Leslie crazy telling you the whole story."

"Which is what my mother does!" said Ilka. "She tells the whole story of how she left my father sitting by the road just outside Obernpest, the week before the end of the war, and she never saw him again."

"I did it again!" said Ilka in the car. "I told my father story and stopped Eliza from telling the story about the baby! How long ago was this?"

"It will be fourteen years next April 15."

"Doesn't that take some of the pain away?"

Leslie thought about that and said, "It seemed intolerable when it happened, and it seems intolerable today."

Ilka silently resented the Shakesperes' intolerable loss. She imagined it as a wound in their lives, a flaw in their every pleasure. This flawed the pleasure Ilka wanted to be at liberty to feel when she was with them. Ilka wanted that baby unlost.

Before he left her off at her gate, Leslie invited Ilka to breakfast next Sunday. Again he called and offered to pick her up. Again Ilka worried about not helping, but Eliza wanted them to sit and drink their Bloody Marys and talk in the kitchen, where she could hear them. And she said, "Winnie's back. He wanted to come for brunch, but I said we had other plans."

"I'll phone him later," said Leslie.

"I told him to come and get his boxes," Eliza said.

"What's Winterneet like?" asked Ilka.

"Looks like something out of 'Peanuts,'" replied Eliza. "A swelled head walking on his little shoes."

"You don't like him?" asked Ilka doubtfully.

Leslie said, "Winterneet and the Bernstines are our oldest American friends."

"How did you meet him?" asked Ilka.

Leslie said, "When we were graduate students in Chicago. Winnie was an assistant professor—"

"—and already polishing his Nobel Prize acceptance speech," Eliza said.

Leslie uncrossed and recrossed his legs and reached for his glass. He said, "We were short of money. Winnie's first marriage was breaking up, and he moved in with us—"

"—and, having spread his papers over every surface of every room in our apartment," Eliza said, "he moved out."

"He moved in with his second wife, Dorothy," said Leslie.

Eliza said, "Leslie collected all the papers in one cardboard box, which stood in our little hallway all summer and fall. Came the first snow, I put it out in the driveway."

"You didn't!" said Ilka.

"Yes, I did," said Eliza.

Ilka looked at Leslie, who said, "She did."

"Leslie brought it back inside and put it up in his study. When Winnie left Dorothy he brought us his second box of papers."

Presently, Leslie stood up, handling his car keys inside his jacket pocket. Ilka said, "I love it that you let a person know when you've had enough."

"Always the gentleman," said Eliza.

"It means that I can sit and enjoy myself without worrying about whether the time has come for me to go home. Eliza and Leslie, I want to make you a proposition: May I elect you to be my cousins? I'm low on the kind one has by blood."

Leslie and Eliza agreed to be Ilka's elective cousins, and Eliza invited her to come over after dinner, Saturday. The Bernstines were dropping by for drinks. Leslie said he would pick Ilka up.

Saturday, and Ilka walked into the Shakesperes' living room. On a chair, with a drink in his hand, sat a man whose thinning hair was the color, exactly, of the expanse of his cranium. His shoes were child-size. It was the actual Winterneet, regarding Ilka with a smile that revealed a small, charming gap between his two front teeth. Ilka felt looked at longer than was comfortable. She lowered her eyes, raised them, and the actual Winterneet was still smiling. He was taking her in. Now came the Bernstines, and Leslie bringing drinks, and Eliza with a platter of what Winterneet, with his delightful smile, persisted in calling "the eats."

Ilka meant to keep looking intelligently engaged in a conversation that these old friends must have been having for the past two decades. Once in a while Leslie threw Ilka a scrap of data, a gloss on a name. "It was Frank who introduced Dorothy and Winterneet in—Winnie, was that in '63 or '64? Dorothy was Edwin's half sister," Leslie explained. The phone rang and Leslie walked out into the hall.

"'63," said Eliza. "We had the baby in '64." Ilka observed Joe Bernstine plant his hands on the arms of his chair, ready to rise. She saw Jenny's forehead corrugate.

"It was in '65, Winnie, that we moved your two boxes to Amherst along with our things," said Eliza, and Joe settled back; Jenny still looked anxious.

Winterneet said, "When I get back from London, I'll come over and spend the day, and sort out what I want to throw away."

Leslie returned and said, "It's Una. She's at Kennedy."

Eliza said, "Tell her no."

Leslie said, "She just got in from London."

Eliza said, "No."

Leslie went out.

Joe Bernstine asked, "And how is our little Una?"

"I was happy, until a minute ago, to have heard nothing about our little Una for the last six months," Eliza said.

"She wrote me," said Leslie, returning to the room.

"Well, I was happy to hear nothing about it," said Eliza.

"Well, I thought you would be happy," said Leslie.

"Our little Una in the granny dress, with straw in her hair!" said Winterneet.

"That," said Eliza, "is our Una."

The Bernstines offered to give Ilka a lift home. Winterneet said he'd stay if someone would offer him a nightcap.

In the car, Ilka asked the Bernstines about this Una.

"Poor Una! She fell rather in love with Leslie and Eliza. Leslie-and-Eliza as a unit."

"I can understand that," said Ilka.

"The Shakesperes brought her back to the States with them. Her father is the theologian Paul Thayer," said Jenny.

"Uncle," said Joe, and they argued about Una's relationship to this Paul Thayer until they arrived at Ilka's gate.

"They've adopted Ilka," Joe said to Jenny, as they drove away.

"I like Ilka," said Jenny and frowned anxiously.

"The Shakesperes have a new adoptee," Joe said to Zachariah Zee over the phone later that evening.

"Ah!" said Zack Zee. "Ilka."

"Joe says Leslie and Eliza have adopted Ilka," Zack said to his wife, Mary, at Sunday breakfast, and Mary said, "I wish her lots of luck."

That morning, Leslie called and came and got Ilka. Ilka walked into Eliza's kitchen and Winterneet was already sitting at the table, smiling his delightful smile at Ilka.

Ilka was not some young thing: it annoyed her not to be able to keep her end up like Eliza, who could keep the conversation flying like some high-wire act while she cut, sliced, corrected the seasoning, and performed last-minute maneuvers at the stove. Eliza, tossing and tasting the salad, elaborated a very tall tale that Winterneet topped with a deliciously nasty quip. Ilka wanted to play with them up there in the middle air, but the palpitation of her heart preempted her breathing. She hunkered down, waiting for the laughter to take its course so she could take a running start and get her own joke airborne with enough breath for the punch line; but Eliza, passing around the beautiful French bread, had started a story that grew naturally out of Winterneet's point, which Ilka had missed because it took off from what she suspected herself of not having recognized as a quotation. Ilka crouched—awaiting the next opening in the hope that she would have thought of something to fit whatever might, by that time, be under discussion—but she grew discouraged and stopped listening.

She looked at Leslie. He attended to his bread, buttered it. Now he sat back in his chair and observed his wife and his friend with the air of a man eating the world's best bread and butter, and listening to the best conversation, in his own house, at his own breakfast.

Eliza had glided two coddled eggs onto Leslie's plate when the doorbell rang. Leslie looked regretful, reluctantly got up, and went to answer. He came back. He said, "Dear. Una."

"No!" said Eliza.

"She's come straight from the airport," said Leslie. "She has all her bags."

Eliza said, "I recommend the Concordance Hotel, corner of Euclid and Main, clean and well lighted."

Leslie went out.

"You can't do that, can you? Can you do that?" asked Ilka in an excited whisper. "Can you tell someone to go away?"

"Watch me," said Eliza. "Or watch me tell Leslie to tell her."

"Only . . . imagine having just arrived from New York—"

"London," said Eliza.

"What do you *say* to her?"

"You say, 'If you bother me, I'll set the Concordance police on you.'"

Leslie returned. Eliza gave him back the eggs she had kept warm for him, poured Winterneet more coffee, and said, "I always make Leslie go and do the dirty work."

"Yes, you do," said Leslie.

Ilka said, "What actual words did you say to her?"

"I said, 'There's a nice enough family hotel on Main—medium priced.' I wrote the address on a piece of paper and hugged her goodbye."

"You hugged Una!" cried Eliza.

"Yes," said Leslie.

"She's Paul Thayer's niece, no?" asked Winterneet.

"Niece by marriage," Leslie said. The doorbell rang again. Eliza took Leslie's eggs and covered them with foil.

When Leslie came back, he had his car keys in his fist. "Her driver's driven off. I'll take her to the hotel."

"Exit Leslie," said Eliza. "She's *driven* her driver off! Our Una likes to have *Leslie* drive her. Una is always having to be driven. Una *always* needs picking up."

Ilka reddened and said, "But didn't you used to like her?"

"Una was a chilly little English schoolgirl, who came to America and caught the sixties."

"Why isn't that a good thing for a chilly girl to catch?"

"Because she had to work so hard at it. Have you ever seen a hedonist with gritted teeth?"

"Poor Una," said Ilka.

"Poor, poor Una," said Eliza. "Remember the baby kangaroo in Pooh Corner? It keeps saying, 'Look at me jumping!'? Una kept leaping out of her pouch, saying, 'Look at me screwing everybody!'"

Ilka said, "But, Eliza, imagine having been born chilly. What was Una *supposed* to do?" Ilka looked to Winterneet for help, but he kept eating. Ilka said, "Don't you think there's something gallant about warming yourself up by your own bootstraps? What do you want her to *do*?"

"Go back to London," said Eliza.

When Leslie returned from driving Una to the Concordance Hotel, he ate his eggs and salad and then he drove Ilka home to the Rasmussens'.

Eliza was not present at the institute's reception, which poor Una gate-crashed.

Ensconced together in the embrasure of the window, Leslie and Una looked like the classic couple one pretends not to have noticed on a couch or a park bench—she in tears, he consoling, sorry for her, and implicated, although her trouble, one knows, is all hers. Leslie offered Una his handkerchief and waited till she had finished wiping her eyes and blowing her nose. Seeing Ilka looking toward them, he beckoned. He introduced them. Ilka said, "Hi."

Una stared at the new entity before her with humorless eyes. She was a lovely, clever-looking young woman. Her no-bra, bedroom-hair style seemed grafted onto a Reynolds beauty. Una's little, elegant face was exaggeratedly shapely and pointed, her mouth tiny, moist. Instead of an amplitude of crackling satin, Una had on the inevitable anorexic pair of jeans. She sobbed. She said, "Isn't the criminal supposed to be told her crime? What did I do that was so wrong? Why has she dropped me? I rang her, and she picked up and said that she was out."

Ilka and Leslie did not smile. Una had begun to cry again. Leslie offered to drive her back to the hotel. "You want a ride?" he asked Ilka, who understood that she would be a welcome buffer.

Ilka, in the back seat, was no help in stemming Una's grief at her expulsion from the paradise of Eliza's kitchen. "All I want is to sit down face-to-face and talk this thing out!"

"Talking out face-to-face! It's an overrated activity," said Leslie sadly. At the hotel he walked the weeping young woman to the door, hugged her goodbye, and patted his pocket, but Una had kept his handkerchief.

Leslie got back into the car and said, "Come to the house?"

"Love to."

Winterneet was sitting at the kitchen table. Eliza was on a tear. "Can't pick up the telephone without finding Una howling at the other end. Leslie, you remember the day Una wove a circle round you thrice?"

"Round us both, you and me," said Leslie.

"Aren't Jewish brides supposed to walk circles around the groom?" Eliza asked Ilka.

"Are they? Viennese like me tend to be inefficient Jews."

"She's a spider spinning you into her web," said Eliza.

"A magic circle," said Leslie.

"A mandala," said Winterneet. "She was incorporating you. I think our Una was into a little bit of witchcraft."

"*Into* witchcraft? As you are *into* destroying the language," said Eliza, but Winterneet said that he was rather fond of this "being into" things and smiled into Ilka's eyes. It was a nice example of what Mencken called "judicious neology," he said, but offered to give it up if Eliza could come up with a better English formulation that expressed that particular human relation to a human activity.

"It's a syntactic barbarism," said Eliza. They were off. Leslie leaned back and smiled at them, and Ilka was jealous. She contracted and relaxed her several muscle groups beginning with the ones she sat upon. She draped her left arm with what she meant to be an easy carelessness across the back of Leslie's chair; the arm cramped. She ungritted her teeth, relaxed her jaws, temples, cheeks, and achieved the unnatural expression of a person intending to look natural.

Ilka did not think she had impinged on Una's consciousness and was surprised, when she answered the Rasmussens' doorbell, to find the girl on her front step. "Leslie gave me your address," said Una. Una had come to talk about the Shakesperes. "It's like living a whodunit that opens with the hanging, and it's me who's being hanged. What did I do? I think it was the ice cream. Once Eliza made ice cream. It tasted lovely, and I *told* her it tasted lovely, but I shouldn't have said I liked the *consistency* of the bought kind, because she didn't talk to me the rest of the night."

"It's weird," said Ilka, "the way we can't, any of us, bear being faulted."

"But I didn't even fault her. I didn't say I didn't like her ice cream; all I said was that I liked the consistency of the bought."

"I'm wearing a blue dress," said Ilka. "Somebody says, 'Green is a nice color,' and I think, I'm never going to talk to this person ever again."

"But that's silly," said Una.

"That's what I mean," said Ilka. "All we hear is someone saying we are less than perfectly perfect."

"I never mind being told when I've done something wrong."

Ilka said, "Will you forgive me if I don't believe you?"

"What I can't stand," said Una, "is *not* being told. I don't understand people not sitting down face-to-face." Una wiped her eyes and said, "What I actually think is, I think my opinions are too difficult for Eliza to assimilate. She's a very uptight person. I threaten her because I hang very loose."

Ilka looked surreptitiously at her watch, but Una had just started in.

Leslie sounded his horn outside Ilka's gate on Sunday at eleven. "Eliza is on a rampage," he said. A new phase had begun in what Eliza had taken to calling the Una Initiative. Leslie had gone to bed early the night before. Eliza, staying downstairs with a book, had raised her eyes and seen Una staring in the window.

The version Eliza told Ilka and Winterneet at the kitchen table was elaborate. "I walked into the kitchen to get myself a glass of wine, walked back into the living room, and settled myself on the sofa. Where's my book? Nothing like being in the middle of a book, all set to go on reading, and you don't know where you put it. I got up, I walked around, looked everywhere, and there's a maenad, a bacchante—wild eyes, nose flattened against the glass, hair full of fruits and leaves—mouthing at me! I let out such a holler that Leslie came bounding downstairs, and it's something to see Leslie bounding in his blue pajamas with the navy piping."

Leslie said, "Eliza was going to call the police and report a trespasser."

"It was our Una peering through the cherry tomatoes! Leslie pulled on his trousers and drove her back to her hotel."

"She came to my door to complain about you," said Ilka.

"Can't open a door or look through a bloody window without finding Una outside," Eliza said. The front doorbell rang, and she said, "I'm calling the police," but it was the town deli with a delivery: Una's peace offering, a heroic basket, a cornucopia. "Bourbon-spiked marmalade! That's disgusting."

"Let's try some," said Leslie.

"Canned jugged hare! Toss it out. Baroque pears! Look at the size! They're obscene."

"Superfruit, like in those—what kind of still-life paintings am I thinking of?"

"The kind where a worm crawls out of the apple, or a bug, a wasp. A spider."

Ilka said, "But, Eliza, you have to imagine being Una and not knowing what to do about you. I think she really is in pain."

"She's a pain in the neck," Eliza said.

"Really, though," Ilka said to Leslie when he drove her home, "what *did* Una do that made Eliza drop her?"

"Eliza *and I*," said Leslie. "We have both dropped Una."

Ilka understood and accepted the reprimand. In a moment, she said, "But imagine you have friends whom you love, whose kitchen you are used to walking in and out of, and one day they won't let you in, and won't tell you why they won't."

Leslie was silent for such a long time that Ilka said, "Why won't you tell Una *why*?"

"I'm trying to think what the answer to your question is," said Leslie. "I don't want to answer you until I have thought."

"Sorry," said Ilka.

Leslie said, "I'll get you a copy of Winterneet's little book called 'Tales from the Mouth of God.' They're quite nice. In each of Winnie's stories God irritably corrects a Bible story that misrepresents what he had in mind. God says why would he have expelled Adam and Eve for eating fruit? He says they *bored* him, but he didn't want to tell them so. It's devastating to know you are a bore, because it's not something you can do anything about. Much kinder to let them think it was something they had *done*, so that they could hope, if they stopped doing it, to get back into paradise. So God said, 'Let there be sin.'"

"Do you think Una is a bore?"

"Don't you think so?"

Ilka said, "But wasn't she the same bore when you liked her and brought her to the States with you?"

"In another of Winnie's stories," Leslie said, "God says, 'Let there be falling in love.' It makes the other person's sin smell like our own sin—that's to say, not at all. Ah, but the stink after we fall out of love, or out of friendship!"

"That's terrible!" said Ilka.

"Yes. It is," said Leslie.

Back in the kitchen Eliza was filling Winterneet's glass. She filled her own glass and said, "The phone rings. Una is strapped for cash, and the bank is about to close. Leslie drives right over to take her to the bank. The phone rings. Una is suicidal and about to jump out of the window. Leslie runs right over to catch her. *Oh, but you have to imagine being poor Una being strapped!*" She spoke in a mincing voice, with an extravagantly innocent gape of the eyes, and a full Viennese roll of the "R." *"You have to imagine being suicidal!* I don't have to bloody *imagine* being suicidal! And I don't have to imagine Una when I've got her bloody underfoot."

Winterneet tilted the empty salad bowl and picked pieces of arugula off the sides.

Eliza was still going strong the following evening, at a dinner party at Yvette Gordot's. A letter had been slipped under Eliza's kitchen door. "I swear I will call the police if she persists in creeping round the house at night," Eliza said. She read the letter in its entirety, with a good deal of drama: "*'Expulsion and excommunication are cruel and unusual punishments for the commission of a crime of which one has never been accused. I feel that I am living a Kafkaesque whodunit that opens with my hanging as the criminal who has to double as the detective trying to discover my own crime.'* Here," said Eliza, "we come to our central mystery. Una writes, *'Was it the ice cream?'* Una appears to suspect herself of having committed an ice cream! She says, *'Give me five minutes'*—three exclamation marks—*'and I will tell you what I meant about consistency.'* One more exclamation mark and a tear stain. *'Why will you not give me the opportunity to explain or maybe plain apologize?'* Tear stains. *'Of all the people I have ever met in all of my life'* "—here Eliza's voice suggested accompanying violins—" *'I have never been so happy as in your and Leslie's company.'* " Eliza placed her right hand as if to hold up her left breast in the manner of certain neoclassical fountain statuary, and raised her eyes to the heavens above before lowering them onto page 2. " *'I have sat at your kitchen table and have thought, There is no place in all the world where I would rather be than right here, right now.'* "

Ilka was listening, and watching Winterneet walk toward her. Winterneet leaned against the wall beside her. Ilka said, "But that's just how *I* feel about the Shakesperes' kitchen table."

"Me, too, until Eliza goes on a tear."

Ilka experienced the little thrill of a little treachery. She said, "I *am* getting a bit weary of Eliza and the Una Initiative."

"I," said Winterneet, "am getting out of town."

"How long do Eliza's rampages last?"

"Until she finds the next old favorite to demolish. I'm going to London for the weekend," said Winterneet.

"No, you're not, and I can prove it." Winterneet turned his face to look at Ilka, who went on, "People I stand next to leaning against a wall at a party don't go for weekends to London."

Winterneet said, "Come with me."

Ilka said, "That'll be the day!" and laughed and caught the sound—or caught the small, violent commotion to the right of her right ear—of Winterneet's face responding, as if to one of those empty movie slaps. Ilka, unaware of having administered it, turned in surprise to see only Winterneet's left ear and his slack jaw turned in a direction radically away from her.

"First a week in Copenhagen, now a weekend in London!" said Ilka, who thought she was flattering the famous old man. "Sounds just too damn glamorous."

"Does it?" Winterneet turned his face to look not at Ilka but straight before him. He said, "It's a gas from the time I get out of bed in the morning until sometime around five in the afternoon. Then I want to die."

"But don't they give you lots of receptions?"

"Every night they give me a reception," said Winterneet.

"Don't you get to meet everybody? You can have any damn body you want!"

"Evidently not," said Winterneet glumly.

Sunday, Leslie beeped his horn outside Ilka's gate. He said that Eliza was fit to be tied. "Winterneet has taken Una to London with him."

"He took Una? You mean he meant it!"

Leslie turned in to his drive and pulled sharply up. "Oh, for goodness' sake!" In the middle of the driveway stood four cardboard boxes. Ilka and Leslie got out of the car and Leslie said, "I'll get this if you'll go and talk to Eliza," and he picked the first box up and carried it into the house and up the stairs and into his study.

Eliza said, "I'm fit to be tied."

"I think," Ilka said, "that travelling solo is Winterneet's memento mori. The fact is that no one can bear being alone, except most people keep right on bearing it, and Winterneet can't, and he doesn't need to."

"Must be why every time he leaves another wife he moves in with us—breakfast, lunch, and dinner," said Eliza. "And deposits another box of papers." She smiled blackly at Leslie, who had walked in rather out of breath. "We moved two boxes of his to Amherst with us, stored three with our things when we went back to Oxford, and brought four to Concordance. For fifteen years Winnie has been going to take his boxes home as soon as he sorts out what he is going to throw away."

"Which he will never do," said Ilka, "because the papers we are always going to throw away are the papers we are never going to read again, and we won't know which they are till we've read them again."

"That's so," said Leslie and looked at Ilka with pleasure, the same pleasure he looked at his wife with when she said something he recognized.

Eliza said, "And Winnie would come across the Nobel Prize acceptance speech he wrote when he was twenty-nine."

Leslie uncrossed his right leg from over his left knee and crossed his left over his right leg.

Leslie said, "Dear."

Eliza said, "You know what Winnie did the week I lost the baby?" Leslie got up and went and stood beside her. She said, "Winnie got out of town."

"He had an interview at Stanford," said Leslie."The Bernstines, to all intents and purposes, moved in," Eliza said. "The Bernstines sat with us, and howled with us, and talked with us, and were silent with us, and Winnie got out of town."

"I think," Ilka said, "that we feel shy around friends something has happened to."

"That's true," said Leslie.

Ilka said, "We don't know what it is okay to say."

"That's true," said Eliza. "I haven't called my friend Sarah, who wrote to tell me her son has leukemia."

"I wrote her," said Leslie.

"The hell you did," said Eliza, swivelling her chair to give Leslie a pretend kick in the shins. Maybe it was not pretend.

Ilka said, "You can't not mention what has happened, and you can't mention it, for fear of reopening the wound."

"And Winnie," said Eliza, "couldn't bear to watch the blood flow, so he got out of town and let it flow behind his back."

Leslie very quietly said, "That'll be enough."

Ilka had supper with the Shakespeares on Wednesday, and afterward the Bernstines dropped over. Jenny looked worriedly at Eliza and said, "Winnie's back. He's installed Una in his house."

Joe, looking sheepish, said, "We've offered Una an internship."

Several subjects were started, and dropped down the abyss of Eliza's silence, so it seemed to come out of left field when she presently said, "Will no one take my part? Nobody is on my side. Leslie chauffeurs Una around town. Joe gives Una a job. Ilka imagines Una's point of view. Ilka imagines Winnie's point of view. Ilka imagines every point of view except mine."

Ilka said, "I think I'm doing sympathetic magic. I think what I think is that if I argue Una's and Winnie's points of view, someone, when Leslie and Eliza have had enough and dropped me, will argue my point of view." Ilka, who had thought that she was kidding, discovered that her throat was blocked.

"Leslie and I are your elective cousins," said Eliza. "What do you plan to do that you will deserve to be dropped for?"

"Ah," said Ilka, "that is what I want you to promise you will tell me."

Eliza said, "Make you a deal—if you'll quit imagining everything and everybody and making me look like the wicked witch of Concordance, I promise to bad-mouth you to your face."

"And you, Leslie? Do you promise?"

But the best Leslie's conscience would suffer him to do was to offer to open another bottle of this quite-nice white wine.

Mark Blickley

The World's Greatest Saxophone Player

I'M ERIC TESLER. I'm here because Doctor Wandaplatt says I have to be here. And because I know this group therapy session is good for me. As Doctor Wandaplatt says, the time has come for me to take the bull by the tail and face the situation.

I was in a coma for nearly five and a half years. A little over a year ago I snapped out of it. Doctor Wandaplatt says these bones are going to heal, but that my mental health is kind of shaky.

But so's yours, right? Or else why would you be here, too, right? I'm supposed to tell you what happened to me, how I got here. That'll be kind of easy. I spent five and a half years doing nothing but thinking about what happened.

This past year I talked to lots of people who helped me piece together the events leading up to my appearance in this hospital recreation room. I understand what happened. I'm not sure why it happened. I don't even know where to begin except for this typically gray, late autumn afternoon in Rantoul, Illinois, when I was twelve years old.

Now when I say it was a typical Sunday afternoon, I mean that all over town television sets were screaming out half-time scores and town fathers were critiquing football games from bar stools while their kids were in the streets pretending to be the Chicago Bears.

It was after a particularly vicious tackle on me by the Levitzki brothers that I flung down my helmet, threw off my makeshift shoulder pads, kicked Wayne Levitzki in the nuts, and trotted off into my living room where my father was lying on the couch, watching a Bears game on TV. I stood in front of the set, blocking his view, and said, "Father, I don't want to play football. I want to take music lessons!"

My father propped himself up on the couch, angling his way past me and yelled, "For Christsakes, can't you call me Dad or Pop or Old Man? What's wrong with you? Go outside and play some ball and don't go botherin' me again about music lessons."

Then he launched into his, "When I was your age I was playing half-back and defensive tackle, and damned hard, too. 'Cept for Iggy Bolton, I was the best."

Just as he finished that sentence my mother walked into the room. At the time she was a chain-smoking woman of thirty-seven. My mother was famous for two things. One was an enormous capacity for migraine headaches; the other was her punctuating of each sentence with a cough—which isn't all that surprising when you consider she smoked six and a half packs of cigarettes a day.

Anyway, she walked in because she heard my plea for music lessons and was pretty sick of my whining about it. You see, I'm cursed with a photographic memory and I'll never forget what she said:

"C'mon, Eric, give me a break. I can just imagine you honking a horn around here (cough). I'd be dead in a week (cough). I hear enough car horns from the street to last me a lifetime (cough)."

Now mind you, I never said anything about playing a horn. I didn't know what kind of instrument I wanted to play. I just wanted to play something.

But after she told me this she starts gagging real bad. My father instinctively reached out and slapped her on the back without taking his eyes off the game.

At this time I was reading the book that was to influence me more than any other book I'd ever read. It was titled: *Beauty Knows No Pain* and subtitled *Biographies of Obscure Musicians Who Overcame Personal Handicaps in Pursuit of Their Art.*

I remember the characters in that book as clearly as if they were my next door neighbors. I was inspired by an oboe player with asthma, a drummer with metal hooks, a midget conductor, a hare-lipped flutist, a pianist with six fingers on one hand, and a seventy-two-year-old woman who learned to play the tuba after undergoing surgery for the removal of a lung.

My father once caught me reading *Beauty Knows No Pain.* I was stretched out on my bed, totally absorbed in the chapter about Maestro Arnold, the midget conductor, when my door slams open. I panicked and tossed the book under my bed.

"Caught you," laughed my father. "What are you tryin' to hide from your old man?" he asked.

"Nothing, Father. You just scared me, that's all."

But as father approached me, grinning, he pointed under my bed. "You got somethin' under there you don't want me to see?"

"No, Father."

He groped under the bed until his hand latched onto the book. Then he slapped me on the shoulder with his other hand as he pulled the book out and said, "Don't worry. I won't tell your Ma. Us men gotta know when to stick together. When I was your age, I useta keep these playin' cards from Japan with pictures of these gorgeous. . . ."

He held the book up, frowned, and then flung it at me. "What's this shit?"

"It's just a library book, Father."

"Then why were you hiding it?"

"Because I knew it would upset you."

"I ain't buyin' that. What are you usin' this book for?"

"To learn," I whispered.

"This book been exciting you, boy?"

"Yes, Father."

"When I was fourteen this ain't the kinda books excited me. Where's the broads?"

"It does have an incredible story of woman who learned . . ."

He pulled me off the bed and dragged me into the hall.

"You're weird," he screamed at me. "I'm showin' this to your Ma!"

My mother was sitting on the living room couch, coughing, as she stripped her colorful nails with a cotton swab and a bottle of polish remover. Father held the book out to her as she crushed a cigarette butt into the ashtray.

"You wanna see the stuff your son is reading?"

Mother took the book, looked it over, and put it down. She put the bottle of remover on her lap as she continued to work on her nails. I told her it was the best book I ever read.

My father became enraged. "I'm tellin' ya the kid don't use both hands to turn the pages. Look at them rings under his eyes."

Mother said, "That's because he won't eat his vegetables (cough)."

I thought I heard an ally so I told her all about the musician characters. She was quite interested in, or more accurately put, obsessed with the tuba player. She lighted a cigarette and kept badgering about how the woman had lost her lung. I told her I didn't remember. She asked me if I was telling the truth.

"Who cares about that old broad," my father screamed. "Midget conductors! Whatta role model."

Just then mother had a coughing fit. Her cigarette dropped out of her mouth and on to her lap, igniting the highly flammable nail polish remover. Flames roared up. My father and I reacted quickly and with seasoned teamwork. We successfully extinguished the fire. Mother came away with only minor burns, a scorched eyebrow, and some singed bangs.

You know, the more I thought of what these musicians had to go through to learn their craft, the more I would plead with my parents to buy me musical instruction.

Because they wouldn't let me have music lessons, I devised a unique system of creating music. It's the nearest I could come to musical composition.

You see, I'd take my two transistor radios, plug an earphone into each one, stick an earplug in each ear, and then tune into two different stations at the same time. One station might be playing classical, the other jazz or rock. I was always flipping the selector dials, making different match-ups. And when the two musical forms would meet inside my head, I would create a new sound that no one else could hear but me.

I knew my father would rather roast in hell than have any son of his taking music lessons, so I concentrated my campaign on my mother. My mother was never a demonstrative woman when it came to showing affection. In fact, the only thing she ever puckered her lips for was a cigarette. But I knew she loved me when she finally agreed to give me the money she had been secretly saving for a chest X-ray.

It wasn't difficult finding a music instructor. Rantoul boasted only one such man, Professor Theodore Bindt.

Professor Bindt was a tall, skinny man of fifty-nine, permanently bent over as a result of constipation cramps. These cramps were due to his daily staple of fried chicken. You see, the professor's music studio was located above a Chicken Lickin' franchise.

Bindt was a bachelor who didn't know how to cook, so he depended on his business neighbor for meals. It seems convenience always won out over cramps. Besides, after nine years on such a diet he craved the grease.

At one time I thought he had self-destructive impulses because of his diet, but now I think it was just money. Inflationary times always cause men like Bindt hardship.

"Zee little brats"—that's what he called his pupils—would happily sacrifice their music lessons to the family budget. I'm sure these sacrifices made the dollar and fifty-six cent three-piece Lickin' Special with fries and a bun a necessity.

By the time I was ready to seek out the professor things had gotten so bad he was forced to hock most of his instruments. I remember his studio containing trombones minus the slides, pianos without brass pedals or benches, cellos without their bows, and the electric guitars—which Bindt claimed was the only thing "zee little bastards vonted to play"—were missing amplifiers.

The first thing that struck me about the Professor was his teeth. When he gave me his professional smile I noticed his teeth were the same color as the yellowed newspaper clipping taped to the wall behind his desk. After freeing myself from his desperate handshake I glanced at the clipping.

Underneath this picture of a kid taking a check from a fat man the caption read—Teddy Bindt, child prodigy, wins Rantoul's Annual John Philip Sousa Memorial Award.

I was impressed.

Professor Bindt stood up and bent over me. "So, you vont to be a musician, eh son? Vise choice. I could tell by your bearing you have zee sensitivity for a creative instrument. Are you zinking of becoming a pianist?"

I told him I wasn't exactly sure what instrument I wanted to play.

Professor Bindt clutched his stomach during a particularly fierce attack of cramps and looked around his studio. "You don't own an instrument?"

If I'd have owned an instrument I wouldn't be in this room right now.

Bindt's sister, who's a big fan of mine, sent me the professor's journals four months ago. She thought they would help encourage my recovery. Obviously she hadn't read them.

According to his journal, on the day I arrived in his studio Bindt was in the midst of his most severe financial crisis. He had no money and no working instruments.

When I told him I didn't own an instrument Bindt spotted a saxophone in one piece and lunged for it. And when he handed it to me, he knew it was missing a reed.

A reed is a thin piece of cane attached to the mouthpiece. It's set in vibration by the breath and is the sound producing agent for the instrument. In other words, no sound comes out of a saxophone without using a reed. If a sax has a mouthpiece it looks like a complete instrument.

The professor ran out of reeds because he had the nasty habit of using them as toothpicks to dislodge annoying bits of chicken that stuck in his teeth.

Anyway, I'm standing there caressing this big beautiful brass thing. I'm instantly hooked on the saxophone. Professor Bindt tells me the saxophone is one of his most expensive instruments. He says that my rental fees will be higher, but they can go towards purchasing it.

I immediately agreed.

Then Professor Bindt explained the romantic history of the saxophone—that it was invented by Aldolphe Sax in 1846 and how it is one of the few instruments that has no exotic forbear. "A complete original," Bindt says.

A complete original.

I stood there hugging this saxophone like it was my first girlfriend. Then I carefully brought its neck to my lips, bit into the mouthpiece, and blew.

Silence. I blew harder. Nothing, except the sound of me exhaling and the rumbling of my teacher's stomach.

"What's the matter, Professor Bindt? Is it broken or am I doing something wrong?"

Professor Bindt wrapped an arm around my shoulder. "No, no, zere's nothzing wrong. Listen, Eric, anyone can pick up an instrument and create noise. If you step on a dog's tail you vill create noise. But you, you're special. I sense it. Together vee shall transcend musical tradition. Ve'll bypass creating music for zee ear and concentrate strictly on creating music for zee soul! You must never forget zat every great musician who has achieved historical immortality is not remembered for his technical expertise, but for his soul!"

I wasn't exactly sure what he was talking about, so I kept staring at the yellow newspaper clipping while gently running my fingers over the saxophone keys.

"Vot do your parents zink of you taking music lessons?"

I told him they're not too interested. I explained that my Mother had given me the money for instruction, but she said that I was on my own.

Bindt clapped his hands in joy. "Vonderful! Vonderful! No outside interference." I asked him again why no sound came out of my saxophone?

"You veren't using your imagination, son. You tried to take zee short cut from here"—he pointed to my throat—"to here"—he pointed to the sax mouthpiece—"instead of having zee music travel from here"—he traced a line from my heart to my forehead—"and zen to here"—his finger traced the length of the saxophone.

"You vere being artistically lazy, but vee shall overcome zat."

"I'm not a lazy person, professor. I'll work very hard." Bindt squatted by my chair and put his arm around my shoulder. "It is not zat kind of laziness, my boy. It is ignorance of zee spirit of creation. You must tame zist spirit, put it on a leash, before you can qualify as an artist."

I want you people to understand that I was lonely and Bindt was the first adult I'd ever met who genuinely seemed to care about me. I trusted him because I needed someone to trust. It's that simple. I needed to love and trust this man. I was convinced that some cosmic force led me to pursue music lessons just so I would establish contact with this caring genius.

Despite the ridicule of family and friends, I kept to a strict daily schedule of six soundless hours of practice in addition to Professor Bindt's instruction four times a week.

No one at home said anything about my mute instrument. My father was ashamed of his sax-toting son and was too angry for words. My mother thought that her X-ray money was put to good use. There were no more whines from her son or his new toy.

God, I loved my saxophone! With the professor's guidance I entered a trance-like state whenever my lips touched the mouthpiece. I can't describe the joy I got from playing my sax. My eyes would automatically close and I'd just drift.

Not only could I hear this rich music, but I'd see such incredible colors and visions. And the smells! Oh, the smells! It was beyond joy! Sometimes I'd capture this penetrating sorrow, but that, too, was exquisite and always left me refreshed.

I had tapped that special place Professor Bindt assured me I'd find. I know it sounds strange but the vibrations inside my instrument shook my spirit and released these . . . these . . .

Gershwin once said he had more tunes in his head than he could put down on paper in a hundred years. With Professor Bindt's revolutionary approach, a musician didn't need a hundred years to complete his vision. Music isn't marks on a paper or grooves on a CD or even the noise from the instrument. It's here. Inside your head.

The saxophone supplied a structure. It channeled my musical energies. I may have played without a reed, but Professor Bindt taught me all the fingering and breathing techniques any saxophonist needs to be accomplished on the instrument.

Look, anyone can play an instrument. Only a select few can compose, can create art. The Professor's teachings didn't limit me to the sounds a saxophone could make. When my saxophone took off it wasn't an instrument, but instrumental in producing a music no single woodwind, or even orchestra, could reproduce. It was energy and love and anger.

When I was seventeen Professor Bindt died. My last meeting with him is forever burned in my memory. It was a sunny Saturday afternoon. I walked up to his studio for my lesson. He wasn't there. That was quite unusual, but I knew he was probably downstairs at Chicken Lickin, having a snack. I remember shielding my eyes as I looked through the Chicken Lickin' large plate glass window, trying to find my teacher. When I couldn't locate him, I went inside. I surveyed the entire restaurant. Professor Bindt wasn't there.

I spotted Lickin's manager. "Excuse me, has Professor Bindt been here today? I have a four o'clock appointment. He's never been late. I'm worried."

This skinny guy in a shiny red jacket tells me that I have a right to worry. He said that the night before, my professor was eating his dinner at the table that he always eats at when he sort of squealed and collapsed.

I grabbed the manager by the lapels. "What happened!? Where is he!?"

The Chickin' Lickin' chief pleaded with me to calm down. Then he tells me that he thought Bindt had choked on a chicken bone or something, but that nobody had heard him gag.

"Where is my professor!" I shouted.

By now the entire restaurant had turned in our direction. I relaxed my grip on him. He recovered his breath and told me he had called an ambulance and that as far as he knew, Bindt was at Rantoul General.

When I walked into the hospital room, I saw a doctor fidgeting with some life-support equipment attached to the sleeping professor. When the doctor asked me if I was a member of his family, I nodded and told him I was the sick man's son. He then informed that Bindt had suffered heart failure and had been slipping in and out of consciousness for the past sixteen hours. My saxophone was slung over my shoulder. I caressed it as I looked down at my ghostly white mentor.

"I think it's important you're seeing him now," said the doctor. He stared at my saxophone and asked if I played. When I nodded, he told me that he had played sax in his medical-school band. He said he was a real big fan of Bird's.

"Birds? What birds?"

"Bird. Charlie Parker. You know, Bird. The greatest sax player who ever lived, with the possible exception of Red Gorky, Jr. After your visit please report to Nurse Pinkley at the reception desk to fill out the proper forms, okay?" Then the doctor patted me on the arm and left me alone with my spiritual father.

I leaned over my comatose instructor and pleaded with him to live. "Don't die, professor. Please don't die."

I held out a small paper bag I had brought with me. "I guess you can't hear me, professor, but I brought you a gift. It's soup. Chicken soup. Want some? C'mon, Professor Bindt, eat some soup. Please?"

Bindt didn't respond so I removed the container from the bag and waved the soup underneath his nose. His eyes popped open.

"Atta boy, professor." I began feeding him with a plastic spoon. Most of the soup spilled down Bindt's chin, but his eyes were wide with anticipation.

"Can you speak, Professor Bindt?" He moved his mouth but all you could hear were groans. "Take it easy, professor. Maybe you shouldn't try to speak. Save your strength."

Bindt began clenching and unclenching his fist while his mouth moved stupidly. And then I heard a hoarse whisper, "Wrong . . . wrong."

"What's that? What did you say, professor?"

"Wrong," he choked out.

"Am I doing something wrong?" I asked.

"Me . . . wrong."

"Yes, professor?"

"Need . . . money," he said.

"Don't worry about money. Just concentrate on getting better."

Bindt raised his clenched fist. "Me . . . wrong . . . need . . . money."

"Please don't make yourself upset. Is there anything you want me to do?"

"Go," he croaked.

"I'm not leaving you, Professor Bindt. I'll never leave you."

"Go," he insisted.

I hugged Bindt. "As sick as you are you still try to spare me from anything that's not connected with beauty. I won't leave."

He spit chicken soup in my face.

"You don't like the soup? I'm surprised, professor. I got it from your favorite deli. I'll get you whatever you need. Just try to relax."

"Ears . . . ears . . ." he whispered.

"What's that about ears, Professor Bindt? Can't you hear me?"

"Me bad . . . need money."

"What's money got to do with anything? You're not bad because you don't have a lot of it. That's what you've always taught me. You're an artist, a pure artist, and you've made me one, too. I love you for that."

Bindt used his last remaining bit of strength to pull himself up. He glared at me and said, "I confess." I asked him if he wanted me to get a priest to hear his confession. He shook his head.

"No . . . you . . . you . . ." Professor Bindt let out a death rattle and fell backward with his mouth open.

"Come back! Come back here, Professor Bindt! You can't leave me! I won't let you!" I buried my face in his neck and cried. Then I started pounding his chest with my fist, trying to pummel his heart back into motion. "It's too big to stop beating. Too big. Too big. C'mon, beat. Beat. Beat. Beat."

I quit pounding on the dead man's chest. As I reached over to close Bindt's eyes, my saxophone slid off my shoulder and hit the professor in the face. I put the mouthpiece between Bindt's lips and positioned his still warm fingers onto the keys. I tried not to cry. I tried to think clearly and responsibly.

I told Professor Bindt that he would remain alive as long as I lived. "I'm dedicating my life to the completion of your vision. I'm dedicating my life to *our* art."

And then the professor lets loose with a really humongous death rattle. Every bit of gas that was trapped inside that corpse had to have been expelled. It both frightened and excited me. And the smell wasn't too pleasant, either.

My saxophone was still inside his mouth. This meant my sax had captured Professor Bindt's final breath! It was no longer a musical instrument, but a monument to his genius and devotion!

"I won't let you down ever, professor. I swear!"

Strange. I tried to close Bindt's eyes but they wouldn't stay shut. Believe me, it's not like in the movies. They kept popping open. He stared up at me with a mixture of terror and anger that gave me nightmares for years and years.

The autopsy attributed his death to a cholesterol induced stroke. I was devastated. I dropped out of school and drifted around Chicago trying to peddle my sax to the clubs. But no one would listen to me.

To tell you the truth, I almost packed it in. But every time I picked up a phone to call home, I'd remember the professor, eyes half shut, lips twisted, conducting me with a half-eaten chicken leg.

By the end of my first few weeks in Chicago I was tired, hungry, and broke. I slept on park benches at night, but I did have an interesting artistic experience early on in the Windy City. It was quite late at night and I was sitting on a park bench, gently polishing my saxophone.

A wino staggered by. I shot him a quick look and continued cleaning my sax. I prayed he'd go away. But instead of leaving, he stuck his face right up to mine and said, "You gotta use elbow grease, boy. Don't be lazy."

I told him to keep moving. Then he says, "They's a sayin' round this city that if you rub that thing hard enough, a genie'll appear."

I ignored him.

"You don't believe it?" He extended his hand to me. "Hi, my name's Eugene, but friends call me Genie."

I asked him if he was going to make some magic?

"Hell, no. I ain't making no magic. You're the one supposed to make magic with that thing." He points to my saxophone.

I smiled and told him I hope to. Then he asked me if I had any money. When I told him I didn't he asked me if I had a song. I shrugged. "Maybe."

The wino got ticked off. "I said you got a song? Don't give me this maybe shit."

"Yes, I have a song, Genie."

"Good," he says. "You also got yourself a partner."

"Why do I need a partner?"

The wino shook his head. "Don't you know who I am?"

"Genie. You're a genie, right?"

"Damn straight," he said, "and my magic is in my feets." And then Genie breaks into an earnest, if somewhat clumsy, dance. Without his history of booze I could easily imagine him a dancer of merit.

After Genie danced his dance he paused to catch his breath. "How's that? Did I pass?"

"Pass what?" I asked.

"The audition. Will you take me on as a partner?" I asked him again why did I need a partner? Genie plopped himself down on the bench and offered me a sip of his Thunderbird wine. I declined.

"Look, kid, I make my livin' dancing. But it's gettin' harder and harder to turn some change these days. All those damn hippies been cuttin' into the action. People losin' interest in the solo performer. All they wants is the spectacular. The spectacle."

"So what's that got to do with me, Genie?"

"Ain't you got no vision, kid? I need music for my show. We'll be partners. I can dance to anything. We'll do a sixty-forty split."

"With you getting the sixty, huh, Genie?"

"Course. I've scouted the best locations. I know which corners are jumpin' any hour of the day. Besides, I been performin' in Chicago for nearly thirty years. People know me."

I was feeling bold so I asked him if I was paying for his reputation. He told me, "Don't be so smartass. Maybe you ain't even any good."

I grinned. "Maybe."

"I told you to lay off the maybe crap. Let's see what you got."

I explained to Genie that I had already played today, that I haven't missed a day of practice in years. He just shrugged and said, "I could say the same thing about drinkin'. So what?"

"So listen to this!" I took a deep breath, closed my eyes, and tore into an imaginative, pulsating rhythm. Next thing I know Genie's snapping his fingers and I heard him say, "I get it, man."

Boy, he starts dancing like mad. Over the bench, under the bench, on top of the bench, just kicking and swinging his arms like a man possessed. It ended when he hurled himself against the bench, smashing the wine bottle in his back pocket.

The explosion of broken glass and the wino's scream jolted me back to reality. What I saw was Genie sprawled out on the bench, whimpering.

"What happened, Eugene? Are you alright?"

"No, I ain't alright. You broke my bottle!" He held out a handful of wet, broken glass.

I couldn't believe it. I hugged my saxophone. "You mean I got up that high?"

"To hell with your high! What about mine? I ain't got nothin' to drink."

I pulled a dollar out of my pocket. Genie snatched it out of my hand. "You're a dangerous man," he said. "You had me jumpin' and twitchin' like a worm with a match underneath it."

I was delighted with my fiery performance and told him so. "You're a cruel son-of-a-bitch," he said as he walked away, pulling shards of glass from his ass.

I got real good at shoplifting. I managed to survive by sleeping in bus terminals and hustling my sax on the sidewalk.

The breakthrough came one freezing night in the Chicago Greyhound Bus Terminal. I was having a restless night—no matter what I did I couldn't get comfortable. Professor Bindt always maintained that great musicians needed plenty of sleep. He'd say, "you can't perform for zee gods if you're denied zee sweet embrace of Morpheus."

Since I was unable to sleep, I took a stroll on the upper platform where they kept the buses. I was hoping the exhaust fumes would make me drowsy.

A chartered bus pulled in and unloaded a group of yawning musicians carrying expensive instrument cases that filled the air with the obnoxious smell of fresh leather. These musicians were followed by a short fat man in a three piece suit.

He was scribbling something into this notebook and growling at the bus driver, demanding to know if the driver's superiors "were aware how rudely their employees treat the manager of the Monk's Corner Ridiculously Juiced Jazz Ensemble."

When I heard who he was I ran downstairs and squatted on the curb outside the Greyhound building and began playing my sax.

I heard a band member say, "Check out the Road Runner dude." Another guy asked me if I was gigging for the Lung Association. Then someone else laughed, "Beautiful Jim, beautiful." But I was just warming up, saving my best stuff for the manager.

I closed my eyes, took a deep breath, and tapped out a rhythm with my shoe. When the band manager noticed his men crowding around the sidewalk he shouted at them to, "get your butts over to the hotel."

As the crowd broke up, he caught a glimpse of me, sitting on the icy sidewalk, playing my sax. He reached over and shook me. "Hey, kid, watcha doin'?"

I couldn't believe it! It was the first time I'd ever been interrupted during a performance.

He asked me if I was serious. I said, yeah. Then he asked me how long I'd been at it. I told him I'd been playing for years but was having a rough time.

He laughed and said, "No wonder." Then he stared at the tip of my saxophone and with this smirk asked me, "You ever notice anything a bit peculiar 'bout your style?"

I jumped into my familiar defense. I told him I hear symphonies in my head. I explained that the only value my heart has is as a metronome.

He shrugged and said, "Yeah, I know watcha mean." Then he ripped a piece of paper out of his book, scribbled out an address, and handed it to me. "I tell you what. We got a gig over at this club on the South Side. Stop by tomorrow night at nine and we'll see how your act goes over."

"It's not an act," I insisted. "It's my life!"

"Yeah, yeah, gotcha kid. Clean yourself up. And why don't you practice up your leads a bit. We can't have you blowing any clams 'cause this is a class gig." Then he laughed, slapped me on the back, and disappeared inside a taxi.

At ten to nine I managed to stagger into the Jicama Jazz Emporium. What a place! I squinted through thick clouds of smoke and saw two men in tuxedos making their way towards me. They grabbed me by my shoulders and lifted me three feet off the ground.

"Hey, wait a minute! Let me down! I'm a musician! Let go of me! How dare you! I'm an artist!"

One of the men kicked the saxophone out of my hands. It crashed to the floor. A couple of musicians at the bar recognized me and came to my rescue.

I dropped to my knees, opened the case, and examined my saxophone. There was no damage. When I thought about what this guy had done I threw a down-field block on him that sent him crashing into the bar. I wanted to kill him! I was dragged away by some musicians before the man could get up and avenge himself. The crowd was applauding me.

I was taken backstage to Mr. Hackersby, the band's manager. "That's some ballsy thing ya did, kid. Them Godzillas had it coming."

I told Mr. Hackersby that I didn't care what people did to me, but when they started abusing my saxophone I wouldn't permit that. I told him life would be nothing more than exertion and excretion if my sax was ruined.

Hackersby said there were other saxophones to be had, that my life was certainly more important than an instrument. I explained that this saxophone represented a legacy—the immortality of a departed master survived through the fellowship of my lungs and this hallowed brass.

Hackersby shook his head and agreed that my sax was, "the hollowest damn brass," he ever saw. Then he said, "if you can put half the effort into playing your sax as you can defending it, you'll be a smash." He pushed me out of the wings.

The moment I stepped on stage there was applause and I heard someone yell out, "Atta, boy, play like you slay!"

I bowed, put the saxophone to my lips, drew a professionally calculated breath, and vanished into my silent world of misplaced trust.

I learned what really happened that night. It seems the audience was impatient and then shocked when it became clear no music would flow from my saxophone. The crowd, I was told, grew restless and offended. Insults were yelled at me but I was too absorbed in my music to know where I was or who I was with.

Luckily my absorption, coupled with my burlesque exaggerations on the saxophone, transformed a hostile crowd into one convulsed with laughter. Hackersby's gamble paid off. I must've looked pretty stupid out there.

At the conclusion of my set I was given an ovation. A standing ovation! Since I was ignorant of the laughter during my trance, I blew kisses to the audience and mumbled a thank you to Professor Bindt. I felt that we were both vindicated.

Mr. Hackersby signed me to a contract on the spot. The Monk's Corner Ridiculously Juiced Jazz Ensemble now had its first touring soloist.

I was euphoric over my success and determined to work harder than ever at perfecting my craft. It was all hard work for me, not fun.

We toured the United States and parts of Canada. Everything was going pretty smoothly. After a grueling gig in a tiny club in Nova Scotia, most of the musicians headed for the seedier parts of the island. Not me. I went back to my hotel room to practice.

As I inserted my key into the lock a blanket was thrown over me, my ankles were bound with rope, and I was hauled, kicking and screaming, to a car. My abduction ended when I was rolled onto a marble floor.

I sprang up, swinging wildly with my fists. When my eyes made the transition to light, I saw my abductors. They were six members of the band.

I was confused. I asked them what they were doing. "You know, guys, what's the idea?" They all laughed and Ezra, this bald guy in sunglasses, put his arm around me. He said the guys were grateful for the creative lift I'd given the band and had decided on showing me a good time.

"But you know I can't miss a day of practice!" Ezra bit down on his moustache and said, "We know, Ric. But why not try loosening up a bit. Relaaaaaaaaaaaaax."

I told him I was anything but relaxed. "Where are we?"

He grinned and pointed to these scantily dressed women circling the room. Ezra puckered his lips at one of the women and said that we were in the hottest little whorehouse in the Commonwealth.

One of the women, this six-foot three-inch blonde in flesh colored leotards, crept up behind me and stuck her fingers through the belt loops of my pants and started nibbling on my ear.

I broke out of the Amazon's grip by using an old football move which resurrected images of my father lying on the couch denying me music lessons, and of Professor Bindt, staring at me with the disgust he usually reserved for discoveries of cold french fries inside his Chicken Lickin' boxed lunch.

I sprinted out the door and hid inside some bushes by the side of the road. When Ezra found me, I was still shaking. He apologized for getting me upset, but he thought if anyone could put a smile on my face Skyscraper Sally could.

I told him I wasn't angry. I knew they were acting in my best interests. I also knew I was slightly dull. It wasn't that I disliked women or anything weird like that. I explained to Ezra that long ago I asked Professor Bindt if I could cut down on my lessons and spend some time and money on girls and that the professor sat me down and explained the medieval belief that when a man expends his precious bodily fluid it upsets his internal chemistry and drains him of a large portion of his intellectual and creative energies. Bindt said that a woman's purpose on this earth is to zap up a man's vitality by having him transfer it into her. "It is artistic destruction by injection, if you know vot I mean."

I knew what he meant.

Ezra pulled me to my feet and walked me back to the hotel.

For six years I toured with the Monk's Corner Ridiculously Juiced Jazz Ensemble. I loved the travelling and the respect of my peers. After that embarrassing incident in Nova Scotia the guys never interfered with my privacy or practice sessions.

When I was twenty-three my life was altered during a gig in Goose Creek, South Carolina. In the audience that night was a debt-ridden millionaire named Tony Pranklin. He was the innovator of the Pet Stone craze. You people remember that, don't you? Through greed and neglect Pranklin squandered the fortune he made from his conception, advertising, and marketing of the stones he swore "would bring comfort to millions without the mess and expense of a breathing pet."

Tony Pranklin was lazy, but he was no fool. He immediately saw the appeal of a silent saxophonist. When he visited me a couple of months ago he told me he had learned to "exploit the universal fear of casting the first stone."

Pranklin claimed although my popularity originated through travesty and as the years went by the novelty of a reedless saxophonist might wear off, I would endure because he would promote me as an artist.

Now if this all sounds like a crock all I can say is Pranklin pulled it off. I became known as the World's Greatest Saxophone Player—but that comes later.

Pranklin offered Hackersby one hundred and fifty thousand dollars for my contract. I wasn't happy about the sale, but Pranklin promised me complete artistic freedom and the chance to reach an audience of millions.

Pranklin pulled strings and within weeks I popped up on national TV. My father saw me one night on a talk show. He wrote me a letter apologizing for his behavior towards my music lessons. He said that the solo I performed on television reminded him of when he was in the army in '43 and saw Woody Herman's band . . . but that he couldn't hear anything.

I didn't know people were laughing at me. I didn't! I felt I was achieving artistic maturity and touching my listeners. Every time I finished a tune all I heard was applause. How did I know? How could I know?

Nine months after leaving the Juiced Ensemble I cut a solo album produced by Pranklin. It was called *Music for the Disenchanted* and released by the Avantgardarama label. Although I heard elegantly textured orchestrations when I played the record, all anyone else heard was the clicking thud of sax keys against the pads, and my breathing.

But that didn't stop Tony Pranklin. He contacted a music critic for *Art on Parade* and coerced the man into publishing a favorable review of my album. I have it here, in my shirt pocket. I originally kept it out of pride . . . now I keep it for . . . I don't know. This is it:

> "Eric Tesler may be the most dynamic musical innovator on the scene today. Known throughout the nation because of his prolific television appearances, this is the young man's first attempt at recording and he succeeds admirably. Like any pioneer of creativity, Mr. Tesler has attracted the indignation of some critics. These short-sighted men people hate change. I believe these critics would even resist the change of a dollar bill at a grocery store. They claim it is absurd to purchase an album that only offers the sound of an artist inhaling and exhaling. Let me say this: *Music for the Disenchanted* may, on a physical level, be just breathing; but as I replay Mr. Tesler's recording, it reminds me of God breathing life into Adam. Eric Tesler breathes life into a fresh musical genre."

Can you understand how I felt when this came out? I had published proof that what I was doing was valid, don't you see? I'm not a fraud. I wasn't lying to myself or the public.

In twelve years I never missed a day of practice or a rehearsal. I was oblivious to fame, and oblivious to the huge sums of money regenerating Pranklin's bank account.

The concert halls grew in size to accommodate The World's Greatest Saxophone Player! This epithet was dreamed up by Pranklin after he engineered my election to the South Carolina Music Hall of Fame and my winning of the Annual Rantoul John Philip Sousa Memorial Award. This last honor truly touched me.

On my twenty-fifth birthday Pranklin produced my second album, *Quarter Century Blues In A Half-Assed World.* By this time Pranklin had learned from his mistakes. Instead of the LP being a solo venture, he hired a backup group. Three of the eleven tracks were my solos. On the remaining tracks I played with accompaniment. *Quarter Century Blues In A Half-Assed World* was a huge success. I was told recently that it's become a collector's item known as "The Birthday Album."

My popularity was at its peak. I was such an enormous box office draw that Pranklin was able to book me into Lincoln Center in New York City.

The flight to New York was one of the most exciting afternoons of my life. Immediately after my plane touched down at Kennedy Airport I made my way to a taxi stand and asked the cab driver to take me to the hippest jazz club in New York. He dropped me off at a place called The Cookery on Eighth Street.

There was a long line of people stretching from the club's entrance and all around the block. When I told the doorman (who happened to be the owner) that I didn't have a reservation he recognized me and said no problem. He directed me to a stage side table—his table.

Within minutes the houselights dimmed and a tall man with a beard brushed past me. The stage lights reflecting off his silver saxophone blinded me. I was rubbing my eyes when I heard my host announce, "And now, Ladies and Gentlemen, a musical legend, your friend and mine, Red Gorky, Jr."

There was applause. I squinted up at the stage because the light reflecting from the saxophone made it impossible for me to look directly at the musician.

And then it happened.

Red Gorky, Jr. sucked at the air and produced the sweetest, most hauntingly beautiful sounds I've ever heard. My eyes became moist and I started to shake. For years I hadn't followed contemporary saxophonists. Professor Bindt insisted it was dangerous to my development.

For the first time in my life I felt terror, true terror that—oh, my God!—my God!—I'd been living a lie for thirteen years.

The music soared out of that man's saxophone like a celestial conversation between the Creator and the human spirit. I mean, it was a feeling I always experienced whenever I played, but as I looked around the club I realized it was a feeling not limited to the artist, but shared by his listeners as well.

I mean, when I played one tune it would excite a hundred people a hundred different ways. But you know, never, not once did anyone ever come close to describing what I felt while I was playing with what they had heard. Sometimes that would bother me. That's when Pranklin would say, "Your music is much more sophisticated than you realize. And if you ever realize where this sophistication comes from, you'll probably be ruined as an artist."

But listening to Red Gorky, Jr.'s sax, I knew all that mystic mumble jumble about playing for the heart was a bunch of crap. It was the ears! The ears! I'd been trained not to use my ears. I don't care what the music critics wrote about me. It's the ears that count!

I got up out of my seat and ran out the door. I was shattered. Fifteen minutes later I was perched on a bar stool, sipping a G and T, when I heard a high, squeaky voice.

"Psssssssst, pssssssssst, are you Eric Tesler?"

I spun around but didn't see anyone so I went back to my drink.

"Hey, man, you Eric Tesler?" I felt a tug on my pants cuff. I looked down at a smartly dressed midget biting a cigarette. "You Eric Tesler, The World's Greatest Saxophone Player?"

I cringed at the title. I told him I was Eric Tesler.

"Who are you?"

"Just call me a fan," he said. "Mind if I join you?"

I reached down and lifted him onto a stool. This angered the little guy. "Lemme go, will ya? I ain't no baby. Wanna smack in the mouth?" I asked him what he wanted. I suspected it wasn't an autograph.

The little man grinned, adjusted his tie, and handed me his business card. It read: Turner Arnold, The Entrepreneur of Avenue B. I immediately recognized the name. He was the midget conductor that inspired me when I was young.

"Turner Arnold! You were one of my heroes when I was a kid! I read all about you in *Beauty Knows No Pain*."

I expected him to be flattered, but he looked at me with disgust and said, "You did, huh? I'm a musician who overcame my handicap in pursuit of my art, right, kid?"

I nodded. Right. I was excited. This was a great musician! But he just laughed and asked me if I believed everything I read.

Turner Arnold told me the book was written by a second-rate writer who needed cash. Turner Arnold seemed to get pleasure out of telling me that this hack writer lied like a dog about him and everyone else in the book.

I couldn't believe it!

Turner Arnold said, "Sure, I went to a fancy music school. But that stuff about me finding work after I graduated was pure bull. Nobody wanted me. Nobody. They didn't even want me at the school but I had enough bucks to get in so they took me. I was always treated like somebody's joke. But I ain't here to talk about myself. I been following your career for some time now. I run a pawnshop down on the East Side. I trade mostly in weapons and musical instruments—guess I can't get it outta my blood. Anyway, I got a present for you."

He reached inside his jacket and pulled out this cane object that he held up in front of him like someone repelling a vampire with a cross.

I asked him what it was and he called it, "a reeeeeeeed."

Turner Arnold said he knew I was playing Lincoln Center later that evening and had hoped to give it to me after the show. Then he explained how to position the reed on to the saxophone.

I asked him if Red Gorky, Jr. used one and the midget smirked and said, "you're catching on." Turner Arnold assured me I couldn't go wrong if I used the reed at my concert that night.

I put the gift in my shirt pocket and looked at my watch. I was going on in little more than an hour. I opened my wallet to pay for my drink but Turner Arnold insisted on treating me. I thanked him again for the reed and hurried uptown.

Lincoln Center was mobbed. The audience consisted of all types. I was told there was even a balcony filled with senior citizens representing the New Jersey Geriatric League for the Deaf and Hard of Hearing. They were bussed in at taxpayers' expense to show their support for a music form that did not discriminate against their handicap.

At 9:04 PM I dragged myself to center stage. I was bombarded with applause. The instant I stepped up to the microphone the crowd fell silent.

"Ladies and Gentlemen, my first number will be a composition I wrote backstage tonight titled, *A Legacy of Laments for Lunatics, Listeners and Lickin' Liars.* In F minor."

For the first time in my career I didn't close my eyes and drift into a creative vacuum. I filled my cheeks with air, toyed with the keys, and stared at the audience that had paid eighteen dollars a ticket to *watch* me.

It was my first appraisal of an audience and it made me sick. I released the air from my cheeks, pulled the saxophone out of my mouth, and disappeared backstage to vomit.I reappeared on stage to a standing ovation. Muttering curses under my breath, I shook my head and bowed. As I leaned forward the reed fell out of my shirt pocket and bounced off my shoe. I smiled, picked it up, and attached it to my sax.

The ovation lasted nearly five minutes. When it finally died down I bit into the mouthpiece, took a deep breath, and blew as hard as I could.

The initial blast stunned me and the audience. As I manipulated the keys, the raucous sound dissolved into a crisp, blue-tinted rhythm. The audience gasped, but no one was more surprised than me. Employing the technique I forged out of years of silent practice, I made a smooth transition from a natural romantic flow of melody to a series of forceful jazz riffs.

I lost myself in the delightful music—not imagination, MUSIC! I didn't hear my fans shouting at me to stop. All I heard were the beautiful tunes I was producing. It was incredible! It'll always be the happiest moment of my life.

A little while ago I received a cassette in the mail from a fan of mine who was at my Lincoln Center performance. His recorder was smashed in the excitement, but he saved the tape. It's the only record I have of my music; it's my most valuable possession.

I was oblivious to the orchestra section running towards the stage, cursing me. The sounds coming out of my saxophone took me far, far away.

But not far enough.

My fans surrounded me and the last thing I remember hearing was a plea to "PLAY WHAT WE PAID FOR!"

The first blow landed on the back of my neck. It caused my teeth to clamp down on the mouthpiece. The follow up blow knocked out three of my teeth, two of which I swallowed. Blood gushed out of my mouth, splattering the attacking mob.

They pulled me to the floor and kicked my face. All of my ribs were cracked and my leg was broken and still they swarmed over me. Despite this punishment, I hunched over my saxophone and cradled it like a protective mother.

Eventually my arms went limp. That's when the crowd turned their anger on my instrument. They stomped on my sax until it was nothing more than brass flecks!

But I hurt, Doctor Wandaplatt, and I don't mean from the bruises covered by these bandages. You say that my injuries could not heal while I was in a coma because my body was using all its resources just to maintain my survival. I wished I never opened my eyes.

You claim that my condition won't improve until I confront a saxophone. But it's over! My saxophone was destroyed, Doctor! Will you stop trying to force me to touch one? I told you I want to stop feeling things!

I've listened to the other patients, Doctor Wandaplatt. I've heard them explain how experiencing a closeness with death clarified some kind of meaning or direction in their lives. Well, it hasn't happened to me. But then you can't always trust what you hear, right Doctor?

I'm scared, Doctor Wandaplatt. Real scared. But I'll get through it on my own, thank you. I've always been a solo act.

Ed Falco

Sexy Chat

YOU HAVE JUST ENTERED ROOM "SEXY CHAT"

ApeMan: Any Wild Woman wanna cyber?
DeepThrust: <---givin LadyLove's butt a squeeze on her way out . . . . . . LOL
Chuck2359: Any girls interested in private chat?
OnlineHost: "BUBBA B" has entered the room.
ApeMan: Hello Lazy
SkippinOut: yeah, right.
DeepThrust: <-----she's hauling butt now
OnlineHost: "BUBBA B" has left the room.
ALLAIN666: chat?
OnlineHost: "MrBgnHd" has left the room.
OnlineHost: "GINOGINO" has entered the room.
OnlineHost: "ThicknNice" has entered the room.
Seductres2: well... tell what next.
GINOGINO: hello room
OnlineHost: "Imyors2day" has entered the room.
ApeMan: Hello Vicky
DeepThrust: <-----uh,oh she's got me . . . . heheh
SINBAD: Help me, ples. My Daddys going to hurt my Mommy.
OnlineHost: "CMUNDRME" has entered the room.
SkippinOut: Why don't blondes make koolaid?
OnlineHost: "ThicknNice" has left the room.
GINOGINO: Hello All
SkippinOut: They can't fit all the water in that tiny little packet.
OnlineHost: "HIALEAH" has left the room.
Sweatlicker: *welcome*
OnlineHost: "GGreat082" has left the room.
OnlineHost: "REPOMAN" has entered the room.
CNTRYBOY69: What's up with SINBAD?
OnlineHost: "Cindy35819" has entered the room.

OnlineHost: "NottoFast" has left the room.
CNTRYBOY69: Anyone home?
OnlineHost: "ChugIt69" has left the room.
DeepThrust: Anyone for private?
CNTRYBOY69: What's SB's story?
Sweatlicker: Hey, Sinbad. What's that?
LabiaLady1: Sinbad, where are you?
OnlineHost: "VAVAVOOM" has entered the room.
OnlineHost: "Seductres2" has left the room.
Sweatlicker: What is happening?
OnlineHost: "Roberto518" has entered the room.
OnlineHost: "DeepThrust" has left the room.
CNTRYBOY69: Sinbad, Tell us who you are.
Roberto518: Any horny ladies here?
OnlineHost: "REPOMAN" has left the room.
CNTRYBOY69: Should we do something bout SB?
SkippinOut: <sneer>
Cindy35819: Sinbad's a guy. I cyber'd him.
SINBAD: PLES,PLES HELP. DAD'S HURTING MOM.
Cindy35819: He gives good cyber
OnlineHost: "CuteButt" has entered the room.
CMUNDRME: Hello all you crazies
OnlineHost: "JUSTIN0836" has entered the room.
OnlineHost: "VAVAVOOM" has left the room.
CNTRYBOY69: Think we should report?
ApeMan: ooh, ooh, that's goooood.
GINOGINO: Hi, everyone.
CNTRYBOY69: SINBAD, Tell us where you are?
OnlineHost: "WhipIt" has left the room.
OnlineHost: "Rimmer" has entered the room.
GINOGINO: Hello Everyone
SkippinOut: How do you drown a blonde?
OnlineHost: "PauliJeann" has entered the room.
Cindy35819: I don't get this Sinbad situation.
SkippinOut: Put a scratch-and-sniff sticker at the bottom of her pool.
BobAdder: Hello, hello, hello Ladies!
OnlineHost: "Slikker" has entered the room.
SINBAD: I'm at home.
Roberto518: hi girl
CuteButt: Bob, I love those big strong shoulders.
OnlineHost: "PoetTaster" has entered the room.
BobAdder: Do you really have a cute butt?
JAKE3702: {{{{{{{{{{{{{{{{{{{{{{{{{{{{Cindy}}}}}}}}}}}}}}}}}}

Roberto518: Hello Sweatlicker
CMUNDRME: hi Cindy and Sweatlicker
OnlineHost: "Rimbaud" has entered the room.
LabiaLady1: Where is your home, Honey? Can you tell us?
ApeMan: Hello Cindy
PauliJeann: ANY LOVELY LADY PRESS 69
OnlineHost: "BDRad835" has left the room.
PoetTaster: I'm a tomcat! I'm a tomcat!
OnlineHost: "Rick936" has entered the room.
JAKE3702: Where did WhipIt go?
OnlineHost: "Voracious83" has left the room.
LabiaLady1: Can you tell us your name, Honey?
BadGrrrl98: Hey, SkippinOut. How does a man take a bubble bath?
SINBAD: My name is Alicia.
CuteButt: Here. I'll just slip out of these jeans and let you see for yourself.
CNTRYBOY69: Where are you, Alicia?
OnlineHost: "Roberto518" has left the room.
OnlineHost: "Rick936" has left the room.
BadGrrrl: He eats beans for dinner.
CNTRYBOY69: Maybe we should just report.
OnlineHost: "PDuncan465" has left the room.
LabiaLady1: How old are you, Sweetheart?
GINOGINO: Hi Everyone
SkippinOut: What do you call it when a blonde dyes her hair brunette?
CNTRYBOY69: I reported.
BobAdder: Oooh, that's nice. Feels sweet runnin my hand over your smooth ass and down between your legs.
SkippinOut: Artificial Intelligence.
OnlineHost: "TheRevrnd" has entered the room
Cindy35819: Alicia? I had cyber with a girl? Does that make me gay?
OnlineHost: "DONTCHWANA" has entered the room.
PoetTaster: hi CuteButt
SINBAD: I'm sevn years old. I'm in my Dads office.
CuteButt: Your hand feels good, but I know something that feels better. I'm taking my blouse off now. I'm not wearing a bra.
JAKE3702: You all see who just entered the room?
OnlineHost: "WindSail69" has entered the room.
OnlineHost: "Dilapidate" has left the room.
TheRevrnd: The lips of a strange woman drop as a honeycomb, and her mouth is smoother than oil: But her end is bitter as wormwood.
Cindy35819: I cybered a seven year old girl? That's perverted. If I'd known I'd never have.
OnlineHost: "Elvira719" has left the room.

Rimbaud: Take a walk, Rev
JAKE3702: Elvira719 is a prude.
OnlineHost: "CMUNDRME" has left the room.
BobAdder: I'm standing behind you, kissing your shoulders lightly, holding your breasts in my hands, touching your nipples with my fingers
WindSail69: Are you back again, Rev
PoetTaster: Why do you show up EVERY ***KING DAY!
SkippinOut: Cindy, you wouldn't happen to be a blonde, would you?
PauliJeann: Would you guys take it private, please.
LabiaLady1: Alicia, Sweetheart. Tell us what the problem is.
DONTCHWANA: Ooooh, I love to watch!
CNTRYBOY69: Where's your Dad and Mom, Alicia.
Badgrrrl: Skip, you know what you call a man with IQ of 50? Gifted.
Rimbaud: oh man, an end bitter as wormwood! bummer. guess you'd better get your tongue out of it, rev.
Cindy35819: As it so happens, I am blonde.
OnlineHost: "UpInAtIt42" has entered the room.
OnlineHost: "DONTCHWANA" has left the room.
OnlineHost: "BruteAl" has entered the room.
HOTTOTROT: Hey, LabiaLady. You're not a woman at all, are you?
SINBAD: Dad's screming at Mom. I'm afrad he's going to hurt her.
OnlineHost: "Sweatlicker" has left the room.
Cindy35819: <wetkiss> Bye, DONTCHWANA.
CuteButt: <shivers> I turn around, lift myself up onto my desk, hook the heels of my feet on edge of desk so my knees touch yr chest.
HOTTOTROT: Admit it, LabiaLady. You're a man.
OnlineHost: "Rpd25680" has entered the room.
OnlineHost: "PDuncan465" has left the room.
TheRevrnd: Who can find a virtuous woman? for her price is far above rubies.
Rpd25680: Why do you think LL is a man, Hot?
OnlineHost: "Luke486" has entered the room.
OnlineHost: "MGrat26743" has entered the room.
OnlineHost: "HIALEAH" has entered the room.
JAKE3702: There's something in the way she moves. Oh, yeah.
Rimbaud: A virtuous woman has a price, Rev? How much? I'd like to buy me a couple for housework.
LabiaLady1: Is there someone you can call, Honey? An aunt? A grown-up friend?
OnlineHost: "AHower123" has entered the room.
SINBAD: Mom and Dad are in the kitchn dwnstair
BobAdder: I kneel, kiss your knee, then run my tongue down the inside of your leg, your thigh, till I reach your hot nexus and lick, lick.
HOTTOTROT: Because a woman wouldn't call herself LabiaLady. Would you call

	yourself ScrotumMan?
Cindy35819:	What's a nexus?
OnlineHost:	"Lunchbuket" has entered the room.
OnlineHost:	"PauliJeann" has left the room.
CNTRYBOY69:	Do your Mom and Dad know where you are, Alicia?
OnlineHost:	"CATDAD5002" has entered the room.
OnlineHost:	"AHower123" has left the room.
OnlineHost:	"JUSTIN0836" has left the room.
OnlineHost:	"MGrat26743" has left the room.
SkippinOut:	How do you know when a blonde has used your computer?
OnlineHost:	"BoomBox" has entered the room.
SkippinOut:	There's white-out all over the screen.
CuteButt:	I'm holding your head in my hands, pulling you into me. I'm close already, close . . .
OnlineHost:	"WindSail69" has left the room.
OnlineHost:	"Luke486" has left the room.
BoomBox:	anybody wanna cyber?
GINOGINO:	hello room!
BruteAl:	Will you guys please find a private room!
Cindy35819:	BoomBox is back!
OnlineHost:	"JUSTIN0836" has entered the room.
HOTTOTROT:	bye {{{{{{{{{{{{{{{{{{{ WindSail}}}}}}}}}}}}}}}}}}}}}}}}}
Badgrrrl:	What do men and bottles of beer have in common?
OnlineHost:	"RobinJ974" has entered the room.
LabiaLady1:	Can you call a grown-up, Darling? Tell us.
Badgrrl:	They're both empty from the neck up.
OnlineHost:	"TRex9826" has entered the room.
OnlineHost:	"DONTCHWANA" has entered the room.
BoomBox:	Badgrrl's jokes are too angry to be funny, no?
Cindy35819:	Is a nexus what I think it is?
SINBAD:	I herd something brek. Im afraid. Ples, can you help me.
TheRevrnd:	A virtuous woman is a crown to her husband.
ApeMan:	What's everyone's age?
BoomBox:	I'd do it for you, oh yeah.
OnlineHost:	"Rpd25680" has left the room.
LabiaLady1:	Can you tell us your phone number, Honey?
OnlineHost:	"ZWeeks69" has entered the room.
GINOGINO:	hi room!
Lunchbuket:	Round and round we go!
BobAdder:	Oooh, oooh . . . Delicious . . .
CNTRYBOY69:	I'm reporting. Be right back.
ZWeeks69:	What tit sizes we got in the room?
Rimbaud:	I had a virtuous woman once. she like to do the doggy dog.

CuteButt: Ummmmmm Ooooooh Yes, yes, yes
BruteAl: Will somebody shoot the Rev? Hurry!
OnlineHost: "CATDAD5002" has left the room.
OnlineHost: "AUSTRAILA5" has entered the room.
Trex9826: Someone get her last name and address and call the cops.
BobAdder: Lights a cigarette.
SkippinOut: What do blondes say after sex?
BoomBox: Yes what you think, Cindy. Bob prbly read too much H. Miller.
SkippinOut: "Are all you guys on the same team?"
OnlineHost: "PDuncan465" has left the room.
CuteButt: <cuddle>
BoomBox: 28/M
HOTTOTROT: Rev and Rimbaud should duke it out elsewhere.
Cindy3589: 21 / f
OnlineHost: "TBird69" has entered the room.
Rimbaud: 29/m
CuteButt: 23/F
OnlineHost: "LongJohn" has entered the room.
ApeMan: 25/ M
Lunchbuket: 19/M
GrndMaster: 29/M/
TRex9826: 19/M
HOTTOTROT: 22/F
Cindy35819: 36C
Badgrrl: What dick sizes we got in the room?
BruteAl: 25/m
OnlineHost: "Lunchbuket" has left the room.
BadGrrrl: Why are blond jokes so short?
BruteAl: 9 inches
OnlineHost: "Trudy9147" has entered the room.
Badgrrl: So men can remember them.
BruteAl: Let's do it, do it, do it!
ApeMan: 10 inches
Trex9826: 9 inches
DONTCHWANA:foot and a half, soft.
HOTTOTROT: 38 D
BoomBox: 11 inches
CuteButt: What have I been missin'
PoetTaster: 10 inches
CuteButt: bra size? 38C
Rimbaud: 10 inches
OnlineHost: "Rimmer" has left the room.
SINBAD: I don't know a grownup

CNTRYBOY69:	I reported.
BoomBox:	I'm taking off my shirt
SkippinOut:	Why dont Blonds use vibrators?
OnlineHost:	"Coyote 328" has entered the room.
SkippinOut:	Chips their teeth
Trudy9147:	40 D
LabiaLady:	Tell us your last name, Honey.
BoomBox:	Would you really do that?
FOXXY000:	41 C
Cindy35819:	;-)
SINBAD:	My nme is Alicia Welling. I liv in Huntington, Long Island. My phne nmber is 586-348-2222
BoomBox:	Do you guys believe this SINBAD crap?
BadGrrl:	What's a man's idea of foreplay?
LabiaLady1:	That's good, Darling. You just stay up in your Dad's study, okay?
CuteButt:	Is SINBAD a joke or what?
OnlineHost:	"JUSTIN0836" has left the room.
CuteButt:	It's like really off-the-wall, isn't it?
BadGrrl:	A half hour of begging.
TRex9826:	Is anybody checking SINBAD out?
LabiaLady1:	What grade are you in, Alicia?
OnlineHost:	"UUreskinska" has entered the room.
OnlineHost:	"ImDaOne" has entered the room.
Trudy9147:	Someone should do something.
GINOGINO:	Hello everybody!
OnlineHost:	"DONTCHWANA" has left the room.
OnlineHost:	"SAL93623" has left the room.
SINBAD:	What's it to you what grade Alicia is in? Who the hell are you?
FOXXY000:	WHAT?
OnlineHost:	"BoomBox" has left the room.
OnlineHost:	"9INCHES" has entered the room.
CNTRYBOY69:	Who the hell are you?
LabiaLady:	Who is this?
9INCHES:	I'M HERE AND READY TO PARTYYYYYYYYYY!
OnlineHost:	"PoetTaster" has left the room.
SINBAD:	I'm Sinbad. Will you guys quit calling us up! My wife and I are having a fight. Nobody's hitting anybody. Alicia exaggerates.
OnlineHost:	"SlipStream" has entered the room.
OnlineHost:	"AlxRs" has entered the room.
CuteButt:	Anybody wanna cyber
9INCHES:	Yeah well I like it too sweet sweet
OnlineHost:	"Thruster" has entered the room.

LabiaLady:	You ought to be more considerate of your child's response to your fighting.
OnlineHost:	"LNGnWd" has entered the room.
AUSTRAILA5:	oh man
CuteButt:	Somebody do me
SlipStream:	hello room
OnlineHost:	"LNGnWd" has left the room.
AUSTRAILA5:	What have u been up to CuteButt?
SINBAD:	***k you,L.
9INCHES:	K Y Jelly
CuteButt:	Thruster's back!
OnlineHost:	"FstEddy69" has entered the room.
CuteButt:	I love your muscular shoulders, T
OnlineHost:	"BD'sGirl" has entered the room.
OnlineHost:	"IntoIt666" has entered the room.
LabiaLady:	You did, S. A couple of months ago.
CNTRYBOY69:	You're scaring your kid, you assholes. They shouldn't let people like you be parents.
CuteButt:	Thruster likes it private. Bye, all.
OnlineHost:	"FlickFlack" has entered the room.
OnlineHost:	"AlxRs" has left the room.
FstEddy69:	hi all
OnlineHost:	"CuteButt" has left the room.
SINBAD:	***k you, too.
Zweeks69:	This is better than watching a soap opera
SlipStream:	What's all this Sinbad weirdness anyway?
FstEddy69:	Any hot woman wanna cyber?
OnlineHost:	"ImDaOne" has entered the room.
SINBAD:	Oh, shit. Here come the cops. Will you guys quit calling, please!
AUSTRAILA5:	Bye, NA
OnlineHost:	"Wilder323" has entered the room.
AUSTRAILA5:	Is that what you do with those?
OnlineHost:	"ZipitUp" has left the room.
FstEddy69:	Any Babes want phone sex IM me
OnlineHost:	"ImDaOne" has left the room.
9INCHES:	I heard it was gerbils.
SINBAD:	Now Daddy's fiting with the poleecemen.
AUSTRAILA5:	Is there like a set number of beads?
OnlineHost:	"JAKE3702" has left the room.
OnlineHost:	"RoxyTime2" has entered the room.
TRex9826:	Please if yr under 18 don't IM me
CNTRYBOY69:	What's happening now?
OnlineHost:	"Nitedreams" has entered the room.

OnlineHost: "ApeMan" has left the room.
OnlineHost: "ImDaOne" has left the room.
TheRevrnd: As a jewel of gold in a swine's snout, so is a fair woman which is without descretion.
SINBAD: Daddy's yeling at the polleecemen. Mommy's on the phone. The phone keeps ringing.
OnlineHost: "BeatMePles" has entered the room.
OnlineHost: "Nitedreams" has left the room.
OnlineHost: "LongJohn" has left the room.
BeatMePles: Anyone well hung to cyber
9INCHES: I think hamsters are too big.
SINBAD: What is this? Some kind of a dirty talk chat group?
GINOGINO: Hey Everybody.
OnlineHost: "SnowBunny" has entered the room.
OnlineHost: "Gene Al B" has left the room.
OnlineHost: "Bigguy826" has entered the room.
CNTRYBOY69: Who are you?
FstEddy69: I happen to know CuteButt's a guy. He's a systems engineer. I know where he works.
OnlineHost: GlmNDmTU has entered the room.
BadGrrrl: How can you tell if a man is sexually excited?
SINBAD: I'm a cop. Are you people aware that there's a six-year old girl reading this filth?
BadGrrl: He's breathing.
OnlineHost: Tchitbaby2 has entered the room.
SkippinOut: What goes vrrroom—screech, vrrroom—screech, vrrroom—screech?
OnlineHost: Lv2Doit50 has entered the room.
RIMBAUD: She's too young to think it's filth yet, asshole.
SkippinOut: A blonde at a flashing red light.
OnlineHost: LvConectun has entered the room.
BadGrrl: How many men does it take to screw in a light bulb?
SINBAD: Are you located in the state of New York? How about telling me your name, big shot.
OnlineHost: Sally9875 has entered the room.
BadGrrl: One. Men will screw anything!
SkippinOut: What's the difference between a blonde and a lightbulb?
RIMBAUD: ha, ha, ha, ha, ha . . . Hey, is it true cops have to fail two IQ tests before they qualify for the force? Or is that only in New York?
GINOGINO: Hi, Folks!
SkippinOut: You can unscrew a lightbulb.
SINBAD: This is Sinbad, again. Will you guys please, please stop calling. My wife and I are not arguing anymore. They police are gone. Alicia is

	in her room. All is quiet here. Except the damn phone.
BadGrrl:	Why do men find it difficult to make eye contact?
OnlineHost:	Swordfisher has entered the room.
TheRevrnd:	The way of transgressors is hard.
SINBAD:	This is one of those sex chats, isn't it. I want you to know I think you're all perverts.
BadGrrl:	Breasts don't have eyes.
SkippinOut:	What do you call a skeleton in a closet?
LabiaLady:	Who's this?
SkippinOut:	Winner of an all-blonde hide'n'seek game.
BadGrrl:	Why don't men eat more M&M's?
OnlineHost:	Lmost873 has entered the room.
SINBAD:	I'm a firefighter.
BadGrrl:	They're too hard to peel.
SkippinOut:	What did the blonde mom say before her blonde daughter's first date?
LabiaLady:	Hey, Fireman? Do you have nice pecs?
SkippinOut:	If you're not in bed by ten, come home.
BadGrrl:	How many men does it take to change a roll of toilet paper?
TheRevrnd:	As a dog returneth to his vomit, so a fool returns to his folly.
CNTRYBOY69:	What now? Is Sinbad's house on fire?
BadGrrl:	We don't know - it's never happened.
OnlineHost:	Hard Drive has entered the room.
SINBAD:	The little girl started a fire in her room.
BadGrrl:	What is the thinnest book in the world?
OnlineHost:	Bbracken986 has entered the room.
OnlineHost:	LKMYBUSH has entered the room.
LabiaLady:	Is she okay?
BadGrrl:	What Men Know About Women
OnlineHost:	Sizzler has entered the room.
SINBAD:	She's fine. Just lots of smoke. I didn't know perverts cared about kids.
SkippinOut:	What did the blonde say when her doctor told her she was pregnant?
OnlineHost:	KLB 222 has entered the room.
SINBAD:	This is Sinbad. The phone's off the hook, you clowns.
SkippinOut:	Is it mine?
BadGrrl:	How can you tell if a man is happy?
OnlineHost:	RASONDET has entered the room.
SINBAD:	This is Sinbad's wife. I think you should all know that Sinbad is a tax accountant. Sinbad . . . What a joke. How many of you has he had cybersex with?
BadGrrl:	Who cares! ! ! !

OnlineHost: LEZLVR69 has entered the room.
SkippinOut: What does a blonde do first thing in the morning?
LabiaLady: A tax accountant! Read his profile, dear. He's supposed to be a twenty-eight year old professional fitness trainor who works with corporate executives.
SINBAD: Are you guys happy? You're ruining my whole damn life.
SkippinOut: Introduces herself and goes home.
OnlineHost: WIZARD06 has entered the room.
OnlineHost: FlyBoy333 has entered the room.
SINBAD: I just read his profile. Wait . . . I can't stop laughing. Wait . . . wait . . .
OnlineHost: RndBuns has entered the room.
BadGrrl: How do you save a man from drowning?
SINBAD: My wife thought AOL stood for Airports On Line. Honest.
OnlineHost: GotBalls has entered the room.
BadGrl: Take your foot off his head.
SINBAD: Sinbad's name in Harvey, he's fifty-three years old, 25 pounds overweight, and he has one eye.
SkippinOut: What is the mating call of the American Collegiate Blonde?
OnlineHost: BullDog has entered the room.
SINBAD: I lost an eye in a hunting accident. Is that funny?
SkippinOut: Y'all, I am so drunk . . .
OnlineHost: WldWoman has entered the room.
SINBAD: He lost his eye on a fishing trip!
OnlineHost: CDarden has entered the room.
OnlineHost: MClark has entered the room.
BadGrrl: Why do men always have a stupid look on their faces?
SINBAD: Okay, a fishing accident. So?
OnlineHost: BufmBiffy has entered the room
BadGrrl: Because they're stupid.
Rimbaoud: Getta Outta Here! A fishing accident?
OnlineHost: GARY9251 has entered the room.
OnlineHost: BLUESINGER has entered the room.
SINBAD: What's so funny? We were fishing for Blues on the Atlantic and we got into a school and during the frenzy another fisherman hooked my eye. He yanked my eye right out. Hekjsdk[kkj
BadGrrl: You really think that's funny, Skip? Suggesting that a woman who drinks too much really wants to get raped?
OnlineHost: LkWhtsUp has entered the room.
SINBAD: He's lying with me right here looking over his shoulder! He hooked his own eye, the asshole. And he was on a rowboat in Hecksher Pond. And he didn'kjs[asdk ksdj
TheRevrnd: It is better to dwell in a corner of the housetop, than with a brawling woman in a wide house.

SkippinOut:	Come on, fess up, BadGrrrrrrrrrl. You're a blond, right?
SINBAD:	Do you believe this? We're fighting over the keyboard. We'rkjsaijdj
OnlineHost:	Sassy10196 has entered the room.
BadGrrl:	***k you, you pig.
SINBAD:	I thought AOL stood for Assholes On Line. I thkjkkl
TheRevrnd:	A continual dropping in a very rainy day and a contentious woman are alike.
SINBAD:	Thsjsdlkj Theaklaldj Helcxjvlkjdsf;l
OnlineHost:	Sassy10196 has left the room.
SkippinOut:	That's just what you need, BadGrrrrrrrrrrrrrrrl. A little lovin would straighten you out fast.
SINBAD:	Help me, ples. My Daddys going to hurt my Mommy.
OnlineHost:	CNTRYBOY69 has left the room.
OnlineHost:	LabiaLady has left the room.
OnlineHost:	SkippinOut has left the room.
OnlineHost:	Cindy35819 has left the room.
OnlineHost:	The Revrnd has left the room.
OnlineHost:	BadGrrl has left the room.
OnlineHost:	Rimbaud has left the room.
GINOGINO:	Hello, everybody!

Gary
John
Percesepe

Missionary

So they drew near to the village to which they were going.
He appeared to be going further, but they constrained him, saying,
"Stay with us, for it is toward evening and the day is now far spent.
—Luke 24:28-29

RIGHT AFTER HIGH SCHOOL I spent almost a year at a fundamentalist Christian college in upstate New York where I seduced my English professor and got C's in all the courses not in my major, which was psychology. My papers in John's classes were all weeks late, which explains the C's, if you believe in explanations. I wasn't dumb. I left before we were caught. They didn't have anything on us, but they were on the scent. John was hopeless in the area of deception, and they had ways of finding things out, a whole legal machinery of sin detection complete with informants. Leaving was something I could *do* for him, at least. I never got to say goodbye, which was the way I thought I wanted it at the time. Just check out, like a rehab gone bad. Failed fundamentalist. Don't look back. Lead him not into temptation. Deliver him from evil. I know what people think when they hear all this, and it's okay, maybe I think some of that too, but the thing is, it's been six years since I left and I still don't know what any of it means, or even how to make this sentence keep going until it made sense to anyone who wasn't there. Or to anyone who was.

Like Garbo

Winter is my favorite season. I've always known this. It seems wrong to speak of other seasons, as though they exist. I liked it there in winter. The sky was low like a snowy roof and in the brilliant woods adjoining campus a furious wind was blowing, always. The lake was frozen three straight months. Sometimes John would walk me across it, laughing and moving in a half-skate. We danced, a kind of tortured mock tango there on the lake, remembering bits from old movies that John had seen in videos that he rented and played late at night in his cabin, where I'd go late at night, breaking curfew with the help of my roommate Kit, another fugitive from fundamentalism, who'd let me in the locked dormitory door at six the next morning. When we stumbled and fell we'd lie in a heap on the ice, kissing. After, I'd pull away and stare at him, my face lit by moonlight, immobile, like Garbo. Like that, yes. I knew what he saw when he looked at me, his conflicted desire. It hurt to look at him then, seeing the shape of his care reflected in his cloudy eyes. Poor boy. It was then that I knew he was as lost as me. At these times and no others I'd let myself think "he loves me," but then I'd remember that to him, as a fundamentalist Christian, love and rescue meant the same thing. He's big on salvation, I would think. Then: It's not his fault, it's all he knows.

John

John did his best to impersonate a normal fundamentalist college professor but it was unconvincing to me, as a performance. He'd tell me that he didn't belong there at Redeemer College, that he took the job only because he was desperate for work in his field, that he got the job because the dean knew his father (a pastor), that he'd leave when he finished his dissertation, that something better would come along, and I'd say "What," sweeping my hand in a dramatic gesture that took in the eight by eight square of his office with the droopy tile overhead and the blinking fluorescent lights, "And leave all this?"

John believed that leaving would be the best thing after what had happened between us, but I observed that belief was precisely his problem, that he was *excessive* in his need for belief. Besides, I'd tell him, you're needed here. You're a missionary.

Mr. Darcy

When I was small, the single missionaries would stay with us at the parsonage. My sister and I always dreaded it. The women, with faint moustaches and impeccable grammar in their fund-raising newsletters, always seemed to have the most terrible physical problems; they limped, they gave off a vague medicinal smell, they used no makeup, they wore K-Mart shoes and hose with seams. I changed the sheets when they left, holding them at arm's length as I threw them into the washer. It's possible that the single men, however, were worse. Once, in sixth grade, a man named John Darcy stayed a week with us, and I never saw him come out of his room—that is to say, my room, I had to stay with my sister—until the last night, just before dinner, when he appeared before me and Cassie and our girlfriends and started doing calisthenics with an unholy enthusiasm. Amazed, we watched as he stood on his head in the living room, his glasses awry, his spastic mouth twitching with exertion. I was twelve, and horrified. I wondered what he had done all that time alone in my room. I grew up deathly afraid that I would become a single missionary and do calisthenics in the houses of strangers.

Class Notes

What I remember comes in pieces, like the soft doughy squares of bread my father served at communion in the Baptist church, the crust carefully cut away by deaconesses. I reach inside and seem to pick up a piece of Wonder Bread memory. This do in remembrance of me. This is my body. Broken for you.

I remember John lecturing on the history of romance. It was a morning in early January, missions week at Redeemer. Slouched in my seat against the pale green wall, notebook in my lap, I sleepily took notes. Tall titled columns of them. But when I look, my notebook now looks like the haphazard ramblings of a bright but disorganized deity:

happy love has no history
Tristan lands in Ireland
Iseult the Fair
love has always been nourished by obstacles
romance only comes into existence when love is fatal, frowned upon
doomed by life. what draws us is the story?

It surprised me that a fundamentalist college would offer courses on Shakespeare and the Age of Romanticism, lots of Keats, Byron, Shelley, but I've learned that fundamentalists are very big on love and romance. They're suckers for tales of conquest and heroism, evil dragons slain, fair damsels rescued from distress. They don't really believe in happy endings, at least not in this life. They want to believe that all are sinners, all are lost (*they're right, there*!), that everyone and *everything* can be saved through a personal relationship with Jesus.

I'd say: Jesus saves, Moses invests. Lead us not into Penn Station. Deliver us from Evel Knieval.

This was not what John wanted to hear.

Mother, Milky

I had sex for the first time at fourteen, and by the time I was sixteen I had had four lovers, a drinking problem, and an abortion. My parents were oblivious to what was going on in the house. They were never home, always at church, organizing, or practicing the cure of souls, and Cassie and I quietly became famous in the Grand Rapids underground, a loosely knit criminal network of mostly pastor's kids. It was fun, until Cassie fell off the back of a speeding motorcycle, her pretty brown hair matted with blood and particles of brain, and my parents remembered me, and started to use my name in sentences in a way that seemed to me *excessive*, and began asking to spend time with me, their cadaverous eyes haunted, their skin stretched tightly over remaining flesh.

Late one night I got up for some milk. My mother, drawn like a moth to the light of the refrigerator, silently sat down in the middle of the kitchen floor, naked. I dropped the milk. I laid down next to her, my head in her lap, and kicked the carton away, then drew my milky legs up until they were under my chin.

There was no money for college, but Redeemer offered free tuition the first year for the children of pastors, so there I was. I figured I'd do one year, then transfer some place. It wasn't much of a plan, but it was what I could manage at the time. My parents said they'd find a way to help pay for a secular school later if I gave them that one year at Redeemer. They'd say it just that way, like a prayer: "Give us this year."

Like it was a gift.

To them I guess it was.

To me it was a life. Or half a life. A half-life.

I was eighteen years old.

Chapel

The first week of winter quarter was missionary week at Redeemer. Did I say this? We were required to attend chapel twice a day during missionary week, in the morning and again at night. The missionaries that came to the conference were the real item, all the way from Chad and Brazil, Zaire, Mexico, the Philippines, Japan, England, France, you name it. And "home missions" people too, from Grand Rapids and Atlanta. I found it odd that they would have missionaries in a lot of these places, especially England and France and Grand Rapids, where there's a church on every corner. Kit said the evening sessions were a great time to catch up on your homework. We'd sit in the back of the chapel in the part we called "The Zoo." We'd pass notes, giggle, set off the occasional alarm clock, and make fun of the nerd boys they had there, who carried gargantuan designer Bibles with their names printed in gold block letters on the cover. (They prayed over ice cream cones when they'd venture out on dates, which was rare.) One night I asked to look at one of these Bibles. A nerd boy had come in late and had to sit in The Zoo, so I reached over and opened it to the inside cover, looking for the inscription Kit said was always there, in the five line space Zondervan made for this purpose. Sure enough, there it was: "To Travis, in the hope that this book will keep you from sin. Remember son, This book will keep you from sin, or sin will keep you from this book. For prayerful study at Redeemer, where we trust you will get a *safe* education, by the grace of God. Your loving parents." I gave the Bible back to Travis and squeezed his sweaty hand, dragging it into my lap. I pecked him on the cheek. I put my tongue in his left ear and smiled sweetly. I did not ask him how safe his education felt then.

Sex

I didn't tell anyone about us, except for Kit, but I knew that we were being watched. At Redeemer points could be scored for bringing someone down; a sexual fall was a biggie. Sex was preached against on a daily basis in chapel, but all *that* did was call attention to it, heightening anxiety and of course, curiosity. Lust was everywhere. The place was a hothouse of love, love, love; everyone was a possible victim, anyone could fall. It was the most sexually democratic place on earth. I'm saying there was an obsession there about sex. Even Hugh Hefner got tired of it, for Christ's sake, but at Redeemer they just didn't know when to stop.

John, II

Somewhere in here I concluded that John belonged there. I say this because I watched him pray (while safely disguised as a good-attitude coed in a navy blazer and plaid skirt). John sat up front on the right side of the college chapel, with the other faculty. His head cradled in his beautiful hands, the long slim fingers threaded through his wavy hair, when he prayed he seemed to be lifting off the pew, as if elevated by an invisible wire. Afterwards, students and colleagues would gather around him to ask what he thought of the sermon. Even if it was a disaster—say the preacher had gotten off one-liners on abortion, the ACLU, how God made Adam and Eve not

Adam and Steve, liberal apostate theologians, all in a commentary on the first chapter of Paul's Epistle to the Romans—John would look each of these petitioners in the eye and speak carefully, without condescension, giving his careful critique. Even-handed. He must have known that it was killing him to be there, that he should leave, but I began to feel that this was because of me, not because he had outgrown the place. How could I take him away from all this when I didn't even know what it was, the life he had there?

I'd think: If anyone finds out about me and John we're fucked. I felt bad about this, because as I said, John was so hopeless in the area of deception. He wanted to turn himself in. He was unprepared to live in the world, that was pretty clear. One day we went to the post office in Albany. He wanted to mail a package to his grandparents. We were in the downtown office, it was crowded, and he drifted from counter to counter, unable to settle anywhere, until finally he found the right one. But then he realized he didn't have the right zip code. He stood there, turned to stone. He was ashen. I asked what was wrong and he said it was impossible, we'd have to return home and look up the address. I told him that was ridiculous, it was a thirty-minute drive back, and besides, one of the clerks at the window could look up the zip code. He stared at me as though I were a Martian, as though this were news from another planet. Finally, he got in line, the clerk addressed the package complete with zip code, and John paid him. But when he counted the change, he saw that he had one dollar too many, so he gave it back to the clerk. Then he walked away slowly, counting again, and in the middle of the staircase he realized that the missing dollar belonged to him after all. I stood next to him, at a loss, while he shifted his weight from one foot to the other, wondering what to do. Going back would be difficult; a crowd upstairs was pushing and shoving in line. "Just let it go," I said. He looked at me, baffled. "How can I let it go?" he said. Not that he's sorry about the dollar, money in itself is of no consequence to him. But it is the fact that there is one dollar missing. How can he just forget about something like that? He spoke about it for a long time, and was very unhappy with me. And this repeated itself with different variations, in every shop and restaurant. Once he gave a homeless person a five dollar bill. The man had stopped him and asked for a dollar so he could eat. Five was all he had, so John asked the man to change the five, but the man claimed he had no change. We stood there for a full two minutes trying to decide what to do. Then it occurred to him that he could let the beggar have the five. But we hadn't gone ten steps when he began getting angry. This is the same person who would have been eager and extremely happy to give the poor man five hundred dollars with no questions asked. But if he had asked for five hundred and one we would have spent the day trying to find a place to make change, he would have worried himself over one dollar.

His anxiety in the face of money was almost the same as his anxiety over women or his fear of things official. Once I called his office in the morning, begging him to take me away from there that day. I was beside myself, I needed to get away, just for half a day, somewhere, anywhere. I cursed him when he said he couldn't. Afterward, he didn't sleep for nights, he tormented himself, wrote me letters full of self-destruction and despair. Why didn't he come? He couldn't ask for leave. He was unable to bring himself to ask the department chair for release from his one remaining class that day, the same department chair he admired in the depths of his soul—I'm not kidding—because of the chair's skill with computers. How could he lie? he'd say. To the chair? Impossible.

Lying is possible for most of us because it gives us a safe place, at least momentarily, a refuge from some situation which would otherwise be intolerable. At one time or another all of us have taken refuge in a lie, in blindness, in confusion, in enthusiasm or despair. But John had no refuge, nothing at all. He was absolutely incapable of lying, just as he was incapable of getting drunk or high. He lacked even the smallest refuge, he had no shelter in the world. He was exposed to everything that most people are protected from. He was like a naked man in a world where everyone is clothed. This is why he could not continue seeing me, and also why he could not continue teaching there. He knew this but was unable to leave either me or Redeemer. Like at the post office, I thought: He will move from counter to counter trying to find a space to work it out, a place from where he can see through to tomorrow. He couldn't leave because of me, but he couldn't stay either. But what would be his reasons for leaving? He loved what he did there, he felt he was needed by his students. And of course, he was. And if he were to leave, where would they go? Had he left last year he would have never met me, and then my suffering would have been greater. I know that he thought about this, but for him it was more than a practical problem, it was also a theological issue: How could God do this to him?

I told him: "Lying is inescapable." If he stayed there he lied, because he couldn't remain and be the type of person that he was. But if he left that was a lie too, because there was part of him that very much belonged there, that would be misplaced anywhere else.

I told myself: maybe we are all searching for places where we can stay the longest without lying.

Later, I thought: Who knows? Maybe he reached his place of optimum truth there.

Cabin Stories

When we met during Fall quarter, John was a virgin. He told me there was a girl once when he was in high school but they broke up before it ever got to that. One had to know how to listen with John. He tended to leave things out.

One night I followed him home to his house on the north end of College Street. The street was lined with run-down shacks, with broken-down cars on the dirt driveways and little kids playing tackle football in the street. No faculty lived on this side of town. As we walked our shoes clacked on the concrete pavement, then afterwards crunched on the long cinder path that led up to his little cabin at the edge of a dark wood. Dry leaves rustled. It was Thanksgiving break. I'm sure that to him I was a waif, lost and errant. It's true that I had nowhere to go. Everyone else had gone home, most to their parents' houses. For many reasons, my parents' house was out of the question. I called and told them I was staying with a friend. They sounded relieved. Over wine at dinner I got the rest of the story out of John. It turns out that he had never even kissed this girl, Colleen, whom he had met at a dance when he was fifteen. She was the great love of his life, there had never been another, and he hadn't so much as kissed her.

There was a black coal stove in the center of the main room, but the bin next to it was empty. The tiny bedroom was in the west corner of the cabin. The bed was covered with animal skins. It was funny to see John's white hands shooting out of those dark skins at dawn, like some prehistoric creature with good reflexes. We'd laugh and squirm around to get warm, grinding ourselves into the cotton sheets while John re-positioned the skins above us. I'd ask him to tell me a story, and he'd tell me how he used to tug his little brothers on a sled up a snowy hill in Peekskill, or about the time when he was four and his older brother's dog bit him, and his parents made Matt destroy the dog in the back yard, in front of him. Right here was when I told him about Cassie. I mentioned her wavy dark hair and did her laugh for him and made him get up to get my jacket, which had been hers, for her scent, and we both put our noses into the collar and runted around, and when he cried I knew I wanted a different story. After that he began telling stories about God and I got less and less interested, and finally I just told him to stop and then there were no more stories.

We stayed in that cabin almost a week. John found some coal for the stove, and it was a good thing, because on the second day it snowed. The windows frosted over, and snow blew in through small gaps between the logs in the northwest corner. When we talked, we could see our breath. John said it looked like something out of *Dr. Zhivago*. I took his word for it.

We got into a routine: Wake up, cook breakfast, back into bed, up for lunch and long walks in the woods, drive into Albany for dinner at a different restaurant each night, bed again. There was no talk of Redeemer College.

The day before classes resumed, we were lying in bed. We talked past noon. I took a deep breath.

"John, how did you get into this whole fundamentalism thing? Why are you here? I mean, you can't really believe all this stuff?"

"Jesus made as though he would go farther."

"What?"

"That's it. That's why I believe."

"What are you talking about?"

"Luke 24. After his resurrection Jesus is on the road to Emmaeus and he meets up with two of his disciples, but they don't recognize him. They think he's just another guy and they're amazed that he hasn't heard about this Jesus person, so they say, "Haven't you heard? You must be the only one in town who hasn't, he's risen from the dead!" Then Jesus finally reveals himself to them, going back through the Old Testament and showing them how all this was speaking of him, how he really is the messiah. The first time I read this story, Zoe, I thought to myself, this is sad, this is really *so* sad. I mean, to have to explain yourself like that. After all the great things he did, all the miracles and the healings and to top it off Jesus rises from the dead, and here these guys that claim to be his followers don't even recognize him. He was traveling through the world incognito. Even the ones who claimed to know him best didn't recognize him, or denied him, they all somehow *missed him*, or betrayed him with a kiss. After three years they still didn't know who he was, they still didn't get it."

"But what is this, Jesus made-as-if-he-would-go-farther stuff?"

"After Jesus goes through this whole routine with them, and now they recognize him, and believe again, it's dinner time, and the disciples were going to spend the night somewhere. But the text says that Jesus made as though he was going farther, and they had to persuade him to stay with them. I think that's why I love him. I think that's why I'm here. He was just so incredibly polite, he didn't force himself on anybody, he had the most incredible manners. He didn't want to offend. He wanted to help them to *see*. Jesus—"

"Wait a minute. *That's* why you're here? Because Jesus made as though he was going farther, because he had good manners, that's a *reason?* You're saying that you came to teach at a fundamentalist college with weirdo rules and a pervert for a president, and you choose to stay here, the whole thing, because Jesus was polite to these bozos?"

"Because Jesus goes unrecognized in the world, Zoe. Because we've been in the presence of grace and we didn't even know it. Because the greatest mysteries in the universe have been revealed to us and we've forgotten or overlooked them or somehow screwed things up but he's too polite to embarrass us again. Because he travels through the world, travels *through us,* incognito. We keep pushing him away, out of the world, out of our lives, *and he lets us!* Because he's been right there with us, hell, he's *carried* us and we didn't even notice."

He sighed, and looked into his hands.

Outside, the wind was picking up. Voices of children could be heard at play in the street, and farther off, the low rumbling of a train. I watched the grimy curtains move toward us, disturbed by the wind, then lie limp against the window pane, suddenly still.

John got up and threw some more coals on the fire, then came up behind me and waited. I didn't say anything.

Then he said, "I know I'm not saying this very well, Zoe. I just think I can help here, that's all."

Kit

One day during missions week a vice president of one of the big missions boards used maps and charts to share with us missionary possibilities all over the world, particularly in the former Communist bloc, and could it be that God would like to use us in Russia for His glory? Five hundred students raised their hands and came forward down the aisle to go to Russia. That's one third of the student population. I thought, What are all these people going to do in Russia? I felt sorry for the place. I pictured all those Bible thumping classmates tearing up the countryside, knocking on doors and handing out tracts in poorly translated Russian. I thought, if I were in the Kremlin I would pass laws immediately to stem the tide of evangelistically minded American students with large Bibles. The way I looked at it, the country had enough problems. But then, Kit and I figured that 498 of them would change their minds. They'd get married, get a mortgage, have kids. Most of the students I knew there would rather die than think of themselves in a country without shopping malls. What would they wear, these students, in Russia? Kit and I tried to imagine the Redeemer girls with their blazers and pearls, trying to talk to vodka-smirched Russian women waiting in line for brown bread. We cracked up.

Besides me and Kit, there were our trainees, Alix and Jennifer and Sara. After the missionary conference ended at 9:30, we'd sit around complaining about how we were expected to get any work done when they had us going to meetings all night. We'd trade favorite missionary stories. Sara thought she had the best one, about this missionary from Brazil who used to tell repeatedly, every time he spoke, about how this giant bug was in his skull for three weeks, how they eventually prayed that bug right into oblivion, and Alix recalled a missionary who somehow failed to tie up the livestock on a plane and wound up with goats chewing things up and raising hell in the cockpit, but we all sat there in amazement when Kit told us about her mother.

"I grew up in West Virginia, right, and down there we take our religion seriously. No room to fuck up, I mean you've got to toe the line sister, or whump, they'll toss your sorry ass out the church. So my mom tries, right, really tries, to please my dad—who incidentally is the pastor of the church—you know, to be the total woman. She even wears only Saran wrap when he gets home from work, kinky sex to the Song of Solomon, the whole funky thing. But she knows that she's going nowhere in that small town and she's itching to get out and back to school so she can get herself a life before she's too old."

Jennifer stopped looking at Kit, and stared at the wall, a vacant look in her eyes. I put my arm around her.

"So one Sunday night at church my mother shows up with three roses, each in a Dixie cup of dirt. One rose is completely closed, the other is partially open, and the third is in full bloom."

"What was she doing with three roses," Alix asked.

"They were her props, see. She was about to give us an object lesson, just like she might have done in junior church or something, but that congregation was about to hear something it never heard before, I promise you. Us kids are sitting quietly in the pew, we've got our coloring books, our Barbies, the whole thing, like a normal Sunday night. But nothing was normal that night.

"So now my dad, who remember, is the pastor, says it's testimony time, and the minute he says that my mother stands to her feet and in her hands she's holding her three roses, and she starts in on her testimony.

" 'My dear sisters and brothers in Christ, I want to share my heart with you. You see these three roses? They represent my life. As you can see, the first rose is unopened. It signifies my life as it has been for the first thirty-three years. All this potential, all of my *possibilities*, going to waste. Do you know what it is like to have a good mind, a sound mind, that the Lord God has given you, but you are unable to use it? Well, that has been my life. This is the old me, a beautiful rosebud, unopened, yearning to burst out into bloom.

" 'And this second rose you can see is in bloom. Its petals have opened, all the world can see its beauty, but it is still a veiled beauty, isn't it?' My mom held the second rose aloft in her hands. I could see old Mrs. Bartle sitting on the edge of her seat, following that rose with her eyes. 'But something is still wrong,' mom said. 'This rose is not all it can be. It has yet to become all the rose that God intended it to be.' Now she had her head bowed. She was weeping. 'This is my life now, this rose. I've opened up to the Lord, I'm willing for the world to see me now, but not all of me, just a part. I'm still only half a person.

"'But this rose.' She waved the third rose in the air now, triumphantly. 'This rose is in all its glory! It is the rose in full bloom. Nothing can be more beautiful than a rose that has completely opened to its possibilities. And this rose is what I want to be. What I shall become, by the grace of God.'"

"God, Kit, that is *so* beautiful," Jennifer said.

"Yeah, they all thought so. Mrs. Bartle was bawling so loud you could hear her across town. But what no one knew is that I had heard my mother and father earlier that day. They were having a huge fight. They thought I was outside playing with my sister. My father was pleading with mom to stop having the affair, to stay with him and her family and she kept screaming, over and over, 'Leave me alone, leave me alone, you're smothering me!' That woman was heading for the door long before the trinity of roses speech, I'm telling you. It was a great performance, and it bought her some time and a lot of sympathy afterwards, when she left town. Masterpiece theater."

"God, Kit," Jennifer says. "How did you stand it? Did you tell her that you knew?"

"I've never told anyone," Kit said, "till now."

On The Ward

Kit was the rebel. I didn't have the energy for rebellion. For that, you had to care. I was just there for observation. I told myself constantly, "You're on the ward, pay attention." But it was weird, since *they* all thought the same thing, they were observing *you*. After all the church services at home, all those Redeemer chapel messages, all the Bible classes, I had internalized a fundamentalist voice. It talked back to the other voice, the one that was mine. I heard these lengthy conversations all the time.

—It's wrong to have sex. The Bible says so. Whoremongers and adulterers God will judge.

—That's ridiculous. Sex is the most natural thing in the world. You see a gorgeous guy, you think you're going to live forever. God gave us sex, he made us this way.

—You must learn to overcome these lustful thoughts. God will judge.

—Then God's judging himself, since he gave us these bodies in the first place.

—That's blasphemy.

—Your God's perverted. Do you really think he's hanging around the Ramada Inn, checking out what's going on in Room 208? Shouldn't he be more interested in Northern Ireland, or Lebanon, Bosnia, something more worthy of his time?

—He's working on that. Besides, God knows everything about everybody. He is not only omniscient, He is omnipresent.

—So he's got the Holiday Inn covered too.

—You have a bad attitude.

—So what?

—You're headed for hell.

It's like fundamentalism is a double-voiced sickness, but the ones who observe it are themselves observed, so no one knows how to chart it. It's a standoff.

Chapel, II

I did some math: If you stayed at Redeemer for four years, and went to chapel and the special bible and missionary conferences at the beginning of the semesters, and to church twice on Sunday and Wednesday night prayer meetings you would have heard 255 sermons per year, for a total of 1020 in four years. Redeemer was in session for thirty weeks a year, fifteen weeks per semester. This means that a student could hear 255 sermons in 210 days in one year; graduating seniors will have heard 1020 sermons in only 840 days. If you want the prayer figure, take the sermon number and double it: 2,040 public prayers, minimum, not counting required dorm bible studies and prayer meetings. Many of these were about sex. Not having it was the idea. There was no mention of child abuse, homelessness, poverty, racism, or sexual harassment. Math was not my strong point, but I checked my figures three times. I thought these figures were not widely known. When I told John, he suggested I write a letter to the school newspaper. When I told Jennifer she said that's not counting the summers, when you attend church and prayer meeting at home with your parents. She went off to calculate the number of times that worked out to in terms of hosiery bought and put on. When I told Kit she said, "What'd you expect, that they'd leave anything to chance?"

The President

The President of the College frightened me. His name was Jack Sampson. Since Redeemer was so small, we all got to see him way more than we'd want. When he looked at me, it sent shivers down my spine. One day, waiting for John after Chapel, he looked at me; well, not at me, he looked at my body. At my legs and butt. It was a "degree day," meaning it was below zero and the girls got to wear pants. Pants on girls were so unusual that when we got to wear them, we'd flaunt it, whatever we had. So I had on Jennifer's too tight striped pants and he looked at me in this really ugly way, and I knew he wanted to undress me. I wanted to take John's hand and run out of the building.

That night's topic of dorm conversation was President Sampson: Was he a pervert? Kit thought so. "Think about it, this guy comes right out and says he is a friend of Jimmy Swaggert, I mean this guy knows that weirdo! He has Swaggert's home phone number, can you believe it?"

"Did you see the news when Swaggert asked forgiveness from his congregation? Wasn't that nauseating? His poor wife."

"I saw the interview they did with the prostitute Swaggert was with. She has a kid. She said the stuff he asked her to do, it was sick."

"I don't know, Zoe. I don't think Sampson's a pervert. The president asked for prayer for him, is all. And besides, we're different from Swaggert in doctrine, right? So Swaggert doesn't really represent the Christian community. I mean, Swaggert *is* a charismatic, right? We don't believe that stuff about tongues and all."

This was Jennifer. She was somewhat in awe of us.

"Right, Jennifer." Kit said, "Sampson doesn't speak in tongues so he can't possibly be a pervert."

John, III

I worried about John constantly. It was unbearable. He was wrecked with guilt. I didn't believe in guilt. I thought it was a false emotion that we manufactured to torment ourselves. I had watched my parents manipulate each other and my sister with guilt. Fundamentalists are expert at guilt, but this is a cliche. What's not widely known is how much they suffer.

I looked at it this way—I'd been around fundamentalism enough to have received an inoculation. I mean, I think I'm immune to it now, that enough distance has been created, but I know it's still in my blood, traveling in me, silent and potent.

Saved Sex

John sometimes wondered if he was still saved, what with all that we had done together. I'd tell him we need saving from something every day, what makes this day any different? Then I would take his hand and place it on my breast.

Kit and Me

One of the weirder rules at Redeemer was that if two girls were on a bed, they both had to have both feet on the floor.

I ask you.

So one night Kit and I were lying in bed in our underwear with the door locked. Kit was admiring my panties, which were white, with red hearts. My mom sent them to me for Valentine's day, but they were too big. I knew Kit didn't have much money. After her mom ran off her dad lost his church. He got another one but it was a small congregation and couldn't afford to pay him much. I said what the hell. I took the panties off and gave them to her. My bra too.

Kit gave her professors fits. That day in New Testament she had embarrassed her prof by asking him if he had sex before marrying his wife. He deserved it, he kept going on and on about the biblical view of sexuality and Kit just couldn't take it anymore. I had to put my head on my desk to keep from laughing out loud. The prof asked if he could see her after class. He questioned her attitude. She had an appointment with the dean the next day at 8:00 AM.

Anyway, we're lying in bed, me naked now, regretting my decision to stop seeing John outside of class, when Kit jumps me. We wrestle till we're panting with exhaustion, our sides splitting with laughter, but she has a good twenty pounds on me, and it's clear I'm going to get pinned, so I decide to just lay back and enjoy it. Kit pins me, then counts slowly to three in a referee's voice, and calls me a wimp. She lip synched to the illegal tape I had playing, "Got it bad, got it bad, got it bad, I'm hot for teacher." Then she kissed me on the lips, and asked me out to dinner.

I got back to the room the next day after classes and found a note on my bed. From Kit. They'd kicked her out. I ran down the hall crying. I found the Residence Hall Advisor and asked her what happened to Kit. She looked at me like I'd dropped in for the day from Jupiter. Then she said out of the side of her mouth, "Kit had an attitude problem. As you know. She's gone."

It's been six years. I made my escape the day Jennifer was kicked out for attitude in The Zoo. I piled all my Redeemer clothes in the middle of the floor with a note saying "Help Yourself!" and caught the next bus out of town. I didn't say goodbye to anyone. I called my parents from the bus station and they freaked. But they didn't ask me to come home, I'll give them that.

I stayed with Kit in Ithaca until I got a job cutting hair and an apartment. I took some night classes and tried to get into a degree program at Cornell, but I couldn't get my Redeemer credits to transfer. Whenever I said that word, Redeemer, I'd get this look, like I was bad meat. There were fights with the registrar, and scenes in the admissions office. Finally I just gave up.

That was years ago.

I am twenty-four.

Last year I got married to this guitarist. We're on the road a lot. It's okay at night, when there's so much set-up work to do and then the band is playing and everything is moving by so fast, the lights winking at the dancers on the crowded floor and the crashing wall of sound that seems to flatten the room, picks us up and throws us down again. But the days are slow. Sometimes, after dinner with the guitarist and his friends, I stand up and walk outdoors, and keep on walking till I'm in sight of a church.

I just found out that I'm pregnant. I haven't told the guitarist. I haven't told anyone, yet. I've given a lot of thought to what I'm going to call the baby if it's a girl. Katherine Anne, after Kit and my grandmother. And if it's a boy? That's easy.

There's this song playing at work. I hear it all day long. The one about God on the bus, trying to make his way home.

I think: What if God *was* one of us?

I don't know what happened to John. For a while Kit was getting Redeemer newsletters at her house but she called and told them to fuck off. I never got any. I guess to them I never existed.

I still think about him sometimes, and yeah, about our conversation that last day in his cabin. And I see John's point in the Luke story. But I think Jesus made as though he would go farther because he just wanted to get away from those two guys. Maybe that's the difference between believers and non-believers when you get right down to it: the believers think it all comes down to this one person, and they know how to hang on to what they have.

And then I remember: We were in bed when he told me that funny story about Jesus walking on the road. John's hands were there on my belly, like mine are now, soft and warm, and he was sobbing, shaking so hard I thought he would fall apart, and he kept saying my name, over and over, *Zoe, Zoe, Zoe, Zoe.* I tell myself I may be remembering this all wrong, that things change and your life plays tricks on you, but I mean, there we were, in that little cabin at the end of the road, and I was in his presence and I never knew what it was, what he meant, what was mine.

Jodi Bloom

Triple X

THE DAY THAT I GOT UP the nerve to challenge him, Royce paused for a minute, then wandered around the counter to where I was standing—real deliberate and slow, with his fat lower lip stuck out like he planned to teach me a lesson—and he grabbed my arm until it hurt, just a little.

"I ain't selling Smooth Johnny's magazines," I repeated for the third time. "You can do what you like Royce, come in here on your own and sell whatever garbage you please, but I ain't participating."

"May Jean," Royce said, staring at me hard, as if we were still snot-nosed kids and he could maybe scare the living shit out of me just by giving me the evil eye, "you and me is going to settle this idiotic and ridiculous dispute right now."

I knew Royce wasn't going to hit me or anything. I'm not one of his girls, and besides, even Royce would never hit family. So I just eyeballed him right back and stood stubborn in my position at the cash register. Royce maneuvered his fat self around behind me, gave a little shove, and then waltzed us both out the front door and down the walkway, still holding my arm like I was his prisoner.

"Little sister, what does that sign up there say?" he asked, spinning me around to face the house as though we were doing some kind of disco dance routine, thrusting his hip out and pointing his chubby finger up toward the sky *Saturday Night Fever* style. I didn't bother answering the question on account of I didn't feel the need at that moment to prove to my own low-life brother that I am a grown woman of twenty-six who can read just fine *thank-you very much*, even if I am a high school drop-out. I narrowed my eyes up at Royce who, in addition to being overweight, was a good deal taller than me.

"You *can* read can't you, May Jean?" he asked, raising an eyebrow just like Papa used to when he expected a particular answer out of you, or else.

"Yes Royce," I said. "I sure as hell can read." The sun was burning bright and piss-yellow in the afternoon sky and I squinted up at the house, our folk's house, which Royce inherited 100% a few years back and then proceeded to transform into a trashy business venture on the first floor with a two-room apartment for me on the second.

"Well then sis, in case you are having difficulty with your eyesight, that sign up there says 'Royce's X-X-X Newsstand.' I am assuming since you can read you can also count. There ain't one X, and there ain't two. There's three of them X's on that sign May Jean, and I'm not about to get my ass sued by John Q. Public for false advertising." Royce held tight to my arm. Lucky for him, I thought, that this house is on the edge of a one-horse town and no one seems to care what goes on here at our place, no one ever has. Royce continued with his lecture. "Here's some very simple math for you May Jean. Bare naked bodies, that equals one X. People fucking? That adds up to two. People fucking things they ain't supposed to? Now that's what gives you your triple-X status.

"And in case you are having trouble with your memory," Royce added, giving my arm a squeeze, "let me remind you that it is only due to my good and generous nature, and what they call business acumen, that you have this roof over your head and food on your table instead of being left out in the cold to starve your skinny ass off. You are unskilled and uneducated May Jean, and you don't have two dimes to rub together. So go on back inside and do your job. And stop getting all political on me. It ain't good for business."

Earlier that morning, Smooth Johnny had come by to drop off another disgusting shipment of his wares.

"Hi there pretty lady," he said when he came in the door, his smile flashing like he was running for president except that I doubt any politician worth his salt would go around with a missing front tooth. "How's my favorite hillbilly feminist?" he asked. I didn't smile back and I didn't answer his stupid question because I ain't no hillbilly or no feminist. And because Smooth Johnny is the main reason that I am in my current predicament and I prefer to say as little to him as possible. Besides, I know better than to trust a man who wears a black toupee and who has a stud-earing the size of the Hope Diamond twinkling from his left earlobe. "Where's Royce?" he asked, hoisting a brown cardboard box up onto the counter. I watched a bead of sweat run down his ugly face.

"Haven't you noticed?" I said. "Royce is the owner of this establishment. I, on the other hand, am nothing more than the minimum-wage slave girl. Royce is probably over at his place sucking down a cold beer, getting a foot massage from one of his whores, and watching a baseball game on TV. Now is there something I can help you with Johnny?"

"Ain't no baseball games on TV this time of day," Smooth Johnny said, wrinkling his brow as if I was speaking a foreign language. He took the box and walked around the counter, dropping the damn thing right beside my feet. I didn't say a word and I didn't look at him either.

"My you have pretty red hair," he said. "You could be *my* slave girl if you weren't so damn cranky all the time. You tell your brother I came by," he added as he walked across the room and turned the doorknob to leave. The sleighbells which Royce has attached to the top of the door—so I can hear customers come in when I'm in the toilet—tinkled and made me think of Christmas, like they always do, no matter if I've heard them a thousand times. "You ought to be pleasant to me May Jean, if you know what's good for you. I'm gonna be a partner in this business real soon," Smooth Johnny said, and he was gone. I heard his raggedy-ass two-toned Bonneville backfire out front, just the way it did when he pulled into town six months ago and started all this trouble.

When I first told Royce that I refused to sell Smooth Johnny's pornography—sleazy home-spun magazines that featured technicolor snapshots of people getting horny with barnyard animals and faded Polaroids of buck-naked underage boys, known in the skin-trade as chicken—he said, "Well, ain't you high and mighty for someone who got herself knocked-up the minute she hit puberty."

Anyway, he accuses me of harboring what he calls an *irrational hatred* for Smooth Johnny just because Smooth Johnny drives the same kind of down-and-out car as the no-good son of a bitch who knocked me up and ruined my life when I was sixteen.

"You have a psychological problem, May Jean," Royce explained. "See, you are wrongly associating Smooth Johnny with that long lost man and that long lost baby of yours and the fact that you got written right out of Papa's will for being . . . well, let's not spare any words here little sister . . . for being a teenage slut. It ain't Smooth Johnny's fault," he reasoned. "Smooth Johnny is just keeping customers—my customers, *our* customers—satisfied. It's a simple supply-and-demand thing, May Jean. And you got it all tangled up in your mind with something else. Matter of fact you could say you got Smooth Johnny to thank for that cream of wheat you chowed on this morning. You still eating cream of wheat every morning May Jean?"

Did you think I wasted my time answering that question? I was busy wondering where Royce got all that psychological mumbo-jumbo. Probably from watching Oprah Winfrey or from some magazine article he read in the dentist's office while he was waiting to get another tooth capped. Royce's life is a fantasy starring himself as a small-time Larry Flynt, living it up in a high-priced townhouse on the other side of town with two women—in what the French call a *ménge à trois*—and buying himself a movie-star smile, one sparkly white tooth at a time.

Maybe Royce is right about some things. The truth is that directly after Smooth Johnny started bringing his filthy smut around, I did become obsessed about my baby boy, who I gave up for adoption ten years ago purely in the hopes of giving him a chance for a better life.

Royce had cracked into that first box of Smooth Johnny's magazines and tossed a few across the counter at me, without saying anything about the contents. I opened one called *Beauty & the Beast,* and I can't say that I felt anything but sick to my stomach looking at pictures of naked girls fornicating with horses and dogs. A little T & A is one thing; this was something else altogether.

One day shortly after that, Royce's girlfriend Lovely stopped by the shop when I was on the register. She's a retired ex-porno star who claims to have worked with all the greats, including John Holmes himself. "Fucking him," Lovely said, "was pure heaven. Like having a baseball bat shoved in and out of you." I took it upon myself to show her a copy of *Beauty & the Beast* and I asked her, "Lovely, would *you* do it with a horse?"

Lovely is AC/DC and she swears she always worked in porn because she wanted to, because she loves fucking and sucking men and women both and she can't get enough of it. She is damn grateful, she says, that someone was willing to pay her money (*good* money, mind you) to utilize her talents, which she considers to be a natural god-given gift. But even Lovely said that she ain't anywhere near fuck-happy enough to do horses and dogs, and she don't imagine any girl really is. "That there is exploitation," she said, shaking her head back and forth, and she promised to talk to Royce. But as you can already see, there is no talking to my brother, the king of pornography here in Hicktown, U. S. A.

The chicken magazines Smooth Johnny wanted us to sell were even worse, like seeing snapshots of your darkest nightmare and I didn't need an ex-porno star to tell me so. Because although the fact is that I am only a mother in the technical sense of the word, I looked at the pictures of those kids, some of them ten years old if they were a day, and I thought: This here is somebody's child. This could be my own little boy.

My boy had red hair, just like me by the way. The nurses let me hold him before they took him away, placing him ever so gentle in my arms, even though they said it would make things twice as hard, and that as professionals, they could not in good conscience recommend it. I now believe that holding that teeny baby was the best and worst moment of my life all rolled into one. Sometimes in my dreams I see my boy standing in the front yard here, under the maple tree, and smiling up at me with his fat pink cheeks. After I saw Smooth Johnny's magazines though, other pictures started appearing in my mind's eye, things not nearly so pleasant.

Those glossy magazine photographs burned into my memory and I stayed awake at night hating myself more than ever for giving away my boy and hating Smooth Johnny for bringing his sick perversions into our otherwise (well, relatively speaking) normal lives. Of course I hated Royce plenty too, but that was nothing new; I've hated him since I can remember. Still, I stood firm on my principles and Royce himself had to haul his lazy ass in here on Saturday nights to sell Smooth Johnny's illegal pornography, which he kept hidden behind the counter, under a pile of newspapers. Of course, having to actually do some work—other than deciding which TV channel to watch out of the several thousand his satellite dish pulled into range—put Royce in a worse frame of mind than usual toward me, and my life has been hell for half a year now.

So like I said, maybe Royce was right about some things. I do miss my boy and I regret giving him up. In fact, there are times that I think that one act has drained the very life out of me. But Royce was wrong about other things. For example I did not long for my boy's daddy, who ain't worth the raw energy it would take to miss him. And for another, I did have two dimes to rub together; I had started saving up a pile of cash money from my measly cashier's pay the minute I saw the new merchandise Smooth Johnny was peddling to Royce. And the day after Smooth Johnny made his prediction of becoming Royce's partner in the business, I got me a money order from the post office and I sent away to the Murray McMurray Hatchery, Incorporated, way out there across the United States in a place called Webster City, Iowa.

Mr. Buddy, an old man who lives down the street and happens to be my friend, loaned me the Murray McMurray catalog; he used to raise a few chickens himself in his own backyard. I ordered 100 baby Orpington chicks—all females, because I figured with Smooth Johnny and Royce in my life I had plenty enough roosters parading around. And besides, I was fixing myself up in the egg business and nothing else, so there wasn't any use for some old rooster cockadoodle-dooing and fertilizing everything in sight.

The picture of the Orpington in the Murray McMurray catalogue showed a fine white chicken with a red comb on its head and cute little pink feet. The description below said: *These Orpingtons are large, quiet, and gentle, with a pinkish white skin and easy to dress. They are good winter brown egg layers.* It was the part about them being gentle and quiet that sold me on them above the Rhode Island Reds and the Bantams and all the other breeds. I didn't imagine I'd be wanting to dress my chickens, like they suggested you could, but I laughed out loud, picturing my brood running around the backyard in various sweet little outfits, puffy polka-dotted sun dresses and flowered aprons, and one very fat chick twirling 'round and 'round in a ballerina's pink tutu. Of course, I know that's not what they meant.

The chicks cost $113, plus 10¢ apiece for vaccinating against something called Marek's Disease, which affects their poor little central nervous systems, and which I didn't want my babies to suffer even a hope of catching. Besides, I figured 100 baby chicks traveling all that way from Webster City, Iowa already had enough odds stacked against them. I spent another $84.61 on a special electric floor brooder, and last but not least I bought a book about raising them and enough feed for two months.

"What you got in there May Jean?" the postman was saying as he carried the boxes up the front porch. "Are they making dirty magazines with sound effects these days? One of these boxes here is peeping."

I had to giggle when I heard it—squeaky little peeps coming out of a flat cardboard box that otherwise looked like it might be holding a dozen glazed donuts from the Krispy Kreme. "I'm going into the egg business," I said to the postman. "Couple of weeks and you'll be able to buy the best-tasting fresh eggs ever. Brown eggs," I added.

"Mmm," the postman said. "Sounds real good May Jean."

"I wonder if the Murray McMurry Hatchery only sent part of my order," I said, when the last box was loaded onto the porch and still only the one was peep-peep-peeping. "How can a hundred baby chicks fit inside a donut box?"

The postman frowned. "Don't know," he said, "but that's all they sent."

Inside the house I carried everything down to the basement. I took a deep breath in an effort to try and quiet my heart which was beating so loud I thought it might scare the baby chicks. Then I opened the donut box.

Every person in the world should mail-order baby chicks sometime just for the sheer joy of opening a plain brown box and seeing those sweet little darlings, squiggling around and making their chickadee noises, like fluffy white cottonballs come to life. Sure enough there was probably a hundred of them, give or take, jam-packed into that box end to end. I looked down at them and they seemed to look right up at me, blinking as if to say: *Now what?* I couldn't help but think of my little boy, his wide-eyed stare from his position in my arms, and the same question dancing across his innocent face. Only this time at least I had an answer that didn't break my heart in half.

Mr. Buddy came over to help me get the baby Orpingtons situated in their brooder. Only three of them had died—in transit as Mr. Buddy put it—which he said wasn't bad, not bad at all. I read the book *Backyard Flock* by one Mike Strecker, from cover to cover, and visited with my babies before turning in for the night.

"May Jean, what the *fuck* is this?" Royce said. He was standing up at the top of the basement stairs and looking down at me and the brooder. Royce is so absorbed in himself that it took him three full days to notice the baby chicks. "I thought I heard something funny," he added. "Thought I smelt something too for that matter."

"Ain't nothing funny," I said, "it's chickens. Orpingtons," I added, to let Royce know he wasn't dealing with an amateur.

"Okay," Royce said. "Let me ask this another way. What the fuck are you doing with chickens, May Jean? You starting a restaurant or something? We ain't got no license to sell food here. Besides, there's room for one business and one business only at this house."

"No Royce," I said. "Don't you worry, I ain't selling no chicken. That's yours and Smooth Johnny's business—which like I have said from the beginning, you can keep to your perverted selves. I'm fixing to sell eggs."

"I don't know about this, May Jean," Royce said. "I don't know about this at all."

After that incident, I locked the basement door and hid the key under my mattress, on account of I was afraid Royce might come after the baby Orpingtons. Then, lo and behold, a week later, Royce had done a 360 with regard to my new business venture.

"You go ahead with them chickens, May Jean," he said, like he felt sorry for me and was giving me permission. "It's good for you to have something to occupy your mind. Maybe you'll stop obsessing over things so much."

Although I sure didn't need Royce's permission, I was glad he didn't give me any more trouble because I wasn't in the mood for something else to fight with him about. I made up a sign, hand-painted on an old piece of wood, that read, "Coming soon! May Jean's fresh brown eggs. A bargain at only 99¢ per dozen."

Those chicks doubled in size just about every day, growing faster than weeds or kittens. A month later, when they were fat fluffy white hens, just like the one in the catalog picture—and me and Mr. Buddy had them nicely situated out in the garage on the back of our property—I crossed out the "Coming Soon" and wrote "Available Now," because my precious Orpingtons had started to lay.

Every morning at the crack of dawn I was out in the garage harvesting the smooth brown eggs from underneath the warm sleepy bodies of my chicks and they'd squawk a little and sit up as if they might start an argument. I got to thinking they hated the fact that I was out there in the garage disturbing the peace and quiet, not to mention snatching their eggs, so I sang a little tune to the chicks in an effort to try and distract them. Each day I'd test a different song out there in the dark and it was "Loving You (is Easy 'Cause You're Beautiful)," by Olivia Newton John, that finally made the Orpingtons calm down and quit their fussing. Imagine that.

Mr. Buddy says I shouldn't worry at all about taking their eggs. "That's a chicken's job, he says. That's her lot in life, like it or not." Truth is, I wasn't sure. But I was damn sure that selling Royce and Smooth Johnny's triple-X pornography was not my lot in life. And I was also damn sure that the Orpingtons were my ticket out.

I personally stopped eating eggs because of seeing first-hand the distress it caused those poor hens. But the folks in this two-bit town kept right on gobbling them up and my business grew and grew. I give Mr. Buddy some of the credit. I mean aside from him helping me to set up on my own, it was him that gave folks around here the taste for fresh eggs—years ago before he got "plum tired of getting up at the ass crack of dawn," as he likes to say.

Yes sir, it wasn't long before me and my Orpingtons could barely keep up with the demand for our fresh brown eggs. Mr. Wallace down at the Super Mart said he'd take whatever leftovers I couldn't sell myself, so each and every one of my eggs was spoken for before it was even laid.

Sunday was my number one selling day because folks liked to stop by after church and pick up a fresh dozen or two for the week. It was old Mrs. Nuttle who told me that I was doing God's work because an egg is actually one of the symbols of the lord Jesus Christ himself. And it was also old Mrs. Nuttle who spotted a copy of *Boys, Boys, Boys* which Royce was dumb enough to leave laying out on the counter after his booming Saturday business the night before.

We had these old drapes we would pull over the shelves that held the magazines, for times when even Royce didn't want anyone to see what was being sold, and I always made sure to clean up and close them for my Sunday customers—out of respect, I suppose. The rest of the week, I figured everyone knew just exactly what it was besides eggs we were selling here at Royce's X-X-X Newsstand, because you'd have to be a complete idiot to think it was *Time* and *Newsweek*. Although we stocked those too. "It's a marketing thing," Royce says. He says some men like to pretend they're coming into the store for one thing, and then they just so happened to walk out with something else.

I sure had to laugh at times, watching people stroll into our place, right under Royce's sign, to buy a dozen eggs—folks that wouldn't have set foot on our walkway previously and folks that knew damn well the nature of our other merchandise. Fact was, it all made me feel kind of proud, like finally something was going on in my life that my daddy himself—if he was watching from Heaven—would have thought highly of me for.

It's a mystery to me what happened the day Mrs. Nuttle found that magazine, because like I said, I always cleaned up the place for my after-church customers. Royce likes to accuse me of subconsciously leaving it right there in plain view as a pre-meditated strategy to cause him the trouble that followed in the days to come, but that's just another of Royce's fantasies and I'll swear that on a stack of bibles.

There was a small crowd in the front room at the time, like there always is on Sunday afternoons, and Mrs. Nuttle was about third in line to collect and pay for her eggs. I saw, out of the corner of my eye, her scrawny wrinkled arm in its moth-eaten navy blue sweater sleeve, as she reached out to the counter to lift up the magazine that had honestly appeared out of nowhere. I looked up just as Mrs. Nuttle's gnarly old fingers were opening to the center spread and I can't say just exactly what terrible thing she saw there, but she let out a cry which sounded like someone was pulling out her eyebrow hairs one by one. Then she dropped the magazine and ran out of our house screaming bloody murder.

I got so scared I dropped a dozen eggs and me and my customers all stood there watching the yellow slime ooze out of the carton and onto the hardwood floor.

After that, Royce and Smooth Johnny started having their talks with me. They'd both come over to the store together, trying to double-team me like a couple of schoolyard bullies.

"May Jean," Royce would start out. "You and me have got to talk."

"Nothing to talk about," I'd say.

"Oh yeah there is," Royce said. "There is plenty to talk about. Let's start with the fact that you are robbing those poor chickens of their own babies, their *offspring*, May Jean, just like you were robbed of yours. Did you ever think about that little sister? Hmm? I think they call that *irony*, is what they call that."

"What the hell does ironing have to do with it, and who's *they?*" I asked Royce.

"Don't be a smart ass, May Jean," Royce said and he narrowed his eyes at me. Smooth Johnny just stood there in the background like a deaf-mute, but with a sharp look on his face like he might cause me a slow and agonizing death if I didn't see things their way.

"Aside from that," Royce continued, "you and your little egg business are endangering the hell out of our livelihood here. You keep bringing them old church bitties around, we're going to get into trouble, you can see that can't you? Johnny and me are hoping that even you can understand that church bitties and pornography can't live in the same god damn house, May Jean. And in case you've had another of your famous memory lapses, pornography is our livelihood and *our* livelihood is *your* livelihood, sweetcakes, you dig?"

"No it ain't Royce," I said. "In case you haven't noticed, those chickens out there are bringing in some pretty cash themselves. And," I added, remembering what Mr. Buddy said, even if I really wasn't 100% sure I believed it myself, "laying eggs for eating is a chicken's lot in life, that's just the way it is. So don't be trying to spread your guilt trip all over me. And don't call me sweetcakes. I ain't one of your whores."

Royce looked down at me and shook his head back and forth. "Eggs," he said. "You really think that you can pay the mortgage on this house, and put food on your table selling *eggs?* You are dumber than the day is long, May Jean, you know that? But, okay. Okay." He put his hands up above his head in the "I surrender" pose, and Smooth Johnny mimicked him in the background, his hands high, that big diamond stud-earring winking at me from the shadows.

I thought it was over. I thought we'd had the argument for the last time. But we had it about nineteen times after that.

What happened next you might already know if you read the newspapers anywhere near this part of the world. Old Mrs. Nuttle, who never had the energy to do much of anything but drag her creaky bones to church and the grocery store, on account of she was about a hundred and six years old, became the leader of our very own local chapter of WAPs—Women Against Pornography—which consisted of Mrs. Nuttle and a dozen of her old cronies. There they were every Sunday afternoon, in dresses and hats dating back to the year zero, marching along the sidewalk in front of our place, with their signs and sandwich boards that said things like: *Honor the Children*, and *Remember the Sin of Adam,* and all kinds of religious hoo-ha that made no real sense to the situation. They'd stop in for eggs when their old feet got tired of parading, then they'd go on their way down to the police station and march around in front of there for awhile.

Finally, as summer turned into fall, the police came by and shut down Royce's X-X-X Newsstand and that was that.

Captain Williams himself brought over a CLOSED sign and said, "Royce, May Jean. I'm sorry. I don't really have no choice here. Let's just do this nice and quiet so I don't have to arrest nobody. Nobody wants a stink," he concluded, then he nailed the sign on the door while we stood by and watched.

"Fuck you, Captain Williams," Royce said, when the sign was up, and I couldn't believe my brother was stupid enough to talk to the captain of the police that way. Then he farted, real loud. "There's a stink for you," he said and stomped into the house, slamming the door behind him. The CLOSED sign fell to the ground and Captain Williams (who is very handsome by the way) nailed it right back up again. He shrugged his shoulders and said, "I'm sorry May Jean, real sorry." And I believe he truly was, being that he was one of what Royce called his most consistent customers.

That night I had an awful dream that my boy was in deep trouble with the law. I mean he was just a boy, so what kind of trouble could it be? I'm not sure because the dream was fuzzy around the edges the way dreams are. I just knew he was in deep. Then the trouble was over and we were all at a Bar-B-Q right here in our backyard. And it really was a dream because Royce and Smooth Johnny were sitting there eating coleslaw and chicken from the grill with Mrs. Nuttle and the WAPs. Everyone was getting along fine and having a good old time. The food smelled so delicious I woke up hungry, wondering what might be down in the fridge that I could go and round up for a midnight snack.

Then I noticed it still smelled like some kind of Bar-B-Q even though I was awake, or at least I thought I was. I sat up and pulled back the curtain on my bedroom window, and I pinched my own arm to make sure I was not still asleep because what I saw was so terrible.

The old garage out back where my sweet innocent chicks were nesting was on fire, flames licking upwards from the ground all the way to the roof and ripping a bright yellow tear into the black night sky. I raced downstairs in my nightgown, grabbed a big knife from the kitchen, and flew out the back door. Out in the yard the smell was strong, like the biggest chicken Bar-B-Q you ever attended, and the Orpingtons were screeching and squawking for their very lives.

"If I can't sell chicken, you can't sell eggs, May Jean," Smooth Johnny said in a whisper, his breath hot on my ear. I turned around fast because he had come up behind me and taken me by surprise. "I guess them chickens of yours is done *roosting* and now they're *roasting,*" he added and he laughed real sinister. There we were, face to face, my eyes burning from the smoke, and his breath stinking like beer, and I didn't mean to, but I stuck the kitchen knife right into him and gave it a mean twist. I hated that man so much at that particular moment that I couldn't think of anything else to do. Smooth Johnny sucked a big gulp of air and collapsed onto the ground. His toupee rolled right off his head and lay in the grass like a dead skunk.

"You ain't stopping us, May Jean," he said, looking up at me. "You can bring your old raving bitties around, and the cops and whoever the fuck you want. You can stab me in the god damn heart if you want and watch me bleed," he said, "but you can't stop what's natural. Fucking is natural, only I don't guess you remember since you probably ain't been laid since you were sixteen." Smooth Johnny clutched his stomach and blood oozed between his fingers. The chickens were screeching their tiny lungs out but I knew I couldn't save them. I started humming the opening bars of "Loving You," out of habit I suppose.

"Come here, May Jean," Smooth Johnny said. "I always thought you were sexy as hell. Stop singing that god damn song, and come give a dying man his last rights," he laughed, and he grabbed his crotch with his bloody fingers. "You can't stop the natural male urge, May Jean, not you and not an army of your crusty old hens." His eyes rolled up into his head and I knew he was going to die right there in front of me.

I thought about dragging Smooth Johnny into the flames and watching him burn. But then, I told myself, he's headed south anyway. Looks like Satan himself has come for Smooth Johnny and he'll be burning in the flames of Hell soon enough. I waited a half an hour or so, which was all the time Satan appeared to need in order to finish his job of letting Smooth Johnny bleed to death uninterrupted in my backyard. Then I went inside and called 911. While I was waiting, I got out my catalog from the Murray McMurray Hatchery. And although I was crying real tears over my poor dead Orpingtons and my long lost boy and the whole entire mess, and those tears were dripping right onto the pictures of the Leghorns and the Bantams, I began to think about just what kind of baby chicks I would order up this time around, as soon as things calmed down some.

Floyd Skloot

The Wings of the Wind

He came swiftly upon the wings of the wind.
He made darkness his covering around him.
—Psalm 18

MY SON ISAAC, adopted at twelve weeks of age, turned twenty on September 15. That day, he measured exactly seven feet five and three quarter inches tall. When he was home last summer, I stood beside him posing for a photograph and my head came up to about his pancreas.

Isaac outgrew Loretta when he was eight and me when he was ten. But until he was sixteen or so, he loved to walk between us holding hands, towering over us like a spike on a graph. He would giggle at our reflections in shop windows and at the looks on the faces of passers-by. Isaac weighs exactly what my wife and I do combined, 290 pounds. And as you can see, I'm accustomed to using precise numbers when I speak of my son.

Loretta and I got him from an orphanage in The People's Republic of Romania at the zenith of Ceausescu's power. All we knew was that he had been born near Sibiu, a small industrial city north of the Transylvania Alps, his mother had been a textile worker, and he had such raging impetigo around his nose and mouth when we first saw him that it looked as though someone had drawn on a bright red clown's face.

We named him Isaac after my father, but the name would have had a nice resonance for us anyway. According to Genesis, the biblical Isaac was born when his parents were quite old and thought themselves well beyond child-bearing age. Same as us. He was also the fulfillment of a promise, which felt right in our case as well, a kind of entitlement due to a couple who loved as deeply as we did. Then what does God do after giving Sarah and Abraham their son? Right. No wonder Loretta and I were overprotective, despite our Isaac's size.

He was virtually silent during the entire plane trip from Bucharest to New York. He slept for long periods, waking with a soft whimper wanting to be fed, then sitting in his carrier with his eyes wide open, hands moving vaguely in front of his face as though warding off something strange and unpleasant. His smiles seemed wholly inward, prompted less by anything he saw than by forces going on inside his body.

Probably you've heard of him. Isaac Berg, the great basketball star. Most people call him Ike and the press dubbed him The Ikeberg, a huge mass afloat in the middle of the lane. They say he may be the best collegiate center since either Wilt Chamberlain or Kareem Abdul-Jabbar or Bill Walton or Shaquille O'Neal—depending on your era—and maybe the best big man ever. In his freshman year at the University of Oregon, Isaac averaged twenty-six points, fourteen rebounds and six blocked shots a game, leading the Ducks to the NCAA Final Four where absolutely no one had expected them to be and where they had never been before. People in and around the game thought he would leave school then and make himself eligible for the pro draft, but he stayed on and had an even better sophomore year. In a press conference last spring, to stop all the speculation, he announced that he was staying in school for his final two years. He wanted to get his degree, help the team to its third straight final-four appearance, and play in the Olympics as a true amateur before basketball became a job for him.

I hope you got to see my Isaac during that press conference. Except for his size, everything about him said Gentle Scholar, said Books, said Soulful. For the first time, his nickname seemed to make sense, to reflect the truth that so much of Isaac was hidden below the surface regardless of how much there was above it. After every question, he looked down as though to collect his thoughts, smiling shyly, humble, unwilling to seem the smart-ass like so many other young athletes. It was the proudest moment for me, prouder than all his on-court honors, prouder than the night he scored 67 points and grabbed 28 rebounds against UCLA.

The name Isaac Berg, I would be the first to admit, fits a little strangely on him now. We had him circumcised when he was an infant, brought him up within the Reform movement as a moderately observant Jew, and kept telling him that he, of all people, was truly one of the Chosen. Of course, he looks about as Jewish as Vlad the Impaler, but who knew that when he was six years old? He was a dark infant, had huge hands and feet, a mop of curly black hair and deep-set eyes that followed me everywhere I moved, and while I didn't think he was necessarily of Jewish parentage, I didn't imagine he would look quite so gentile either. His features became enormous, everything growing at an accelerated pace, and, with his basso profundo voice thrown in, my son could be quite terrifying to encounter. Which is so ironic, since I believe it worries him to box opponents out for a rebound lest he accidentally crush someone.

At his Bar Mitzvah, Isaac stood six foot five and towered over the rabbi. Most thirteen year olds have to stand on a stool to see over the podium when they read their Bar Mitzvah portions to the congregation; Isaac, clean-shaven but heavily shadowed with stubble by 10:00 AM, had to stoop so that Rabbi Herschorn didn't hurt his neck looking up to bless him. As Isaac carried the Torah in a slow march through the congregation, some of the little old men reaching up to touch the scroll with the hems of their prayer shawls suddenly backed away as though seeing a Cossack on horseback. But he was oblivious, blissful at being a newly consecrated member of the tribe, his face literally glowing as he passed into light that poured through the stained glass window at the rear of the sanctuary. That night, at home after his party, Isaac could not stop talking about feeling hugged by God—those were his exact words. He had been embraced in that light, taken over, and felt himself to be loved and protected forever. It was a feeling I have never had myself, even at his age, and I remember hoping that whatever caused him to lose it would not be too great for him to bear.

Like so many extremely tall young people, Isaac had his social difficulties, especially as an adolescent. He didn't join clubs, didn't have any close male friends, didn't date much. The first time, near the end of his sophomore year, he asked me to drive him and the young girl, a foreign exchange student from Paris named Laura Quost, to the downtown cinema where a French film was showing. I dropped them off, went by myself to another film in a theater across the river, then picked them up at the Metro on Broadway, where they had gone for snacks and sparkling water, four hours later. Isaac's relief when he saw me walk through the restaurant's doors was so palpable that I felt like crying for him.

He knew he was strange-looking and, I think, secretly agreed when kids called him Frankenstein, called him Moonman, Geek or Bronto. But that all changed halfway through his junior year in high school, when Isaac's talent as a basketball player asserted itself and he became a hero over the course of one frigid Portland winter.

I will never forgot the silence that fell over the gym the first time Isaac's rage was expressed on the court. The silence only lasted for two seconds, a kind of collective stoppage of breath, before turning into something like joy as the fans erupted in whistles and wild cheers. But it was those two seconds I will never forget. Isaac had been taunted by the opposing fans and, worse, by players on the other team, throughout the first half of the season's opening game. He had refused even to consider joining the team during his first two years in school, refused to be seen with a basketball anywhere except on the driveway beside our house, and as the game progressed he had played mildly, passing the ball off whenever he got it, sticking up his arms but not moving aggressively to block any shots, reaching for rebounds but not boxing out or jumping. It seemed as though he was afraid to stumble and look awkward, though I knew it had more to do with his fear of causing harm. As the third quarter was drawing to a close, I saw his eyes narrow and his nostrils flare and I felt that something had snapped in Isaac. After all those years of being razzed, of trying to act small, denying his essential isolation, he had finally grasped some essential truth about his situation and reached an instantaneous decision. He moved into position at the top of the key and raised his arms, calling for the ball. The point guard, as shocked as I was to see Isaac asserting his will, bounced the pass to him. Isaac planted his feet, spun to his left and took one incredibly long step toward the basket. With the ball securely stuck in his right palm, threw down a slam dunk in one great windmilling motion. The ball tore through the net and bounced back up off the floor so high that time seemed to stand still as everyone watched it reach its apogee before reacting to what they had seen. Isaac had dunked from the foul line, moving through the air with such power, authority and grace that he looked like a seasoned professional. Or a prehistoric bird riding a zephyr. Back on the ground, he stood there glaring into the middle distance while the gym filled with noise. Then his eyes changed again, found me where I sat at midcourt as he trotted back on defense, and the expression on my son's face was a terrifying mix of triumph and grief.

Believe me, there was never a spoken plan. However, Loretta and I understood that Isaac intended to buy us a new home on Lake Oswego as soon as he signed his first professional contract. He thought we might also like matching leather recliners for the new living room, a big screen television on which to watch his games, a dark green Lexus, a summer trip to Israel after the basketball season. Where he came up with Israel, I don't know; my fantasy has always been a month on the beach in Rio.

This idea of Isaac's was something we knew from hints and suggestions he would drop into conversations. We'd be sitting in the living room after dinner, all three of us immersed in our books, and Isaac would suddenly wonder if it would be nice to listen to some Mozart right about now, maybe that *Piano Concerto in C Major* that we all went to hear last year in downtown Portland. Be nice to savor the crystal clear sound one of those new CD players is capable of. Then furniture and electronics catalogues started to arrive for us in the mail after his freshman season at Oregon. We were suddenly on the mailing lists for travel agencies and fancy automobile dealerships. Taking care of us in this way was probably the only thing that made Isaac hesitate to turn down the professional inducements and stay in school till he graduated. I'm glad he did.

These dreams on our behalf were pure American dreams; they certainly weren't Romanian ones. So equating personal success with waterfront homes or luxury cars is not in our genes after all! Tay-Sachs disease is in our genes, a hundred times more than in anybody else's, but not the need for a big screen television. Excuse me. I've been a bit emotional lately.

Although Isaac's dreams for us were contagious as airborne viruses, and we couldn't help talking from time to time about when we would be living on the lake, I would have been happy—and I'm confident Loretta would have been happy too—just to see Isaac at ease in this world we had brought him to, see him pleased with his achievements in it and smiling as he looked it in its eye. Of course, I'd also like to have a view of water. But so would my friend Henry Ah Sing, who owns a Szechuan restaurant in Old Town and is far more likely to get such a view than I am.

Because three months, one week and two days ago, on a typically dark, windy December night in eastern Washington, I watched Isaac follow his own missed sky-hook shot with a brilliant rebound and slam dunk over the seven foot Nigerian center who plays for Washington State, turn to head back downcourt, come to a complete stop while everyone ran by him, raise his arms a few inches toward his breastbone, and crumple to the court as though he'd been shot. He hit the wood floor so hard that I could hear the sound of it over the wildly beating drum that Cougar fans were using to whip themselves into a frenzy as they urged their team on. I swear I could feel it through my toes.

The team doctor rushed onto the court. He threw himself onto his knees and skidded to a stop beside Isaac, jerking open a bag as he reached toward my son's chest. Almost instantly, they were surrounded by members of the team, all of them too tall to see past.

The image that stayed before my eyes was of Isaac's utter stillness there. He lay sprawled across the top of the key, his face down and twisted slightly to the left in a position exactly like the one he always slept in as an infant. My first thought, odd and unbeckoned, was that I was glad Loretta's arthritis was acting up so that she had decided against coming to Pullman with me.

I got up to run onto the court, but was restrained by some people sitting nearby. Their collective grip on my arms and shoulders—part embrace, part shackles—felt as though it were cutting off my air supply. I shook myself free and ran onto the court. The videotapes shown over and over again on the news, especially the one on ESPN, shows my mouth opening and closing as though I were screaming, but nothing was coming out. To me, it looked like I was trying to breathe for Isaac.

Technically, he was already dead when he hit the floor. But I didn't need to be told that. As I watched him fall, I swear I glimpsed a faint spray like the sweat that comes off a boxer's face when you see a slow-motion film of him taking an uppercut to the jaw. I understood that this was the spirit rising out of Isaac, a soft blue incandescence, it seemed to me, the actual formation of an aura around his collapsing form. When I knelt beside him, Isaac's gigantic body seemed vacated and when I touched the center of his limp palm—his most ticklish spot—there was nothing.

Miraculously, it turned out that Marius DePino, the west coast's premier heart surgeon, was in the crowd. This was certainly the first and most profound of our blessings that night.

Dr. DePino had come from Seattle to tour the campus with his youngest son, who wanted to become a veterinarian. When they'd heard that Oregon would be playing at Washington State, they stayed to see the great Isaac Berg in person. Dr. DePino quickly made his way down from the stands and trotted onto the court, working through the circle around Isaac's form until he was beside my son. His hand brushed my shoulder gently, asking me to step aside.

Marius DePino brought my son back and kept him here, turning the visitors' locker room into an emergency room (while getting me to scribble a waiver of liability on the back of a Cougars-Ducks souvenir program) and working on my son's heart before my eyes. The inventor of the DePino Procedure for correcting mitral valve prolapse and of the DePino Technique for grafting veins in bypass surgeries, the author of two cardiology textbooks and a popular novel about the mystical bond between a heart transplant recipient and his donor's daughter, the man was both brilliant and bold. I don't remember anything after seeing DePino's hands begin moving toward Isaac's chest. The team doctor got to work on me while DePino worked on my son.

There was more surgery later, after he was stable, to correct Isaac's hypertrophic cardiomyopathy, a thickening of the inner wall of his heart's pumping chamber. Usually, this disease can only be discovered after its young victim has died a sudden death. This is why I'm supposed to regard Isaac as lucky. They put a small electronic defibrillator behind his stomach muscles to shock his heart back into rhythm whenever it goes haywire on him.

Isaac always wondered how to get closer to God. To me now, it feels like he is—the Lord's hand present in tiny heartshocks emanating from Isaac's belly. But what it feels like to me is not what it feels like to my son.

You see film clips on the news all the time. These very tall young men in the greatest physical condition imaginable, these invincible kids on the brink of vast fortunes, suddenly collapse on the court. One minute, they slam dunk and make the whole backboard shake or they swat a shot into the fourth row; the next minute, they're dead. Hank Gathers of Loyola Marymount, dead. Reggie Lewis of the Boston Celtics, dead. Marcus Camby of Massachusetts, prostrate on the court, out of action for a few weeks, then coming back to play and no doubt terrify his parents. It even happens to women athletes, always the long and lanky ones, basketball or volleyball stars, the ones with slender fingers curling under toward their wrists, great specimens, dead. Marfan's Syndrome, a hole in the heart, a faulty valve, a heart too large, a heart hiding its flaws until the sudden failure.

There were three hospital beds turned sideways and pushed together with their side-bars down to accommodate Isaac's body. His first coherent post-operative words were spoken in a raspy whisper five days after his heart had stopped.

"Dad, I'm sorry."

"And I'm overjoyed, Isaac. You're still with us." I let go of his hand and stroked the side of his face. "Now let me go outside and get your mother."

"Wait." He squeezed my arm. In the past, he could bruise me with such pressure but now his grip was weak, child-like. "It's all over. They made that clear yesterday. No more basketball. No running. A very quiet life. What, I'm suddenly going to become a physicist? Everything we planned for is out the window."

"I never planned for any of that stuff."

He closed his eyes and seemed to drift off. I shifted my weight to get up and leave the room, but he squeezed my arm again. "The house, the car, the trips, all out the window. I can't believe it."

"It doesn't matter, Isaac. Look," I pointed to his right, "all that's out the window this morning is sunlight." I couldn't believe that these were his primary thoughts after all he'd been through, after all he'd lost for himself.

His hand fell back to the bed. He swallowed dryly. "What good is a seven-and-a-half-foot-tall non-basketball player? I've never done anything else. Never even thought about it."

"Don't exaggerate."

He blinked and looked at me closely, as though seeing me there for the first time. "I don't think I am, Dad. This is serious, what happened to me."

"Well I think you're exaggerating. You're only seven feet five and three quarters. Now let me go get your mother. She'll want to hear your voice."

When I brought Loretta back into the room, Isaac was asleep again. She looked at him, then back at me, her face filled with questions and worry. I bent over the bed and stroked Isaac's brow.

"What?" he whispered, opening his eyes.

"Nothing. You were dreaming, I think."

He moved his eyes back and forth. "He was here, it wasn't a dream."

I started to shake my head, contradicting him, but Isaac grew more agitated. It worried me and I thought about going out to fetch a nurse, but Loretta held me in place.

"I think I may be getting nearer to God," Isaac whispered.

"He's gotten near enough."

"I don't think so." He reached vaguely in my direction and I handed him the cup of water. "Just the outskirts, where the light turned me around."

"You can remember that?"

He nodded. "And a sound, something like a windstorm in the darkness, but filtered through a long stand of trees. I don't know." He sipped and handed back the cup. "This is something I can tell people about."

"Sure. When you're ready, maybe we can set up some kind of speaking tour."

He blinked. "I think maybe this is what I'm supposed to do, you know? Maybe it's why I'm so tall, to be closer to Him than most people."

Loretta nodded. But I didn't get what Isaac meant. He was so tall, we'd learned, because of a combination of genes and a pituitary disorder.

"Maybe," I said. "But you need to rest. You need to heal for a while before you even think about what to do next."

"This has to have happened for a reason," he whispered, closing his eyes.

"You were born with a thick wall in your heart. The pump was bad, that's the reason. You should get some sleep, there's plenty of time to talk about what you'll do."

"Nothing happens by accident," Isaac whispered. "Do you think Marius DePino was there by coincidence?"

"Yes," I said. "We're lucky his son didn't want to be an electrical engineer or they might have been watching the Gonzaga game instead."

Isaac closed his eyes. A faint hiss came from the machinery beside the bed.

Out in the hallway, Loretta took my arm and gently led me toward the waiting room at the end of the hall. We plopped down together on the brown plastic couch, sighing as one, relieved to have him talking but, I believed, a little shaken at what he was saying.

Loretta patted my arm, always a bad sign, and announced, "Well, you handled that about as badly as a man could, I would think."

"I'm not even sure someone who's a Jew by adoption *can* become a rabbi."

"We're reformed Jews," Loretta said. "So almost anything is possible."

I looked out the waiting room window into a parking lot where cars all neatly fitted into their diagonal slots gleamed in winter light. It seemed possible to rearrange their pattern, to shift them so they faced the other way, noses to the street instead of noses to the hospital wall, just by fluttering my eyes or twitching my pinkie.

"For some reason, I just don't like it. The idea makes me squirm."

"Who says you have to like it?" Loretta asked. Her tone wasn't particularly challenging, just curious, a gentle questioning. "I never much liked the idea of his being an athlete, myself."

"You're kidding me."

She shook her head. "So I didn't come to very many of his games. Big deal. You could skip his services, or start going to the Conservative temple, whatever." She paused; I could hear her swallow. "The point is, George, you don't have to like what Isaac does."

I nodded, but a person would have to be looking closely to tell. Of course she was right, I should just be glad he was still here to do anything. "Tell me something." I paused, still looking down at the cars, picking one long Lincoln and changing the angle of my head so that the reflected sun pinged off the fender like a shot. I got lost in the game of it.

"All right. But first you have to ask it."

I turned to face her. "Why do you think I'm uncomfortable with this?"

"Beats me." She got up and came over to me, putting her arms around me from behind and hugging me to her. "No it doesn't. You're terrified, my love. You're in shock. You want everything to go back to where it was two weeks ago."

I nodded, leaning back into her. "Probably right."

"And you've had enough God for a while, I think. You don't want Isaac inviting Him back into our lives any time soon."

"What if it's something else?"

"Well, then it's something else. Now why don't we go for a walk and let him sleep."

"In a minute."

"Okay, George, what is it?"

"The new house, the recliner, the trip to Rio . . ."

"You hate the beach."

When we brought Isaac home two weeks later, the house immediately seemed tawdry to me. It felt too small to contain him, though he'd lived there with us all his life, and our furnishings looked shabby in a way I'd never seen before.

I've worked hard for thirty-one years now, and this is all I have to show for it? Three decades selling people insurance, eventually opening my own office, making nice money, and I live in a house I'm secretly embarrassed to own? We haven't had friends over to dinner in years—I always thought it was because we were too busy, too involved with following Isaac's career or with our little projects, our routines. Now I realized it was out of shame; who wants to bring people in here, with the faded wallpaper and dull paint and threadbare carpet? It was as if we had stopped tending to the place five years ago, almost exactly when Isaac's potential as a basketball player revealed itself. Everyplace there was wood there were chipped surfaces, as though the house had been subject to airborne abrasion. Posters of flowers and vegetables were wavy and sagging behind their glass, windows whose seals had busted were all blurry with contained moisture, there was noise everywhere from appliances that labored to keep up. All of a sudden, I could see the place for what it was, for what it had become. An abandoned home.

While Loretta tended to Isaac upstairs, I found myself sitting in my old easy chair staring out the window. The view, what I could see of it, was east toward a commercial section of Portland. A flickering neon sign with two letters out told people driving on the below-grade freeway that home furnishings were for sale. CAREYS FURN URE. Across the freeway, a new medical center loomed. The day seemed unnaturally dark. I turned back and listened for the sounds of my wife and son, his deep murmuring voice, her high breathy melody of comfort and devotion.

The doctors had told us that Isaac had a very good chance for a satisfactory outcome, whatever that might mean. His heart was essentially good, which I could have told them without holding it in my hands, though slightly enlarged by years of extra pumping action. His circulation and respiration were all good, he was in great condition, under the circumstances.

It was just that he couldn't play basketball again, or engage in strenuous activity, or do much of anything he'd always done and always dreamed of doing. Perhaps what bothered me more than all this was Isaac's reaction. He seemed happy, relieved. He was still tormented by the feeling that he had let us down, broken his promises, but with help he was getting beyond that. He seemed, in fact, gradually to have grown joyous about the new direction his life would take.

What, did I want him to be depressed? To be immobilized by despair over his losses, to be so angry that he jeopardized his recovery? No, of course not; but giddy, as though he'd been let off the hook? It was all very confusing to me.

We had made inquiries about how Isaac could begin studying for the rabbinate because that's what he asked us to do. I'm sorry to admit that if Loretta hadn't taken over, it might not have gotten done. Neither of us—nor Isaac—had realized how many credits in philosophy and religion he'd already accumulated. Still, it would be a good five more years, provided his recovery continued apace, before he was likely to stand before a congregation of his own.

I turned back again toward the window and began to drowse. A glimmer of color erupted outside the window. At first I thought it was just the Carey Furniture sign blinking, but then it came back, a small bird darting quicker than any point guard I'd seen on the basketball court. It was the most outrageously bright yellow, with hints of black on the wings and tail, a brilliant red head, and it zoomed across my field of vision like a flash of sunlight bright enough to cut through the barrier of the cloudy window. I thought I could even hear its hoarse call, its *pit-ik pit-ik* over the traffic sounds and the voice of the refrigerator cycling on in the kitchen. What's a western tanager doing a half mile from the Banfield Freeway, I thought. What's it doing with a red head in winter?

Then, jerking up with a start, I realized that was where I really wished we were, the three of us, where the bird was. We should be in a small house in the woods, in springtime. One of those yurts maybe that come pre-designed so you can assemble them yourself in the middle of your acreage. Not by an urban lake in a big house paid for by my son, but a cozy little place without many walls, located halfway between the city and the shore, precisely the kind of home I'd always dreamed of having. I had five years left for selling insurance before I was ready to retire. By then, Isaac would be finished with his studies. Could he find a congregation for himself in rural Oregon?

I stood and went over to the window. Nothing. At least, nothing in the way of yellow birds. Still, it would be nice, I thought, and turned to head upstairs to see what Loretta and Isaac might think about my dream.

Hart Schulz

Trout Fishing in L.A.

THREE WEEKS AGO I met a woman named Luanne, an adjuster who started snooping around the shop. She had eyes for me from the start, despite her suspicions, her long list of probing questions.

"Can you *hear* a crack in an engine block, or do you actually have to lift the car? . . . Are rubber mounts pretty much interchangeable? . . . Is there engine damage on *all* the near-totals we send you for salvage? . . . If too much torque will cause a crack, what happens with too little? I mean in the long run?" She's a person who sounds like she knows, but probably doesn't.

Actually, I admit, there are times when I've cheated, but only when Gonzalez, the shop foreman, made me. Gonzalez is the one she should be watching. "Huevo," he says like a robot, pinching an egg, a raw chicken egg, between two fat fingers. He holds it up in front of his big teeth. "Drop this into that radiator, little man. No more headgasket leak." He calls me "little man." He's an old machine without much imagination. He makes me fill hair-line cracks in motor blocks with pink Bondo, then cover them up with axle grease; he thinks of this as artistry. It's what happens when you work in a machine shop too long. "Little man with the big rod," he calls me.

"Is it hard getting all that grease off your body when you get home?" Luanne asks. This surprises me. She strokes her ring finger on my arm quickly, delicately. "Ugh," she says. I notice a ring, but I ask her to lunch anyway. On the way she gets real interested in my fishing gear and asks me about *that*. So what winds up is she's sitting in the truck with the binoculars watching me work Cat's Creek. I tell her it's the best spot in the city. Then I make a buffoon of myself—not a rise the whole lunch hour. On the way back she looks at me like I'm crazy. "I liked the way you flicked your pole through the air," she said sarcastically.

That place is less than a mile from my work, just off Figueroa. I've really learned to fish it; I know that stream. What you do is lay your fly into the trickles that feed from the overhead culverts just beyond the Glendale Freeway Overpass. Someone has painted cat's whiskers and ears on the huge disks that cover the outlets on the canyon wall there, and the water lumbers, slow and heavy, so you can drift a Black Gnat or a Gadfly nicely. Just when it meets faster water—the city's main drainage—

a quick tap of your rod tip will get a hit every time. You'll actually see them making passes just before the notch; then, as the water turns from lead to silver, you'll get a strike. I've caught half a dozen native spawners, steely rainbows from who-knows-where, just like that. On my lunch hour! It's what you know that counts.

Fishing on my lunch hour is what keeps me sane. When my head starts to buzz with the torque wrenches or the screaming customers, I take my break and climb down the embankment behind the shop. Pure spring water ambles down from the San Bernardinos a hundred miles east, through the Flood Control District's concrete channels (along the Golden State Freeway), past the shop, and off to the Pacific Ocean twenty-five miles west. The hot spot, Cat's Creek, four miles downstream at the Los Feliz Offramp, is where I began trout fishing in L.A.

I followed some fool in a pickup one day as he left the shop. Plain as day he had his rod propped up in his slider, and I'd learned long ago to follow the locals to the holes. He uses his key to the padlock on the hurricane, opens the gate, drives down into the riverbed, gets out of his rig, and takes a quick look around. He's all flustered, with his hands on his hips and his shoulders hunched over like, "Man, what'd I come *here* for!?" And I'm just sitting in my truck watching. I've got binoculars on this clown. The guy's standing a short cast from a round of water the size of a tire, and he doesn't so much as bring on his tackle! So when he leaves, I jump the fence and get down there fast. I tie on a big gray streamer that rides smooth just under the fast, brown current. It wobbles down like juicy shad. I get a hit-like electricity, and before I know it, I've got a twelve-inch native Brown in my creel. That thing has big onyx eyes like the kind at the taxidermist. You need persistence and confidence.

Most people don't think of the L.A. River as a western "blue ribbon." It's not Hat Creek or the Yellowstone, but I've taken some near-trophy fish there. It's surprising what you can find, places you'll never see written up. The gravel pits behind Hansen Dam way upstream from here, for example—the lake dried up long ago and the fishermen disappeared. But after a rain especially, the pits there at the bottom of the San Bernardinos become pristine ponds, and nobody knows. A lot of these quarry ponds are fenced-in and looked over by rent-a-cops, but the last thing they expect is a flyfisherman in waders. The security guard at *Conrock* even unlocks the gate for me. I think he fishes himself when I'm not there. I explained to him once that you have to spray your dry flies thoroughly with silicone. You need the float because the water is so clear. And use your best fly. "Oh really," he said.

I use a Royal Wolfe there, Curt Gowdy's fly, with an ultra-light tippet to fool those wide-eyed Goldens. You have to fish at dusk, cast flies as the water turns black with the sky. In the city's violet haze, peace overwhelms until it doesn't matter if you catch any fish at all. It doesn't even matter if the purple in the sky is poisoned air. You can, from the pits, hike up the talus of gravel to the crest of the concrete-slab dam. From there you can see the course of the L.A. River severing the city with a straight, dark line through a canyon of chalk and charcoal.

Another of my favorite quiet-water spots is the evaporation pond at the Hollywood Freeway and Arleta, in the Valley. The Valley is another basin, another drainage entirely, and not without its own mesh of neglected waterways. It's where I grew up, and fishing there is a pleasant regression to days long ago, when everyone had the dignity of fly-fishermen. Luanne drove me there recently because she suspected we were discarding perfectly good engine casings there and replacing them with damaged ones—to double our business.

"You mean to say you're going to *fish* here?" she asked.

"I grew up here."

"And you're going to go fishing here, is that right?"

"Well, not now," I said, "not when there's no water. But when there's water, I mean." She looked at me like I meant to poach a hatchery! "Check it out, Luanne, Not a block in sight. So who's the crazy one, huh?"

"Nothing fishy here, I have to admit," she said with this smirk, throwing her right leg over her left so her skirt climbed up an inch or two. Her arm was up behind my headrest and she went like to whisper in my ear. "Of course we don't know what's just under the surface, do we?"

"There isn't even any water!"

"I *mean* the sand," she said. Then she kissed me on the jaw and fingered the earring on her right lobe. The thing is a dead ringer for a Mepps Spinner. "I swear to God," she said, "you're certifiable."

All the while I was remembering a rare Humpback Cutthroat I took there, big and beautiful, on a hellgrammite, with the distinctive lines like laces along the hump of its back. My hands trembled with the weight and life of that fish before I threw it back.

"It's what I do to stay sane," I said.

Actually, I've caught trout in most of our better storm drains, for example, just by dropping big, dry dragonflies through the notch in the street curb (especially if there's a running gutter). There *are* fish there. And I don't cheat with a feather jig and spinning rig either, I drift a hand-tied Silver Dragon tactfully down the curb and let it tumble into the dark basin. It can be argued that a blind hit is even more exciting than a calculated one. Like in night fishing.

It's even possible, in the middle of the night, in the suburbs, to fish neglected swimming pools: when the water is allowed to stagnate, trout will migrate up the drains! You just have to know *which* swimming pools to fish.

After a while, Luanne became convinced that I wasn't cheating her insureds, and that I wasn't crazy. Spending the night with her made it seem as though everything would work out. So I took her to my secret spot through this culvert under a metal works a few miles downstream from the shop.

It's dark and she's tripping on the corrugation in her spiked heels. Her hair is coming out of its clips. Steam is hissing overhead, and trucks are rumbling outside on the freeway.

"It's not much farther, Luanne. Be patient."

A stream of water arches over our heads as we reach the end of the tunnel and come upon a huge, lighted cavern, an enormous main room laced by countless jets of spray from the cooling system.

"There," I say and point. Four rivulets flow and settle beneath big smelters forty feet above. A burnt orange haze, like a sunrise, falls on the drifts and flows of the four little brooks. Steam floats overhead like bulbous Montana clouds. When you go fishing, you sometimes imagine things, things that are better than what your life really has to offer.

"There!"

"It's a scrap-metal casting plant!" she says. "You've been melting down good ones and putting in cracked ones." She wipes sweat from her forehead with the back of her wrist. "I don't appreciate your way of telling me this, you know."

She sits down on a wet spool of metal cable, her knees together, her ankles apart. Her hair has come loose and a fish-shaped spot of moisture grows from the center of her blouse. "I really thought we were going fishing." She sighs and shakes her head.

"But we are."

"Here?"

"Exactly, Luanne, it's my most secret trout stream."

A smile gathers on her face like ripples on a pond.

Annie La Ganga

Tandoori Chicken

ONCE, I HELPED A WOMAN move and clean out her house. She had every craft, every appliance, every style of purse, and every self-help book ever written. We threw it all out in a big pile for these moody boys to take to the dump. She said, "Do you see all this? What was I trying to do? Be something?" I told her that it didn't matter, she didn't need to figure it out. I'm not sure I believed myself. Later, at a Mexican restaurant, she told me that people are the real joy, the real adventure, the reason. She also said that once at a hypnotherapy session, in a recovery house, she realized that her dad raped her when she was two. She told me that she had a kundalini awakening one day at work and then started furiously canning vegetables. She dated a physicist. Once, she committed herself to an asylum. Out of all the useless stuff in her house, we both liked the painting she did there the best. I wonder how she is now. I am a little sad thinking of her. Maybe I should think about flowers or something. Once, I was in a work-out class and the instructor ordered us to abandon all thoughts of obligation, work related issues, and grocery lists and think about something nice. I decided to think about flowers. I love gerber daisies the best. They are bright and obvious. Daffodils and tulips are nice, too. Here in Seattle, the tulips are a big thing. There's a place off the freeway somewhere and you can see tons of them during a couple of weeks in spring. I didn't make it out to see them, despite my boyfriend of last year continually bugging me to go on little day-trip car excursions. I resisted a lot. Usually, I was tired after work at the restaurant serving breakfast to people preparing for day trips to the tulips or something equally dumb, and I just wanted to be left alone to smoke. Neither of us got what we wanted. We would strike some lame compromise that lead to a long, annoying drive through the city to get an overpriced lunch. I think that sums up our entire relationship. We didn't want any of the same things; but, we were completely willing to abandon our independence for a nice meal. We did it over and over again. On the plus side, I learned to really love Indian food. My favorite is spinach stuffed nan and vegetable pekora with that beautiful mint cilantro sauce. I also like Tandoori chicken with grilled onions. Grilled onions are so delicious. I told a friend once, knowing it was a cute joke, that I really do hope reincarnation is true because I'm positively certain I will not get to eat enough grilled onions in this lifetime. I've eaten a lot of grilled onions, I've also spent a long time calling myself a creative person, an artist. Believe me, anyone who says that of herself is saying, "I know how to make everything, except a decent living." I spent time with last year's boyfriend this weekend. I begged him to tell me what I should do with myself and all this brilliance. He suggested fancier restaurants. I guess that's where I'll go. Restaurants are like convents for nuns who drink and/or fuck. I remember a long time ago at this restaurant in Southern California, I worked and drank cocktails with creative names like "Red Silk Panties" and "The Blue Whale." The Blue Whale was awesome. It was very popular at the restaurant because it came in a pint glass with a wedge of pineapple and a big, plastic whale. As an employee, you got it without the whale; but, with extra pineapple. It was vodka, blue curaceo, pineapple juice, and seven up. I called it "Hawaiian Punch for Adult Children" or I would have if I knew what an adult child was then. I remember the day I came to work aglow with the news that my boyfriend at the time had asked me to marry him. Everyone was very happy for us and asked to see the ring. I wonder if they were truly happy for me or just saying it. Now, when I hear a girl in her very early twenties tell me that she is getting married, I smile and say, "How wonderful!" and think, "You dumb ass." Anyway, there was no ring. We boiled our brains in Jack Daniel's the night before in a seedy bar in Pasadena. We got carried away professing our undying psychotic love for each other. He popped the question. It was a moment I anticipated and hungered for since fifth grade when I wrote boys love letters sprayed with Avon perfume in a swan shaped bottle I stole from a weekend trip to my grandmother's house. The moment held slightly less importance for him because as soon as the words wheezed out of his sharp, drunk face, I think he forgot about it. He was literally shaking in fear when he arrived to pick me up from work and everyone was patting him on the back and congratulating him. We drank so many Blue Whales that night, the fantasy marriage proposal was flushed away with all my blue puking. It was okay. At the time, I was blind in love with one of the bartenders, who was from New Jersey, and was writing a screenplay about a boxer while he took classes on how to channel an entity named, Ralston. Oh, how I loved him. He was a lush. He disappeared from my life. He moved to Arizona with some rich lady. For years after, I called Arizona directory assistance to beg for a listing. I never found him. I think I would still give my big toe to see him again. Is he bartending or writing or both? What happened with the rich lady? Is Arizona nice? I've only been there once myself. I was on a reckless identity quest road trip with an equally identity-less boyfriend. We were scouting the country to find the perfect place for our band and genius to flourish. We drank a lot of beer in freezing-cold campsites. We stopped in Seguarro National Park, where I climbed this little mountain so high I was shaking. We didn't find the perfect spot or even a good bag of pot on that trip and if it wasn't for my sister's credit card, we wouldn't have made it home, where he would break up with me a month later only to enter a completely ridiculous relationship with a brain damaged girl whose good fortune I sorely resented. They stayed together for about a year. He lived off of her SSI check and was her flaky caretaker. He finally left her after a big TV-smashing fight one night when they were both without meds. He ran home to his over-protective Swedish mother who once said to me in all earnestness, "Now you take care of my little baby." He was a little baby. He didn't know how to work at a job. He loved puppy dogs, pastel colors, and fucking me up the ass. That lady was right, people are the real joy, the real adventure, the reason.

Harriet Doerr

The Extinguishing of Great Aunt Alice

GREAT AUNT ALICE broke her hip when she was eighty-two. Walking about her garden one summer night, she fell over a hose that had been left across a brick path. She lay there until morning with her cheek pressed against candy-tuft and her feet on a clump of white dianthus. Her thoughts, rising like star shells over the pain, were various. She remembered the girlhood excursion when her long poplin skirt caught in the spokes of her bicycle. She remembered when the chipped beak of her grandfather's grotto-blue parrot had clamped onto her finger until it bled. She remembered the gestation and delivery of Theodore, her son. And she earnestly hoped that when daylight came she would be found by her driver or her gardener and not by Theo.

During her three week confinement to a hospital bed, the only family visits Aunt Alice endured with grace were those of her great niece, Elizabeth, then eleven years old. Elizabeth brought strange maps she had drawn of India, France, and Peru, striped with rivers, crocheted with mountains, shaded with forests, dotted with wheat, rice, and corn, red-circled with capitals, and all bounded by shores of a thousand parentheses. She brought recent school compositions which might start, "When I give my dog, Old Moll, a bath she smells like seaweed," or, "Things I hate: roller coasters, Brussels sprouts, 'The Phantom of the Opera.' " Great Aunt Alice felt more akin to the second generation than the intervening one. Her son, niece, and nephews tended to cloud issues. Elizabeth and Great Aunt Alice shared the same crystal vision.

Through the open door of her hospital room, Great Aunt Alice sometimes heard protracted weeping. It seemed chronic rather than acute, a way of life rather than a trauma. During the fifth night of her stay she woke in the dark to the sound of steady sobbing beyond the foot of her bed. Switching on the light, she saw a woman sitting in the visitor's upholstered armchair. Long strands of uncombed white hair fell over her shoulders and she was naked. Great Aunt Alice understood very little about senility, everything about eccentricity, and was not alarmed. She rang for the nurse, then regarded her caller. The sunken red-rimmed eyes, the mouth half-open in lament, the sagging lines of the body, shaped like a wrinkled winter pear, gradually took form as a painted image.

She has struck a pose, Great Aunt Alice thought, and wished for the reincarnated presence of Picasso or Matisse.

With her new artificial hip, Great Aunt Alice regained much of her former mobility. She resumed attendance on Sunday mornings at her church. This was a modest ivy-covered stone structure in a decaying section of the city. Here it was that she had gone to Sunday school. She recalled coloring and cutting out pictures of David and Goliath, and of the baby Moses lying swaddled in his craft among the reeds.

Great Aunt Alice, an inveterate non-believer, went to church because she always had, just as she took off her glasses when men were present, and called her car the machine. At an Easter service she suffered a painful muscle spasm at the beginning of the Apostles' Creed. Feeling sharp pain, she rose at once, tall and erect as always, to tower over the lilies at the altar and the bowed heads of the congregation until she felt she could walk unassisted and without a limp.

Soon after the hip operation Great Aunt Alice became the victim of a series of small strokes. These were apt to cause temporary spells of what her doctor called disorientation. At the onset of one particularly trying lapse, when Bridget, her close friend and cook of forty years, was in Ireland for her sister's funeral and Theo was away at a college reunion, Brooke, Elizabeth's mother, had to have Great Aunt Alice admitted to a nursing home. Or, put more accurately, locked up.

The patient imagined that she was vacationing at a second-rate motel and, being naturally gregarious, soon had a dozen acquaintances among her fellow guests. One of these was an ash blonde widow, willowy to the point of emaciation, and given to apologetic coughs. It was to her, one tedious afternoon, that Great Aunt Alice said on impulse, "Let's go out to tea." Shortly after that the two ladies exited through the empty kitchen, thus eluding their wardens.

Once on their own, they walked a few blocks until they reached the freshly sprinkled lawns and flowerbeds of a residential neighborhood. In the driveway ahead of them a woman was backing her compact station wagon from the garage of a white-washed bungalow.

"There's a taxi," exclaimed Aunt Alice, hurrying on and signaling the driver with an urgent wave. She and her friend approached the car, now idling at the curb, opened the door to the back seat, and got in.

"To the Maryland Hotel, please," said Great Aunt Alice. She had conjured out of a rainbow kaleidoscope of the fragmented past the site of her first dancing class and her first lemonade served on a palm-shaded terrace by a waiter wearing gloves. The Maryland Hotel and its gilded chairs lining the paneled walls of the ballroom, its gold and crystal chandeliers, its polished floors, and Great Aunt Alice herself in tucked dimity and high white buttoned shoes, were now of one flesh with thirty stories of concrete and black glass. That is, if Great Aunt Alice, and her niece Brooke, Elizabeth's mother, and inevitably Elizabeth, were correct in their notion that nothing was ever lost. That the theaters, where they once had played, could produce on demand the voices of Maude Adams, Ethel Barrymore and Harry Lauder, the boards of the great stages the faint tapping above the orchestra of Anna Pavlova dancing backward *aux pointes*. That the tree still held all the birds that ever sang there.

The driver of the station wagon wore thick, brown-rimmed glasses and a lime green pantsuit. She had planted both feet on the ground when she was one and a half, and an aura of common sense hung about her like the aroma of wholesome food. Today she had realized at once that she must pilot the rudderless into safe waters, and set off with purpose and without surprise.

On arrival at the police station, she took the desk sergeant aside and hazarded a guess that her passengers were from one of several nearby institutions for the failing aged. The sergeant picked up the telephone.

Meanwhile Great Aunt Alice and her friend had been served coffee by a pair of young policemen, and the four sat together, two chairs having been drawn up to face the bench next to the wall. Great Aunt Alice, assuming they were midshipmen, immediately began an account of the June prom at Annapolis in 1901. After their second cup of coffee and some packaged Nabiscos from a vending machine, the sergeant interrupted to report that a car was waiting to take them home, and the ladies entered a black-and-white automobile whose revolving red lights and siren were temporarily stilled.

The nursing home, when finally hunted down by the police sergeant, had called Theo's apartment and found him there, returned prematurely from his alma mater. He had made a thorough search of the anniversary classes and encountered only eight alumni of his year, all so altered by time and varying levels of despair that none recognized the others.

Theo, reached in time, was standing at the yellow stucco entrance of the nursing home to meet his mother when the police car drew up and discharged its two passengers. He was still wearing his straw reunion hat, a boater whose ribbon band bore in golden numerals the year of his graduation.

"Theo, dear," his mother said. "We've had a lark. So many young men, and such good manners. They wined and dined us." Then, aside, "I don't have my purse. Would you give the driver something?"

In a later lucid period, Great Aunt Alice, perhaps more perceptive than the family would acknowledge, filled out a Living Will, the instrument by which she expected to be discharged into eternity with a minimum of fuss, discomfort (as agony is often called), and the inept ministrations of Dr. Hilford, the family physician. The esteem in which he was originally held had been undermined long since by familiarity.

"Doctors should be strangers," Great Aunt Alice always said. "The only common meeting ground should be the examining table."

From the Living Will she deleted clergyman, lawyer, and doctor as witnesses and wrote in driver, gardener, and hairdresser. Once this was executed, she sent a copy to Theo, who wished neither to antagonize nor encourage her.

"Gee whiz, Mother," is all that he was known to have said. Theo had married late and been left a widower early. He remained alone, having sought in vain for a mate as considerate and self-effacing as Amy. For his first wife, fifteen years younger than he, had skidded in a dense fog off a coast road and died on the rocks below. Even now, thirty years later, he often said to himself, She might have chosen a different route.

Great Aunt Alice's driver and gardener were a father and son named Joe. Big Joe, small and wiry, took care of the garden, and Little Joe, tall and muscular, drove Great Aunt Alice about in her machine. When the car was not needed, Little Joe helped his father with the flower beds and rye grass lawn, occasionally trying out inventions of his own. One of these was his rooting out of two eucalyptus stumps by means of a personally conceived mixture of explosives. The force of the ensuing blast flattened one wall of the toolshed, lifted its roof and splintered the old water tank above it.

Big Joe and Little Joe were originally Portuguese, from the Azores, and without demurral or curiosity signed the document at her request.

The hairdresser was Oliver, born in Cheapside, London. Great Aunt Alice associated him, because of his address, his name, and his accent, with Shakespeare, Dickens, and a nurse she once had who called her Halice.

She had patronized his shop for years. When she suffered her penultimate stroke and could hear and see but not speak, Little Joe delivered her weekly, by car and wheelchair, to Oliver's mirrored booth. Here he brewed and shared a heady concoction of frivolity, fantasy, and unswerving friendship. Great Aunt Alice had concluded that in time of need Oliver would be of more use to her than oxygen.

Later on, this proved to be the case. When Great Aunt Alice was at last brought low, not to rise again. Oliver went to the room where she lay, unconnected to any life-prolonging apparatus. Three pillows were behind her and her eyes were closed. Oliver opened his black case, took out a brush and comb, and arranged her hair. After that, he stepped back to survey her.

"High style's your style," he said loudly, in the event that she could hear. And yes, he detected the remote beginning of a smile. Or believed he did.

Two weeks after Great Aunt Alice died, Theo found a note in her bed table drawer. It must have been written on various occasions, months ago. The separate lines, penned and pencilled, slanted independently across the page. For a moment, he thought it was a verse, unpunctuated.

Theo, it was headed.
Your father's Mesopotamian journal might
Perhaps the piano tuner should
The Helen Traubel roses need
I had hoped

Alan Cheuse

Little America

IN THOSE DAYS, that was how we did it, never a trip anywhere that wasn't business of one kind or another. My then-wife and I and our two children had spent the winter in California, where she had been teaching, and now we were heading home, or I was, since she and the girls had flown on ahead while I began driving our station wagon east. I had a brief stay-over scheduled at a fabled truck stop and motel in the Red Desert on the high plains of the Continental Divide. There I would spend a day or two so that I could write a piece about it for a travel magazine and thus pay the air fare, highway tolls and for my gasoline.

Little America—that was the name of the truck stop—was situated on the edge of a dry (in summer) windy (always) plateau and accommodated weary travelers passing between east and west, to and from Cheyenne, Laramie, Rock Springs, Salt Lake City, San Francisco, Grand Island, Omaha, Des Moines, Chicago, New York, all those names, destinations here and there. It didn't take more than a few hours to speak with several of the managers of the place, to suffer a tour of the kitchen and the gift shop—I would soon know what it was like to spend the night in one of the tidy little rooms smelling of disinfectant and the dull perfume of synthetic drapes—and then to take photographs—I took my own photographs back then—of the sign above the entrance. LITTLE AMERICA. Bold by day, glowing neon at night. We Americans are always so big on signs.

I visited some of the ranch-houses behind the motel complex where the year-round staff lived in a little enclave all their own, though a lot of the waitresses and sales clerks stayed only for the summer (and it was just this side of Labor Day that I was making my journey east for another year of family and marriage). Many of these summer employees were smiling, pink-cheeked Mormon blondes from a nearby church college in Idaho. I asked the restaurant manager if I could visit one of the houses where they lived, and I spent about twenty minutes conversing with the girls, some of whom seemed almost young enough to be one of my own daughters (though one of them emerged from a bedroom, her hair in curlers, a Coke can in her hand and a special look in her eye, suggesting that the Eden of the Mormons, perhaps the last trace of Eden in America, had already begun to erode).

Late afternoon, and I wandered out to the truck-stop garage, as big as an airline hanger, where teamsters with major problems could find a twenty-four-hour diesel mechanic on duty, summer, fall, winter, spring. Summer meant dozens of cars overheating every day because of the combination of the temperature and the altitude. In winter, whipping blizzards closed the interstate highway, and eighteen-wheelers gathered here for days, like giant buffalo, waiting out the storm. In the garage at twilight, a young grease-monkey who a hundred years ago might have been a cowhand told me about the saloon in the little mining town just seven miles northwest of the truck stop, the closest place on the plateau where you could get a drink.

I drove out there, crossing a meandering river whose name I now forget, past the signs for the borax mines hidden in the desert to the north, and found a hamlet of about twenty stucco houses and another twenty trailers, and a crumbling old Pony Express station, windowless, surrounded by barbed wire, awaiting a promised restoration. In a great splash of russet and vermillion, the sun slid below the western rim of the country, the kind of display I called familiar after a season by the Pacific. No street lamps came on, though here and there lights blinked in some of the trailers. I was the only person on the road. Across from the Pony Express station someone had taken down the cross from atop the former place of worship and put up a blue-white neon sign which beckoned: THE CHURCH.

I still wasn't sure why I had come here. Certainly the fleeting time I had spent with those silken-faced Mormon waitresses had stirred me up a bit, making the lonely week ahead seem ever more acute. Motels, I told myself I might say in my story, make a solitary traveler so much more aware of his solitude. The families, the couples, those other isolatoes you could spot a mile away, it was hard to say which was worse than the others when it came to contemplating—and I sometimes thought of it—what it was they did when they closed the doors to their rented rooms. So I would drink. That's what we did in those days to ward off the blues, though the feeling of rumpled clothing, aching bones, and sullied mind could make it seem like a losing proposition in the morning.

But that night I didn't care as I pushed open the door to the former church turned saloon. *Check your knives and guns at the door*, said a dusty sign above the entrance, the letters so faint that it didn't appear to speak at all to the present. Two lean, toothless, old men, borax miners I learned later, sat slouched at the bar that ran along the right wall of the old nave. The red-haired woman serving the drinks didn't look twice at me in my beard (still solid-black) and silver-rimmed spectacles. She poured me the drink I asked for (it was bourbon at that time, nothing but bourbon) each time I asked. Another ancient miner came in through the door, found an empty stool and settled in at the bar. Only the sound of the redhead—she had a hard face and her hair was black at the roots—rinsing glasses and the forced breathing of the old man broke the silence. After a while I walked outside, staring off into the wind and dark beyond the border of the old church's neon glow. Seven miles back to Little America. A year to the end of my marriage.

I knew the way.

Maggie Dawson

Treatise on a Closet

MY SISTER RECENTLY left her husband of sixteen years and their two children to live with a "friend." Her friend is named Caroline. Whenever my family mentions the friend, they get that edge in their voice. The edge implying that the uncomfortable thing in question will be left undiscussed. Everyone disapproves of my sister's new lifestyle, everyone who knows that is. The situation is being kept rather quiet.

I don't think I am supposed to know there is even an issue. I know but I'm not telling. What gave it away for me, I think, was when my stepfather (a Southern gentleman of few words and immeasurable tact) said, "You're almost as pathetic as your bitch sister, breaking up her family 'cause she decided she'd rather be licking pussy."

Now I'm not one to judge any one else, so all I could think of to say was, "I don't see why it's such a big fucking deal? You'd rather be licking pussy, too." I *didn't* say it, though. I just blankly looked at him and didn't say anything. I do a lot of thinking and not saying.

Skeleton

My mother's husband, Rick, is pretty hostile toward homosexuals. I remember one day last June the three of us were eating dinner out on the patio. Rick was telling about some guy at his work who apparently had been making passes at him.

The majority of words leaving Rick's mouth sounded like, "Faggot . . . faggot. AIDS faggot . . . fucking faggot, AIDS faggot. . . ." When I had heard enough, I quietly stated, "Not everyone with AIDS is gay."

He came back with, "Yeah, well most of the faggots have It. 98.3% of all the people in the United States with AIDS are faggots."

"I know you're not stupid, Rick, and I don't know where you got your statistics, but when you talk like that you sound really ignorant." I could see his mind's eye aiming a Gloch 45 at the imaginary bull's eye taking form between my brows.

"I am not ignorant, you smartass little girl. I've got an IQ higher than you can prob'ly count, so don't you go telling me I'm ignorant. . . !"

"I didn't say you *were*. I said you *sound* like an ignorant asshole." As Rick's hands reached across the table for my throat my mother jumped and grabbed at his shirt. I took my plate and walked into the house. From my room I could hear them arguing.

Mother saying he could have chosen a less offensive vocabulary, and Rick screaming, "don't you reprimand me!" Later, Mother came into my room to tell me that I needed to make an apology.

"Why did he bring it up? Why does he have to be such a dick about it?"

"I'm not making excuses for him, but Rick went through a lot of bad stuff, growing up in Louisiana."

"Oh, what! Did he get fucked up the ass when he was a little kid!?" I yelled this so that Rick, who was listening in anyway, would have the benefit of hearing it clearly.

She just said, "That's not your business."

Mother

Lately I've had married, middle-aged men falling in love with me. At least they think they love me. I tend to think I am the more the object of their proverbial midlife crises. For one thing they always see me smiling and at my best, and I just listen to whatever they have to say. And they don't wake up next to me every morning. I had one man tell me I remind him of his mother. I had to laugh. I told him I seem to have that effect on people.

At any party, I am designated the designated driver. I am everyone's mother. I have repeatedly been heard saying: *You don't feel good honey? Here, drink this water and let me tuck you into bed. No, you can't drive after that bottle of Jack. Give me your keys and I'll take you home . . . You'll pick up your car tomorrow.* Or my personal favorite: *Don't you want to come inside? I really don't think you want to spend the night in that bush/street/shed.*

I really don't mind. Someone has to do it. I feel better knowing that it's my job and everyone is taken care of. My children tell me they think I'll make a good mommy.

I've decided I love children. I didn't use to. I used to think they were dirty and loud and annoying. The world is overpopulated, so everyone should stop having so many damn babies. Until I realized that for this reason the smart people stopped having babies a long time ago. The only people left with kids are the stupid irresponsible people, teaching their kids to be stupid and irresponsible. At that point I decided that it was my duty to have children. It's my responsibility to give them a loving environment, to impact the human race and assist in the generation of a superior future.

Now I love children. I want at least a dozen. Well, no, maybe two. Yes, two maximum. I want to take my children and live in a commune in the Sequoias or Eastern Colorado. I want them to grow up in an environment where they learn to be free. To be whoever they are, do what ever they want to do. As long as they don't hurt anyone.

Stare

During high school a lot of my friends were experimenting. Yes drugs, too, but I was referring more to sex. I was at a party once where everyone was playing bi-sexual spin the bottle. It was a pretty good bet if I had a thing for one of my male friends, he would turn up gay. I can count at least four instances where it happened like that. There was a joke a friend and I shared, that when someone came out of the closet we would send them a card that said, "Welcome to the Family." It was inside humor.

That was about the same time that I cut off all my hair and started to look like Peter Pan . . . or Tinkerbell . . . something androgynous and not quite human. My solitary ambition in high school was to make people look. I did a damn good job of it. Sometimes a group of football players would get up the nerve to ask me if I was a lesbian. It didn't bother me. I'd usually just laugh. The football players weren't exactly my crowd.

Big Bad Voodoo Daddy

Before my mother married him, when Rick first moved in with us, I made him a cake. It was two layers with yellow frosting and it said, "Welcome Home, Voodoo Daddy!" He got all emotional and teary eyed at my gesture, but pretended he had eaten too much Tobassco sauce. That was in February. By July, he had kicked me out of the house.

Why you no go to church?

I talked to my mother last week. They've lived in Louisiana for two and a half months now. She says she's been praying for my soul. I told her not to bother, that my soul is taken care of. I told her I'd rather she pray for my checking account. Mother says she just wants to know that I love Jesus and I love God. It's suddenly this big God kick. I'm glad she's suddenly found her Answer. I'm glad she's happy, but along with her new fixation comes a sense that she is justified in being judgmental. That is all fine and good, until she tells me that she is praying for my soul. Until I hear that edge in her voice when she mentions my sister's new "friend."

Welcome to the Family

I had a girlfriend. She was beautiful.

I had a boyfriend. He was beautiful.

He didn't work out. She didn't work out.

I'm glad they happened. At least now I know that either way I'm not missing out on anything.

After seeing the family's reaction to my sister, I am also glad I didn't tell anyone.

I'd like to somehow tell my sister about it. Maybe send her a card that says, "Welcome to the Family." She probably wouldn't understand what family I was referring to. The matter is being kept rather quiet. I don't think I am even supposed to know. No one is saying anything, including me.

I do a lot of not saying.

Mark Donnelly

Old Blue

YOU REMEMBER, Blue. I was on my third wife and working for PanAm and living in Florida. I found myself one midnight walking barefoot down the white line of the main drag in Miami zonked out of my mind. I ended up in the drunk tank. Funny because that was the first time I ever got picked up by the cops for drinking. All those years when I was chugging down six-packs and driving you on the freeway back to L.A., I never got stopped. But spending the night in that fucking sleaze-hole jail sobered me up quick. I had no idea how I got on that strip barefoot. I was miles from the house. Peggy came and bailed me out the next morning. But she was no fucking help. She was as big a boozer as me. And she did pills, too. I knew that morning driving back home in her car that I had to quit. Things got real clear as I sat in the convertible afraid of getting the seat dirty because my clothes were so fucked up and funky. Funny how sanctified you get at 6 AM. I told Peggy I was quitting and she just laughed. I said I was going into rehab and I wanted her to go in, too. She laughed some more and then I just got real silent the rest of the ride home.

When we pulled into the driveway, I saw you parked there, safe and sound—"Old Blue." I was glad I hadn't driven you the night before. I would've felt terrible if I'd hurt you. When I opened the door of Peggy's car and my feet hit the driveway, I was wobbly. I thought, Maybe I can't go through with this. I could feel her laughing right through my shirt. But I put one foot in front of the other and it was a start. I told Peggy again I was going into rehab, but she just laughed some more. Then she said to me, "Who are you bullshittin' with that line? You'll be guzzling a six-pack when I get home. Only save some for me, lover. I'll call your boss when I get to work. I'll tell him you were up all night with an upset stomach."

She laughed again and kinda whirled her hair around. I'm glad I couldn't see her eyes when she put on her sunglasses and backed out of the driveway. I liked the anonymous look it gave her. Made me feel more distant, separated. Made it easier for me to leave. And that's what I did. I went upstairs and packed a couple of suitcases of stuff and left. I lost the house in the divorce, but I would've lost a whole lot more if I'd stayed. I might as well have thrown myself in the surf if I'd stayed, because I was going under with Peggy. I was drowning and going under for the last time. I didn't lose you though, Blue. When we pulled out of that driveway I didn't look back because that was the fire . . . I was getting out of a burning house. I remember waving to the neighborhood paper boy, Jimmy. I was more sad to leave him than Peggy. Jimmy was a good kid.

I spent ten weeks in that Miami rehab clinic. You were out in that parking lot the whole time. I wasn't allowed to drive you, just turn over the engine once a week. But I could sit in you and that was a comfort, always a comfort —you could take me places even when we were dead stop in the parking spot. I was glad I could at least look out at you from my room at night. Draw back the curtains and see you in the moonlight. Ready to roll if I needed you. But I stayed there—toughed it out the whole time. I still smoked a lot then—couldn't kick the booze and cigarettes at the same time. Used to fill up your ashtray when I'd sit in that parking lot with the door open and turn on your radio—late night Miami talk radio. I'd drink a lot of coffee in rehab, too, sitting in the day room watching *Perry Mason* and *Fugitive* reruns. *The Fugitive*. The whole idea of being on the run, being alone in the world. No car even.

I liked driving into the sunset with you. I liked that look as the clouds took on black shapes but were still visible in the blue-black sky. Heading into the west, fading, fading sun. Remember that drive cross-country when I first got out of rehab? Texas was really hot and it was only May. That state goes on forever. I'm glad I was alone on that trip, just me and you, Blue. I needed to test myself —to see if I could make it across without intentionally crashing. It was because of you. You would never deserve ending up in some ditch on fire. I fucked around enough drinking—like when I flipped that Camaro on 101 north of Santa Barbara. Never flipped you though. Maybe you were my good luck charm. Maybe that's how I got through all the shit.

I used to like driving up on Mulholland Drive at sunset. Remember? It made living in L.A. seem all right from up there. And at night the lights below were even magical. Like a fantasy land—and Disneyland was just stretches down the way, past the airport. You liked climbing those hills, taking those curves. I remember going up there one Christmas Eve with you. And then New Year's Eve of '87. Or was it '88? Driving up from L.A. to my cousin's party in Modesto. The long drive didn't bother me. I liked the solitude. Started out mid-afternoon and then it was dark. I liked the darkness closing in. I felt solid driving you, felt good behind the wheel. Always did—that was one constant in this fucked up world. Almost skipped the party. Got to Modesto around eight and went to a diner. Watched the clock go by, marching time. I never was too nuts about New Year's Eve. Used to be great in the old days when I was drinking—another big excuse day. But no more. Like time eroding, passing time, fucking time, every day, every minute, sand, sand in my brain, on my brain. Like those ancient timepieces shifting. Yeah, I'm shifting all right, right out of time. Stopped drinking, but I can't stop this pain.

Sometimes it's not one day at a time, it's one hour at a time or even a minute at a time. The counselor in rehab told me, "You just have to live in that one moment, live in the present. Work it on the smallest scale, whatever you have to do."

I tried, Blue, I really tried. That job at the treatment center—I liked the kids. But my boss. You know how much trouble I had with him. It's the loneliness, Blue. Like I'm on patrol, like I'm a pointman for loneliness. Other people deal with it. Being alone used to be okay for me. I even wanted it, just getting away on the road with you anytime I wanted. You and me riding away, me getting the fuck out of bad marriages. Me sleeping off bad drunks in your back seat.

Man, you seen me in bad shape. Can't go back to the drinking, Blue, just can't do it. No matter what. You understand. Mom will understand, I hope. Maybe, maybe. I don't know what to do. What's the answer, Blue? Is it the river underneath this bridge? Pretty far down there, Blue. Cold, too, I bet. But blue like you. A little darker in color, maybe, like that blue-black Scripto ink I had for my fountain pen in grammar school and I used to get that stain on my finger, right where I held the pen, and I'd pretend it was a wound, a battle scar. Is that what we all get, Blue? Up here in this beautiful state of Washington? Up here in God's country? GOD'S COUNTRY! Where are you? Where are you? Fuckin' Prozac!

Working at the treatment center was good in some ways, Blue, counseling kids from really fucked up families. Their mom or dad being boozers and the kids starting to get juiced early, too. Like when I was fifteen and starting out. Reminds me of the basketball games that I'd go to in high school and I'd get drunk outside in the parking lot with my older friends and then go in to the game. That was all before I got you. We'd get thrown out by the ref because we were yelling so much at the other team. Then we'd go get some more beers—the older guys would buy another couple of six packs with their phony proof. And being dumped on my lawn at one or two and puking my guts out. One time I ended up there really late on that lawn. And the grass was wet, and I fell asleep shivering cold. Too embarrassed to wake up my folks for fear I'd knock something over when I came in, my legs so shaky. And my dad coming out in the yard in the early morning and almost carrying me into the house like a little kid again. Like when I was a kid and we'd get home late from my Grandma's and he'd carry me into the house and me half-asleep. He'd lower me down on my bed and he'd always say, "You're getting so heavy you're like a big sack of potatoes." And he'd smile and wipe my brow to get the hair out of my face and give me a "Goodnight, pal" and turn out my light. I miss him. Would've been nice to go fishing up here with Dad, Blue. Like we used to when I was growing up. My dad liked you, Blue. Thought you were a good old car. It was at his friend's used car lot, Mr. Gunderson's in Fresno. That's where I picked you up in 1972.

I don't know why it's tougher up here than it was in L.A., Blue. December doesn't help. Supposed to snow over the weekend, for Christmas. I remember when Dad gave me that fleece-lined cover for the driver's seat, for you. That was a nice Christmas. Mom liked it when I'd take her last-minute shopping Christmas Eve day when I'd be home from college. Remember, I'd put that old green army blanket down and I'd lay the Christmas tree on you, all wrapped up in rope and hanging out the rear? With that blanket down I wouldn't get the pine needles on you.

This will be okay. This place is okay. Remember we saw it in the daytime when we first got up here last spring? It was nice then in the sunshine with the grass over there and those pine trees. Be nice if someone would put Christmas lights on those pine trees. Kind of give it a cozy holiday feel. I always liked the colored lights at Christmas. Liked to drive through town as a kid with Dad and look at the different houses and see which had the prettiest lights, which had the most, which looked the dumbest. Some lights on that tall pine would be really something. Probably need a cherry picker to get up to the top branches. You know what I liked best about Christmas though? Picked up on this when I was a kid. I must have been around thirteen or so. I used to like to sit late at night in the living room those days before Christmas and the whole week after, with all the lights off in the house except the lights on the tree. Made the colors shine deeper, brighter. Kind of like sitting in church alone in the dark with just some candles. That's the kind of church service I liked, too, silent and dark. Be nice to get you something new for Christmas, Blue. Maybe the next person who gets . . . Be nice to see Mom, too. She made the best cookies for Christmas, with those green and red sprinkles—cookies in the shape of Christmas trees with white frosting to look like snow. Bet those trees look great with snow on the branches. Like a calendar. You think this bridge ever appeared in any magazine photographs? Maybe *National Geographic*. A shot of the river with this bridge standing in the background.

Water's not running too fast right now, Blue. You can sure hear that current though, constant. Wonder where this empties into the ocean. Should look at a map. Got one here in your glove compartment. There it is, Blue. Probably about 50 miles out to the ocean from here.

Lot of damn good miles we covered, Blue. Plenty of trips. It just didn't work out the way I planned. Not with you, I don't mean with you, Blue. I mean the jobs, the wives, the money. I thought getting that masters in counseling, then coming up here and getting the job . . . It just didn't work out like I thought—brought up too many bad memories, Blue. But not about you. It was always okay with you, Blue. It'll be okay now, Blue. I know it. We're both gonna be okay. Bye, Blue.

Robert
Reid

The Rock Garden

FARGO WATCHED THEM come through the gates of the walled city. The large black motor wagon that his grandfather had called a hearse led a long parade of black motor cars. They would take the box covered with flowers to what he called the rock garden, bury it and cry, as his small sister cried when she was hungry. They wore black and wept incessantly. He wondered if they were hungry.

The guards that would kill children who came too close to the parade must not have been hungry. They did not cry. Last year, he had seen a small boy, attracted by the flowers, break through the bushes and run toward the large motor wagon. He turned red, almost immediately, from the machines that the guards carried. That angered Fargo. He felt that mothers should watch their children.

Fargo's father, angered by Fargo's disgust with the mother, called him a fool and told him to mind his own business. Saying it was a good lesson for all of them. Something about "curiosity killed the cat." These phrases often tossed out by Fargo's father came from the Holy works written, apparently as messages from God. Nobody could remember anyone they knew having said them.

Every month, as a group they all gathered in a clearing not far from the rock garden and sacrificed a dog or a cat, something valuable only to the children, on a large limestone slab to President. A priest spoke of how President provided the herbs in the forest and the bits of food in the large metal containers outside the walled city, and how kind it was for President to do this. Then the choir would sing, "What a friend we have in President. All our sins and griefs to bear." And chant bits of phrases like "we the people, to preserve freedom, what's good for business, our inalienable rights, we go now to a better place, boots are made for walking and if you don't like it here."

After this ceremony, a Holy man would speak of his call to express thanks to President who made bits of food rain into the large containers from above and deplore selfish people who allowed children to cry from hunger, saying that the youth who cried today did not understand the sufferings and death of President to give them bits of food and freedom. He would speak of how it rained fire and President ran into the rain, sacrificing himself for us to go to prepare the place in the sky called corporation where the bits of food were much larger and made you sick less often.

He even spoke of happiness from drinking a liquid in corporation and orgies like those before fire rained from heaven. Saying in those orgies in corporation everybody loved everybody else and drank the liquid all day long. At times he became very emotional and Fargo knew that if he would subdue his earthly anger, he too would one day go to corporation.

In the end, the people would break into song, singing, "How beautiful corporation must be. Sweet home of the loving and filled."

Once a month Fargo's elders sacrificed a small male child rather than the pets of the children. This pleased President, who understood that they gave their all, subduing their emotions and living as he would want them to live.

Fargo asked his father why they never sacrificed any adults and his father told him to shut up unless he wanted to be sacrificed. That was the way they'd always done it and that was the way President wanted it.

Fargo seldom asked questions. He watched and listened. He watched the walls behind the metal cans and when the gates opened he tried to see behind them. Once his father caught him watching from the edge of the forest and beat him severely. Fargo understood this. Children seen by the uniformed men on the walls were killed on sight. Fargo thought that President must love the uniformed men. They never cried from hunger. Fargo always hid when they forged into the forest. They would beat and drag the larger, less malformed of the forest people behind the gates. More than once while rummaging for bits of food in the metal cans, Fargo had found pieces of girls and boys that he had known among the bits of food. The city people seemed particularly fond of cutting the sex organs of the forest people and "disemboweling" them.

Fargo himself was better formed than most. His belly was not distended and he limped only slightly. President had been good to him in this way and Fargo learned that when President was good to a forest person, he was likely to be butchered. The Holy man said that the butchered were taken up past the skies to live in corporation with the beloved President, but Fargo doubted. He doubted many things, so he watched the walls more than anyone he knew and he had escaped capture, although his father beat him regularly. Fargo believed that the beatings were better than the dripping groins and holes that he found in the bellies of some of the other children so he continued to watch from the edge of the forest and only took bits of food from the metal cans in the darkest hours of the night. He never ventured out with the groups to feed from the cans. For this his father beat him, saying, "He who does not trust President to protect him is damned. All things are ordained by President. His will be done."

Fargo hated his father and remained in the tent because he felt much sadness for his mother. He knew that this was not natural. He often cried when he thought of the time that she would grow sick and die as all forest people did. At times he believed that he hated President and worried that this would bring some catastrophe on his mother. If one cared for anyone President was likely to make that person die.

Fargo tried very hard not to care and was afraid that President, who read all thoughts, knew that he, Fargo, hated President.

Fargo knew that his mother was less malformed than other forest women and feared for her safety when the uniformed men, who were favored by President, came into the forest to collect people. He would run quickly when he saw the guards leave the walled city and watch her dig collard greens or roots from a hidden position. He watched her blonde hair flowing across her dark face and was aware that her firm tan body, flat belly and voluptuous hips sloping into unusually well formed thighs and long legs made her attractive to all men, especially his hideous father and the forest men. He had seen their loin sacks bulge as they watched her work and he hated them. He knew this care for his mother was no more natural than his hate for President, so he protected her quietly from his hidden position. He feared President knowing and reading his mind, but he continued to care. The horrors he'd seen in the metal cans frightened him more than President.

Today as he watched from the underbrush at the edge of the forest, he saw the gates open for another parade to the stone garden. He was now seventeen and could tell the difference in the costumes worn by those who rode or marched in the parade to the stone garden and whether it was a man or a woman in the box. A man wearing a guard's uniform decorated with ropes and bits of metal wailed horribly over the flower covered box at the grave and had to be pulled away when he lurched forward, jerked the box open and violently pulled a woman dressed in purple and white cloth from the box. He screamed and fought when they held him and took her from his arms, then fell on his knees in fresh mud heaving torturous sounds and begging his captors to let him take her home.

That night, in the darkest part of the night, as rain soaked the muddy grave, Fargo took a tool and violated the most stringent of President's taboos. He feared, but he did not fear for himself. He had discerned by watching the parades that the costumes of the city people were what made them valuable even to each other. He cautiously, without soiling them in spite of the mud, took the woman's clothes from her body. He discovered, to his surprise, even the silk garments beneath and, protecting the clothes from the rain with his body, stashed them carefully in a well hidden earthen pot before returning to push the mud back over the nude body lying in the ivory box.

John
Rybicki

Inside the Dog

RED THORTON PUSHED through the barber shop door like a man capable of moving through physical matter. The white ball light on the ceiling started knocking all over on its chain, bleeding shadows out of everything: the lather cups, the dancing girls with their scissor legs, the ink blot spot stretching in and out of itself below the barber's chair. Red Thorton wanted a body hollowed out like this room, a huge hole for a neck where the street began. Red Thorton wanted the barber's hands in his hair but had to wait.

There were movements to make—the hanging of the coat, the newspaper shake. He sat down beside a man who had snow boiling down on his cowboy boots, his eyes slipping over at Red and pricking. Soon there were two sets of newspapers snapping open, two sets of eyes floating above the wooden bench, gazing around and below and through that newsprint. There was hair flying all over the room, enough to pack maybe halfway around a hot heart. The hair wooled against the bottles of lotion, wooled against the lime green cabinets until the room looked time-licked, time-rubbed.

The barber thumbed off his razor and the room jerked like some animal muscle twitching. He pressed his lips down close to the man's throat and blew a white-gold filament out into the room. The hair swarmed around the bare bulb, catching fire. Then the barber filled his hands with lotion and started smacking the man left then right on each cheek. The two men on the bench were touching their hair and letting go of it, folding the papers flat in their laps.

When the man rocked out of the barber's chair, the room bucked again, violently, and the white ball light started crashing all over on its chain. The barber was flying in and out of himself in wild shadow shapes. Red stood up on the bench and caught the bare bulb in his mouth, steadied it, let it slip down the back of his throat like a peach. To Red, that room was like walking inside a dog that had been in a cold rain too long.

Ten minutes into his haircut, the second man started clicking his cowboy boot heels together and purring. Red Thorton's veins were screaming all over his body, but when the barber spoke, Red's veins possumed back down into his flesh. "I've been shot at before," the barber says, pressing his lips down close to the man's throat. "Hit once," he says, cocking his eyes up at Red Thorton, and blowing a red-wick fire off into the air. Christ, his turn! Christ!

Tobias Wolff

Nightingale

DR. BOOTH TOOK SEVERAL wrong turns during the drive upstate. It vexed him to get lost like this in front of his son, especially since the fault lay with the lousy map the Academy had sent him, but Owen was in one of his trances and didn't seem to notice. His eyes were fixed on the far distance and his lips formed whispery sounds in a cadence that suggested poetry or music. Dr. Booth knew better than to try and make sense of it, but he couldn't stop himself. He thought he recognized one word—"nightingale"—and that word awoke a memory of three children, himself and his older sisters, sitting in a garden at dusk while somewhere above them a bird sang. It was, he knew, a trick memory, a mirage; there had been no such garden and no such evening. But the thought of his sisters, one drowned in a boating accident courtesy of her dimwit husband, the other far away and silent for years, made him even gloomier than he already was.

Owen did not want to go to the Academy. He had made this plain when the idea first came up, but as Dr. Booth and his wife continued to discuss it, doubtfully to begin with, then slowly surrendering to its tidal pull, the boy had less and less to say. He receded further into the very remoteness Dr. Booth had been trying to lure him out of, and now, having failed, proposed to force him out of with the help of the school.

Until another doctor mentioned it—he had a patient who'd praised its method of handling difficult boys—Dr. Booth had never heard of Fort Steele Academy. But a few days after the name came up, and without his having requested it, a brochure arrived. The cover showed a pair of uniformed boys standing guard on either side of a gate. It was snowing, and they appeared to have been there for some time; a good two inches had gathered on their epaulets and caps. The last page of the brochure carried a statement by the Commandant, Colonel Karl: "It is no kindness to the young to pretend that life is not a struggle, and that the meek shall inherit anything but a boot on the neck. The world belongs to men of unbending will, and the sooner that lesson is learned, the better. We at Fort Steele are dedicated to teaching it by every means at our disposal."

Dr. Booth could well understand why Owen didn't want to go to the Academy. He was comfortable at home. He had his foolish dog, his lazy friends, the big house with all its sunny corners for reading, or for staring at nothing and making funny noises, or whatever he did all day. When Dr. Booth went into the kitchen, there was Owen. In the living room, Owen again. The front yard, Owen; the back yard, the basement, the hammock—Owen! As a boy, Dr. Booth had delivered a hundred and eighty newspapers before school and hustled subscriptions at night. He played football. He ran for president of his class. Those memories of his own youth had figured heavily in the decision to send Owen away, but now, reviewing the list yet again, he thought he must be leaving something out, something conclusive. There was more; surely there was more.

"It won't be so bad," he said.

Owen was silent.

"Give it a chance, son. You might even like it." When Owen still didn't answer, Dr. Booth said—almost cried out—"It's for your own good."

"I know," Owen said.

"You do?"

"Yes."

"How do you know?"

"Because it's what you want."

This was the very answer he would have hoped for, and Dr. Booth knew that he should be satisfied with it, but he wasn't. It troubled him. Just then the road came to a fork not indicated on his map and he had to do some guesswork. He decided to take the right branch, then at the last moment swerved onto the left, which led through a dense stand of maples that hung darkly over the road and opened up to reveal, across from a field golden with hay, the gates of Fort Steele Academy. Dr. Booth slowed down. He wasn't ready, he wanted a moment to probe the unease he felt, but when his car came into view the two cadets on either side of the gate snapped to attention and held their salutes until he had driven between them into the grounds of the school. Owen braced his hands against the dashboard; Dr. Booth heard him take a deep breath. They bumped over the cobbled lane toward a courtyard bordered on three sides by gray stone buildings. Two flags waved from the pole in the yard: Old Glory on top, the school crest below—sabers crossed above a castle. A line of cadets waited in the circular drive at the end of the lane, legs slightly apart, arms behind their backs. Like the guards at the gate, they wore black uniforms with white belts. Their eyes were shadowed by the gleaming bills of their caps.

"Son," Dr. Booth said, "what did you mean, it's what I want?"

Owen stared at him without comprehension, then looked back at the line of cadets.

Dr. Booth stopped the car. "Well? Owen? What do I want?"

"For me to grow up," Owen said, watching one of the cadets march toward them. He was tall and his chin was long and sharp and his belt buckle flashed like a beacon. He was carrying a clipboard in a crisp, prescribed-looking way. The cadet stopped in front of the car and waited as Dr. Booth and Owen got out.

"Name, sir?"

"Booth."

The cadet ran a finger down the clipboard. "Booth, Owen G., blood type A."

"That's my boy." Dr. Booth smiled at Owen, who stared dead ahead. He had attempted to square his thin shoulders and was holding his arms straight at his sides. He had never looked so young. Dr. Booth made up his mind to have a talk with Colonel Karl before he left. He wasn't going to leave his son here without some definite assurances.

"Private Booth is late, sir. Roll call for new men was 1300 hours."

"I'm aware of that. We had some trouble getting here. A lot of trouble, in fact. That map is practically worthless."

"I'm sure you have excellent reasons, sir. The fact remains, Private Booth is late. Private Booth will report immediately to the quartermaster. When Private Booth has drawn his gear, he will move smartly to D Barrack and await orders. Corporal Costello will escort him. You can leave his bags here." The cadet snapped his fingers. Another cadet stepped forward from the line.

Owen turned quickly to Dr. Booth and held out his hand. Dr. Booth understood that he did this to prevent the embrace he'd known was coming, which the doctor, wounded, was tempted to impose on him anyway. But he took his son's hand in his own.

"Goodbye, sir," Owen said. Then he fell in behind Corporal Costello and followed him across the courtyard, trying to match the cadet's precise stride and rigid carriage. He didn't even come close, and Dr. Booth knew that he never would. The distracted saunter he kept breaking into was not an accident of age, something to be outgrown or overcome; it was, in truth, nothing less than Owen himself.

"I need to speak with Colonel Karl," Dr. Booth said.

"Colonel Karl is busy, sir," the cadet said.

Dr. Booth insisted, and finally the cadet had another boy take him to a windowless lounge in the basement of the far building. He was alone there. An aerial photograph of the school occupied one wall; otherwise the room was bare of ornament. Four overstuffed chairs faced a coffee table bearing an Academy brochure identical to the one Dr. Booth had received. He picked it up and slowly turned the pages, then set it down and paced the room. A silent grandfather clock, hands frozen at 6:18, stood in one corner, an empty umbrella stand in another. Time passed: more time. Dr. Booth went upstairs to the door of the building. The courtyard was empty. The flags drooped on their pole. He stepped outside and, seeing no one, followed a brick pathway around back in the direction Owen had gone. The path skirted a deserted football field with bleachers on one side, then led past a pond covered with lily-pads. On the opposite bank, black against the hazy sky, rose the stone walls and battlemented tower of what Dr. Booth recognized from the brochure as Memorial Chapel. The path he was on turned away in the opposite direction. He left it and pushed through clumps of sumac and elder to the other side of the pond.

One half of the arched door was locked, the other slightly ajar. Dr. Booth listened, heard nothing, and entered the chapel. Weak light fell aslant through the long narrow windows—windows like gun slits. It seemed to dim rather than brighten the oak pews and stone floors. There was no organ. The altar was bare. On the platform in front of the altar, facing the pews, someone had placed a high-backed wooden chair. Dr. Booth could not make out its purpose. If one wished to address the congregation, surely one would use the carved pulpit with its superior elevation and authority. One would stand, not sit. He studied the chair from the rear of the chapel, then started down the aisle. In obedience to an impulse he was hardly aware of but could not resist, Dr. Booth held his upper body stiff and paused for a beat after each step, one foot trailing, heel raised. He had never marched before, but he marched in this fashion the length of the aisle and climbed to the altar, where he executed a perfect about-face and then, as if on command, lowered himself onto the chair, back straight, hands in his lap.

How quiet it was. Dr. Booth looked out into the chapel, at the somber pews where the cadets would file in and stand waiting and then take their seats in a single motion—one great creak, then silence. Whoever sat in this chair could see the face of every cadet. Dr. Booth could almost see them himself, row after row of them, faintly luminous in the shadows. He could feel them watching behind their unblinking eyes, weighing him in the scales, and then it came to him that this was the place of judgment. This was where you sat to have your faults revealed and to receive your sentence. Dr. Booth looked away, at the heavy beams overhead, the roof slanting up into darkness. He closed his eyes. Still he saw the faces of the cadets, taut and pale above their black uniforms. He strained to find among them some glint of fellow-feeling, some intimation of mercy; he found none. Mercy there was none.

The door swung open at the rear of the chapel and a cadet stood silhouetted in the doorway. "Sir," he said.

Dr. Booth stood clumsily, knocking over the chair. He set it right and hurried up the aisle. "Coming," he called out, and again, more softly, "Coming."

The cadet held the door for Dr. Booth and followed him outside, where another cadet—the tall one who'd scolded him for being late—passed on Colonel Karl's deepest regrets that, due to prior obligations, he was unable to speak with Dr. Booth this afternoon. The doctor could return the next morning if he wished or call for an appointment at some later date.

Dr. Booth supposed he could raise a fuss and make it impossible for Colonel Karl not to see him, but he was worried about the trouble this might cause Owen, and anyway he had to get back on the road if he was to reach home before dark. He was ready to leave Fort Steele Academy; he was ready almost to the point of panic. So he accepted Colonel Karl's message without protest and allowed the two cadets to take him back to his car. They led him like a prisoner, the tall one in front, the other at his heels, but saluted elegantly when he started the engine and drove back down the lane. The guards at the gate also saluted. In the field across the road a green tractor moved slowly along the fence, pulling a mower. The smell of fresh-cut hay filled the car, and lingered until Dr. Booth was several miles away, and lost again.

He parked on the shoulder of the road, engine ticking, and choked back his rage just enough to hold the goddamn sonofabitch map without tearing it to pieces. With a trembling finger he tried to retrace his route: he'd taken this road through the maple grove beyond the school, yes, then it must've been this one, here, that had carried him over an unmarked bridge and thence to a triple fork, also unmarked, where he'd been forced to make the first of a long series of choices for which he had received no guidance, before finally coming to rest in this vast flatland whose very existence went completely unremarked by the map. Dr. Booth did not know where he was.

A water tower gleamed in the distance. The reek of manure lay heavy on the air. Three white-faced cows watched from the fence to his left as Dr. Booth continued to study the map, this time in reverse, trying to find the various roads he and Owen had followed from home to the Academy. Only the first couple of turns off the interstate were correctly indicated; everything else was wrong or nonexistent, a chaos of misinformation. It was a pure miracle he had ever found the school, given that he'd been forced to make his way there almost entirely on hunches. The map simply did not correspond to the countryside.

He crumpled it and threw it out the window. One of the cows took a step backward, then continued to ruminate and stare. Dr. Booth was thinking about the aerial photograph in the lounge. Why he should have remembered it at this moment he couldn't have said, but he saw it again in detail, and did not like what he saw. There was no pond in the picture, and the chapel stood a quarter mile from its actual location, forming part of a quadrangle where the football field lay. That quadrangle did not exist. Like the map, the aerial photograph was a fiction.

Once Dr. Booth recognized this, he had to entertain a number of questions he'd been trying to shrug off. During his time at the Academy, he had seen only a few cadets—the guards, and the ones who took charge of Owen. Where were all the other boys in this school of five hundred? Why hadn't he run across any of them out marching around, or heard their voices? How had *their* parents found the way? Why wouldn't Colonel Karl see him, or at least send a deputy?

And how had this happened? How did it come to pass that he had given up his son to powers of which he knew nothing, except that they were without patience, humor, or mercy? Of all mysteries, this was the most perplexing.

Dr. Booth turned the car around and started back the way he'd come, driving slowly so as not to lose his way again and delay his return to the Academy. He was determined not to leave Owen in that place one instant longer than he had to. He saw a crossroad approaching and knew without doubt that he should turn right. The certainty he felt was surprising and tonic, like the first deep breath when he left the hospital at day's end. He knew where he was going now.

How had this happened? It was unaccountable to him. The Academy had been mentioned, the brochure had arrived—but how? And why had he considered it at all, the surrender of his boy to unknown disciplines and judgments? His wife had resisted at first, but in spite of his own doubts he bullied her along until she, like Owen, saw the futility of argument. They had no choice in the matter; nor, it then seemed to him, did he. From the moment he heard the name of the school, he had known, unhappily, miserably in fact, that Owen would go there. His attempts to talk himself out of it left him even more helplessly snarled in reasons for sending the boy away, reasons that now seemed trivial, unjust, baffling.

He had compared Owen to himself—how, in his youth, he had sold newspapers and played sports and run for office. That much was true. But he'd never actually been elected; he had offered himself up year after year and received nothing for his pains but more humiliation. His father had made him take on the paper route because they needed the money, and he'd hated every minute of it, the waking in darkness, the cold and rain, the way his customers cried poor and hid from him. He'd played varsity football, yes, but only in his senior year, when his little brother took over the route. Owen was much younger than he had been then. Much younger. How had he forgotten?

Reason, reasons. Owen's remoteness. Time for the boy to wake up and get out of the house, show some pluck, some drive, some will power—that was always the closing argument, the clincher. But why? Owen did well in school. He was quiet and liked to read and wasn't much of an athlete, but he wasn't lazy or lacking in courage; he and his friends routinely rode their bikes up and down hills that verged on the perpendicular. It took inestimable courage to learn to ride a bike at all, to swim, catch a hardball, even to walk . . . how had he forgotten his pride in these victories?

And those sounds Owen made—what was the harm in them? Why shouldn't he dream up poems, or songs, or whatever they were? Why shouldn't he dream? He was a child, for the love of God.

Dr. Booth turned left at a fork and navigated a run of sharp turns as if he'd spent his life on this road. The haze was gone, the late afternoon light almost painfully clear. Pumpkins gleamed in a passing field.

He had wanted Owen out of the house. That was the truth, and it made no sense to him now. The impatience he'd felt, coming upon his son reading or playing with his dog, doing nothing, dreaming—why? What was the crime? As a boy, he himself had wanted nothing more than the chance to dream. It came seldom in that crowded, industrious house, and never lasted long. Why should he begrudge his son what he had most desired? Why should he begrudge his son his childhood?

Impatience . . . impatience. He'd felt it from the day Owen was born. All the distractions of having young, the complications, the sheer frivolity. One night Dr. Booth used the word "quadruple" while talking on the phone to another doctor, and Owen fell to the floor in a fit of hilarity. For days afterward he broke himself up by repeating the word. Dr. Booth finally got tired of all this silliness and spoke sharply to Owen, but couldn't help laughing himself, which made him feel giddy and foolish and angry at the same time. Here he was, a grown man, a surgeon of the heart, acting like a child. Owen often did this to him—made ordinary words, ordinary things, seem ludicrous oddities. But quadruple *was* a funny word, when you thought about it. It was a very funny word.

Neat files of tall corn flicked past. Dr. Booth drove faster, fast as he dared, through corkscrew turns, down straightaways, over gravel fire roads and glistening blacktop, past marsh, past field, up hilltops awash in light and deep into valleys abysmal. As he drove, he pondered the face of his son as if it were a map, as if he were learning where to turn from the curve of Owen's neck, the slant of an eyebrow. And then it began to fade. At first he barely noticed. The long fine line of the nose blurred subtly, that was all. Then the cheeks paled; the smile grew faint; the light dulled and died from the eyes. He fiercely studied every feature even as it ebbed away, trying to hold the ghostly image there, keep it in mind long enough to find his way back to the true face. And then it vanished. He entered a dark wood, and as the trees closed overhead he forgot that he had ever had a son. He didn't know where he was. When he left the wood he slowed down and pulled to the side of the road. The sun was going down over the field to his right, where a tractor moved slowly in the distance, cutting the last rows of hay.

Dr. Booth got out of the car. He crossed the road and gazed up the hill. Another field, also full of new-mown hay. The smell went to his head. He stood there a moment, then ducked through the fence and walked farther into the field. He kept staring up the hill as he climbed, looking for something, though he could not remember what. When he reached the top, he stopped to catch his breath. All around him the fields rolled empty away. He felt a stone under his shoe, nudged it aside, then bent to pick it up. Not a stone, after all. A button—a metal button caked with mud. He picked at it until the brass was revealed, then examined it in the last of the light. Under the verdigris he could make out a pair of crossed swords. A military button, then. An old one. Something must have happened here, long ago—that was why he'd been drawn to this place. A battle had been fought, no quarter given; boys became men, and were lost. Wasn't that the way of it? He slipped the button in his pocket and started down the hill.

Peter Pryor

Heavy Air

I do not believe in a fate that falls on men however they act; but I do believe in a fate that falls on them unless they act.

—*G. K. Chesterton*, 1928

VERY QUIETLY, he moved among the rocks, taking care to step only on stone, leaving no trace of his passage on the soft, damp desert ground.

Silence was his friend; the cool, still night air that transmitted even the faintest sound an astonishing distance with utter clarity the potential traitor.

He felt the slow release of the day's heat from the rock as he sat, back resting against the weathered outcropping of granite. His own weariness felt as ageless as the stone. "Maybe," he thought, "you never do finish paying the price of the fire." He drew his knees up nearly to his chest, closed his eyes and slowed his breathing, suppressing his rising sense of urgency.

The .308-caliber Browning was cradled diagonally in his lap. The rifle had been given to him years ago by his father. Its walnut stock was polished by the contact of hands over years of use and it bore the more-recent refinements of an old German gunsmith who understood that firearms were tools that performed best when individually tailored to the user and was wise enough not to ask unnecessary questions: every part hand-matched to precise tolerances, glass-beaded barrel ending in an adjustable muzzle break and bearing a Pentax Lightseeker 4-16X60 scope. A Nossler 150-grain partition round was chambered, a second in his jacket pocket. There would be no need for more than two rounds. At three hundred yards, the rifle was deadly accurate.

He opened his eyes and continued to breathe slowly, deliberately, taking the range finder from its case on his belt. He flipped open its front and back covers, uncoiled into an angular prone position, turned his ball cap bill-backwards on his head and sighted.

He centered the cross hairs on the target and waited for the range finder to stabilize: two-hundred-and-ten yards. He had estimated two hundred.

He moved the finder slightly to the left and sighted the second target and waited as a vagrant, black cloud passed across the moon, darkening the night. "There's no difference between this and the jungle," he reassured himself. "Different place, different time, different targets; thirty years later but still the same."

A slight breeze came up from the night, carrying with it the smell of burning mesquite, of rain-damp earth. It came straight into his face. It would carry away any inadvertent sound he might make. In the distance, a brilliant blue bolt of lightning running its jagged, forked course to the desert floor split the sky. Its thunder rumbled lazily across the night.

The summer thunder showers had been wandering through the desert since late afternoon; columns of heated air rising from the furnace floor of the day, cooling as they ascended until they reached condensation temperature and formed dark-gray clouds that occasionally gave up their moisture in heavy, violent downpours.

He retreated to his position of rest against the granite, put the range finder back in its case, readjusted his cap and zipped up his nylon flight jacket against the night air. He felt the safety on the rifle casually with his thumb and waited, eyes closed again, drifting on thoughts and memories, still cat-like in his awareness of the sounds and smells of the desert night.

A hundred-and-eighty miles to the west a slightly drunk movie studio executive and a casting-couch would-be actress turned off Pacific Coast Highway onto Mulholland and headed up into the coastal mountains, on their way from an elegant seaside restaurant to his Lake Sherwood estate.

She hit the change-disc button on the CD player, adjusted the volume, slouched deeply into the leather seat of the BMW, turned the sun visor up into the open air to deflect the wind flow and lit a joint. She took a hit, moved her left hand to his thigh and passed the joint to him. When it was finished, she flipped it outside the car.

"Jesus," he said, "you 'gotta be careful with that shit up here. This whole place is like a bomb waiting to go off in the summertime."

"Sorry," she said. "It was done. Not a problem."

The roach nestled in the dry grass at the side of the road for a moment and then glowed a bit more brightly, its ember freshened by the canyon breeze.

It was two years earlier when the phone rang at three in the morning.

"Shit," he mumbled in half sleep as he knocked the lamp off the night table in his reach for the phone.

"Hello."

"Sean, it's Eamon."

"Uh huh," rubbing his eyes with his free hand, sitting up on the edge of the bed, trying to right the lamp. "Eamon? Jesus, brother, it's the middle of the night. You guys have another baby or something?"

"It's three in the morning, Sean. Look . . ." and then silence. "I've got bad news."

"What," wide awake and alert now.

"It's dad. He's . . ."

"He's what? Is he okay?"

"He's dead."

"Dead? How? What happened?"

He heard a heavy, deep sigh in his ear.

"He . . . was killed. Shot. Some cops shot him."

"What? C'mon, this is a pretty sick joke at three in the morning."

"It's no joke. He was shot in the house last night. It was a raid."

"A raid? Whadyamean, a raid? Shit! How's mom? Is she okay?"

"She's all right. She's here with us. She's pretty sedated. Christ, she was hysterical. They killed him right in front of her. Jesus, they even killed the dog. I think she's finally asleep now. You need to come down here."

Sean finished a hurried preflight on the twin Navajo, taxied out to the runway and took off in the predawn darkness.

Eamon met him at Camarillo airport.

At seven o'clock, his father and mother were ready to sit down to dinner in the kitchen.

"Let's see," his father said, "roast chicken calls for white wine. A Chablis. No, a chenin blanc. I will repair to the wine cellar and return with a fine chenin blanc, yes?"

"The chenin blanc is in the 'fridge under 'C'," his mother replied. "I put it in an hour ago to chill."

"Ever thoughtful. I don't think I could survive without you," he said in jest.

"Nor I without you," she replied, encircling his waist with her arms from behind as he turned toward the refrigerator. She kissed the back of his neck.

At sixty-eight, she was seven years his junior; tall, striking, with chiseled features, short hair of natural silver, flashing green eyes and a trim figure that defied her age. They had been married fifty-two years.

Michael Cleary was born in 1919 in Dublin, Ireland. Seventeen years later he left home to go sea, where he would spend the next twenty years sailing dry-cargo ships to most every major commercial seaport in the world.

He began as a boatswain's apprentice and by the time he was thirty had his master's papers and was commanding ships for Sweden's Sandviken line. His education beyond high school was nautical-formal, general-self taught and entirely eclectic.

When he was twenty-five he married Ingrid, a beautiful Swede of seafaring stock he had first met in the Swedish port city of Malmo. Eamon was born two years later and Sean two years after that. They lived variously in Malmo, Stockholm and Dublin, finally emigrating to the United States and California in 1956 when Michael gave up the sea to pursue a burgeoning interest in painting and sculpting.

Eamon was fourteen and Sean twelve when they began working side by side with their parents and local artisans and craftsmen building their new home in the then-largely-barren coastal mountains of northwest Los Angeles County.

The home they built was constructed with care and precision of the finest stone and wood; situated to become a part of, rather than intrude on, its natural surroundings; burnished floors pegged, not nailed; positioned to take advantage of the warmth of the sun and cool of the sea breeze.

It was conceived with an artist's vision, planned with an engineer's mind, executed with a master craftsman's skill and decorated with a fabulist's sensibilities—inhabited by the ghosts of scrimshaw, objets d'art from around the world and the countless memories of a mariner's life.

Outside, insinuated into the mountains through sheer force of will and determination by their mother was an expanding array of gardens that thrived in the Mediterranean climate under her constant care and administrations.

Michael and Ingrid sat in the living room after dinner on the sofa in front of the fireplace listening to music and reading; he sipping a brandy, she chamomile tea, their Siberian husky stretched out on the throw rug by the hearth, legs twitching furtively on occasion as private dog dreams drifted across his mind on the winter's evening.

At nine o'clock Michael set his book down on the end table, stretched, yawned and kissed his wife on the cheek.

"Time for this old man to go to bed. How 'bout you?"

"In a while," she said. "I'm going to read for a bit more."

He got up, and started for the stairway to the second-floor bedroom. "Poke the fire before you come up to bed, okay?" he said.

"Sure."

Robert Ellison was thirty-eight years old, with two ex-wives who considered themselves lucky to be alive, much less have their freedom, and no children. He had been a sheriff's deputy for twelve years. Working in the narcotics bureau for the past six years, his world consisted of snitches, deception and a grandiose but vague sense of duty to something he really didn't understand and didn't much care to beyond a simplistic attitude of moral superiority. Going nowhere in the Marine Corps, he'd opted for the next closest thing, and law enforcement gave him a war, of sorts, to fight. His record, thanks more to luck than virtue, was unblemished.

A down-and-outer he had busted for manufacturing methamphetamine in a beat-up trailer squatting on a land parcel at the end of a seldom-used dirt road deep in the hills behind Malibu had told him of a marijuana plantation farther up the canyon in a desperate attempt to bargain some hope for his own sorry plight.

When Ellison went to look, he found the side road from Mulholland Highway blocked after a mile by a chain-locked livestock gate posted: "Private Property. No Trespassing." The brush on all sides was too dense to allow an easy excursion.

The tweaker was effusive. Thousands of marijuana plants, carefully cultivated around an expansive house tucked away at the end of the dirt road, another mile beyond the gate. He would have described a secret air base and a dozen black helicopters if he thought it would benefit himself.

Ellison was ambitious. He gave free rein to his rising curiosity. He was coming up empty at every turn: Old couple; man an artist of some note; obviously well off; wife an obsessive gardener; both naturalized citizens; older son a corporate lawyer for an oil company; younger son a career-track Vietnam-era ex-soldier who did a one-eighty and left after his third tour, banging around various jobs before settling in as owner-operator of a three-plane charter air service outside of Eureka in Northern California.

"This guy is a weird-ass old recluse. Doesn't even do much of the *artiste* party circuit. And *thousands* of marijuana plants. Shit," Ellison thought, "why not. Guy could be big time into growing weed. Worth a shot."

He broached the project with another deputy, a young up-and-comer in the narcotics division, in an effort to move along his nascent investigation. He'd worked with him twice before. He was okay.

"Look, Jason," Ellison said, "this could really be a big deal. We could nail down the lid on a big grower, but we've 'gotta get enough to get a warrant. I tried going up there last week, but it's a real mess if you have to leave the road. It's like a fuckin' jungle up there. Brush and snakes and shit. We can go up, look around, make a threat assessment. Shit, we nail this one down, could be a big-time forfeiture. Feds already have this guy surrounded on three sides with parkland. Park Service might want to get in on this. Three-hundred fuckin' acres in the hills above Malibu. Big-time forfeiture. Four, maybe five million bucks worth of property. High-profile-artist-big-weed-grower. Jesus, big time. We move up the ladder. I move up, you move up. This is really good stuff."

"Okay. So whatta we do?"

"We get a dog. Not a drug dog. They're too fuckin' hinky. Don't want a handler around anyway. Keep this to us for now. Just a dog. I'll get Janie's Brittany. We just take a walk up the road past the gate and look around. If anybody comes out, we just play dumb-ass hikers that really didn't mean any harm and be on our way out of there."

"Sounds okay. When?"

"Day after tomorrow. Saturday. Lots of dumb-ass hikers that can't read 'No Trespassing' for shit out on a weekend."

"Sounds good. Let's do it. We gettin' overtime?"

They had been looking around for fifteen minutes when they heard a car coming up the road. They moved off into the brush along the side of the house at the end of the rose garden and slipped a muzzle on the Brittany.

The old couple parked on the pad in front of the house and got out of the Cherokee. The husky was on a leash and none too steady on its feet, having just endured forty-five minutes of a veterinarian searching for a foxtail that had entered between the toes of his right front paw and traveled half-way up his leg. It made an effort at sniffing the air and then looked plaintively at the couple.

"Poor baby," Ingrid said. "C'mon, up into the house, then you can sleep it off."

"Damn foxtails," Michael muttered. "Poor baby," she said again.

The two deputies waited for half an hour before gingerly picking their way through the brush to a point beyond where the dirt road curved and they could emerge out of eyesight from the house.

"Shit," Ellison said. "Maybe aerial can find something. It'd take forever to ground-search that place. Looks like a fuckin' nursery or something."

During the course of the next month, Robert Ellison was able to enlist the aid of a Sheriff's Department helicopter, a fixed-wing aircraft through the state's CAMP anti-marijuana program, the Forest Service, some Drug Enforcement Agency officers and the National Park Service in an effort to come up with something substantial enough to merit a search warrant.

The reconnaissance photos were worthless—black-and-white and, at best, open to imaginative interpretation. The DEA agent who went along on one recon flight—at a thousand feet—wouldn't use binoculars because he said they would make him sick to his stomach. After a couple of passes, he saw something he thought might be some marijuana plants; maybe a hundred or so, certainly not thousands, beneath heavy tree cover.

Calling in a marker from a buddy with the Border Patrol, Ellison was able to get a C-RAT team from Bakersfield to conduct a clandestine ground assessment. The team encountered heavy brush, three rattlesnakes and spooked a few mule deer. They retreated back into the deep growth when the husky left the front porch of the house and went out to investigate the scent it had picked up on the evening breeze.

"C'mon," Ellison said to the DEA agent on the phone. "You owe me one. Cut me some slack on this. It's no big deal. We get the warrant, we go in, we probably get a great bust and everyone wins."

"What if it's a wash," the DEA agent said. "What if it turns up shit."

"Then it's a wash. Nobody gets hurt. Old guy and his wife bitch and scream about their civil rights. Fuckin' artist-type. They always scream about their civil rights. We're not 'gonna lose anything. It's worth the shot. C'mon."

The DEA agent signed an affidavit stating he had observed what he thought were possible marijuana plants growing underneath a stand of trees behind the house.

The assistant district attorney who signed off on the warrant request never thought to ask if the DEA agent was using binoculars and if he wasn't just how much he could distinguish in the scrub-oak and tree-grown area with his naked eye from a thousand feet. The judge who issued the warrant didn't ask *any* quesions.

"Well, partner," Ellison said. We've got our warrant. "We need to put a team together and do this deal."

"I dunno," Jason Daniels said, "It's really pretty inconclusive. Doesn't seem like a whole lot."

"Shit, man, you 'gotta go on your gut feeling. This one's 'gonna be good. It's 'gonna be real good. Trust me. We're partners in this. Trust me on this, okay?"

"Yeah."

The husky padded behind Michael as he climbed the stairs and went into the bedroom. The dog circled the round rag rug at the foot of the bed a few times and finally settled down. Michael came out of the bathroom and got into the captain's bed, turned off the light and fell fast asleep.

An hour later, the old husky wakened and raised his head, tasting the air, listening. His ears turned to an all-but-indistinguishable sound and his body tensed. He rose to his feet and left the bedroom, stopped at the top of the stairway and hesitated for a moment.

His concentration was total as he started for the bottom of the stairwell with a wolf's intensity.

The unlocked door swung viciously back on its hinges and crashed against the wall as the first three invaders exploded into the house.

They were dressed the same—olive green pants and shirts, jackets with Sheriff's Department in yellow on the back covering body armor, hands encased in thin, tactile-sensitive gloves, the first in holding a Glock 9-millimeter pistol, the second an AR-15 assault rifle, the third a short-barreled twelve-gauge shotgun loaded with double-ought buck.

Two dozen others from an assortment of county, state and federal law-enforcement agencies held various positions outside.

The husky was in the air on a trajectory for the lead intruder, driven by instinct and reflex, fangs bared and a primal snarl welling up from deep within his protective ancestry when the blast from the sweeper's shotgun disemboweled him and he crumpled to the floor.

Ingrid had time for little more than to raise her head from her book, wide-eyed in terror, and scream before Ellison was on her. He pulled her from the sofa, slamming her face down to the floor, hitting her head on the coffee table on the way. He pulled her arms behind her back and handcuffed her wrists.

Upstairs, Michael was startled awake by the noise of the door crashing open, his wife's scream and the shotgun blast.

He grabbed his .357 Magnum Smith & Wesson from the drawer in the nightstand by the bed and bolted, still sleep-groggy, from the bedroom.

"Ingrid!" he shouted as he turned the corner from the hallway at the top of the stairs.

He saw the room below from the top of the stairway in a series of stop-motion frames—his wife on the floor on her stomach, arms bent behind her back, an armed man crouched beside her; two other armed men in the room and more entering; the husky motionless in a spreading pool of its own blood.

He thumb-cocked the .357 and began to lower it toward the closest of the invaders at the foot of the stairs. He heard someone shout "Police!" as he began to squeeze the trigger of the Smith. He reeled from the impact of two rounds from Ellison's 9 millimeter and two .223-caliber rounds from Daniels' AR-15 fired in quick semiautomatic succession and fell dead where he stood. He never got a shot off.

More officers entered through the battered front door and quickly swept the house, room by room, downstairs and up.

"Clear," one of the deputies yelled outside to the night. "It's clear." The deputies, rangers and agents outside began to leave their positions and congregate in an uncomfortable group in front of the house. The gunfire had added an unwelcome edge to the operation. "This was supposed to be about plants, not people," one park ranger said softly to no one in particular. He had spoken to the couple on occasion in chance meetings over the years. "This is fucked, big time."

"Oh, shit," Daniels said, crouching over the old man's body.

Ingrid was struggling, screaming hysterically on the living room floor. "Goddamn it!" Ellison shouted, "Get her out of here. Somebody take her out of here!"

He climbed the stairs and knelt next to his partner on one knee.

"He's dead," Daniels said, sitting down on the first step next to the old man's body. "Jesus Christ, what the hell is this all about?" he said, taking off his gloves and rubbing his eyes with the heels of his hands. "The shit's 'gonna hit the fan on this. What the hell is this all about?"

"He had a gun," Ellison said, trying to organize his own thoughts. "He had a fucking gun. He was 'gonna fire. I shot, you shot. Shit, we didn't have any choice. Dumb shit. He had a gun."

Daniels looked into his partner's face with questioning eyes. He didn't say anything.

"This is total, unbelievable, bullshit," Sean said to his brother. "Total bullshit! Assholes! Look at this. Fucking morons! They have to turn the place inside out, too? It's not enough to murder him. Assholes."

"He was up there, at the top of the stairs, when they shot him. They say he had a gun," his brother said, trying to go beyond his own emotion.

"No shit he had a gun. Wouldn't you, if some gang of terrorists broke into your house? It's just too bad he wasn't able to get a few of them. Fucking assholes."

"You need to get a grip on yourself," Eamon said quietly. "Going over the edge isn't going to solve anything, isn't going to help anything."

"No? Maybe someone *needs* to go over the edge. How can you be so goddamn calm?"

"I think Mom could use some stability around her now. I don't think any of us going crazy is going to help right now."

Sean sighed deeply and closed his eyes. "I know. You're right. I'm sorry. I didn't mean to go off on you. I'm sorry. It's just so . . . What in the hell were they doing here anyway?"

"They had a search warrant. Drug search. Apparently, they'd been snooping for months. Best I can find out, some junkie gave a narc a wild story to try to save his own ass. It got way out of control. It was bad all the way around."

"Yeah, really bad. Search warrant . . . more like a death warrant. Probably killed the dog just for laughs, threw him in for free. Lucky they didn't shoot Mom, too. Probably pissed 'cause they missed the chance."

"He was at the top of the stairs when they shot him," Eamon said, motioning with his head.

He stopped for a moment to organize a collection of framed photographs thrown askew on an oak table during the raid. He saw their parents, the husky, himself at twenty-five after graduating law school. He picked up the one of his brother, standing by a tree in a jungle halfway around the world.

Sean was twenty-three then, an idealistic adventurer on his third tour with the 9th Infantry Division Mobile Riverine Force. He was wearing tiger stripe camouflage fatigues, boony hat pushed back rakishly on his head, cigarette dangling casually from his mouth. A 9th Infantry Division Recondo badge was on his right pocket, metal staff sergeant rank pinned on his lapels, a Ranger tab on the left shoulder above a 9th Infantry Division insignia, as well as a Vietnamese Ranger qualification badge above his left-pocket name tape. He held an XM21 sniper M14 with Sionics noise suppresser in his hands.

On the front of the boony hat was sewn the unofficial emblem of the Mobile Riverine Force snipers: a wolf's face with fangs bared—The ultimate hunter.

They moved through the house, mostly in silence.

Someone had made an effort at cleaning the hardwood floors where their father and the dog had been shot. They were not entirely successful. What remained were accusatory stains.

"You know," Eamon said as they went out through the kitchen door that opened to an expansive rose garden, "We all thought for a while that you were going to make a career of the Army, 'specially after you volunteered for a third combat tour.

"We were all surprised when you just left it. I always had the feeling Dad knew why, though, that he understood. He never said much about it."

Sean absently fingered a blood-red rose bud just beginning to unfold. "I got tired of the killing, the dying, being lied to at every turn by the government," he said quietly. "I guess I just realized somewhere along the way that there wasn't much point in trying to live up to an ideal that wasn't really on anyone else's agenda. I got tired of being a pawn in someone else's game. I mostly just got tired of the killing; tired of having to pay the price of the fire every day.

"Maybe I should've learned a lesson from you . . . stayed in school, become a lawyer or something, got married, had kids. That'd be different, wouldn't it—me and stability?"

"I don't think you'd do very well in law, brother. I can see you telling some judge who's threatening you with contempt that that's about all you really had for him and his court."

"Probably right," Sean said behind a brief smile.

The Sheriff's Department's investigation quickly absolved itself of any wrongdoing: The shooting was self-defense; the raid was justified based on the information the narcotics deputies had; they had a valid search warrant.

The District Attorney, faced with some embarrassing media scrutiny and on the heels of a Sheriff's Department narcotics bureau that was still trying to clean up the mess from a previous scandal involving misappropriated assets and the dismissal of a dozen deputies, started asking some hard questions.

Six months later, her sixty-page report concluded the shooting was justified. The deputies, she wrote, when confronted with an armed suspect had fired in self-defense. No indictments were sought. She went on, however, to say the officers probably should never have been there in the first place. They had, she said, at best strained credulity and honesty to the limits in their application for the warrant.

Ingrid's health began a quick and rapid decline after Michael was killed, the maiming of the single taproot they shared too much to allow recovery and sustain her own life. She died of heart failure a year-and-nine-months after Michael's death.

"So, where do we go from here?" Sean asked his brother.

"It's been almost two-and-a-half years. I mean, the DA said the warrant was basically bogus. The jerks bullshitted their way into a warrant. She wants to know how come every fucking law-enforcement agency you could think of is involved; wants to know what in hell the Border Patrol is there for; wonders if the property being almost surrounded by national parkland had anything to do with it. Christ, she even went out of her way to point out a big part of the sheriff's narc budget is covered by drug asset forfeitures. They find nothing, zero, zip, nada. No plants, no drugs. Shit, their goddamn dope-sniffing dogs couldn't even turn up anything. Jesus, she all but came out and said they're all a bunch of liars and the whole thing was bogus. Totally, completely bogus . . . and nobody's held accountable. Where's the justice in that? You're the lawyer. Tell me where the justice is in that."

"It's not about justice," Eamon said, "it's about law. You know that. Beyond the civil suit, there's nothing left that can be done. It sucks, I know."

"So what's with the suit? It gets thrown out . . . For the second time. What's that all about?"

"Procedural. Dismissed without prejudice. It'll be refiled. We have an awfully damn good lawyer dealing with this. Whatever can be done, he'll do. It's his territory, he knows it. I trust him, Sean."

"You know what really gets me? After the DA's report came out, when it was all pretty well spelled out that the cops fucked up big time . . . all that worthless fat-fuck county sheriff did was push himself away from the dinner table long enough to make some lame-ass statement climbing all over the DA and defending the fuck-ups who engineered the whole thing. They're all the same. Maybe the real justice is where you make it."

"Sean, you need to let go of this. Don't get crazy. Don't go over the edge. Don't let it kill you, too. You've got to just let the system work through things."

"I'm tired of the fucking system."

"Everything in its own time," he thought, "Everything in its own time. Be patient."

The breeze quickened a bit and he listened as it carried in the sound of a distant pack of coyotes yapping over a kill.

The smell of burning mesquite became stronger and he lay prone again, angling out from behind the rock.

Images of his father, his mother, his brother, an entire childhood drifted with utter clarity and detail in a fleeting moment across his mind.

He locked it away.

"This *is* the jungle," he whispered to himself, "Just another mission."

A faint trace of satisfaction crossed his face and disappeared as quickly as it had formed. "Except that was then. This is now. This is personal."

"Jesus, I'll be glad to see that whole fucking mess be done and gone," Daniels said as he poured another healthy slug of tequila into an enameled metal cup. "Damn near three years and its still dragging on. Wish the judge would just tell those two to piss up another tree; tell 'em to take their suit and shove it. Just'll be fucking glad to see it gone," he repeated, staring up at the desert sky. "You see all those stars, Bob," he said, weaving unsteadily and taking another gulp from the cup.

"That's probably the odds that whole mess would have gone as bad as it did. Gazillion to one."

"It happens," Ellison said. "C'mon, partner, let's not treat the Cuervo like private stash. Pass it on over."

"Sorry." Daniels sat down on the log by the edge of the fire next to Ellison and doodled aimlessly in the dirt with a stick.

"Goes with the territory," Ellison said. "Sometimes they just go bad. Nobody could've know the old guy was 'gonna come out waving a piece. Not supposed to happen like that. We didn't have any choice."

"I suppose. It happens," Daniels said, hoping to find some reassurance in just saying the words. "Still bothers me though. Doesn't make it feel any better. I sure didn't want to wind up shooting anybody. I mean, we killed the guy on an empty raid. Goddamn tweaker snitch. Son of a bitch. It all goes back to him. Goddamn lying snitch. Now there's somebody who desperately needs killing. Little shit."

"You need to get over it, let it go. You can't unring the bell. Don't let it kill you," Ellison said. "Few days out here riding the dirt bikes, hangin' out, kickin' back 'gonna do us both a world of good. It'll work out all right, you'll see."

"Yeah. I hope so."

Ellison got up and stretched. "Think I'm 'gonna hit it. Gettin' kinda late. Wonder if there's more rain coming. Still some big-ass, nasty, dark clouds rolling around. 'Least a camper's a hell of a lot more comfortable than a tent."

Sean followed him up with the scope, cross hairs keeping pace as Ellison rose to his feet and stretched in the cool evening air, silhouetted behind the dying fire.

His arms were spread back at waist level, hands clasped behind him, back arched, head back as he looked up at the sky. "Yeah," he said, "you're probably right. Gazillion to one."

Sean's life narrowed to a single figure in the circle of the scope. "Lot of moisture in the air," he thought. "Heavy air. A quarter, maybe a half-inch drop at most at this range." He adjusted for it and began a slow, steady, deliberate squeeze on the trigger.

Sean walked the four miles back to his Blazer at a leisurely pace, taking in the now-early-morning air. He began the one-hundred-eighty-mile drive back to the ranch without any sense of urgency, adrift in his own thoughts. He stopped for breakfast along the way.

He saw the smoke plume from the crest of the 405 Freeway where it came through the pass and the San Fernando Valley opened up below. He turned on the radio and listened to the reports of the fast-moving brush fire that had burned through the night in the coastal mountains behind Malibu. "They could save those," he thought, "and just replay them every year."

He knew the ranch was gone when he turned off onto the dirt road from Mulholland, scorched-earth wasteland all around as far as he could see. It looked like the aftermath of a napalm run.

His brother's car was parked in front of the remains of their childhood. The stone chimney remained; the rest was rubble; the gardens lifeless, smoking skeletons.

"Started last night. Who knows why. Careless smoker, whatever," Eamon said. "I guess it really is over now."

Sean didn't respond.

It was almost noon when Robert Ellison woke up with a hideous hangover. Jason Daniels was still fast asleep. Ellison splashed water on his face in the camper's sink and stumbled out the door, heading for the fire pit and the tequila to take the edge off his misery. He picked up the bottle, reached down for the cup and stopped, a quizzical expression crossing his face. He knelt down on one knee, took a swallow from the bottle, set it on the ground and stared. "What the hell's that all about?" he wondered.

Both cups were next to each other on the ground where they had been left the night before. In each, standing upright on its base, was a single, unexpended 150-grain Nossler .308-caliber partition round.

Julie A.
McCracken

Disease of Nerves

AMELIA'S HAIR IS BLACK, the black of anthracite, not the black that is first kin to dark brown, and it matches her eyes. Pupilless. Deep water. Helen, Amelia's mother, holds the long black tresses in her left hand, runs her right hand through the warm water in the white face bowl, and moistens her only child's hair.

Helen's hands are the angry red of dried autumn leaves. It's a disease whose name she's forgotten. Her ragged nails and cuticles betray the sharp bites of her own small teeth, and, too, the disease of nerves that sings inside her. These nerves calm their siren wail when she holds Amelia's long hair, when she completes the every morning ritual of making order from chaos birthed during night. She combs Amelia's hair from crown to neck to shoulders, to the tiny waist beneath the lacy undershirt tucked into the cotton panties with pink lace trim. Helen divides the hair into three sections, wets her hands again, and braids the left side, twelve inches, poker straight, black as moonless night.

Amelia complains in her taut seven year old voice. She cries "ouch!" threatens mayhem, screams bloody murder. The stacks of thirsty white towels may hear her cries, but Helen doesn't. Helen's breath moves from her lungs and out her nostrils in a smooth push, and back inward with a soft pull. No whistles, no uneven rushes of panicked wind. Amelia's hair is watered silk against her mother's ruined hands, smoothed momentarily by the water.

She smells her daughter's young girl smell that has no name to her but "Amelia" or "my child, my only child."

The red pack of Winston's are not permitted in this room at this time, nor is the cup followed by cup of weak coffee she will drink before the sun is high over her house, nor the dark-eyed faithless husband, nor his blowzy mother with her bottles of gin who snores within feet of the bathroom door.

Outside the cracked casement window, the circle of crows do not speak to each other and the mice behind the walls make no sound.

The disease of nerves parks itself outside the half-open door. Watchful. Waiting.

The scratch of a match, the red-orange flame.

Smoke.

Mike Maggio

Letters From Inside

April 10

Dear Mary,

Sorry for the break in communication. As you can imagine, the circumstances here aren't the best. Besides, it's always the same routine and there isn't much to write about—get up in the morning, breakfast at seven, morning activity (woodcarving, leather work, etc., sometimes they let us out on the grounds, especially now that the weather is improving, but this depends on how many merit points you've earned). In the afternoon, I see Dr. Schwartz. By the end of the day, I'm really drained.

But then you haven't written for more than a year, as I recall.

They say I'm improving, Mary. They say maybe in another twelve months or so I can go home, go back to work, begin my life all over again. How long have I been here now? Five, six years? Do you remember? Except for the turning of the seasons, you'd never recognize that time was passing in this place.

I think of you often—your little apartment overlooking the ocean, those lunches we used to have over in Venice—the Rose Cafe, wasn't it? —the museums downtown, the galleries—are they still there? It all seems like a fairy tale, a dream where I wander like a ghost—no substance, no reality. How I long to be free, to see the world again, especially you if you're willing to risk it. Or is that why you've stopped writing?

Funny how easily we took freedom for granted. I know we constantly talked about it, theorized, pretended—yes, pretended—to be its stalwart defenders, but did we ever appreciate it? Did we ever know what it meant? Who would have thought it would come to this, Mary? And right under our very eyes. But I'd better not speak like this, not now, not when I'm on the verge of recovery.

Outside my window, I can hear the birds singing. I wish you could hear them, Mary. They sound so beautiful. They must be nightingales. When was the last time you listened to a nightingale, Mary, tried to understand its message? Do you remember that scene in *Romeo and Juliet*, or is that still forbidden? Mary, it's as if they come especially for me. Every once in awhile one enters through the bars and perches on my windowsill, examining me, my surroundings, like a curious spectator at a zoo or a freak show. Then just as suddenly, he flies off, leaving me alone to my confinement.

Did you notice I used "he?"

But I'm good now, Mary, I really am. I *want* to be cured. Not like in the beginning when I resisted, defied them every chance I could. Though I think they still restrain me sometimes. It's all a fog to me, as if I'm on a cloud, floating helplessly, at the mercy of the winds, and the winds have no mercy, believe me. Yet I remember struggling, screaming, pleading with them, begging them to believe me. I told this to Dr. Schwartz today. Silly of me, really. The response was predictable—still paranoid, part of my condition.

This letter has gone on too long. The shorter the better. Trust me. Remember that when you write. Anyhow, it's time I went to sleep. They're good about that here. When I'm in my room, locked away from the world, I'm free to do as I please. Not exactly the way I thought my life would ever be, but one learns to savor these rare moments of freedom. Yes, freedom. Because no matter what the circumstances, there is always an element of freedom. I've learned that. You just have to recognize it, seize it, enjoy it to the fullest and let it compensate for everything else.

Mary, it's been so long. Don't get me wrong. I'm not blaming you. I understand if it's become a problem. It's just that things are difficult enough here, and worrying about you makes it even more so. Please write.

Jack

April 14

Dear Mary,

I forgot to tell you something when I wrote the other day. Dr. Schwartz says I'm full of denial. That the reason I don't know why I'm here is that I've disavowed my crime.

I asked her point-blank what my crime was. She said she didn't know, it really wasn't her business, and even if she did, she wouldn't tell me, that it was something I'd have to find for myself. It's part of the healing process, she said.

Why is it I remember things from my childhood as vividly as if they happened yesterday?

Mary, what did I do? Why can't I remember? I trust your judgment. You know me better than anyone. Of course, there's Danny, but how much can he have learned about me in a place like this, even if we've known each other since the day I arrived. You know, Mary, he'd been here once before, and I remember he told me, one day, in the beginning, when I first arrived, he said trust only what your eyes see, and then only after you've analyzed it thoroughly. Disregard everything else as a trick on your existence.

Anyhow, I had to tell you this before I forgot.

How are all our friends? How's Bob? Is he still seeing that actress? What about Sharon? Tell them all I said hello. God, I can't believe it's been five years. Five years!

Jack

May 21

Dear Mary,

Something rather strange has happened. Danny hasn't shown up to woodcarving class. It's been three days now.

Last week, he had a visitor. That's strange enough around here. They rarely allow visitors, and then only under certain circumstances—you're terminally ill and about to die, or you're nearly cured and about to be released. Then they allow frequent visits to help in the readjustment.

But Danny was neither of these, and this visitor—they said it was his brother, but when Danny went to the reception cell, he didn't recognize him, said he had never seen him before. Well, whoever it was, he smuggled in a small radio, about the size of a credit card, he said. The next day, we're outside on the grounds, working in the flower patch, and he pulls me over, whispers to me, says we're at war. He says the cities are being destroyed, he says the security forces are slaughtering the people like rats.

Mary, believe me, I tried not to listen. I thought to myself he's crazy, suffers from delusions. How can you believe someone like that? Besides, I don't want to get involved anymore. I just want out. But he kept talking, wouldn't shut up. He said he hadn't wanted to take the radio, but the man insisted, assured him no one would ever know. When he got to his room, he hid it under his bed, swore he would never listen to it. Then as the night wore on, it started to gnaw at him, the thought that an opportunity had come to see what was really happening in the world—not what they tell you Mary, not what they want you to know.

And now he's disappeared. I mentioned it to Dr. Schwartz today, thought for sure she would have seen him—three days, Mary, three days he hasn't shown up—and she dismissed it as my paranoia again, never told me whether he had come to his appointments or not.

Mary, I'm afraid. I don't trust anyone here. Especially her.

Jack

July 10

Dear Mary,

They found Danny this morning. After all this time. Dead. Impaled on one of the fence posts that hold up the barbed wire. Except it's not plain barbed wire. It's got lasers at the top, or so I hear. As if they want to encourage you to try, bloody yourself up, get your hopes high, so that just when you think you're going to make it—poof.

And that's what they said about him. An escapee. Did it to himself. But Mary, I know it's not true. Danny had no intention of escaping. If he had, I would have known about it, believe me. And besides, he was impaled, at least that's what everyone is saying.

Mary, do you think they killed him? To make an example of him? I know I'm not supposed to talk like this anymore, but I can't help it. I can't stop wondering what they may have done to him. And to think we've let this happen. But I will not fight them anymore. Even if he was my friend. I want out. I want my freedom. Even if it has to be on their terms.

What's it like, Mary? What's it like to be out there? I've forgotten. The pleasure of picking up a newspaper, a book. To read a poem, a story. To feel the paper brush against your skin, to hear the crisp sound of the pages as they turn. Even those slick advertisements we used to denounce seem so attractive now? Or to go to a restaurant, to dine, to indulge in a bottle of wine. What's the latest in cuisines, Mary? What do the restaurants look like nowadays? I'm starving, Mary, and you're my only source, the only one ever willing to risk writing to me. Why don't you answer? Why do I wait and receive no letter?

Jack

September 5

Dear Mary,

A new phase in my incarceration has begun.

The warden came to see me today. Imagine. As if I'm that important. Do you think it's a test? Do they always start this way? After all, they keep saying I'll be going home soon. Do they want to trick me? Make me slip when I least expect it? Put me at ease, or perhaps frighten me, so that either way my defenses will be down and they'll get inside of me, find out that I really despise them?

Mary, what should I do? How should I behave? Should I go along with him, and if I do, how will I maintain my guard? And if I don't, what will he do to me, what happens to my release? Will they cancel it? Will they keep me here forever?

There was a time I learned to accept my situation. Being locked up, dealing with Dr. Schwartz. Things went along smoothly, things never changed. Somehow I've got to figure out how to deal with this turn in events.

Jack

September 8

Mary—

Dr. Schwartz is an agent. I'm convinced of this now. She works with them, she informs them of everything I say. I know this as clearly as day from night. I'm not surprised, of course. But I thought she followed, however minimally, her oath of confidentiality. Don't they still take an oath like that? Or have things changed that much?

I tested her, Mary, I fished with her, so to speak. I told her Danny was alive, that I had seen him. She said I was deluding, of course. We all know he's dead, she insisted—but it was the way she said it that got me, the stony look in her eyes, the cold, flat tone of her words, as if it were not true, yet still essential that I believe it.

Well today I was called into the warden's office again. There were a few preliminaries, a few niceties, the kind of behavior you don't expect in this context. And every so often, he mentioned Danny—wasn't it a shame about him, he would have been a free man if only, etc., etc. Then he set his eyes on me—hard powerful eyes that seemed to bore through me. You'd better be careful if you know what's good for you, he said to me at last, his voice suddenly callous. And then he dismissed me.

How do you suppose I'll have to pay for this mistake?

Jack

September 15

Dear Mary,

Last night I had a horrible nightmare. I dreamed that they took me from my room—the warden and two guards. They led me away, through long, narrow corridors that seemed to go on and on. They were dark and creepy, and the lights flickered every so often as if the electrical system were being overburdened. We were in a maze of tunnels that twisted and turned and seemed to be leading us down, deep down. I could hear groans and screams and the sounds of men laughing.

Eventually, we came to an iron door that the warden unlocked with a set of heavy keys—the sound as he forced it open rushed through me like a knife—you know how metal sounds when it grates against stone. I wanted to cover my ears but I couldn't. My hands were tied behind my back.

It was dark inside, but I could hear someone breathing rapidly, as if resting after a long, strenuous ordeal. Soon, my eyes began to adjust and through the darkness I could make out a figure standing in the shadows. It was Danny. He was alive, except he was somehow different, not the Danny I had known. He had turned into some kind of vengeful monster. In his hand was a blowtorch. It was unlit, but I immediately detected the smell of burnt flesh, and then I noticed a man strapped to a table, naked, his body blackened with burns.

Danny turned to me. He smiled—a wild, insane smile, filled with sadness and fear, as if he had gone to hell and returned with the knowledge of survival. Suddenly, he lit the torch and applied it to the man's body and, as he did so, he grinned at me. The incongruity jolted me, but it was purposeful, as if he wanted me to understand the horror his life had become. The man made no sound, though his body was shivering like he was freezing instead of being burned alive. The warden and the two guards laughed, as if the scene had suddenly turned comic, and the sounds reverberated violently through the dingy chamber.

I woke up in a sweat. It was morning. I could hear the birds outside, and the light was filtering in gently through the trees. But I couldn't move. I felt groggy, mentally and emotionally drained, my eyes were heavy. It was as if, despite what my senses were telling me, I was still there in that room with Danny.

Later that morning, I was invited to the warden's office. Again. This time I was treated like a king. They offered me breakfast—eggs benedict, gourmet coffee, fresh orange juice—none of that artificial stuff they feed us everyday.

I ate heartily. I didn't want to, but it's been so long. You remember how food has always been my weakness. While I ate, the warden watched me, relishing each bite I took as if he were eating for the first time. He made small talk, like we were two friends meeting at a restaurant—two free men, associating by choice, not by edict. How did I feel this morning? I didn't look well. Perhaps I hadn't slept during the night.

What frightens me, Mary, is that this encounter was more a dream than my nightmare was. What do you suppose is happening to me? I refuse to discuss this with Dr. Schwartz. I refuse to discuss anything with her anymore. The problem is what to do during our sessions. Silence will indict me. And since she knows what's going on, I can't escape not talking about it. I've got to learn to play their game, only I'm not sure what it is.

Jack

September 20

Dear Mary,

Dr. Schwartz has asked me to keep a dream journal. Do you think it's just a coincidence? I know it's a common practice in therapy, but the timing is uncanny. Moreover, she's been skirting around the subject for two days now—as if she knows something.

She asked me about Danny again—not directly. She asked me if I had had any other hallucinations. Of course, she was referring to my little lie—I refuse to tell her about that dream I had. Yet, it's as if she knows.

Mary, do you think it's possible for them to induce dreaming? Do you remember the LSD experiments back in the 60s? Could they have refined it, developed it to a point where they can make you see what they want?

Now that I have to keep a journal, my dreams have become vivid—vibrant as if I'm living them. But I don't write about them. Not exactly. I tone them down, sometimes I even make them up. But somehow, I think she knows.

Jack

September 29

Dear Mary,

The warden can be a kind man. I learned this during a medical emergency that took place today. We were out on the grounds. It was a crisp, fall day, the kind that can only take place in this part of the country. The Northeast, Mary. There's nothing like the Northeast, especially in the Fall. Clear blue skies, dotted with clouds, the leaves crimson and gold, the smell of nature in its last glorious burst of life.

Anyhow, we were out tending the grounds when suddenly Mark—I don't believe I've told you about him, he's former CIA, relatively new here, from what I gathered from our short conversations, they picked him up planting bombs at government installations—anyhow, he had a fit—he's an epileptic. The warden happened to be out on an inspection when this occurred, and he immediately ran over and helped him. He's a medical doctor by training, and he treated Mark with such skill and care, looking at me and smiling in a kindly way.

Things have calmed down, Mary. No more visits to the warden, no problems with Dr. Schwartz. It's as if they've let everything pass. As if it were all a test. Perhaps I'm learning to play the game.

Mary, I'm not going to ask you to write anymore. In fact, I've stopped waiting for your letters. I ask only one thing—please let me continue this correspondence. Leave me at least that.

Jack

November 10

Dear Mary,

My dreams continue to get stranger. Last night I dreamed I was writing to you. It was as if I really were. And what I was writing about was this very same thing - that I dreamed I was writing to you about this dream. And here I am writing to you—except I feel like I'm dreaming. A sort of double deja vu.

Mark came back from the infirmary today—this was in the dream too. He lost his tongue. They said they were too late in getting to him. How did I know that would happen?

Jack

November 22

Mary,

Dr. Schwartz knows about you. Don't ask me how, but she does. Everything. Your friends, what organizations you belong to, where you work. She even described every detail of your apartment.

I remained silent during our session today. This is my new tactic. Don't say a word. Avoid all encounters, all confrontations.

But she looked at me with her miserable brown eyes and started to spew off all this information about you. She must have seen my reaction—my eyes must have reflected the hatred I feel for her—because she stopped suddenly and came over to me, shoved her severe little face into mine.

You think you can hide things from me? she said. You think I don't know everything about you—what you like and don't like, your sexual habits, the way you like to fold your shirts in threes?

She stood up and walked triumphantly over to her desk—that's the only way I can describe it, as if she had conquered me by telling me this information. Then she opened the drawer and pulled out a photo album.

You know what these are? she said. She opened it up and showed it to me. And inside were pictures of me—all sorts, Mary you can't believe it. There I was skinny-dipping at Jones Beach, dining, dancing, speaking with my associates at the party and—at the very end—you.

We know who she is, she said, because you're the one who told us. And she picked up my file and proceeded to tell me when I had told her all these things about you—she quoted specific sessions and told me what I had said in each one.

You want her to remain untouched? she said finally. Cooperate. It's as simple as that.

But what am I suppose to cooperate with?

Mary, you've got to run away, go into hiding. Please, Mary, I'm begging you.

November 24

Dear Mary,

Thanksgiving. I have some visitors. Even as I write these words, they are watching me.

Danny has been here for about two hours. He's been sitting with his blowtorch and his horrid grin, staring at me in silence. It's as if he wants to tell me something but can't. As if he wants to congratulate me. Don't ask me how I know that. It's just a feeling. I don't know why he has the blowtorch or what he intends to do with it. I've been trying to remain calm.

Dr. Schwartz arrived about half an hour ago and immediately asked what the problem was. No one answered. She looked coldly from me to the warden, as if we were responsible for ruining her holiday, then glanced over towards where Danny was sitting, without acknowledging him, as if he were some kind of ghost whose presence she was aware of but refused to confirm.

Suddenly, the warden asked me how I felt about my impending release. I told him I wasn't aware of it, but that when it was granted, I was ready to return to society to lead a productive life. He seemed pleased with this, but Dr. Schwartz immediately objected. She insisted I wasn't ready. The warden brushed her off, as if she were a fly on his lapel, and pulled out a picture from his jacket pocket as evidence of my cure. It was grainy and unfocused, but it seemed to be of a woman, naked, with large black blotches all over her disfigured body, the bare bone just evident. On the bottom was the initial "M."

But I had no time to react because Danny, who had remained silent up to this point, walked over and took it from the warden to examine. Then he turned to me.

Nice job, he said, smiling at me, a big, proud smile, the smile of a master pleased with the work of his apprentice, then went back to inspecting the tip of his blowtorch as if it were a gun that had just been shot.

Now I'm writing this letter. I don't know why or how I came to be doing this. It's part of the process, Dr. Schwartz says. My farewell to malady. What does she mean? They're all waiting around silently—Danny with his torch, Dr. Schwartz with her cold, expressionless face, the warden with his kind smile which makes me feel unsettled. It's as if they want me to write to you, as if this is the reason they have come.

Because I am writing, and they are watching. Because they are allowing me to.

Mary, what have I done? Mary, please, you've got to answer me. Tell me you're alive. Tell me you're okay. Tell me why they're here, why they've been standing around, staring at me for so long. Tell me, Mary, why suddenly they're now gone, vanished, like ghosts, as if they had never been here at all. Have I gone mad? Have they managed to take total possession of my thoughts? Mary, tell me why I now find a big fat turkey on my table with all the trimmings, why there's music, why they have tapped into all my weaknesses, why now I discover, on a bone china plate, under a polished silver server, a tongue, freshly cut, steeping in blood, and beside it a picture I took of you when we were in college. Tell me why I find myself suddenly immune, as if it doesn't matter, why I find myself instead preparing to dine, carving the turkey, laying each slice neatly on the gold-trimmed plate they have provided me, serving myself mashed potatoes, candied yams, arranging the cranberry sauce neatly on the dish. And the wine, Mary. They have provided me wine. Pinot Noir. My favorite. I pour it, savor its aroma, let it linger on my palate and completely forget about you. As if I no longer have any feelings. As if they have torched them away, carefully excised them and left me numb and helpless as only they can do.

Lobotomy, Mary? Remember? *One Flew Over the Cuckoo's Nest*? Only this isn't physical, Mary. This is much more sophisticated. We are, after all, at the dawn of a new millennium.

And now, as I get ready to enjoy my first real Thanksgiving dinner in five years, one I have apparently earned, I pick up the radio from which come strains of Tchaikovsky's *1812 Overture*—oh, how glorious, Mary, complete with canons and fireworks—a tiny radio I never had but which has been prominently placed on my table—a small radio, like the one Danny was given a few months ago, with rich, magnificent sound—and I find myself changing the station, searching for the BBC or some other independent source of information, and I am at last in heaven. I am at last, for a while at least, enjoying life as I imagine I will upon my release.

I'm sorry, Mary. Please forgive me. I want to enjoy this moment. I want to relish every nuance, every second.

Jack

December 2

I'm crying, Mary, I'm crying and I can't stop. Mary, they've broken me. I thought I could play their game, but you can't, Mary. Or maybe you can, but you can never win.

Mary, they've ripped out my tongue. After all I did for them. Why? I couldn't have told anyone even if I wanted to. Don't they realize that? Why don't they let me be? Or kill me, get it all over with? But this is prison, Mary. This is, after all, punishment. For going against them, for defying them. No, death would be too easy. Too quick. Too merciful, even if they tortured me until the last weak breath left my body.

I was a fool to think they would ever release me. Instead, today, I am scheduled for amputation. An "operation," they call it. A "slight correction." Only it will be my left hand. The one I write with. The one I used to draft all those treatises to expose them, to draft all these letters to you. Not so slight, after all, is it?

Mary, I don't know what to say and have so little time to say it. Forgive me? You were a willing partner, after all. Wish you well? Hardly. After all, we do what we must to survive. Do you detect a little Darwin in me? Does that surprise you? I mean we all have our weaknesses and fall so easily into them, allow them be exploited. When push comes to shove, as they say.

Mary, I know you will never read this. As I know you've never read any of my letters. It's the way things are. I know that. So believe me when I tell you I was only doing what I thought was right.

Jack

Mavis Gallant

Scarves, Beads, Sandals

AFTER THREE YEARS, Mathilde and Theo Schurz were divorced, without a mean thought, and even Theo says she is better off now, married to Alain Poix. (Or "Poids." Or "Poisse.") Theo may be speaking the truth when he says he can't keep in mind every facet of the essential Alain. Mathilde moved in with Alain six months before the wedding, in order to become acquainted with domestic tedium and annoying habits, should they occur, and so avoid making the same mistake (marriage piled onto infatuation) twice. They rented, and are now gradually buying, a two-bedroom place on Rue Saint-Didier, in the Sixteenth Arrondissement. In every conceivable way it is distant from the dispiriting south fringe of Montparnasse, where Theo continues to reside, close to several of the city's grimmest hospitals, and always under some threat or other—eviction, plagues of mice, demolition of the whole cul-de-sac of sagging one-story studios. If Theo had been attracted by her "physical aspect"—Mathilde's new, severe term for beauty—Alain accepts her as a concerned and contributing partner, intellectually and spiritually. This is not her conclusion. It is her verdict.

Theo wonders about "spiritually." It sounds to him like a moist west wind, ready to veer at any minute, with soft alternations of sun and rain. Whatever Mathilde means, or wants to mean, even the idea of the partnership should keep her fully occupied. Nevertheless, she finds time to drive across Paris, nearly every Saturday afternoon, to see how Theo is getting along without her. (Where is Alain? In close liaison with a computer, she says.) She brings Theo flowering shrubs from the market on Ile de la Cite, still hoping to enliven the blighted yard next to the studio, and food in covered dishes—whole, delicious meals; not Poix leftovers—and fresh news about Alain.

Recently, Alain was moved to a new office—a room divided in two, really, but on the same floor as the Minister and with part of an eighteenth-century fresco overhead. If Alain looks straight up, perhaps to ease a cramp in his neck, he can take in Apollo—just Apollo's head—watching Daphne turn into a laurel tree. Owing to the perspective of the work, Alain has the entire Daphne—roots, bark, and branches, and her small pink Enlightenment face peering through leaves. (The person next door has inherited Apollo's torso, dressed in Roman armor, with a short white skirt, and his legs and feet.) To Theo, from whom women manage to drift away, the situation might seem another connubial bad dream, but Alain interprets it as an allegory of free feminine choice. If he weren't so pressed with other work, he might write something along that line: an essay of about a hundred and fifty pages, published between soft white covers and containing almost as many colored illustrations as there are pages of print; something a reader can absorb during a weekend and still attend to the perennial border on Sunday afternoon.

He envisions (so does Mathilde) a display on the "recent nonfiction" table in a Saint-Germain-des-Pres Bookshop, between stacks of something new about waste disposal and something new about Jung. Instead of writing the essay, Alain applies his trained mind and exacting higher education to shoring up French values against the Anglo-Saxon mud slide. On this particular Saturday, he is trying to batter into proper French one more untranslatable expression: "airbag." It was on television again the other day, this time spoken by a woman showing black-and-white industrial drawings. Alain would rather take the field against terms that have greater resonance, are more blatantly English, such as "shallow" and "bully" and "wishful thinking," but no one, so far, has ever tried to use them in a commercial.

So Mathilde explains to Theo as she sorts his laundry, starts the machine, puts clean sheets on the bed. She admires Theo, as an artist—it is what drew her to him in the first place—but since becoming Mme. Poix she has tended to see him as unemployable. At an age when Theo was still carrying a portfolio of drawings up and down and around Rue de Seine, looking for a small but adventurous gallery to take him in, Alain has established a position in the cultural apparat. It may even survive the next elections: he is too valuable an asset to be swept out and told to find a job in the private sector. Actually, the private sector could ask nothing better. Everyone wants Alain. Publishers want him. Foreign universities want him. Even America is waiting, in spite of the uncompromising things he has said about the hegemony and how it encourages well-bred Europeans to eat pizza slices in the street.

Theo has never heard of anybody with symbolic imagery, or even half an image, on his office ceiling outlasting a change of government. The queue for space of that kind consists of one ravenous human resource after the other, pushing hard. As for the private sector, its cultural subdivisions are hard up for breathing room, in the dark, stalled between floors. Alain requires the clean horizons and rich oxygen flow of the governing class. Theo says none of this. He removes foil from bowls and dishes, to see what Mathilde wants him to have for dinner. What can a Theo understand about an Alain? Theo never votes. He has never registered, he forgets the right date. All at once the campaign is over. The next day familiar faces, foxy or benign, return to the news, described as untested but eager to learn. Elections are held in spring, perhaps to make one believe in growth, renewal. One rainy morning in May, sooner or later, Alain will have to stack his personal files, give up Apollo and Daphne, cross a Ministry courtyard on the first lap of a march into the private sector. Theo sees him stepping along cautiously, avoiding the worst of the puddles. Alain can always teach, Theo tells himself. It is what people say about aides and assistants they happen to know, as the astonishing results unfold on the screen.

Alain knows Theo, of course. Among his mixed feelings, Alain has no trouble finding the esteem due to a cultural bulwark: Theo and his work have entered the enclosed space known as "time-honored." Alain even knows about the Poids and Poisse business, but does not hold it against Theo; according to Mathilde, one no longer can be sure when he is trying to show he has a sense of humor or when he is losing brain cells. He was at the wedding, correctly dressed, suit, collar, and tie, looking distinguished—something like Braque at the age of fifty, Alain said, but thinner, taller, blue-eyed, lighter hair, finer profile. By then they were at the reception, drinking champagne under a white marquee, wishing they could sit down. It was costing Mathilde's father the earth—the venue was a restaurant in the Bois de Boulogne—but he was so thankful to be rid of Theo as a son-in-law that he would have hired Versailles, if one could.

The slow, winding currents of the gathering had brought Theo, Alain, and Mathilde together. Theo with one finger pushed back a strayed lock of her hair; it was reddish gold, the shade of a persimmon. Perhaps he was measuring his loss and might even, at last, say something embarrassing and true. Actually, he was saying that Alain's description—blue-eyed, etc.—sounded more like Max Ernst. Alain backtracked, said it was Balthus he'd had in mind. Mathilde, though not Alain, was still troubled by Theo's wedding gift, a botched painting he had been tinkering with for years. She had been Mme. Poix for a few hours, but still felt responsible for Theo's gaffes and imperfections. When he did not reply at once, she said she hoped he did not object to being told he was like Balthus. Balthus was the best-looking artist of the past hundred years, with the exception of Picasso.

Alain wondered what Picasso had to do with the conversation. Theo looked nothing like him: he came from Alsace. He, Alain, had never understood the way women preferred male genius incarnated as short, dark, and square-shaped. "Like Celtic gnomes," said Theo, just to fill in. Mathilde saw the roses in the restaurant garden through a blur which was not the mist of happiness. Alain had belittled her, on their wedding day, in the presence of her first husband. Her first husband had implied she was attracted to gnomes. She let her head droop. Her hair slid over her cheeks, but Theo, this time, left it alone. Both men looked elsewhere—Alain because tears were something new, Theo out of habit. The Minister stood close by, showing admirable elegance of manner—not haughty, not familiar; careful, kind, like the Archbishop of Paris at a humble sort of funeral, Theo said, thinking to cheer up Mathilde. Luckily, no one overheard. Her mood was beginning to draw attention. Many years before, around the time of the Algerian War, a relative of Alain's mother had married an aunt of the Minister. The outer rims of the family circles had quite definitely overlapped. It was the reason the Minister had come to the reception and why he had stayed, so far, more than half an hour.

Mathilde was right; Theo must be losing brain cells at a brisk rate now. First Celtic gnomes, then the Archbishop of Paris; and, of course, the tactless, stingy, offensive gift. Alain decided to smile, extending greetings to everyone. He was attempting to say, I am entirely happy on this significant June day. He was happy, but not entirely. Perhaps Mathilde was recalling her three years with Theo and telling herself nothing lasts. He wished Theo would do something considerate, such as disappear. A cluster of transparent molecules, the physical remainder of the artist T. Schurz, would dance in the sun, above the roses. Theo need not be dead—just gone.

"Do you remember, Theo, the day we got married," said Mathilde, looking up at the wrong man, by accident intercepting the smile Alain was using to reassure the Minister and the others. "Everybody kept saying we had made a mistake. We decided to find out how big a mistake it was, so in the evening we went to Montmartre and had our palms read. Theo was told he could have been an artist but was probably a merchant seaman. His left hand was full of little shipwrecks." She may have been waiting for Alain to ask, "What about you? What did your hand say?" In fact, he was thinking just about his own. In both palms he had lines that might be neat little roads, straight or curved, and a couple of spidery stars.

At first, Theo had said he would give them a painting. Waiting, they kept a whole wall bare. Alain supposed it would be one of the great recent works; Mathilde thought she knew better. Either Alain had forgotten about having carried off the artist's wife or he had decided it didn't matter to Theo. That aside, Theo and Theo's dealer were tight as straitjackets about his work. Mathilde owned nothing, not even a crumpled sketch saved from a dustbin. The dealer had taken much of the earlier work off the market, which did not mean Theo was allowed to give any away. He burned most of his discards and kept just a few unsalable things in a shed. Speaking of his wedding gift, Theo said the word "painting" just once and never again: he mentioned some engravings—falling rain or falling snow—or else a plain white tile he could dedicate and sign. Mathilde made a reference to the empty wall. A larger work, even unfinished, even slightly below Theo's dealer's exacting standards, would remind Mathilde of Theo for the rest of her life.

Five days later, the concierge at Rue Saint-Didier took possession of a large oil study of a nude with red hair—poppy red, not like Mathilde's—prone on a bed, her face concealed in pillows. Mathilde recognized the studio, as it had been before she moved in and cleaned it up. She remembered the two reproductions, torn out of books or catalogues, askew on the wall. One showed a pair of Etruscan figures, dancing face to face, the other a hermit in a landscape. When the bed became half Mathilde's, she took them down. She had wondered if Theo would mind, but he never noticed—at any rate, never opened an inquiry.

"Are you sure this thing is a Schurz?" said Alain. Nothing else bothered him. He wondered, at first, if Theo had found the picture at a junk sale and had signed it as a joke. The true gift, the one they were to cherish and display, would come along later, all the more to be admired because of the scare. But Theo never invented jokes; he blundered into them.

"I am not that woman," Mathilde said. Of course not. Alain had never supposed she was. There was the crude red of the hair, the large backside, the dirty feet, and then the date—"1979"—firm and black and in the usual place, to the right of "T. Schurz." At that time, Mathilde was still reading translations of Soviet poetry, in love with a teacher of Russian at her lycee, and had never heard of "T. Schurz." In saying this, Alain showed he remembered the story of her life. If she'd had a reason to forgive him, about anything, she would have absolved him on the spot; then he spoiled the moment by declaring that it made no difference. The model was not meant to be anyone in particular.

Mathilde thought of Emma, Theo's first long-term companion (twelve years), but by '79 Emma must have been back in Alsace, writing cookery books with a woman friend. Julita (six years) fit the date but had worn a thick yellow braid down her back. She was famous for having tried to strangle Theo, but her hands were too small—she could not get a grip. After the throttling incident, which had taken place in a restaurant, Julita had packed a few things, most of them Theo's, and moved to the north end of Paris, where she would not run into him. Emma left Theo a microwave oven, Julita a cast-iron cat, standing on its hind legs, holding a tray. She had stolen it from a stand at the flea market, Theo told Mathilde, but the story sounded unlikely: the cat was heavy to lift, let alone be fetched across a distance. Two people would have been needed; perhaps one had been Theo. Sometimes, even now, some old friend from the Julita era tells Theo that Julita is ill or hard up and that he ought to help her out. Theo will say he doesn't know where she is or else, yes, he will do it tomorrow. She is like art taken off the market now, neither here nor there. The cat is still in the yard, rising out of broken flowerpots, empty bottles. Julita had told Theo it was the one cat that would never run away. She hung its neck with some amber beads Emma had overlooked in her flight, then pocketed the amber and left him the naked cat.

When Mathilde was in love with Theo and jealous of women she had never met, she used to go to an Indian shop, in Montparnasse, where first Emma, then Julita had bought their flat sandals and white embroidered shifts and long gauzy skirts, black and pink and indigo. She imagined what it must have been like to live, dress, go to parties, quarrel, and make up with Theo in the seventies. Emma brushed her brown hair upside down, to create a great drifting mane. A woman in the Indian store did Julita's braid, just because she liked Julita. Mathilde bought a few things, skirts and sandals, but never wore them. They made her look alien, bedraggled, like the Romanian Gypsy women begging for coins along Rue de Rennes. She did not want to steal from a market or fight with Theo in bistros. She belonged to a generation of women who showed a lot of leg and kept life smooth, tight-fitting, close-woven. Theo was right: she was better off with Alain.

Still, she had the right to know something about the woman she had been offered as a gift. It was no good asking directly; Theo might say it was a journalist who came to tape his memoirs or the wife of a Lutheran dignitary or one of his nieces from Alsace. Instead, she asked him to speak to Alain; out of aesthetic curiosity, she said, Alain acquired the facts of art. Theo often did whatever a woman asked, unless it was important. Clearly, this was not. Alain took the call in his office; at that time, he still had a cubicle with a bricked-up window. Nobody recalled who had ordered the bricks or how long ago. He worked by the light of a neon fixture that flickered continually and made his eyes water. Summoned by an aide to the Minister, on propitious afternoons by the Minister himself (such summonses were more and more frequent), he descended two flights, using the staircase in order to avoid a giddy change from neon tube to the steadier glow of a chandelier. He brought with him only a modest amount of paperwork. He was expected to store everything in his head.

Theo told Alain straight out that he had used Julita for the pose. She slept much of the day and for that reason made an excellent model: was never tired, never hungry, never restless, never had to break off for a cigarette. The picture had not worked out and he had set it aside. Recently he had looked at it again and decided to alter Julita from the neck up. Alain thought he had just been told something of consequence; he wanted to exchange revelations, let Theo know he had not enticed Mathilde away but had merely opened the net into which she could jump. She had grabbed Theo in her flight, perhaps to break the fall. But Alain held still; it would be unseemly to discuss Mathilde. Theo was simply there, like an older relative who has to be considered and mollified, though no one knows why. There was something flattering about having been offered an unwanted and unnecessary explanation; few artists would have bothered to make one. It was as though Theo had decided to take Alain seriously. Alain thanked him.

Unfortunately, the clarification had made the painting even less interesting than it looked. Until then, it had been a dud Schurz but an honest vision. The subject, a woman, entirely womanly, had been transfigured by Schurz's reactionary visual fallacy (though honest, if one accepted the way his mind worked) into a hefty platitude; still, it was art. Now, endowed with a name and, why not, an address, a telephone number, a social-security number, and a personal history, Theo's universal statement dwindled to a footnote about Julita—second long-term companion of T. Schurz, first husband of Mathilde, future first wife of Alain Poix. A white tile with a date and a signature would have shown more tact and common sense.

All this Alain said to Mathilde that night, as they ate their dinner next to the empty wall. Mathilde said she was certain Theo had gone to considerable trouble to choose something he believed they would understand and appreciate and that would enhance their marriage. It was one of her first lies to Alain: Theo had gone out to the shed where he kept his shortfalls and made a final decision about a dead loss. Perhaps he guessed they would never hang it and so damage his reputation, although as a rule he never imagined future behavior more than a few minutes away. Years ago, in a bistro on Rue Stanislas, he had drawn a portrait of Julita on the paper tablecloth, signed and dated it, torn it off, even made the edges neat. It was actually in her hands when he snatched it back, ripped it to shreds, and set the shreds on fire in an ashtray. It was then that Julita had tried to get him by the throat.

Yesterday, Friday, an April day, Theo was awakened by a hard beam of light trained on his face. There was a fainter light at the open door, where the stranger had entered easily. The time must have been around five o'clock. Theo could make out an outline, drawn in gray chalk: leather jacket, close-cropped head. (Foreign Legion deserter? Escaped prisoner? Neo-Nazi? Drugs?) He spoke a coarse, neutral, urban French—the old Paris accent was dying out—and told Theo that if he tried to move or call he, the intruder, might hurt him. He did not say how. They all watch the same programs, Theo told himself. He is young and he repeats what he has seen and heard. Theo had no intention of moving and there was no one to call. His thoughts were directed to the privy, in the yard. He hoped the young man would not take too long to discover there was nothing to steal, except a small amount of cash. He would have told him where to find it, but that might be classed as calling out. His checkbook was in a drawer of Emma's old desk, his bank card behind the snapshot of Mathilde, propped on the shelf above the sink. The checkbook was no good to the stranger, unless he forced Theo to sign all the checks. Theo heard him scuffing about, heard a drawer being pulled. He shut his eyes, opened them to see the face bent over him, the intent and watchful expression, like a lover's, and the raised arm and the flashlight (probably) wrapped in one of Mathilde's blue-and-white tea towels.

He came to in full daylight. His nose had bled all over the pillows, and the mattress was sodden. He got up and walked quite steadily, barefoot, over the stones and gravel of the yard; returning to the studio, he found some of yesterday's coffee still in the pot. He heated it up in a saucepan, poured in milk, drank, and kept it down. Only when that was done did he look in a mirror. He could hide his blackened eyes behind sunglasses but not the raw bruise on his forehead or his swollen nose. He dragged the mattress outside and spread it in the cold April sunlight. By four o'clock, Mathilde's announced arrival time—for it seemed to him today could be Saturday—the place was pretty well cleaned up, mattress back on the bed, soiled bedclothes rolled up, pushed in a corner. He found a banquet-size tablecloth, probably something of Emma's, and drew it over the mattress. Only his cash had vanished; the checkbook and bank card lay on the floor. He had been attacked, for no reason, by a man he had never seen before and would be unable to recognize: his face had been neutral, like his voice. Theo turned on the radio and, from something said, discovered this was still Friday, the day before Mathilde's habitual visiting day. He had expected her to make the mattress dry in some magical and efficient, Mathilde-like way. He kept in the shed a couple of sleeping bags, for rare nights when the temperature fell below freezing. He got one of them out, gave it a shake, and spread it on top of the tablecloth. It would have to do for that night.

Today, Saturday, Mathilde brought a meal packed in a black-and-white bag from Fauchon: cooked asparagus, with the lemon-and-oil sauce in a jar, cold roast lamb, and a gratin of courgettes and tomatoes—all he has to do is turn on Emma's microwave—a Camembert, a round loaf of that moist and slightly sour bread, from the place on Rue du Cherche-Midi, which reminds Schurz of the bread of his childhood, a carton of thick cream, and a bowl of strawberries, washed and hulled. It is too early for French strawberries. These are from Spain, picked green, shipped palely pink, almost as hard as radishes, but they remind one that it is spring. Schurz barely notices seasons. He works indoors. If rain happens to drench the yard when he goes outside to the lavatory, he puts on the Alpine beret that was part of his uniform when he was eighteen and doing his military service.

Mathilde, moving out to live with Alain, took with her a picture of Theo from that period, wearing the beret and the thick laced-up boots and carrying the heavy skis that were standard issue. He skied and shot a rifle for eighteen months, even thought he might have made it a permanent career, if that was all there was to the Army. No one had yet fallen in love with him, except perhaps his mother. His life was simple then, has grown simpler now. The seasons mean nothing, except that green strawberries are followed by red. Weather means crossing the yard bareheaded or covered up.

Mathilde has noticed she is starting to think of him as "Schurz." It is what his old friends call Theo. This afternoon, she had found him looking particularly Schurz-like, sitting on a chair he had dragged outside, drinking tea out of a mug, with the string of the tea bag trailing. He had on an overcoat and the regimental beret. He did not turn to the gate when she opened it or get up to greet her or say a word. Mathilde had to walk all round him to see his face.

"My God, Schurz, what happened?"

"I tripped and fell in the dark and struck my head on the cat."

"I wish you'd get rid of it," she said.

She took the mug from his hands and went inside, to unpack his dinner and make fresh tea. The beret, having concealed none of the damage, was useless now. He removed it and hung it rakishly on the cat, on one ear. Mathilde returned with, first, a small folding garden table (her legacy), then with a tray and teacups and a teapot and a plate of sliced gingerbread, which she had brought him the week before. She poured his tea, put sugar in, stirred it, and handed him the cup.

She said, "Theo, how long do you think you can go on living here, alone?" (It was so pathetic, she rehearsed, for Alain. Theo was like a child; he had made the most absurd attempt at covering up the damage, and instead of putting the mattress out to dry he had turned the wet side down and slept on top of it, in a sleeping bag. Who was that famous writer who first showed signs of senility and incontinence on a bridge in Rome? I kept thinking of him. Schurz just sat there, like a guilty little boy. He caught syphilis when he was young and gave it to Emma; he said it was from a prostitute, in Montmartre, but I believe it was a married woman, the wife of the first collector to start buying his work. He can't stay there alone now. He simply can't. His checkbook and bank card were lying next to the trash bin. He must have been trying to throw them away.)

Her picture had been on the floor, too, the one taken the day she married Theo. Mathilde has a small cloud of red-gold hair and wears a short white dress and a jacket of the eighties, with shoulders so wide that her head seems unnaturally small, like a little ball of reddish fluff. Theo is next to her, not too close. He could be a relative or a family friend or even some old crony who heard the noise of the party and decided to drop in. The photograph is posed here, in the yard. One can see a table laden with bottles, and a cement-and-stucco structure—the privy, with the door shut, for a change—and a cold-water tap and a bucket lying on its side. You had to fill the bucket and take it in with you.

Schurz never tried to improve the place or make it more comfortable. His reason was, still is, that he might be evicted at any time. Any month, any day, the police and the bailiffs will arrive. He will be rushed off the premises, with just the cast-iron cat as a relic of his old life.

"I'll tell you what happened," he said, showing her his mess of a face. "Yesterday morning, while I was still asleep, a man broke in, stole some money, and hit me with something wrapped in a towel. It must have been his flashlight."

(Oh, if you had heard him! she continued to prepare for Alain. A comic-strip story. The truth is he is starting to miss his footing and to do himself damage, and he pees in his sleep, like a baby. What kind of doctor do we need for him? What sort of specialist? A geriatrician? He's not really old, but there's been the syphilis, and he has always done confused and crazy things, like giving us that picture, when we really wanted a plain, pure tile.)

Schurz at this moment is thinking of food. He would like to be handed a plate of pork *ragout* with noodles, swimming in gravy; but nobody makes that now. Or stewed eels in red wine, with the onions cooked soft. Or a cutlet of venison, browned in butter on both sides, with a puree of chestnuts. What he does not want is clear broth with a poached egg in it, or any sort of a salad. When he first came to Paris, the cheapest meals were the heartiest. His mother had said, "Send me a Paris hat," not meaning it; though perhaps she did. His money, when he had any, went to supplies for his work or rent or things to eat.

Only old women wore hats now. There were hats in store windows, dusty windows, in narrow streets—black hats, for funerals and widows. But no widow under the age of sixty ever bought one. Young women wore hats at the end of summer, tilted straw things, that they tried on just for fun. When they took the hats off, their hair would spring loose. The face, freed of shadow, took on a different shape, seemed fuller, unmysterious, as bland as the moon. There was a vogue for bright scarves, around the straw hats, around the hair, wound around the neck along with strings of bright beads, loosely coiled—sand-colored or coral or a hard kind of blue. The beads cast colored reflections on the skin of a throat or on a scarf of a different shade, like a bead diluted in water. Schurz and his friends ate cheap meals in flaking courtyards and on terraces where the tables were enclosed in a hedge of brittle, unwatered shrubs. Late at night, the girls and young women would suddenly find that everything they had on was too tight. It was the effect of the warm end-of-summer night and the food and the red wine and the slow movement of the conversation. It slid without wavering from gossip to mean gossip to art to life-in-art to living without boundaries. A scarf would come uncoiled and hang on the back of a chair or a twig of the parched hedge; as it would hang, later, over the foot of someone's bed. Not often Schurz's (not often enough), because he lived in a hotel near the Cafe Mabillon, long before all those places were renovated and had elevators put in and were given a star in some of the guidebooks. A stiff fine had to be paid by any client caught with a late-night visitor. The police used to patrol small hotels and knock on doors just before morning, looking for French people in trouble with the law and for foreigners with fake passports and no residence permits. When they found an extra guest in the room, usually a frantic young woman trying to pull the sheet over her face, the hotelkeeper was fined, too, and the tenant thrown out a few hours later. It was not a question of sexual morality but just of rules.

When dinner was almost finished, the women would take off their glass beads and let them drop in a heap among the ashtrays and coffee cups and on top of the wine stains and scribbled drawings. Their high-heeled sandals were narrow and so tight that they had to keep their toes crossed; and at last they would slip them off, unobserved, using first one foot, then the other. Scarfless, shoeless, unbound, delivered, they waited for the last wine bottle to be emptied and the last of the coffee to be drunk or spilled before they decided what they specifically wanted or exactly refused. This was not like a memory to Theo but like part of the present time, something that unfolded gradually, revealing mysteries and satisfactions.

In the studio, behind him, Mathilde was making telephone calls. He heard her voice but not her words. On a late Saturday afternoon, she would be recording her messages on other people's machines: he supposed there must be one or two to doctors, and one for the service that sends vans and men to take cumbersome objects away, such as a soiled mattress. Several brief inquiries must have been needed before she could find Theo a hotel room, free tonight, at a price he would accept and on a street he would tolerate. The long unbroken monologue must have been for Alain, explaining that she would be much later than expected, and why. On Monday she would take Theo to the Bon Marché department store and make him buy a mattress, perhaps a whole new bed. Now here was a memory, a brief, plain stretch of the past: love apart, she had married him because she wanted to be Mme. T. Schurz. She would not go on attending parties and gallery openings as Schurz's young friend. Nobody knew whether she was actually living with him or writing something on his work or tagging along for the evening. She did not have the look of a woman who would choose to settle for a studio that resembled a garage or, really, for Schurz. It turned out she could hardly wait to move in, scrape and wax whatever he had in the way of furniture, whitewash the walls. She trained climbing plants over the wire fence outside, even tried to grow lemon trees in terra-cotta tubs. The tubs are still there.

She came toward him now, carrying the bag she had packed so that he would have everything he needed at the hotel. "Don't touch the bruise," she said, gently, removing the hand full of small shipwrecks. The other thing she said today, which he is bound to recall later on, was "You ought to start getting used to the idea of leaving this place. You know that it is going to be torn down."

Well, it is true. At the entrance to the doomed and decaying little colony there is a poster, damaged by weather and vandals, on which one can still see a depiction of the structure that will cover the ruin, once it has finally been brought down: a handsome biscuit-colored multipurpose urban complex comprising a library, a crèche, a couple of municipal offices, a screening room for projecting films about Bedouins or whales, a lounge where elderly people may spend the whole day playing board games, a theater for amateur and professional performances, and four low-rent work units for painters, sculptors, poets, musicians, and photographers. (A waiting list of two thousand names was closed some years ago.) It seemed to Theo that Julita was still around at the time when the poster was put up. The project keeps running into snags—aesthetic, political, mainly economic. One day the poster will have been his view of the future for more than a third of his life.

Mathilde backed out of the cul-de-sac, taking care (he does not like being driven), and she said, "Theo, we are near all these hospitals. If you think you should have an X-ray at once, we can go to an emergency service. I can't decide, because I really don't know how you got hurt."

"Not now." He wanted today to wind down. Mathilde, in her mind, seemed to have gone beyond dropping him at his hotel. He had agreed to something on Rue Delambre, behind the Coupole and the Dome. She was on the far side of Paris, with Alain. As she drove on, she asked Theo if he could suggest suitable French for a few English expressions: "divided attention" and "hard-driven" and "matchless perfection," the latter in one word.

"I hope no one steals my Alpine beret," he said. "I left it hanging on the cat."

Those were the last words they exchanged today. It is how they said goodbye.

Victoria Lancelotta

Festival

THERE WERE THESE THINGS I saw through the window: our parents' coffee table, askew, furrows in the carpet from where it usually sat—that's how well I could see, how clearly. The light was on, dim light but enough—it was dark where I stood in the backyard, outside the living room window. So: there was the table, the couch of nubby plaid, my sister on her back, head hung over the armrest, blonde hair brushing the floor, and on my sister was a boy whose name I've since forgotten, jeans crumpled to his knees, skinny hips, white ass, rocking himself into her like that.

Then I was fifteen, old enough to know enough to watch—that would be me in a year, I thought, standing in the backyard, waiting for the dog to finish, cold wet grass and weeds scratching at my legs. I moved closer to the window, to the side, my cheek almost against the brick of the house, angling, squinting. Watch, I thought then: this is a thing I need to know.

This boy on my sister, on her pretty white skin. We'd slept together, my sister and I, curled into her narrow bed after our mother turned out the light. After she shut the door I left my own bed, fit myself against my sister like a snail to its shell, my face in her tangled hair. She smelled like yewberries then, at eight or nine, still taller than me and thin, dirty feet, hands stained red from berry paint.

I pressed my face against the house, shooed the dog away, watched this boy on top of her. I watched the shadows on the ceiling, shaped, humped, moving in almost even time, sharp above the lamp and blurry farther out. I watched my sister's hands on his back, gripping the cheap fabric of his shirt and my own hands I know now were clenched, fisted tight against my legs. I was afraid to open them. I watched until I saw the last thing, the thing I saw before they finished: beyond the couch, up three steps to the doorway of the kitchen, the wall there covered with pictures of us, straw hats, sunburns, sand, our father lifting us both above a wave, one on either hand, tracking the steps up to the kitchen landing, to where our father stood.

If my sister had lifted her head, had opened her eyes enough to see, their eyes would have met. I watched our father watching them, my sister in between us with her hair dragging the carpet and her arms twisted above her head in her tangled sleeves.

I cannot, now, imagine his face, shadowed, outlined, nothing more. I thought he must have had no face, not then, not watching that—how would that face look? Mouth set or slightly open, eyes bleary or not, hooded, red-rimmed, shot through with gin-soaked veins. His little girl, his darling—I knew who he loved best.

My sister taught me this: that our father could be charmed, teased, bought—with drinks at the door when he got home, with kisses to the back of his neck as he bent over the paper, with perfume behind our ears at dinner. Our mother was no competition for her. Our mother, who had been beautiful, had woken one morning in a house that was no longer hers, had woken to find it given over to her oldest daughter while she slept. Walls, windows, doors, fingerprinted and smudged, strands of my sister's hair like voodoo trails all over.

They slept in separate beds, our parents, the reach of a nighttable between them, their door open across from our closed one, and in my sister's bed I smelled yewberries, faint, bitter and early in August. We mashed them in the backyard into paste, striped our cheeks and foreheads, sharpened sticks the length of babies' arms into spears. My arms were mapped with scratches, scabbed and then picked clean. We had the same hands, thin-skinned, backs traced by veins in winter, dark with dirt and sun in summer, too smooth yet to be leathery then. Our feet, too, the same, narrow and bony, toes like monkeys had said our father, long and grasping. My sister could write her name with a marker held in her curled toes.

My sister's husband, the first time we were together, said to me *She told me the two of you were the same.* He wrapped his hands in my hair, darker than hers and not as long, never quite as long, wrapped his hands and pulled until my head rocked back, until I thought my breath would stop. He licked the sweat that slicked my throat, that ran between my breasts. We were in my bedroom which was hot and oven-close, windows facing an alley, the back lot of a church. There was a festival: the bingo hall, the wheel of fortune, the priests who sat at paper-covered tables and ate sausage wrapped in dripping napkins and foil. There were the smells of grilling meat and fried dough, burnt sugar, sweat and sweet perfume.

My sister's husband told me things about her I already knew. He told me he loved her and he told me how much.

Yewberries are poisonous. Our mother scrubbed our hands and faces with soap and disinfectant. She dusted tables and polished mirrors, served us dinner. She never wore an apron. On her dresser were jars and bottles, makeup I never saw her wear. We used this, then, after the berries, warpaint first and then done right, lips red, eyes lined, practicing. We sat for dinner one night like that and our mother said *Get that garbage off your faces. I will not have that at my table.*

For our mother, it was that simple: the protocol, the rules, the things we could not do. We knew not to set the table with napkins laid on plates, with goblets upside down.

Later, through the bedroom wall: *Your daughters run wild, Richard, like trash.* And our father's voice, indistinct, not soothing, and the clink of ice on glass. When the lights were out I heard him walking, his tread uneven, one step heavier than the other. He limped, a fracture badly healed, his car accordioned a year before. I knew when he stood in our bedroom doorway: that tread, the creak of door, the smell of cigarettes still on his shirt from work. This was a smell I hated, a smell I pulled away from when I hugged him every night, the smell of where he'd been. I didn't think of this until later, until after my sister had gone and I stood waiting by the side of the road for a car that didn't come, waiting for that boy to come for me like he had come for her, lighting one cigarette off the end of another.

Now, I time myself. A cigarette on the hour, every hour: not even a pack a day. There are lines around my mouth, at the corners of my eyes. Suck, pull, squint. I am aging by the clock.

The boy that night was Joe, or Jim, I think—the name on the patch of a shirt I'd seen him wear before, the kind mechanics wear. But those are shirts he got used, a quarter from a bin at the back of a thrift store, wrinkled and stained. Our father watched that inside his daughter, a boy in a shirt with someone else's name on it, and I waited outside the window, how long? Only minutes, I think now, with the dog whining at my ankles, waiting. Ten years later I stood next to the altar, watching her on our father's arm, coming almost crooked down the aisle, almost lurching our father was by then, and I thought the limp was hers, that by the time they reached the altar I would have to hold her up. Across from me the groom cleared his throat, coughed, looked down at his shoes. Our father's eyes up close were yellowed, and I thought for just one moment that he would stop, refuse to take another step; that he would pick my sister up and run with her, back up the aisle and out the door.

Her husband called me on a Sunday, after how many months? Not even a year. He called and said *Please, meet me, I need to talk to you.*

It would be a lie for me to say I didn't know then. I dressed: nothing special, not outright, and black silk underneath. He would tell me there were problems, he would say they were her fault, and I would believe him because it would be easy, because I would have no reason not to. I put on lipstick and perfume and got into my car, thinking. I would say: She is difficult, she has always been difficult. You are not to blame if she lies to you, if she hides things from you. We all know. I would put my hand on his and speak quietly, make him lean to hear me. Do you want me to talk to her, I would say.

As it happened: I bought him a drink and listened to him talk about her, things I'd heard before in my mother's voice. *Anything that happens to her will be your fault, Richard, do you understand that?* We sat in a bar for an hour before leaving. He followed me back, parked in the back lot of the church. I thought as I walked up the steps, opened my door, and let him go in first: This is the worst thing I've ever done, the one unforgivable thing, and there will be no witnesses.

And I waited for someone to stop me. I stood in front of him and unbuttoned my shirt, stepped out of my pants, waiting for him to say *Don't do this,* stood in that underwear I'd bought with my sister, let her pick out and never worn because I didn't wear things like that. I stood, waiting, waiting for anything, for my father's voice in my ears, for his face I couldn't see from where I stood that night. My sister's husband put his tongue in my mouth and I thought I tasted her.

Once, not long after my sister had gone, I climbed from my window and ran down the street, ready to spread my legs in the back of a stolen car. I walked two miles. I stood at the locked gate of a park by the road, I leaned up on chainlink fence and smoked. I waited an hour before turning back, before walking home thinking *There was an accident, he got caught, got arrested,* and wanting these things to be true.

When I got home every light in the house was burning. *Stupid little whore,* my father said at the front door, my mother behind him, shaking. He caught me by my hair, pulled me in, his bad leg dragging, catching on the carpet's edge. His glass was on the coffee table, the ice cubes melting, condensation puddling on the wood already shadowed by old water stains. When he slapped me, his hand was cold and wet. *I should take your pants down,* he said, *but that's been done already.*

All right, I thought, think that, it's the easy thing, the thing you've gotten used to.

He hadn't stopped them, that I know. I didn't watch them finish. I sat down in the grass, the dog's head in my lap, wet nose quivering, snapping at nightbugs. I didn't hear them finish, but if I had, would I have known the sound—a choke of breath, a long exhale? I didn't hear our father walk away—it must have been so hard for him, to be that quiet on his leg, to balance all his weight on the sloping kitchen floor. There was no sound that night until the boy's car pulled away, and even that was not so loud; distant, low in the humid air, giving out to crickets and the whining of the dog.

There was, at the festival, a wooden pole, twenty-five feet high and covered in grease that dripped and ran in the sun. Men lined up beneath it, shirts off and given to their mothers or wives to hold, and dipped into a pile of sawdust at the base of the pole. They covered their bare chests with it, slapped it onto arms and legs, rubbed it between their sweating palms, and each, in his turn, attempted to climb. There was a cloth affixed to the top of the pole: this was what needed to be gotten.

From my bedroom window I could see them climb: the tops of their heads, hair matted with sweat and sawdust, faces tilted back or pressed to the slick wood, eyes squeezed shut to the glare of sun. The best came close, gripping with chalked knees and bare feet, taped hands, shoulders bunched and knotted, sunburnt, gaining inches, half a foot then slipping, praying for a rough spot where the grease had melted off. Some bled before they fell, each allowed three tries before moving to the side.

There was a band as well, and majorettes around the pole, girls eleven and twelve, most of them heavy, their wide dark nipples showing through the bodysuits, or else in bras that held up nothing, the flesh of their legs jiggling as they tossed and dropped batons. We had never looked like that, never been so soft and doughy. Our mother would not have had it. She starched and ironed t-shirts, made sure our nails were clean before we went to bed.

Our father took us on his lap until we no longer fit, even with our legs curled tightly to one side, and even then my sister kept on, twisting herself, tucking her knees up under her shirt until it was stretched and torn. In the summer, he held her there on the back porch, both of them watching my mother and me kneeling in the garden, digging rows for lettuce and for mint. If someone had seen us then, he would have smiled, thinking only of our parents, how lucky they were with their two girls, their garden and their house.

My mother taught me to pile dead leaves around the lettuce to protect the soil from the scorch of sun. She worked with heavy gloves on, her fingers moving through the earth and leaves, faster than I could barehanded. With me, though, she was patient; she had learned that much.

If someone had been watching he would have imagined our table at night: tomatoes and cucumbers piled, fresh mint and basil, the kitchen door opened onto our backyard, and peach soufflé for after, because our mother's hands could do that, could coax up eggs and milk and fruit, suspended, quivering, impossible to figure.

Her silence I only heard in relief, I only recognized when I heard her voice at night, rising up through the vents in our bedroom floor, or coming shrill from across the hall, and I thought *What has my mother said today, what has she said before now?* I heard my sister's name, enunciated, drawn out, my mother's voice insistent over her husband's slurring. My mother had been to college.

What are you teaching her? I heard my mother say, as clearly as though she were in bed next to me. *Do you have any idea what will happen to her after you're done with her? I won't let you do this with the other one, Richard. Not with her, not both of them, not both my girls.*

I had never heard her call us *mine.*

My face was to my sister's back, scratched by brambles from the woods behind our house, drops of drying blood on her nightgown, bits of bark still in her hair our father's brush had missed. When he came up to our room he knelt beside the bed, laid his head on the flowered sheet. I didn't move or turn: I could hear my mother moving in their room, the clink of jars on the dresser, the creak of closet doors, and our father's catch of breath in a haze of gin and lime. My sister slept on, turned away from me beside our father's hands.

There is no one thing that I remember, not before I watched that boy on top of her, nothing even after. She circled my father like some small moon, kept at no great distance by any force of gravity on either side of that night—before, after, no difference I could see. When she packed to leave, my mother and I sat at the kitchen table, waiting. The kitchen door was open, the grass outside high, brown-tipped towards the field behind our lawn where my father never watered. There was forsythia and pussy willow edging the garden, there was a vase of them on the table. The dog lay between our feet. We drank iced tea with mint.

I thought: If someone gets to the top of the pole, manages to snatch the cloth from it, one quick turn before sliding down and he would see us, would see my sister's husband pulling me to him by my ankles across the bed.

After my father slapped me my mother followed me to my room, closed the door behind us and took me in her arms. I wore no makeup, I had no money, my hips were narrow like my father's. The window I'd climbed from was still open. She turned down my sheets, took my clothes as I stripped. She brought her pillow in from her bed, propped it against the wall and sat.

The next morning she had not moved, not that I could see. My clothes were folded on my sister's bed.

The festival ends today. The crowd is denser, men pressed around the stalls. My sister's husband leans from my window, naked, visible to the line of his hip for anyone who wants to know. His back is slick, his hairline almost dripping. I think he could climb the pole: if he were my husband I would want him to.

He has told me, these past days, that he does not know what to do. He says this over endlessly, as though by saying it he will somehow come to understand. I can't make her hear me, he says.

I have no explanation. I think of her, of sleeping at her back, of the paint striped on her skin. I tell him: I don't know her, I say, I only know the things I saw. She has her secrets.

But this is not enough. I could say to him: Did she tell you what our father saw? Did she tell you what she let him see?

I could say: If it had been me, he would've beaten me until I couldn't move, torn my hair out by the roots. I have no doubts, none.

Or I could say: she planned that, she wanted him to see. She brought that boy into our house and she saw the lights were on. Your wife was on her back, her arms bound up in twisted sleeves, her legs locked around his hips beneath the fabric of his shirt, of someone else's shirt, and her father stood and watched.

We are not the same, I tell him

In my garden, I would plant tomatoes and cucumbers, I think. Peppers and lettuce, dark green and leafy. There is no room here for that, for mosquitoes and caterpillars, forsythia. But I would fill it: parsley, mint, small shoes, plastic shovels, dolls, tiny arms and legs on climbing vines, sun-warmed and fleshy.

Outside my window I can see the procession: the pastor of the church in gold and crimson robes and behind him the other priests, the extraordinary ministers and their wives. The last, finally, are the nuns, habits billowing in the hot wind, rosaries twisted through their fingers. They walk behind the float, a statue of the Virgin Mary crowned with plastic dimestore flowers on a wheeled plywood frame. They walk and parents push their children forward with money clenched in greasy fingers, bills the nuns attach to money clips that line the edges of the float, and their faces shine with rapture.

Lucinda
Ebersole

Suicide Notebook

WHEN BYRON LEFT her for an anorexic waitress who worked in the Caffeine Connection he told Virginia she needed to get a hobby, so she began collecting suicide notes. Not the actual notes, but reasonable facsimilies that she copied into a small notebook. She copied down quotes from biographies, pulled phrases from television and newspaper accounts, bought a tape of Jim Jones delivering his final suicide speech as his followers drank Kool-Aid and she even owned a T-shirt with Kurt Cobain's note silk-screened on the front.

I'm too much of an erratic, moody baby!
I don't have the passion anymore, so remember, it's better to burn out than to fade away

Virginia realized that even in death, Kurt had been derivative and failed to credit Neil Young who actually wrote the final line of his note. Creative types kill themselves when they cease to be creative. One psychiatrist hypothesized that homosexual men kill themselves with guns because they want to be attacked by a penis. Kurt used a big gun. Women rarely used guns, Virginia thought, perhaps because they had already been attacked by a penis, and no woman would leave all that blood on the carpet for strangers to clean up.

I am a nuisance

Virginia found it impossible to drink coffee. Byron had chosen the very open and public Caffeine Connection to break up. He dumped her as the anorexic waitress dumped espresso grounds. She could still smell the roasting beans. On her way home, alone, she purchased a small notebook to collect her thoughts. Byron said she lacked spontaneity. She researched everything. She made incessant lists. She wrote down the words Byron used to dump her and then she tore out the page and wrote a suicide note.

Dear Byron,
I hate you!
Love,
Virginia

The note was spontaneous and to the point, still it needed something. The *New York Times* reported the story of a woman who laid down on the tracks of the commuter train that carried her husband, but Byron walked to work. Jumping from a building into his path would be spontaneous, but required too much planning; after all, she wouldn't want to fall on him. She could wire herself with explosives, tape a note to the window of the Caffeine Connection, and blow herself up in front of his waitress.

You will have to live with this until you die
May you never, ever forget

As Byron steadily retrieved his possessions from the apartment, Virginia expanded her collection to include quotes and facts about suicide. Men with tattoos are more likely to use guns. Byron had a gun but no tattoo. Brown-eyed girls and boys like hanging and poison. Byron had brown eyes. Beautiful brown eyes like a girl's eyes, with long fluttering lashes. There were lies about suicide. Most suicides do not occur during a full moon or around holidays, most are during the new moon and in spring. There are exceptions, like the boy who hanged himself from the family Christmas tree with the note pinned to his shirt like a gift card.

Merry Christmas

Arthur Miller wrote that suicide kills two people, that's what it's for. Though Virginia didn't know when he wrote it, she assumed that he wrote it after Marilyn Monroe died. Freud believed that women who poison themselves want to get pregnant. After Marilyn died, the suicide rate jumped more than 10%. Suicide rates increase with famous victims as do car and plane crashes. Some people try to hide suicide by getting into an accident. That would be too easy and Byron wouldn't suffer enough. Perhaps she could go up in a plane of sky divers and jump without a parachute. Surely someone would get it on film for Byron to watch over and over.

Like cherry blossoms
In the spring
Let us fall
So pure and radiant

Virginia cried incessantly. To the point of being trite. She was drowning in her tears. Menninger argued that drowning is an attempt to return to the womb. Virginia had no interest in returning to the womb, but perhaps she could return home until Byron had cleared out all of his stuff. On second thought, home was not a place she wanted to return to either. Her mother would ask questions after question. Virginia would cry more. Menninger was a quack. It is best to stay curled up in the apartment and gaze at the shrine of photographs of Byron and Virginia when they were a happy couple.

I don't think two people could have been happier than we have been

Virginia made notes in her suicide book. Thoughts and observations. She was brave and cavalier the day Byron came to find a box of papers he needed for his taxes. A vindictive woman would have burned his files. But Virginia still loved him and she couldn't bear to envision him sitting through an audit. He was too bad with math to survive an audit. She sat at the kitchen table, scribbling in her book and fighting back tears. Byron stuck his head around the corner, "I found them." Then he left and Virginia cried. She wrote in her book—I am totally pathetic. Then she stopped her commentary. Suicide kills two people. Why not cut out the middleman?

There are many things I should like to write you about, but I feel it is useless

Ann picked up the black notebook and flipped through it. "Weird little book," she said. "Byron said I needed a hobby and I hate rollerblading." Ann felt the book could sell but it needed illustrations. A skull torn away by a bullet, a floater, and actual typed letter. Especially if . . .

You hate to think so,
but suicide helps sell books

Virginia had a horrific headache, due in large part to her recent withdrawal from caffeine. Regardless of the bad association, she was going to brew a large pot of coffee and drink it all. She put on her tape of Jim Jones. Something about his words urging the flock to drink the Kool-Aid made it easier for her to swallow the dark, acrid fluid. When the pot was empty, Virginia still had a headache and was unable to sleep. She drew a hot bath and sat in the tub. There was speculation that Diane Arbus photographed her own suicide, but there is no proof. Virginia didn't own a camera. The bath water was cold as the first light of dawn came into the bathroom window. Virginia climbed into her bed to sleep alone.

I'm going to put myself to sleep now for a bit longer than usual
Call the time Eternity

In the afternoon, Virginia crawled out of bed and went directly to the kitchen coffee maker. She had overindulged the previous evening and there were hardly enough grounds for the next pot. Virginia sprinkled what she had on the cold congealed grounds from the night before and hoped for the best. She surveyed the kitchen as the coffee dripped. The refrigerator held a head of brown, slimy lettuce and milk that was now cottage cheese. There were containers of yogurt that could officially be classified as antibiotics. Small white Chinese containers held the residue of the final meal she and Byron shared.

The Last Supper

Virginia cleaned out the refrigerator and finally washed the dishes and put them away. She stripped the bed of the sheets that smelled like Byron and tossed them in the hamper. She threw away the plastic razors that he shaved with. She searched the closets for telltale items of clothing. In the back of the closet she found the small box with Byron's gun. She took it out and pointed it at the pictures in the shrine. Virginia laid the gun on the table as she drank coffee. She tore out a sheet of paper from her suicide notebook and began making a list. It was a much more simple list than the one she had been keeping. She wrote milk and cheese, chicken, lettuce and in the end she wrote coffee. She knew what coffee she wanted. Not Folgers nor Maxwell House, she wanted Peruvian Delight and there was only one place to get it.

Someone had to do it
Self-awareness is everything

Virginia entered the Caffeine Connection with her hands stuffed deeply into her pockets. She came up behind the anorexic waitress who hadn't noticed her. "Two pounds of Peruvian Delight," Virginia said to the waitress whose smile melted when she saw Virginia. Virginia tried to look pleasant. She didn't want to look like a psycho ex. "Grind it fine," she said, "and watch your fingers, we wouldn't want you to get hurt." Virginia felt her fingers on the gun. The waitress began to fidget, which at this moment could not be attributed to her vocation. She spilled part of the fine grounds and had to get another scoop of beans as the other employee rang up Virginia's purchase. The waitress slid the two pound bags into a larger bag and handed it to her as Virginia pulled Byron's gun from her pocket and pointed it at the new girlfriend. "Jesus Christ," she screamed. Virginia held the gun for a few long seconds and then she laid it on the counter. "I thought Byron might need this," she said as she took her coffee grounds and turned toward the door.

Judas did not leave a note

Kyle Jarrard

The Watch

I ADMIT I thought about the Grandy's chicken lady for a long time after that. Then she just faded away, though I do still see her in a dream now and then. Standing there in the humid Waco dawn by the pumps.

Watching me get gas. You can tell right away when they're not right. She had on pink nylon stretch pants and a tight white mohair sweater. But she was about 90 and it had to be nearly that hot, too.

I truly hate how they'll come out of the blue like that, right straight up to you. "Is there a Grandy's chicken place around here?"

I was still a little drunk. It was clear she'd walked all the way from somewhere. No telling where though—in off the interstate, all the way from downtown, from the nut house, who knows? I looked to see if she was wearing one of those plastic hospital bracelets.

She wasn't. She was just there, whoever she was, with all her long gray hair down like she was looking for a customer. Just there in those stretch pants and that sweater.

Like an idiot, I said, "Ma'am?"

She came a couple steps closer. I'd finished the fill-up and was turning to put the nozzle back, but without meaning to I turned it toward her, like a gun. This slung some gas on the ground, but she didn't even notice. "Is there a Grandy's chicken place around here?"

That sweater. I knew I had to have either a nut on my hands or some burned-out whore from stupid place like San Angelo.

I didn't have a lot of time to waste. People'd be showing up back at the apartment anytime now. Best to get right to the point.

"Lady, I don't have any idea if there's a Graydy's chicken place around here. Why're you asking me?"

"Grandy's," she corrected.

I slammed the gas nozzle on its hook. "Whatever."

The magic word. No sooner than I'd said it, up she rushed to passenger side of the Toyota, got in and slammed the door. Can you imagine?

I lost my cool, though. There was just no way someone could just get into your car like that. Old lady or not. What did she take me for? A taxi?

I went over, pulled the door open, got between it and her. "Lady, I ain't taking you to no chicken place. Will you get out of my car, please?"

She had a little satchel of makeup out. The visor was down and she was checking herself out in the mirror. Like we were fixing to go out on a date.

"May I ask what you think you're doing?"

She gave me a look. "Fixing my face." Then she gave me another look. This time it was the way you look at an animal that's been injured, hit on the road, left for dead. She gave me that look and then slowly shook her head. "What'd you do, forget?"

"What?"

She pointed. "There."

I looked down. I had my pajamas on.

Dickey and Donna are good people, I know that. And I truly am sorry about their boy and all—wait, why am I even saying that? I don't mean like he died. I doubt he did, anyway, the way we whipped their asses. I mean I am sorry about the rest. I am.

They came over to see me a little bit after Christmas and said the boy'd got his orders and had to go. Would I apartment-sit his place until he got back? I was the nice guy across the street. They always come to me. They always will. Draw them like flies.

I like Dickey and Donna. We go way back. Every time they came to visit their boy we'd all get together on the steps on one side of the street or the other and have a few beers.

We're in the same age-bracket, and all military people. Dick, he did Korea. USAF. Lot of missions over the North he *still* ain't allowed to talk about and it's been almost forty years now—something about carrying nuclear bombs, I think.

Donna, she is just a love. Saw Dickey through hell and back all these years since then—clinics and tanks and hospitals all up and down creation. That's the part about war that always forgets to get talked about on the TV.

Of course I said yes to the deal on the boy's apartment. Why not? They acted like they were even going to pay me to do it. I say acted because they only half-hinted. But I didn't push it. Should have, though, needed the money.

They were going to mail in his rent to the owner every month for however long it took him to get back from Saudi. They'd get the utilities, too, just like it was him using the place. They'd already gathered up all the kid's stuff and put it in one room.

I gave back the rent furniture in my place, then the keys and moved my clothes and some little things over. Not a bad setup. I even got to use his Toyota.

I told Dickey and Donna that everything would be just fine, and then they went back North where they live.

I remember saying, "Free rent" that night when I looked out through the screen at my crappy old place across the way. "Can't beat this."

He had a good color TV, so I watched the war and drank beer. Sixty-two years old and as excited as a kid on the Fourth of July. I mean, did you *see* that triple-A going up that first night? And how about them Tomahawks? One of them reporters holed up in a Baghdad hotel said he'd seen one of them cruise missiles come right by the window, go on down the street like it was looking for something, you know like it was sniffing, then popped through a window into a government building and—Goodbye, Ragheads!

I told the postman—big idiot named Ernie—about them missiles, too. But I don't know, I think maybe it spooked him some because he didn't laugh when I said that someday they are going to be making missiles like the ones on the cartoons, you know the ones that'll come up behind you like on the Road Runners show, tap you on the shoulder and go *kerplow!* when you turn around to see who's there.

Now I thought that was really funny. But Ernie just stared at me. Oh well, Ernie will never be anything more than just Ernie. The postman on that stupid street in Waco. I don't even know why I'm talking about him. He just doesn't matter.

I watched and watched that war. Ate a lot of junk food, too, which is pretty stupid but then, hell. It is *my* life, two-bit retirement and all. I had a free apartment and a damn color TV that made my old rent set the biggest rip-off in creation. So down went the Doritos and Fritos and sour-cream potato chips while the planes, the thousands of screaming American and British and French fighters, went in on that godawful country and did their parking-lot work. I even made up a joke about how somebody somewhere was going to get smart and figure out how to make a billion dollars off the yellow paint contract for the stripes on the parking lot we were putting in.

I remember thinking how there were some other countries in that neighborhood just asking for it, too. Asking to be miles and miles of nothing but black searing parking lot.

The TV picked up 30-something channels, and since almost all of it was tuned in on the war, there was hardly ever a dull moment. It was like having your hands right on the controls. Once in a while I'd yell out, "Zap those bastards!"

This went on day after day, night after night, until I looked up and realized it'd been several weeks. I'd hardly gone outside and nobody'd come over. Who did I know? Dickey and Donna hadn't called, either. But then why should they have?

Nobody'd come to hassle me about no bills or rent so I figured everything was still on track. Just the same, every two or three days I picked up the receiver to be sure the hum was still there.

I got kind of stupid one night, though, called one of my old honeys (one of the ones before Sharon) who lives up in Arkansas, got a man who quickly informed me that this particular old honey was now Mrs. Something or Other and asked if there was anything else I'd like to know.

This got me mad. I get mad easy, always have. So I told him, yes I had another question and then asked Mr. Something or Other if my old honey still liked to do that special thing she used to beg me on her hands and knees to do to me. Click! I laughed a half-hour straight.

Another night I finally opened the door to the boy's room. Boy? Hell, he's a grown man. It wasn't like I was snooping or anything, I just wanted to see what there was to see.

Dickey and Donna had done a good job. Amazing how much stuff they'd got in there. All around the king-size bed were boxes taped shut, in places piled up to the ceiling. You couldn't even walk around.

They'd done that to give me more room. They'd given me so much room I didn't know what to do with it all. I mostly lived on the side of the living room where the kitchen and bar were, let the sea of celery green shag stretch away empty.

They'd left me the twin bed in the spare room, the fish to feed in the tank in the hall, and all the angel fish food.

I guess I was on the third little shaker of food for the angel fish when I got sick of the war and waiting and everything else.

I waited until it was cheaper hours one morning, then phoned Dickey up there.

"What are you doing?" I said. That's the way I always do on the phone, just start right in like I was in the room with whoever it is.

"Nothing. Who's this?"

"Chi Chi Rodriguez who do you think it is."

"Chi Chi who? Is that you, Al?"

"How about them boys, huh? Think we're just about to wrap this sucker up. What do you y'all think?"

"You okay down there, Al? Honey! Honey, it's Al on the phone."

"Don't trouble her now."

It was Donna then. "Trouble? What trouble?"

"No trouble, honey," I said. "Everything's just fine. How are you holding up? Had any word?"

"We're just fine. Doing just fine."

I could hear they were watching television, a Western from the whooping and gunshots. "Had any word?"

"He's fine," she said. "Can't tell us where he is but he says he's okay. Thank God. Our prayers have been answered. He's doing all right. He's doing fine. That's what he said when he called. Sunday. He called last Sunday."

"I'm glad to hear that. I am."

"How are you doing? Is everything okay down there?"

"Just fine, just fine. I just wanted to call. Be sure y'all were all right, holding up and all."

"Dickey, you want to talk to Al?"

There was some whispering. I waited, running the channels with the sound down.

"Al?"

"Yes, Donna."

"Dickey says to say take care. He's doing something. I don't know what."

"Okay then. I just wanted—"

"You take care, Al. You need anything?"

"Not a thing."

"Goodbye, Al."

"When y'all thinking about coming down?"

She'd already hung up.

I like them a lot. They are such nice people. It may sound crazy but, you know, I felt better after that. I mean I somehow got through the rest of the day easier. With just the thought that, yes, I did have a couple good friends even if they didn't happen to live in the same town or even in the same state.

Damn sure would've been fun to go out to the Star Wheel with them in our checkered shirts and boots like we used to and do a little of that two-step. I know Dickey won't mind me saying that Donna is a real looker out on the floor. Gets everybody's eye, rightly so. I don't mean anything by it, but he ain't so bad himself. They're just good people, that's why. That's got to be why. In fact, that's got to be the why of a lot of things.

I had a bad feeling about their son. Couldn't help it.

I was going to say Happy Birthday out loud to myself, since nobody else was going to, finish off my Bud and get on to bed. Instead, I stayed up, all sixty-three fat-ass years of me, and had another one. In the dark with the TV sound low. That's where the night sort of veered.

Because just as soon as you put four or five beers in me, just as soon as the middle of the night is floating in cool through the screen door and there ain't nobody around here or anywhere else on the planet, I'm going to think about my dead wife, Sharon.

You want to know how I picture her? I picture her in a sand trap with her ball stuck up under the lip of the green. You know, where you can't get it out even if you had all day. I see her doing that, cursing, belly-aching, her pile of red hair sticking out of that big old green billcap and practically on fire.

Did she ever love golf. I'd go around with her in the cart, watch. You won't get a club in my hands, though, no way.

The thing that made her maddest was me getting tickled when she got herself into those impossible situations. This may sound vulgar, but when she got mad, real fired-up mad, I wanted to go up and grab her. I wanted to something bad. That was Sharon. Mrs. Mount Vesuvius. We got along.

I remember going on in the boy's room and getting the clubs out. I remember because those damn angel fish got to darting around when I kicked on the hall light. It was a full set, Spalding, looked new. I stood them up against the dinette table, then scrounged around until I found a roll of masking tape and a marker.

One hundred dollars. No, fifty. I had to be sure someone would take them. Forty-nine ninety-nine. Like a real sale.

That done, I must've thought what the hell—and just kept going. I mean I had to have done that, said that to myself because I damn sure knew better than to do what I was doing.

But I loved Sharon more than anything in this world. And, damn it, shit like this is the price you have to pay for loving another person for all that time, all those years. Because, in the end, it will always hurt just as much as it felt good. Nothing will ever change that.

Hell, in my opinion, they should've just put all the boy's stuff in one of them storage places. Why'd they need me to sit there and watch it all, those boxes, the celery carpet, the damn TV, damn war, damn world?

There was a grave in Missouri I wanted to go see. I wanted to go stand by it a while. I needed some extra cash to get up there and back. It was not complicated.

Too bad Dickey and Donna never had the chance to meet her. Everything might've—no, everything has its own time to happen. We can't do anything about that.

I remember somewhere along in there, with all the boxes out in the living room and opened up, half of the things priced and ready, I got really mad inside, got the Ajax under the sink and went and shook a whole ton of it on them damn angel fish. The idiots came up to the surface, then hightailed it to the bottom and hid in the plastic shipwreck. Ajax came down like snow, covered the whole slimy bottom of that tank.

I get mad like that, do things even though I'm thinking at the same time that I know better. But, damn it, I get tired of knowing better, get tired of having to stop myself, to say no. I want to say yes, just do it, whatever it is. Some guys get rifles and ammunition and get up on an overpass and let the world have it. I killed them fucking angel fish.

About 5:30 or so I had to get down the coffee and try to get the lead out before it was too late. I'd damn near passed out there in the middle of that carpet pulling things out—a book on baseball, a red cowboy shirt, a tennis trophy, a chipped blue bowling ball, a good iron frying pan with some egg left on it, six gorgeous green wine glasses from Germany, tons of stuff. I mean at any time I could've just leaned my head back against the chair bottom, dropped the whole deal and slept it off. I could have, but then again it was all kind of beyond me, wasn't it. I had to keep going. The angel fish had sort of made it that way.

They broke in on the Godzilla movie to announce that there was going to be a cease-fire over there. The instant analysts jumped on that like fresh meat, and before you could blink they were all saying the war was over for good. Sure, I can get to acting like a kid, don't we all sometimes. But can you believe I went over and looked out the front door to check and see if he wasn't already driving up? I sometimes wonder about myself.

Of course there was no one there, just a red dog rolling somebody's trash can down the sidewalk in front of my old place. What a nice guy I used to be, I thought, when I was the nice guy across the street.

I blew on my coffee, watched that dog making the awfulest mess, god mad again and went out there. "Get out of that trash you son of a bitch. Get out of here. Go on, get."

I was yelling. Got coffee on my house shoes. And that made me even madder. I took that damn cup and chucked it as hard as I could at that damn dog. Coffee flew all over, but the cup fell way short, bounced on the grass and into some holly bushes. The dog raised its head a second, then jammed his snout right back in the steak bones and baked-potato skins.

It was already getting warm. Which meant I didn't have time to be standing around out there trying to shoo off a dog in somebody else's trash. I dragged everything out of the apartment, set it all up on the 10x10 square of dead Bermuda. I even parked the dying fish out there. It was enough stuff to make a small fortune.

So I began to believe I was going to get to Missouri after all these years and see her grave again. I began to start repeating that to myself, even though at the same time something else in me was starting to say other things. And those other things were pretty clear, like why are you on this tear all of a sudden about going to see your old lady's grave? What do you expect that to accomplish? What are you really running away from? Mightn't it have something to do with the fact that you've got yourself into such a mess you can't even afford a bus ticket to Kirksville and back? Just what is it you want?

"What are you doing?"

I about jumped out of my skin. But it was just the upstairs neighbor, out on his balcony. High school basketball coach, I think. Didn't care, really, what he was.

"Going to have a garage sale."

"At six in the morning?"

I looked down the street at the savings and loan clock. Eighty-eight degrees, 6:22. "I'm just getting everything ready while it's still cool."

He didn't say anything, just stared at the stuff. Then he said, "You're selling Randy's things."

"Going to be hot," I said, like I hadn't heard him.

I needed to go gas up the Toyota, have that over with. Then it'd just be a matter of getting through the day, getting together some of my own junk, throwing it in the car and I'd be out of there.

I dug out the keys. "Got to get some gas. Keep an eye on it, will you? Take me five minutes."

"Sure. I can do that. He say you could sell his stuff?"

"Needs some money over there in Saudi. Be right back."

"Don't they pay him over there?"

"Who the hell knows what our government does," I said.

He appeared to think about that. Then he said, "Well, that's right."

"Be right back."

It was Saturday morning. Only the beer and bread trucks were out. I wondered if he would figure something was wrong and call the cops. Then I thought, Why the hell would he do that? It was just my old paranoia again.

In my pajamas at the gas station. What the hell was I doing? I don't think I had any earthly idea what I was doing. Sure, I was on a tear about Sharon, but what was I doing with this old lady?

Looking back, I know these things just happen, that there isn't anything anybody can do about it. The steps have to be taken, that's all, because whatever it is up there or out there, it's got each and everyone of us on a rope like a cow.

I paid for the gas and drove her to the nearest Grandy's chicken place.

"Closed," I announced.

"I can see that," she said.

"Opens up at ten, sign says."

"This one always opens at 9:50."

I had a pro on my hands.

"9:50, sometimes 9:45," she said. Her light little head vibrated like a lamp shade when you bump it.

"Well," I said. I was hinting for her to get out. "Well."

She looked straight out over the hood at the glass door and the Closed sign hanging there. The lot was empty.

She said: "They are very clean. Some of the other places are not clean. Here, they are."

"Well," I said.

She smiled, without turning. "And polite. Very polite. No rudeness such as you can encounter."

That was neither here nor there to me. I grunted. "Well, what's it going to be?"

"Oh. I always get the box of 10 Golden Nuggets. That's the best. And a bargain. I get a Coke Cola with it as well."

"No, I mean do you want me to leave you here, drop you someplace else, or what. It's only 6:45. You ain't going to wait that long are you?"

"We can wait."

"I have to go. I can't wait."

"Of course you can. Don't be silly."

"Lady, I—"

"Arlene."

"Oh. okay, Arlene, look—"

"Tell me your name, too. Don't be rude."

"What?"

"Your name. Tell me your name." This time she glanced at me.

"Al," I half-shouted. Then I turned the car back on. "You're going to have to get out. I have to go. If you don't mind?"

"I don't mind at all," she said.

"Well, then, fine," I said.

I don't know, but this kind of froze her. She seemed to suddenly be smaller, as if she'd drawn herself in. I felt bad, but then, damn it, you can't just let these people take you over.

"It ain't that long to wait," I said quietly.

There was a perfectly good bench by the kiddie playground.

"Look, there's shade on that bench there, see? I just can't wait with you here. Do you understand? Hey."

The head stopped vibrating, settled back. I'd killed her.

Just like that. I can't describe the chill that blew through me. I'd never seen anybody die, not in real life. And there she'd died, right there in the Toyota, right there next to me. Got in the car at the gas station, forced me to take her to a goddamn Grandy's and up and died in the parking lot.

It was like she'd picked me out to die on. Like she knew she was fixing to check out or something. Maybe she'd just wanted to be with somebody, anybody, and I just happened to be the one. But I didn't believe what my head was telling me. This kind of crap only happened in the movies. This was me. Right there on the Grandy's parking lot. Maybe I even killed her by carrying on, telling her to get out. Maybe I'd scared her to death.

The air-conditioning air was stinking funny. I needed some real air, and began punching the electric window buttons. Hers flew down, then I sort of panicked and shot it back up. I got the back ones down, and so that helped some. But there wasn't much real air around. It was as if it'd all been sucked away, leaving some sort of invisible flame, even though that doesn't make any sense. I busted out sweating.

Now what. What was I supposed to do now? Where do you go? To the police station. Not half-drunk and in pajamas, you don't. To the hospital. But questions there, too. No, I had to go get dressed. Go on back to the apartment, get my clothes on first.

But could I just drive off? With a dead lady like this? Would that be a crime, moving a dead person? This was crazy. Somebody would see. Would see what I was doing and jump up and point, "Hey, look there! That guy is driving around with a dead lady in his car! Stop him, stop him! I bet he killed her! Hey, you, stop!"

I looked at her, tried to calm down. She didn't look dead yet. Of course not. Just sleeping, sleeping there in the Toyota next to me. Like somebody's mother. The hands were holding her purse on her lap.

But the V-neck sweater was sagging down disgracefully. I took a look around to be sure no one was watching, then reached over and pulled it up some to hide things.

Then I felt sick to my stomach. I was sure someone was looking out from inside the restaurant. Some kid there early cutting up fryers on the band saw in the cold box coming out for a warm-up. But I didn't look to see. I never have been able to look and see in situations like that. Never.

I pulled out of there. I took it slow. All the way. I kept thinking the body's going to pitch over on the dash. But she had her shoulder harness on. I watched for cops, took it easy, very very easy.

I parked across the street from the apartment and stayed there a moment to try and figure out if anybody would be able to look over and tell she was dead. There was already a family of wetbacks looking around at the sale. A grandmother was testing the recliner, getting the kids to crank her back. It was going to be all right. Nobody was paying the least attention.

And they ignored me as I came up the sidewalk, except for a little girl who giggled and said something about my pj's. The upstairs guy was nowhere to be seen. I went on inside like it was nothing, like it was somebody else in the complex who was having a sale.

I had a flash as I opened the door that there they'd be—Donna and Dickey, and their boy back from the war. There they'd be standing around with their arms crossed, waiting for me to show up and explain why all the stuff was out in the yard with a price on it. And me in my pajamas and a dead old lady in the Toyota.

I got dressed. Then I got a paper sack from the pantry, stuck my toiletries and some clothes in it, folded the top shut.

I left all the keys on the bar. The watch was over.

Pulling the door to, I scanned the customers. Nobody I knew. People were just shuffling around, leaning over a little to check a price or turn a knob.

I went to the side so I could see if the neighbor was on his balcony again. There was a woman inside up there who yelled *ouch* two or three times, and so they were busy.

"This your sale?" a kid on a banana bike yelled at me. "What you want for that aquarium. Ain't got no price on it. Give you five dollars."

"Not my sale," I whispered.

Couple other people looked around. "This your sale?"

I shook my finger no.

"Well, whose is it?" said the kid.

I just looked at him. I wanted to slap the hell out of him. But then that'd mess everything up. For once, I controlled myself.

"Hey," he cried, "maybe it's all free! You think so? Huh?"

I turned east down the sidewalk. It was only a few blocks to the interstate. In two or three days I'd be in Kirksville, and the Grandy's chicken lady'd be laid to rest. I wondered if she had any kin or somebody who'd show up. Or if the city'd end up having to do it. They probably would.

But that really wasn't any of my business now. That's right. You just walk away.

Richard
Peabody

E is for Elephant

NOTHING SCARED the Colonel more than tight spaces, so it took a hell of a lot of sweet talk to get him into the tunnel of the MRI. One young intern had been pretty convincing and so the Colonel sighed and rolled his bulk off the gurney to please the blue eyes, big lashes and black hair, took a deep breath and climbed onto the platform.

"Are you Italian?" He liked Mediterranean types.

"No Sir. Greek."

"Greek, you say." The Colonel swished the word behind his teeth like a new mouthwash.

"What's your name son?"

"Nick."

Then Nick warned him that the noise would be so loud he'd have to wear the proffered thick gray headphones. The Colonel had balked at that too. The machine was formidable enough.

"But Nick, what if I can't take it in there? What if I need to have you pull me out? How will you hear me son?"

"We won't leave you alone, sir. Someone will be standing right here by your side. There's really nothing to fear."

They always say that. There's never anything to fear. A year ago he'd fallen and he'd had only the vaguest notion of something slamming into him. His right arm and shoulders were numb and he was aware that something was very, very wrong. An electric door had been opening into him, where he had fallen. And his bulk had somehow confused the electronic mechanism. The door opened and closed, over and over again. Banging into him with the regularity of a porch swing. And yet he couldn't move. And he'd been afraid. Afraid like he'd been in the hold of the freighter, a stowaway en route to America, beginning all over again in America. One of RCA's well-dressed young men had finally lifted him out of harm's way. He'd been mortified. How on earth did such a thing come to pass.

The Greek orderly once again convinced him. The noise was impressive—an infernal clanging like one of those new British groups. The metal crunching seemed to crawl right under his skin, wending its way down his body like a dog's teeth on a bone, all the while maintaining a racket that seemed more internal than external. A psycho gong from hell or perhaps something from the movie *Metropolis*. The Colonel licked his lips. A bead of sweat traced a line down his forehead.

The Colonel found himself thinking about his youth. He'd slept with a hooker named Marte in Amsterdam, before the carny days, the midget weddings, the elephants. Before the kid.

The kid was nothing more than a big elephant. The big E. He laughed. The Colonel had crawled into Marte's boyish arms and tried, really tried. But he couldn't shake the sight of the cockroaches. He'd faked sleep and positioned himself so the streetlights made a pool on the floor. And there in the light where it had been flung after the grunting, after the slapping of skin on skin, lay a condom, a little trail of cum on the linoleum floor around it. And something moving. Cockroaches. Fucking cockroaches. Crawling all over each other to squeeze inside that tiny opening. The entire membrane coming to life with them. Fucking cockroaches eating his cum. He'd jumped out of bed, put on one boot and stepped squarely in the middle of the seething mass. Watched the roaches pop out both ends of the latex, leaving a sticky glaze of cum and carapaces adhered to the sole of his boot and to the tile.

The Colonel couldn't tell you why he'd worn a Hawaiian shirt and baseball cap to the kid's funeral. It's true that he used his poor health as an excuse to avoid being a pallbearer. But really, the idea of supporting the person whose career had supported him for twenty years just didn't sit well. Besides, the kid was just another lost puppy and he'd had his share of funerals at the Tampa Humane Society. So, while most of the mourners were preoccupied with the spectacle, he was thinking. There had to be a way to make more money out of the kid's empire even with the kid cold and in the ground.

But he could be excused. Surely the media would forgive him. The boy meant everything to him. Everything. The kid's father inherited the estate. But he'd badgered him. Vernon was in line. No problems there. When the white cadillac hearse deposited the kid at the cemetery, he thought it was all going to work out. Hell there was money to be made off of all of this.

Lot's of it. Once the eulogy started he drifted away. Sat on a cop's motorcycle.

Of course he'd known better. Knew he didn't have to push it to the limit like that. The same way he knew the films were awful. But who cared? The idea was to make money and they'd done that. Hell, he'd made tons of money. He couldn't believe he wasn't gambling in Vegas even now.

"Listen Colonel, I want to do something serious. I want to star in the James Dean story. No more songs. No more girls."

"But your public wants to see you sing. They love you."

"But that's what I want to do. Doesn't that matter?"

"Look. Why do you want to be James Dean? James who? He died young. Nobody will even remember him in a couple of years. You're better looking. Isn't he Bitsy? Isn't he better looking?"

They never guessed that he wasn't really a Louisiana Colonel and not one of their own. It was amazing how well he'd fooled everybody. The Dutchman. He thought about nights in Amsterdam. The city never slept. He'd never gone back of course. No passport. Couldn't get back into the U. S. Couldn't risk everything. Now his secret was out. That bitch Priscilla had seen to that.

The thought of the German hookers draped all over him in Berlin was too much though. God. The shower scene in the army movie. Pure beefcake. And the kid's thick lips. A shiver started at the base of his neck and traveled quickly to his waist. He was getting an erection. The robe was parting beneath the burgundy tie and even with his girth the erection was touching the top of the machinery. Right here in the damn MRI.

Most of the boy's audience never realized the Colonel was a fraud. He'd fought hard to fool them. Of course the kid knew. Of course he did. But it was part of their act. Their sweet act.

He found himself wishing he could undo everything. He missed the kid. That was no way for anybody to go. Dying on the toilet! Like his face had stretch marks.

"How long you people going to keep me in heah? Hello. C'mon now, stop joking around. Somebody get me out of heah."

There was no answer. The claustrophobia was getting worse. He couldn't move. And his erection was brushing the metal. He was going to cum unless he could move. And of course the flogging scene slipped into his mind. The kid getting whipped in the jailhouse. It would come to him now. Trapped in this machine. He couldn't move, couldn't lift a hand, and his jowls were sweating under the metal, under the awkward gray headphones. His nose itched and he tried not to think about it.

Marie had never understood. He'd provided for his wife, but it was all for show. Your typical celebrity wedding. The kid on the other hand had to get married. The media would have destroyed him. No way he'd let that happen. Why he had too much riding on it. Too many people depending on him.

When he walked into the Casino he was really totally alive. The croupiers smiled, called him Colonel. He liked that. Free drinks. Free room. He sent some of the boys ahead and then he'd pick a machine for each one. They carried baskets of change. It made all the blue-haired women from Peoria and Oshkosh stare. He'd stroll behind with his handrolled Havana and he'd bark orders. The young men would crank those handles for him. That was the life. He didn't have to crank handles on slots any more by god, he paid people to do the work for him.

The ferris wheel stopped at its pinnacle and the wedding march bombarded the assembled crowd from makeshift speakers.

"Why don't you come back to my wagon later," his pseudo bride teased. "You look like you could do with a little honeymoon."

The Sears catalog wrapped in black crepe looked like a *Bible* to the crowd and they'd never guess that the justice of the peace in the car below them, was just one of the roughneck crew, that the bride was a coochie dancer. The Dutchman knew that his stunt had worked. He was pulling crowds. P. T. Barnum was right about suckers. Every Tar heel sucker in the vicinity of Charlotte, North Carolina, was assembled around the base of the big wheel watching this weird wedding. And then they would stay for the rides and see the shows and spend all of their money.

"We called him Colonel."

"And what did he say?"

"He said you can go spit and then rot for all he cares."

The colonel snorted. The kid was really mad at him this time. He'd signed him into another couple months of touring. Took the cash right up front. And now the kid was tired and cranky.

"Now here's what I want you boys to do. You call the doctor to see me here in the hotel. I'm sick I tell you. It's my heart. You tell him that. Tell him he's killing me with this nonsense."

Running the kid's life was like running his father's horses around in circles. Or the elephants. Who didn't want to control, really control, a big dumb animal. That was everything.

"Why are you doing this Colonel?"

"Doing what boy? I'm sick or haven't you heard."

"Sure Colonel, you're sick. All right."

"Haven't I made you rich. Haven't I made you famous?"

"That's true but—"

"No buts about it son. Just trust me on this."

"Why can't we tour Europe?"

"It's too cold over there. How about we set up a concert in Hawaii instead. You'd like that wouldn't you? All those Hula dollies."

But Priscilla and the lawyers had really fixed him. Just like some straggly assed stray cat. Here he was in Palm Springs with no reason to live. What was it they called Palm Springs? God's Waiting Room.

"C'mon now. Stop joking. Get me out of heah. I want to get out. Somebody. Please get me out. Help." His voice was muffled because of the headphones. He didn't know if he was shouting at the top of his lungs, or if anybody could possibly hear him over the sound of the machinery. His abdomen was getting cold from his ejaculation. He didn't know how long this test was supposed to take but he was cracking. He felt like he'd been in the machine for hours.

"Please somebody. Please."

And for the first time in a long time . . . the Colonel actually cried.

Allie Bullock-Kagamaster

Swamp Princess

A FADED GREEN TRACTOR protruded from the rear of the store like a stallion at the trough. It was hard to believe that all I wanted was inside a swamp shack in the middle of nowhere. I'd waited until the end of the vacation to search for a down-home country store for some mango marmalade and Spanish moss. Spanish moss would pack well around the tiny glass-blown alligators I left wrapped in tissue paper on the hotel bed by my tweed suitcase.

Once inside the store, I sensed an uninvited presence. I felt noticed, almost stalked. An enormous old pickle jar, filled with brown water, sat on a splintered ledge above the postcard rack and jams. As I pushed my hand against this jar, a dead coral snake rose up through the murky liquid, twisting toward me. A cold feeling sifted through me. I *hated* snakes. I knew I should've stuck to the beaten path. I grabbed the citrus preserves and abruptly headed for the register.

"Ma'am, I killed it myself with a crowbar after it failed to respond to my bare hands," bragged the mossy-neck behind the counter. I was sure he noticed goosebumps crawling up and down my arms.

"The thing squirmed in the grove for darn near an hour," he continued. He wore overalls with no shirt. An armadillo tattoo covered his right upper arm. His muscles flexed as he leaned forward. "Got plenty more if you're interested," he babbled. "Just like the one in the jar," he laughed with a wheezy cough.

"How comforting that it's dead," I said.

There were pictures of Seminole Indians with long carbon hair on the wall behind him. A dingy gauze curtain hung inside the entryway below the pictures. The curtain swayed slightly as if air was trying to escape into the store from the back room. A rainy smell came up from this back room. It lifted the curtain revealing a long table with a single cleaver wedged into its splintered surface. Shelves filled with jars like the one I ran from lined the wall to the left of the table.

"Smells like the weather's going to kick up," he said, interrupting me.

His breath smelled like an ashtray but his teeth were straight and white. I guessed he was in his mid-thirties. I wanted to leave the items and forget I ever left the safe atmosphere of the hotel for a drive and a few souvenirs.

"You live out here in this orange grove?" I asked.

"In a manner of speaking," he replied, sizing me up. "My ex-wife possessed brown hair and dark eyes the likes of yours, only her eyes weren't blue. She wasn't so skinny, either, and there was no freckles across her face," he added.

I felt embarrassed by his remark and began to fidget. The clasp holding my hair in place opened and fell to the ground causing my hair to cascade over my face. It startled me and I blurted, "Where is your wife now? In a jar somewhere?"

"Nah, couldn't catch her!" He laughed. "She's long gone. The woman married some stud, has a slew of kids from what I hear."

I quivered.

"Shoot, you're too fine to be so fretful," he said, clearing his throat.

"I'll also take two bags of kumquats and a clump of Spanish moss," I said trying to ignore his remarks.

I rummaged for money in my purse. His dishwater hair followed his shoulders. It was parted down the middle, thick and straight, moving when he shifted to fill the paper sacks. He popped several Chicklets into his mouth and chewed rapidly. As he moved in closer, I detected a spicy scent to his skin. I always liked that smell because my Uncle Brother wore Old Spice.

"Someone will cross your heart with his heart," Uncle once said when I was almost thirteen, and full of silly questions about love. "He'll wind up as your counterpart, like a discovered shape in a 5,000-piece puzzle of a white cloud; but," he added, "most important of all, he'll smell like me."

I felt unnerved. Just because he smelled like my future didn't mean he was buried treasure. I looked into the tropical forest as a swarm of insects appeared. They increased in number—whorled against a backdrop of gray clouds. The bugs reminded me of my luck with men. The good ones were either married or divorced with baggage. All the rest stung when they left.

The spice-scented stranger approached me. "Hey, you scared of critters, ma'am?"

"I don't like things that sting." I gazed past the screen, continuing to deny the jars in the other room yet unable to concentrate on anything but seeing more.

"Them bugs bite like the dickens," he said.

I looked into his ruddy face. Except for his eyes, his was the face of the familiar redneck: well defined nose, smooth flesh-colored lips, T-shirt tan, beefy muscles.

"Shoot, those fogger trucks run by the government take care of plenty of skeeters, but those bugs multiply worse than rabbits." He paused for a moment clicking the wad of gum before spitting it into a tin bucket by his feet. By now, his tobacco breath had faded into mint. "It sure gets lonesome in these woods," he said.

The moisture in the air made the store smell like a stale bait shop. It was stifling, yet a shiver managed its way up and down my spine.

"The truth is, I imagine one place is as lonely as the next for a guy like me," he continued.

"Well, there's no word for lonely down under," I said. Why not perpetuate this myth? I read about it on Quantas Airlines not so long ago.

"Why's that?"

"Well, the story goes," I said backing away. "in the middle of the desert, there's an underground world."

He leapt onto the counter and sat with his denim-clad legs dangling over the side. I stepped back further to avoid him brushing against my bare legs.

"What do you mean 'underground?'"

"The town's built under the ground," *Maybe he was into mushrooms or cocaine in the back of his store.*

He slapped his hands on his knees. "Here I thought Aussies was known for their beer."

Or better yet, and far simpler, he might be the farmer with the whiskey still. He was hauntingly beautiful for an uneducated man.

"So, why ain't it lonely?" he inquired.

"Something to do with close quarters. Initially, it was smothering to be hemmed in, but before long the closed space became an intimate room." *I felt like a poem inside of an envelope. Like something I would mail only to myself.*

"So, everyone's sort of folded into each other?" It was an intelligible thing for a swamp man to ask, and hinted of something deeper within a creature who strangled creatures and put them in jars.

"When I was there, trucks full of explosives drove over the hot red sand blowing through rocks for jewels like opals and diamonds."

"What are you, part of a demolition team?"

"No, I'm a freelance writer. The photos I shot for *Gems and Rocks* to go with the piece I wrote look like stills from a science fiction movie. That's about as exciting as it gets."

"No kidding? You've got a weird-ass job," he jerked his head and swatted his thighs through his jeans. "My wife left me for another man like that damn blasted book about the photographer who stole into the farmer's wife's house and stole her heart right out from under him."

"*The Bridges of Madison County*?" I asked.

"Yeah, whatever," he said. "She's not here; she's with him and not with me."

It was suddenly too quiet. I broke the silence.

"At night, in Australia, the locals took me on walkabouts but my camera was forbidden."

"How come? They spooked?"

"They're superstitious," I said.

"Ghosts, that's what they are. You can't take a picture of no ghost."

"I don't know about ghosts but they do have this bogey-man called the Bunyip."

"What in hell is a Bunyip?"

"It's a lost soul lurking in the lakes of the Outback."

"They're spooked all right."

"Well, the Bunyip is never seen," I said. I looked into his slightly crinkled eyes. I re-figured him for forty. "It's getting late, Bub, and I have to catch a plane tomorrow, so could you bag this stuff up?"

"As a matter of fact, Princess, my name *is* Bubba. And I'm pleased as heck to make your acquaintance." His hand grabbed mine under one of the bags.

"I'm Penelope," I managed as my stomach churned. *Wonderful, I thought. If I linger, I could get into this swamp princess thing.* "I've really gotta go, Bubba," I added.

He tallied up the order on a ten-key and I paid him. I collected the sacks off the counter and noticed the sun sinking into the cypress trees. With my teeth, I grabbed the plastic holder attached to the car keys and headed for the thicket.

"Sure are a skittish thing," he said, waving as I hurried into the grove, away from the impulse to stay.

I longed for the dirty boulevard near the hotel in Florida City, east of Alligator Alley, back to the civilized world. Back to Franklin Bend, the bed and breakfast inn in upstate New York where I spent half my time since Brother died; was it last spring? Back to the small wallpapered-room up in the loft where my ideas flowed.

I got into the car. I figured it was a mile and a three-quarters back to the highway. I mulled over Bubba. He was unpretentious, maybe that's all it was. I spun along the dirt road. The sun sank lower. It paled over top of the citrus grove, blending a pink sky into mottled greens. The snake was at least half a mile back. I glanced at my wrist and, realizing my watch was at the hotel, guessed I had about twenty-four hours left to pack and fax and finish volume two of C.S. Lewis's *Chronicles of Narnia*. At the moment, I felt like Lucy, exiting an enchanted forest in Narnia through the inside of her uncle's magic wardrobe.

A fogger truck dusted the orchard in a spray of noxious fumes. Two sluggish over-sized dump trucks, filled to their brims with oranges, trailed the fogger. They swerved around me and forced me to dodge off the road. I held my foot to the gas a little too long, while in neutral, and flooded the engine. The starter clicked dead. *I shouldn't have talked for so long. I'd be on the road by now.* I snapped on the radio. The crackling sound clapped, then abated. Minutes later, the thicket blackened and I felt followed by Bubba's dead snake. A racket of crickets covered the inside branches above me while below me squirrels crunched through leaves in the new darkness. I felt dizzy.

I lit a match. The windshield was covered with sticky tree-frogs, transparent and grunting, falling like augmented raindrops from the low-hung kapok trees. Cobras with open hoods whirled through my mind in a distant memory of the unforgettable trip to Taiwan which resulted in countless sessions of group therapy: field trips to the zoo, jungle films, and boxes filled with rubber snakes.

Time to think. The rain pelted against my camera lens as I made my way through a grassy mud-drenched road to Snake Alley. The photographer was heaving in the hotel so I had to take the pictures *and* write the story. Crates of the most poisonous snakes in the world lined the ancient street. Rows of open-air bars served worn Chinese men venom-laden cocktails as milk-white as the fu-manchus attached to their shrunken chins. I was told I wouldn't need a translator, just a tape recorder, and a good eye.

"Vipers, cobras or hundred-pacers are milked," Asia said.

He compressed a hundred-pacer. White nectar oozed from its fangs and he immediately filled a tall urn with the semen-like liquid.

"Next, it is emptied of all blood and bile," he narrated. "One bite from him and you die within one-hundred paces"; he continued with a toothless simper, adding, "but, most of us are unharmed by this serpent's bite."

He wrung the thin snake of all essential and non-essential fluids. I clicked the shutter throughout the gory process.

"When does this become a drink?" I asked from behind my camera.

"When it is mixed into yang. Do you know yang?"

"That's a new one on me," I said.

"The medicine from the snake is blended with natural spirits into an antidote: Potent. Yang. Protects you like a mongoose from within."

He threw the snake onto a messy pile of limp reptiles, stirred the vile concoction into a dingy glass, and handed it to me. I sipped it trying not to think about the pile of dead serpents. Hundreds more slithered inside wooden boxes secured on the outside with a fine triple-layered wire-mesh. The tangy drink reminded me of a black jelly bean at Easter-time. It was a resurrection to my taste buds.

"This is actually good," I said. I placed the milky potion on the ledge of the bar and shot successive photos of it.

It was dark by the time I shuffled back to the old hotel. Cobras wove up and down through the tall blades of grass in the small courtyard below the lit verandah directly outside my room. I decided to shoot a night sequence for Jeremy who was still reeling. I thought an angle from the verandah would capture these snakes, would show their strangeness from an astronaut's point of view. The terrace lights blinked on and off as I loaded the camera. My khaki shorts and denim campus shirt wrinkled next to the shine in my hair. The strap from one of the camera cases brushed against my leg. It felt like one of the snakes and startled me. I tumbled off the balcony in slow motion toward the yard.

Flares shot through the courtyard grounds lighting up the long grass as I fell toward the weaving hoods. In a daze, I heard sing-songy voices mix with the beat of gun shots and tapping sticks. Within seconds, officials wearing mongoose badges encircled me. But it was too late, even for the *Chinese Snake Patrol*, for I felt the scrawl of vipers all through me. I was caught between death and screaming. "You are safe; we are here to rescue you," words bounced in English and Chinese, echoing into the night, over my dazed body. No one could convince me that I wouldn't die from those snake bites. I felt numb as if Novocain ran through every vein.

The time I spent in hospital I learned about cobra populated areas and the fact that the yang drink neutralized the poison. The small black-haired nurses called me lucky. I knew I was fortunate to be alive, but, from that day on, even a wisp of my own hair touching my face would send me into a frenzy. I went from fiancee to boyfriend to acquaintance to my work.

So, what was I doing in a swamp? My therapist suggested I take the plunge and vacation in the Everglades exploring facts about my "enemy." A healing trip. So far, I'd graced the modern air-conditioned interiors of the Florida ranger stations and photographed gator shows in a controlled environment. I rummaged for a flashlight in the glovebox and felt a warm breeze coming up from the back seat. One of the electric windows was open at the top. *Things could crawl in an opening that size.* I decided to walk through the thinned out mosquito population to the road.

I tripped into the darkness in the dim of the flashlight. Airborne palmetto bugs, the size of baby hummingbirds, brushed against my bare arms and legs as I fled on foot trying to shake them away. *Just what I needed—flying roaches.* The dirt road eclipsed with shadows cast by slow-moving crocodiles. *At least they're not low flying gators.* At ranger headquarters, I had learned the basic differences between crocks and alligators. Besides size and color variations, mouths hinged up for gators and down for crocks. A crock rubbed his belly slow across the ground while alligators dodged at light speed over land, searching out sink holes or creeks. I viewed them as fat snakes with feet.

A form appeared from behind a multi-rooted banyon tree. I froze.

"Better watch them live ones, Ma'am."

Bubba walked me to his cottage on the grounds, said I could use the phone. The white picket fence enclosed a vegetable garden: tomatillos, leafy greens and some sort of cabbage I didn't recognize. Once inside I was surprised by a large Goya painting. The flamenco dancers on the canvas seemed to be enjoying life. Tendriled vines, draped up a wall, fell toward their garden table in the background. I felt like I was dreaming. Bubba's house smelled like tomato sauce and beer. He led me into the kitchen toward the phone and the bar. The last two shelves of the wine rack were filled with gourmet cookbooks and Penguin classics such as *Robinson Crusoe, The Old Man and the Sea* and *Treasure Island.*

"Like I told you before, I don't get much company around here," he said as he poured two drinks over ice. He loosened the buckle on his overalls and mentioned something about the foul heat. I fumbled in my pockets for the slip of paper with the phone number that would rescue me. The line rang several times before someone picked up.

"Floyd's Road Service. How may I help you?"

Another car was on its way. I heard Bubba's persistent cough from the other room. Drawn by the flicker of the TV, I crossed the terrazzo floor. He lay sprawled in boxers on a leather lazy boy with the TV on low. The local news reporter said the lowlands just sank lower that afternoon as another missing tourist turned up in pieces just off the Tamiami Trail. Bubba pushed the mute button and I slipped back into the front room. Vertigo. The room swayed. Thin black snakes moved along the baseboards. His small house was crawling. I turned back towards Bubba in delirium.

"Hey, doll, you scared of my pets?" he said smugly. He revolved in his chair as he downed the glass of whiskey. I felt woozy from my drink. He faced me while simultaneously reaching for the Kentucky label. He motioned over his head for me to come to him. I felt trapped. I slid by him too close and imagined him reaching for my hair.

"It's soft and it sure smells good," I thought I heard him say as he slowly dragged the strand past his nose.

Snakes in every room. No place to run or hide. I hoped for the car rental service. I thought I felt Bubba press into me. I was aroused and repulsed all at once. In my mind, I instinctively recoiled his hand just as it began to explore. I had to find a way out. Instead, I found myself across his lap, his mouth deep into mine. This was no dream. This was a real live man in my arms. The taste of alcohol piqued my thirst. Bubba offered me another drink, and this time I felt him tug at my blouse. I repositioned myself. His hands circled my waist as he wrestled me over the snap on my shorts. Chimes bonged ten times through the small house.

"It's my gram, haunting me through that blasted clock," Bubba muttered.

I straightened my blouse and sat up square on his lap. "I don't know what came over me," I said flushed from head-to-toe. This man was a snake I could touch. I pulled him against me and made love to him with my tongue. My top button lay open, and by now, he had unsnapped my shorts.

"Bubba, I really must go," I gasped, releasing my lips from his.

"Nah, there's plenty of time to get some, sugar." He was sweaty, moving against my thigh.

He ran his hands from my knees up. I fought to stop him. I forced his hands onto the recliner leaving him limp in his chair.

"We was almost there, sugar-girl," he said, moisture pouring onto his brow.

I started to ask for the phone again but heard increased swishing in the other room. A musty odor, like dirty mothballs, pierced my nose. Snakes. Lots of them. My zipper and snap were once again closed. Bubba ran his hand over the double seam of my crotch. It rained a lot in Florida. *A thunderstorm could knock out the power and right in the middle of sex a snake might crawl into our love nest. Bubba would get confused and I could end up in a jar.*

"Get the phone, Bubba," I begged.

"We already called them," he said impatiently. He drew my body down onto his.

"I want to call them again," I said, struggling.

He hardened his grip on me. His hand massaged my abdomen. "Well, they're on their way, honey, but they're apparently running late. Now, where did we leave off?"

I backed away from him. "We leave off right here," I said.

"So, you really want to get away from old hard-as-a-rock Bubba?"

"I only want to get home in one piece." I began to tremble.

Home was suddenly out of focus. *I must be having another one of those reality nightmares. What was the significance of sex mixed with snakes?* My doctor would make me read another book. I was sick of therapy.

"Hey, come on, it's just a little loving we're doing here," Bubba reminded me.

I reached for my backpack with the flashlight protruding. I started for the door. "Bubba, maybe some other time. I really do want to go."

Whether I wanted to go or not, I couldn't let down. It had been this way since the snake accident. I had a terrible sense of insecurity when I was away from home.

He walked me back to the stalled car and said he'd stay with me, that he had nothing better to do.

"Mind if I sit in the car, Penny? Can I call you Penny?"

I bit my lower lip instead of giving him an answer.

"I'm not going to love on you no more, Penny; I just want to sit down. You wore me out and we didn't do nothing."

"Well, it's not that," I said, glancing at the stuck-open window.

"Oh, you think maybe something got inside your car, eh?"

He fished under the front seat, then climbed over to search the back. The front of his body rubbed across the top edge of the cloth seat. As I looked away, I saw the path of a shooting star against the pitch night. He called to me assuring me the coast was clear. I slipped into the front seat and propped my back against the opposite side where I could face him reclined in the rear.

"So, sugar, how long has it been since you've had a man?" he inquired.

"Awhile," I said.

He shut his eyes and said, "I'm right here if you get a hankering."

I opened the leather case and reached for the Minolta. Through the camera lens, I watched the silhouette of the Spanish moss dance upon the trees in the wind, and then I focused on Bubba as he dozed. The thick night-air engulfed us. *Awhile? Who was I kidding?* I slumped in the seat exhausted.

An hour or so later I woke. Something brazed my throat. It was my camera wedged into my neck. I removed it and the throb stopped. A streak of light appeared through my partially open eyelids. Bubba was gone. A big glass jar sat on the hood of the car full of a bark-colored water. It slid toward me. My eyes reflected back as though disembodied in the liquid with the snake in Bubba's jar. I re-focused. An oversized lantern, hung on a branch in the kapok tree, confused the night. I heard a southern voice through the window.

"Hope you weren't waiting too long, Miss," a man said as he reached across the windshield for the jar.

The tattoo on his biceps squiggled as he tipped the jar to his mouth. He had black eyes and short frizzy black hair against Negro skin resplendent in the full moon.

"The dispatch sent me out with a replacer for this here lemon," he said, tapping on the roof of the disabled car.

Where did Bubba go? "You take American Express?" I said, shaking myself loose from the evening and Bubba.

"Sure 'nough," he replied. He stepped over the tow-bar to release the new car. "Sure is a sultry night. This'll take a little bit."

I produced the credit card, and deserted the lemon, as he called it, so he could hitch the disabled vehicle to the tow truck inscribed: *Floyd's 24 Hour Service.* I signed for the exchange, and handed the slip back to him along with a twenty-dollar bill and a small sack of kumquats. He grinned and spit tobacco away from me into the nighttime dirt. He then helped me shuffle my belongings into the new car and I said good-bye as he got into his truck. I popped in Zeppelin's *Stairway To Heaven* recorded from the retro station back home and shot a parting wave toward him. He tossed the tiny orange fruits into his mouth as he zipped out of sight.

The tape player whirred. No Zeppelin. I thought I heard a cough from the back seat. I looked up into the rearview mirror to catch Bubba's hazel stare. Startled, I reached past my fears. *What does he want?*

"Don't be scared, Penny. I wanted to say a proper good-bye."

He draped his arms over the seat and touched my shoulders.

"So, are you going to sit in my car for the rest of your life?" I asked.

He looked up at me. "There's never been anybody like you cross my path before. Since the wife left, I pretty much keep to myself in this sawgrass hell."

I crawled over the seat and sat beside him. "I've never had a one-night stand, Bubba. What about tomorrow? I always think of tomorrow."

Something cold and dry like musty tapestry wrapped around my sandal with a slow intention that scared me. I clutched onto Bubba's hand and he squeezed back. I opened my mouth to scream. He inserted his tongue and began to kiss me madly. I felt the snake creeping above my ankle. I tried to push Bubba from me to tell him about the snake but his grip remained firm. Our bodies intertwined into a hungry motion mixed with refrain as I felt the snake inch up my calf. I dug my fingernails into his side and he tore my blouse open. He slid on top of me as I begged for deliverance in silence. I tightened my hold on him, unable to cry out, hoping he would free me from the snake. He took this as a signal to embrace me harder. I was torn between fainting and letting him all the way in. My body felt divided. One part lay crippled by the traveling snake as if in a deadlock while the rest of me fell into Bubba.

The next evening before the sun set across the New York skyline, the charter plane I'd always taken to Franklin Bend ascended through a bank of cumulus clouds. Twenty-minutes later the puddle-jumper approached the familiar runway of my hometown, and I watched as it met the tarmac. I knew I didn't want to unboard into my life so I lingered in my seat. The cleaning crew came on board with their sweepers and large plastic bags. I got up from my seat and through the window imagined Bubba standing behind the tall link fence, its cold barbs hedging the long airstrip. The chill of the years ahead settled on my shoulders.

I slipped on the last step and dropped my carry-on. The jar of mango jam rolled out of the bag across the asphalt and stopped abruptly against a muddy pair of laceless boots. He coughed through the smoke of his cigarette, bent down for the jar, spit the butt onto the ground, stood up and grabbed me in his arms.

Janice Daugherty

Whereabouts Are We?

"LORD, CHILD," hollers Aunt Imo, ducking around the patched screen door, "don't come bringing Mommer to me. I got my hands full." She spits into a bush of speckled-blue hydrangeas while she's out there.

Luzanne has one foot out the door of her old white Corvair and starts to get back in, but when she glances over at her shriveled grannie on the other side, she just hangs there. The old lady is nursing a white Dixie spit cup, nested with Kleenex. She is so tiny that the top of her age-yellowed head draws level with the split black dash. Cradled in the bucket seat, she fidgets with a wadded handkerchief, legs stuck out like a doll's.

"We just come by for a little visit, Aunt Imo," calls Luzanne, trotting around the rear of the car to get Grannie's walker first. She opens the door behind Granny, takes out her metal walker and unfolds it, then closes the door. "Come on, Grannie," she says, opening Grannie's door next, "let's go in."

Aunt Imo now stands, pouty-thick, on the screened porch, hands braced on her boxy sides. Staring off at the side yard where a Silver Stream travel trailer has been set up in a sandy grove of scrub oaks, desert-like against the backdrop of viny green hardwoods and a lone leafy sweetgum shading Aunt Imo's low frame house. Deadend of the gravel road.

Luzanne takes Grannie's arm, a bone dipped in mushy flesh, and tugs gently. "Take your time, Grannie."

The old lady raises her scabby clay face—she has bad skin cancers, though not bad enough to carry her out of this world. The doctors in Macon have patched her up and given her some salve for the sores, and they shine like wet gator hide in the curried summer light.

She'll be ninety-seven next month, first of August, Lord willing.

"Where we at?" she asks and screws her mouth with her hankie.

Luzanne shouts, "We at Aunt Imo's, Grannie," and yanks at her brittle arm.

The old lady's hazel owl eyes seek a peep space around the open car door. "Imo's you say?"

"Yessum."

Aunt Imo steps out to the half-buried brick walk on big bare feet and crosses her arms under her drooped breasts. She has stuffed olive skin, smooth and hairless. "Mommer, y'all come on in." She brushes a fine loose hair toward the brown bun on the back of her head.

The old lady has made a little progress, has shifted around on the seat with one blue terry slipper dangling out the door. Luzanne, still holding to her arm, reaches down and catches the other foot and wrenches it around the seat.

"Ooch!" the old lady says, sitting like a child on a potty.

"That hurtcha, Grannie?" says Luzanne and helps her stand.

The old lady's nickel-rimmed eyes settle on Luzanne. "I hate to be a bother to my family."

"You ain't, Grannie." Luzanne steps behind her and places her hands each side of Grannie's rib cage, which is surprisingly fleshy. Grannie's arms and legs are sticks. "See, yonder's Aunt Imo."

"My pocketbook," says the old lady and struggles against the bracket of hands. "Where's my pocketbook?"

Luzanne frames Grannie in the walker and reaches into the floor of the car and frees the bone triangular pocketbook from the trap of toys and trash. She takes it to Grannie and threads her crooked arm through the strap and hooks her claw-like fingers to the top rung of the walker.

Poising Grannie by holding under her arms, Luzanne points her toward Aunt Imo, now waiting on the walk, shapeless in a seamed-up shift of floursack print—red Robin Hoods with bows and arrows.

"How you getting along, Mommer?" Aunt Imo says.

The old lady clops the metal walker around a warped aluminum pot of pink sultana, toddling behind it. "Ain't so good," she says and laughs, a rattle in her pea-shaped head. Her white hair is stained yellow, polleny stubble, like a bad wig.

Aunt Imo kisses the old lady on the lips, then hugs her tight. "I do love you, Mommer, Lord knows I do."

"And I love you too," says the old lady, stretching tall in Aunt Imo's grasp, then shrinking again to nothing as she lets go. "I love all my children."

"Yessum," says Aunt Imo, done with loving, and pivots with her broad flat back to Grannie and Luzanne. "Y'all come on in if you can get in."

The old lady stops on the brick walk and speaks to a fat yellow cat. "Whereabouts are we?"

"We at Aunt Imo's, Grannie," says Luzanne, muffling a snicker, and steers her toward the concrete block doorsteps, laid one, two, three in the snuff-rich dirt. Morning glory tunnels through the matched hollows of the blocks.

"Francine ain't get no business sending her to me." Aunt Imo brushes her feet on the rag mat and passes through the screen door to the low-ceiled porch and on into the front room, similarly ceiled—squares of white plyboard with dark grouts.

From outside, you can see the long kitchen table and the white stove behind it. A platter of fried salmon patties sits between the dual stove eyes, decked with assorted pots.

Aunt Imo is at the stove, calming the hissing blue fire of an eye to a whisper, still talking. "Reckon y'all heared about Emmacee Mae?"

Luzanne has wrenched the old lady and her walker onto the porch and hobbles with her toward the kitchen door.

Smell of lard-frying, smell of dry bird dust, smell of sickness.

"I do wish Francine and them would a-give me time . . . to change out of my nightgown," Grannie mumbles.

"You all right, Grannie." Luzanne is almost across the raised board threshold and onto the blue linoleum where the prints of the boards beneath have transferred through in dull brown streaks.

The old lady's brushed-polyester purple gown is hiked under her white sweater with flower petals of pearls along the front. Her hardened ankles are starred with dirty-rose veinbursts.

"You doing fine, Grannie," says Luzanne, almost there.

"Emmacee, honey, look, it's Grannie," says Aunt Imo loudly, bending over the green vinyl couch placed along the north wall to the right of the stove. "She come by to see you. Just for a minute."

Emmacee is sprawled back on the couch, staring up at the bare bulb in the stark ceiling. Her green-rimmed pupils are fixed like tacks on styrofoam. Her drab blonde hair frizzes around her long thin face and mats in strands on her jointed neck. A plate of tomatoes-and-rice and a broken salmon pattie sits on the lap of her chartreuse jumpsuit, which has a huge zipper up the front. One hand grips the handle of a spoon, resting on her plate, and the other hangs in a loose fist by her side. Her long straight legs stick out and her yellow toes nest like new mice.

Aunt Imo picks up Emmacee's hand with the spoon and scoops some tomatoes-and-rice and guides it to her slack drooling mouth. Emmacee's pale lips wiggle, her eyes bat, she smacks. Aunt Imo scrapes the dribble of red rice with the spoon and places it on the plate. Then settles in next to Emmacee.

"She was took bad this time, *bad*." Aunt Imo purses her lips, dips forward, and spits into a tin can of sand by her bloated crossed ankles. "Old stroke, doctors said."

The long living room-kitchen opens into a bathroom on the end near the porch. An orange enema bag hangs from a nail over the white bathtub, and a cage with a yellow-green parakeet sits on a stand between the tub and the commode. The other end of the living room leads into a bedroom with two double beds made up wrinkle-free with white chenille spreads. Wedged in the walk-space between beds, a narrow white cooktable with a red scrolled border is set for two: two plates, two forks, two spoons, and two empty pint fruit jars. Two ladder-back chairs are pushed to the table on each end.

Luzanne has maneuvered Grannie to the kitchen table, facing the stove, and steadies her while she pulls out a chair with a cowhide bottom. "Set here, Grannie."

The parakeet twitters nervously from the bathroom.

The old lady skiffles round and eyes the chair, backs up and sits with her pocketbook on her lap. She wobbles. Luzanne places the walker like a cage in front and steps behind her.

The yellow cat flows into the room and sidles around Grannie's legs with its periscoping tail held high.

The parakeet pecks at its bars, then flits to its perch, a miniature trapeze, and rings a bell.

"Lord a-mercy, I ain't thinking!" says Aunt Imo. "Mommer could a-set right here by me." She pats the couch and leaves her hand there. "I wish to my Lord it was so I could just keep Mommer," she says to Luzanne while gazing at Grannie. "I told Francine as much, but with my own youngun in such a fix, took with a stroke . . ."

Aunt Imo reaches across and tries to feed Emmacee a few golden crumbs of the salmon pattie. Emmacee's long pink tongue snakes out and draws back inside. She swallows.

"Can't hold nothing in her stomach," Aunt Imo says. "No appetite."

"Ain't she living in her house trailer out yonder nomore?" says Luzanne.

Aunt Imo crosses her arms, her greedy lips harden. "Belongs to be." She doubles over and spits; the dry skin of her crossed ankles rasps. "Welfare lady wouldn't give us a cent if she was to catch Emmacee living here with me."

"Bet she would if she seen her in *that* shape," says Luzanne.

"You'd think so, wouldn't you, honey?" Aunt Imo turns her thick face to Emmacee, who still stares at the ceiling. 'Mind ain't never been all that good nohow; now I even have to take her to wee-wee. What's got me down in the back."

Grannie mumbles and stands her triangular bone pocketbook on her lap. The crown of her skimpy yellow head just reaches the top of the chair back.

"What you want, Grannie?" Luzanne ducks to Grannie, curly brown hair hiding the old lady's elfin face. "Says she wants to stay right here till Aunt Francine gets back from the hospital," Luzanne tells Aunt Imo.

The yellow cat curls on Grannie's feet.

Aunt Imo cups her hand to one side of her mouth and whispers. "Francine ain't nomore in the hospital than I am; gone to the beach, I got all idears." She winks, her mouth screws. She sits high, hardened gray soles flat on the floor, palms in praying position.

Then she speaks up, striking the cat-purring peace. "Mommer, honey, you know good and well if I could keep you I would—I would in a heartbeat. But you can see what shape poor li'l ol' Emmacee's in. Can't you now?"

The old lady spits in her Dixie cup and mumbles again.

"What's she saying, sugar?" Aunt Imo asks Luzanne.

Luzanne's rich brown hair again hides the old lady's face. "Says how long's Emmacee Mae been took like that?"

Aunt Imo sits back and crosses her smooth hairless legs. "Three weeks ago tomorrow, Mommer, Sunday week." She studies Emmacee, still lolled with the plate on her lap. Her eyes are closed now, showing candle-white lids.

The parakeet flutters, the cage rattles, the bell rings.

They all watch Emmacee while the wind-up clock ticks down on the mahogany-painted table at the right end of the couch.

Aunt Imo suddenly jumps up and pads to the stove and cuts off the fire under a pot. "Honey, I bet ya'll ain't eat a mouthful all day. Is Mommer eat yet?"

"I don't know; I just picked her up two hours ago." Luzanne bows low over the old lady. "You hungry, Grannie?" She listens with large staring eyes, then relays the answer to Aunt Imo. "Says she ain't all that hungry but she could eat a bite and says . . ."

"Well, I'll just fix her a plate, bless her ol' heart." Aunt Imo marches to the stove, slaps a salmon pattie on a white plate, dips a serving each of steamed cabbage and tomatoes-and-rice and breaks off the browned edge from a pone of cornbread. The Robin Hood repeats on the print of her shift shimmy across her broad backside.

Luzanne finishes what she'd started to say. "Granny says she wants me to go get her suitcase out of the car."

Aunt Imo whirls around and flattens both hands on the white tablecloth. "Mommer, honey, I can't keep you this time—Lord knows I wished I could. Why don't you eat a little dinner and I'll call up Moavie and see if she can't take you till Francine gets back from the beach."

"She went to the hospital, Aunt Imo," says Luzanne, pulling out a chair and perching. "And Mama's got a new boyfriend, ain't got but one bed in her house trailer."

"She looks like a boyfriend!" says Aunt Imo. "Give me a minute and I'm gone call her up and give her a piece of my mind. She can tell me to my face she can't keep her own mommer. Me and Francine's done our part—yeah, I know Francine's done the biggest part and it ain't fair, it all on her. But I been down in my back, and now Emmacee . . .

"Why, you see that table yonder?" She points to the set table in the bedroom. "When the welfare lady comes by, I have to make like Bobo and Suellen have set up housekeeping here. Like they're living here with me in their own quarters, so I can draw my foodstamps. Ain't enough to keep a cat alive.

"And talk about *no beds*!" She points to the couch and stops talking, seems to have clipped all links connected to thoughts in her head. Her bland face flushes and her trenched nape pinks beneath girlish curls freed from the old-lady bun. She swipes at her skirt with the backs of her hands and minces flat-footed to the couch, jerks the plate off Emmacee's lap and gets down on her knees. "Done spilt it, I declare." On all fours now, she brushes at imaginary crumbs like Jesus erasing what's written in the sand.

When she gets back with the plate, empty except for a few soupy red grains of rice, she drops it in the dishpan under the large mullioned window set in sideways—a mural of green viny gumwoods.

She takes Grannie's plate off the stove and places it before her on the table. Then huffily she picks up the spoon, paring tiny crescents of the salmon patty. Done, she stares the old lady square in the eye. "Mommer, don't you want to go to Luzanne's house?"

"I been trying to get her to go home with me," says Luzanne, "but she says she wants to be at one of her own daughter's when her time comes." Luzanne leans close to Grannie. "Will you go to my house, Grannie?"

"What, child?"

"You wanta go home with me, Grannie?"

The old lady cups a spotted-clay hand over Luzanne's. "I would, honey, but I want to be at my own daughter's when I'm took."

Aunt Imo's hazel eyes stay on Grannie, now eating in tiny bites with her floweret-sprinkled ankles crossed and the yellow cat measuring the hem of her purple gown with its tail.

"Pool ol' Mommer," says Aunt Imo, "nobody don't want her but me, and I can't take her."

Emmacee begins groaning and twisting, but stays in the same spot.

"I'm a–coming, honey, Mommer's coming," says Aunt Imo, smartly flouncing across the linoleum. "Gotta go wee-wee, I bet."

She bends over and whispers with her soft cotton shift hiked, then laces an arm around Emmacee's back and lifts up, winching her from the couch, half-dragging, half-walking the moaning old girl toward the bathroom. Emmacee's green eyes roll, her bony knees buckle, her feet drag. Aunt Imo lugs her, grunting in hard labor.

From the closed bathroom door comes all manner of hissing and shushing and shuffling. "How come you had to tell 'em I had a stroke?" "Hush now." The parakeet twitters, the bell rings. Something rubbery slaps the door. "I cain't just set there like that all day. You try it." The toilet flushes, the parakeet screeches. "Least you could turn on the radio." Flesh splats; Emmacee shrieks. "You stay put or else!"—Aunt Imo. You can almost hear her teeth grit. Then quiet.

In a few minutes, the door opens and Aunt Imo half-drags, half-walks Emmacee out, the hose of the rubber enema bag tangling on her ankles. She shakes it off like a snake. This time, Aunt Imo places Emmacee on her side, facing the back of the couch with her knees drawn. Her dirty soles press out. Her feet are trim as wooden shoetrees.

Aunt Imo brushes back that same stubborn strand of hair to the bun, with its brown mesh rattail peeking through and hair pins sticking up like bad wires on a hot plate. She doesn't look at Luzanne and Grannie, heads straight for the bathroom and kicks the orange enema bag inside and slams the door. The parakeet screeches, the door flaps open. Aunt Imo goes on to the dishpan and starts washing dishes.

"Worse thing I ever done," she says, "was teach that old bird how to talk."

After dinner, after Aunt Imo has fed everybody and herself, she sits stuffed and cross on the right end of the couch, holding Emmacee Mae's feet while she sleeps. On her back now, with her hands placed on her chest, Emmacee looks like a corpse.

Grannie still sits in the chair at the table, though she's been turned facing out. Luzanne beside her. A fresh dip of snuff in Grannie's mouth, she alternately spits into the Dixie cup and wipes under her nose and nods. Satisfied, while the purring cat sleeps curled around the back of her heels like fur slippers.

Overhead, the sun ticks down on the tin roof, birds sing in the sweetgum, and the yellow-green parakeet in the bathroom mimics the chirring of crickets.

A car door claps out front.

"Somebody's here, Aunt Imo," says Luzanne, stretching high to see over pots of flowers on the ledges of the screened porch.

"That'll about be Suellen and Bobo, bringing my groceries," Aunt Imo says with her head back.

"No'um," says Luzanne, "it's some woman toting a black case."

By the time the woman's feet set in scratching on the brick walk, Aunt Imo is up and running for the door, fussing with her hair while gazing back at Emmacee and then the bedroom. "Lord a-mercy!" she says low. "It's that old welfare woman. Luzanne, run go get Mommer's suitcase out of your car. Hear?"

She switches faces and tones as she bounds to the porch door, talking through the screen to the welfare woman. "Come on in if you can get in."

"How you doing, Miss Imo?" says the woman, on the porch now with Aunt Imo.

"Ain't so good," says Aunt Imo. "How you getting on?"

Luzanne starts out the door to the porch.

"Miss Hogan, this here's my sister Moavie's girl," says Aunt Imo, spitting around the screen door and ducking back flushed. "Come to bring Mommer back from Francine's."

"Howdy do," says the round woman. Her black hair is parted down the middle and bobbypinned flat over small white ears.

"Yessum," says Aunt Imo, "looks like Macon don't agree with Mommer. But it was good of Francine to take her for a few days."

"Run along now, sugar, and get Mommer's stuff out of the car," Aunt Imo says to Luzanne, who is sidestepping between chairs and potted plants and the two stout women taking up most of the space on the narrow porch.

"Reckon you heared about Emmacee Mae having a stroke?" Aunt Imo says to the woman.

The welfare woman sits in the chair next to Grannie, writing on a yellow pad with one foot tucked behind the other. Aunt Imo is wedged in her spot at the right end of the couch. All of them viewing Emmacee, laid out with her eyelids twitching.

Luzanne lugs the tweedy gray suitcase in and sets it by the table and takes her place on the other side of Grannie.

"Miss Imo," says the welfare lady, "you don't reckon Emmacee's gone into a coma?"

"Can't never tell, honey," says Aunt Imo. "Doctor's said she might could."

The welfare woman writes on her yellow pad. "What's her doctors' names?"

"Lord, child," says Aunt Imo, rubbing her bowl forehead, "I'll have to look it up and get back to you."

The woman twiddles her pen on the pad. "Say your mama's living here all the time now, right?"

"Yes'um," says Aunt Imo, shifting against the pressure of Emmacee's soles. "Course, with Emmacee in such a shape I might have to get Francine and Moavie to take Mommer for a day now and then."

"I see," says the woman, watching Grannie doze with her chin on her chest. "So she might be with her other girls some of the time."

"Just when I have to run Emmacee to the doctor and all."

"Bobo and Suellen," says the woman, turning to eye the bedroom, "they still living with you I guess?"

"Yes'um," says Aunt Imo, crossing her legs primly and laying into the couch arm, "gone to town to pick up some groceries right now. But they still living with me."

"Well," says the woman, getting up, "get me the name of Emmacee's doctors and I'll see what I can do about upping your foodstamps and all."

"I'll get right on it," says Aunt Imo, rising and seeing her to the door. Her Robin Hood print dress is stuck to her sweaty back.

Sun still shining, a shower dances up out of the woods behind Aunt Imo's house and beats out a sweet rhythm on the tin roof. The briny smell of damp dust sifts through the porch screen and courses into the kitchen, where Grannie sits peering out. She looks charmed, her face calm though cavernous. Her pocketbook is on the floor by her worn suitcase. She strokes the yellow cat on her lap. It purrs. Emmacee snores.

Luzanne sits facing Aunt Imo on the couch. They both watch Grannie at the end of the table, who is used to sitting that way at Francine's house: in her own corner with a gas space heater, a quick-change picture calendar on one wall, and a Fingerhut clock with sweeping angel wings on the other.

The rain lets up, though a few drops drip from the sweetgum leaves to the tin and trail down the corrugated eaves to twinkling sand gullies.

"What went with *your* little kitty, Mommer?" says Aunt Imo.

Luzanne answers for Grannie. "Aunt Francine took him off."

Nothing is changed by the welfare woman's visit, but in deference to Grannie and the rhythm of the rain, Aunt Imo and Luzanne have put all business on hold till the shower ends.

Then Aunt Imo starts. "I'm gone call up Moavie." She stands and tips to the square table with the slow-ticking clock and the black phone and opens a blue notebook, running her finger down the page. She licks her finger and turns another page, running names and numbers. Her finger stops. She dials, a lazy spring-back grating. She puts the receiver to her ear, discovering the loose hair pins, and while she talks, she punches them into her bun.

Luzanne gets up and goes into the bathroom, closing the door.

"How you doing, Moavie?" Aunt Imo pauses. "That so?" Pause. "No, I didn't know that, I . . ." She waits, switching ears. "Listen, honey, Luzanne's here with Mommer. Yeah. Yeah. Yeah, she took her off Francine's hands for the weekend, can't get her to go home with her. So . . . Yeah, I know, sugar." She laughs, her broad body quakes, bun to buttocks. "Me too. Yeah, yeah, yeah." She waits, straightening the Holy Bible on the table, picking at the starched points of the crocheted table scarf. "Reckon you heared about Emmacee Mae?" She waits. "Had herself a stroke." She watches Emmacee, who has rolled over, still sleeping, with hands clasped beneath one sallow pouched cheek. Her mouth is open, the undersides of her pink lips glisten wet.

"Listen, sugar," Aunt Imo says into the phone, turning her attention to Grannie now, "It'd shore be a help to me if you'd take her, I . . ." She pauses. "Yeah, yeah, I can imagine . . ."

The fat yellow cat stands on Grannie's lap, arches its back and hops softly to the floor and spirits out to the porch.

"Kitty, kitty, kitty," Grannie calls. "Come on back here, kitty."

The old lady braces on the rim of the walker and struggles to her feet, blue terry slippers scuffing across the linoleum. She smiles, her hazel eyes bleaching in the door-shape of sunshine. Her hair turns to gold. She holds out one hand. "Here, kitty-kitty." She skiffles up to the raised threshold and trips and drops to her knees, going down in a puff of air. "Here kitty-kitty."

"Like I was saying, I'd shore 'prechate it if you'd take her . . . just a minute, Moavie." Aunt Imo chins the mouthpiece of the phone and goes white. "Mommer! Mommer!" she yells, lowering the receiver to her side, and watches the old lady rock on her knees. Then into the phone again, Aunt Imo says, "Never mind, Moavie."

The cat, sunning on the west ledge of the porch, hops down and glides before Grannie's raised face, its tail caressing her chin. Then it circles back to the puddle of sunshine on the end of the porch.

The old lady follows, feebly crawling, one blue slipper on the threshold, the other before the screen door. When she gets to the cat, she curls up beside it and closes her eyes.

Henry Alcalay

We Get Paid on Friday

I LEFT THE MEETING, walked down the hall, closed the door to the first office I came to and spun the chair around so I faced the wall. Then I called this girl I'd met to see if she wanted to go out. My fourth try that week. Even if I'd thought it was going to go well I'd have closed the door, I so hate having my calls overheard, but as it was the girl's roommate answered and when she told her it was me, couldn't get her to the phone. I hung up and waited a few minutes, my armpits wringing wet, hoping the guy whose office I'd appropriated wouldn't come barging in. I looked at the pictures on his desk of his wife, children, and pets and at the piles of paper he shuffled all day to keep them clothed and fed. When I called back, Roberta, the girl I'd wished to speak with in the first place, picked up. "I'm very tired and I'm busy," she said in response to my greeting. "Goodbye and good luck."

After that I didn't care so much whether the guy barged in. Mouth sand dry, armpits wet, struggling to control my trembling, I staggered back down the hall to the conference room, claimed an emergency and left. Then I walked the three blocks from the slaughtered-goods warehouse to the foot of the Fifty Ninth Street Bridge, where I caught a cab into Manhattan. "Ray's place," I told the cabbie like I might have told him Studio 54 or The Garden.

"Ray's Place?" the cabbie demanded, glancing at me over his shoulder, all but cocking his head like a perplexed quadruped. "What in the world . . . is Ray's Place?"

"Ray's place? You don't know Ray's Place? How long you been driving, man?"

His bemused smile angered me. "All right, never mind," I snapped. "I'm too tired and too busy to explain. Just take me to 78th and Second, then."

Ray was home. On the ride over I'd been worried he might not be, forgetting that on Fridays he always left work early; when an elevator breaks on Friday they let it go until Saturday when overtime kicks in. I climbed the four flights to his apartment, struggling against the throb of the jukebox in the Stolen Moments which dogged my every step. Ray's room mate Michael let me in. Ray sat on a futon in the little living room, his back against the wall. He looked up when he saw me, his placid face hard to read.

"Hi, Ray," I said and sat down beside him on the futon. He smelled as usual of patchouli, Pall Malls and resin, but a different resin than the one he usually smelled of—resin being what they used to lubricate the cables. "Say . . . where'd you work today?" I asked, suspicious.

"Brooklyn House of Detention," he said and I knew that was it; usually he worked in Manhattan, offices and residences; he was strictly a commercial and residential man. But now things were changing. The futon on which we sat was all the furniture Ray had. The wide planked, highly polished wood floor gleamed like glass; night or day the sight of it never failed to fill me with optimism. Michael leaned against the sink in the kitchenette, next to the gap in the counter where the dishwasher used to be.

Ray asked me how much I wanted to spend and I told him "Thirty." He got up and went in the kitchenette, banged around some pots and pans for a while and when he came back, handed me a folded piece of white paper containing dope. "I'd like to get off here. Can you set me up?" I asked and Ray went back in the kitchen for a glass of water and a spoon. "Also, I need some works," I said when he reappeared.

"Where's yours, I don't think I have any new ones," he looked down at me.

"Well, shoot, you think I knew I was coming? I'm coming straight from work."

He went back in the kitchen and I heard a drawer open. So that's where he's keeping it, I thought; all that banging of pots and pans was strictly to confuse me. Of course I'd brought my own set which I carried with me everywhere in my inside suit pocket as others, with more to lose, may carry a gun, but every day, ever since I'd robbed him, Ray changed the place where he stashed his stuff and that day, for some reason, I wanted to know where it was. Returning, he handed me a plastic syringe with the markings worn from the side. Smiling, he sat down beside me and urged me to put my sock on. I needed no urging. Taking my sock from my foot, I tied it around my arm. Michael came in from the kitchen and sat on the floor across from us, his back against the exposed brick wall, watching as I drew the solution into the syringe through a piece of cigarette filter like it was some science experiment and I was the teacher.

After I was done and had loosened my sock and the rush surged through me, warm blue salty water from the Caribbean, lush with sunlight and plankton, for the first time since meeting Roberta I found myself thinking, "the hell with her, there are a million others." But when the rush subsided, replaced by that well being that results when the dope has shrunk your doubts like chemo shrinks tumors, I figured, Why not call her? The worst she can do is say no and so what, she's said that already which means there's no where to go from here but up; why not call her already?

Just let me soak up this warmth a little longer and then I'll see where Ray's phone is, I decided. *Just don't wait too long, Old Bean,* a voice inside my head counseled, *A deed undone is like a* . . . The voice tried to formulate a pithy truism but it was too much work and it trailed off into silence . . . I leaned back on the futon, closed my eyes, then opened them, smiling at Ray and the thought I could always buy more.

"Hey, I wanna show you something," Ray announced, reaching beneath the futon, pulling out a battered silver handgun. It was so flimsy and small it looked like a toy, like it could fit in a purse. "Got this for protection," he muttered, playing with the clip. In places the paint was chipped off altogether, exposing what looked like grey plastic underneath. When it went off it made such a bang my eyelids slammed shut and stars flew before my eyes and my jaw clamped shut, grazing the tip of my tongue. Blanks, I assumed, rather unamused at what seemed a childish prank. But Ray and Michael were both bleeding, each gripping a limb. Ray, still sitting, rocked back and forth, grasping his left hand to his chest, blood pouring from it like a mop being wrung, rebuking himself in a reedy, whining voice.

"Man, man, what is this?" he demanded, sounding like a motorist trying to coax a cop into taking back a parking ticket.

Micheal was more vociferous. Hopping up and down in one place in the midst of an ever-expanding pool of blood, clutching his apparently gunshot calf to his chest, he swore at Ray at the top of his lungs, calling him over and over again a "nigger, a shit-fucking, sorry-assed nigger." With every oath spittle flew from his mouth, each individual droplet illuminated by the slanting rays of the late day sun. Blood poured from him and ran along the floor and when it reached the baseboards, turned and ran alongside the wall and when it came to the place the wall ended, turned again and ran into the kitchen, forging on as if imbued with some primordial sense of manifest destiny.

Taking a page from Michael's book, Ray stood up as well. Bent over like he'd been shot in the stomach, holding his shattered hand to his chest, cursing in a high pitched voice I didn't recognize, he lurched into the kitchen where I heard him banging pots and pans around. In moments he returned and bounced around the living room, still cursing, still bent over, blood running down his forearm, pouring off his elbow onto the lovely floor. Then he tottered back into the kitchen, banging pots and pans, swearing in the girlish, operatic manner. And in fact it sounded like an opera, the way their voices contrasted, Ray's birdlike voice demanding of himself some explanation as to how this had happened, Michael in his deeper, more manly way calling Ray a nigger; "You nigger, you shot me, you nigger. If you think I'm gonna forget this . . ." Ray, being white, didn't care, I was sure, if he heard at all. I could feel the spot where I'd bit my tongue.

The sheltered life I lead, I'd never seen such blood. There was something raw about it, its oddly voluptuous consistency reminding me of quicksilver rather than some ordinary liquid. Studying Ray's I noted a somewhat oily sheen but where it combined with Michael's I couldn't tell them apart. I've heard people speak of the smell of blood, but that day there wasn't any. How long it took me to figure out the bullet had passed through Ray's hand and into Michael's leg, I have no idea. Time seemed to have lost its ability to help define experiences, becoming as shapeless and random as the blood on the floor. Later, when I thought about it, still wanting to know how long the whole thing took, I would reflect back on the amount of blood spilled as if that would tell me something but without a rate of spill, still I was in the dark. And I wondered what might have happened had Michael not been sitting across from us; would the bullet have hit the brick wall and ricocheted back, making that sound I've never heard other than in the movies, hitting me or hitting Ray, the same bullet zapping him twice?

"You guys have to go to the hospital now, it has come to that," I announced, excited to be thinking about everyone I'd tell this to. Anyone thinks I lead a humdrum life, just wait till they hear this, I exulted. That Roberta, boy, the things she doesn't know about me.

"Would you please stop smiling, please?" Ray said to me in one of his lucid moments. For the last time before we left, he bounded into the kitchen, still clutching his injured hand to his chest. I was reminded of a picture I'd seen in *Life* magazine a decade before, a medic in Vietnam dashing under fire, clutching a blood swaddled infant to his chest. All of a sudden, who knows from where—it wasn't from "The Stolen Moments"—I began hearing that song, "The Limbo Rock." It was in my head. I hadn't heard it in years but I was sure hearing now. What I was hearing most clearly of all were the bongos and cowbell and cymbals. Never before had I really considered what a skilled percussionist they'd hired for the date. Ray and Micheal seemed to be jumping up and down and staggering precisely to its beat, just as if they were in a movie. It exhilarated me to think that my life had moments in it that were so dramatic they deserved to be recorded and studied and that the only thing missing was a context to put them in. *You just keep piling up those moments*, piped up the voice that earlier had urged me to call Roberta, *The context will come.*

"Ray, come on, you guys have to get to a hospital, maybe I should call 911." I said, picking up from the floor a framed photo of Ray and his mother taken when he was ten. He stood in front of her, smiling, holding a bunch of comic books. Her hands rested on his shoulders. I turned the picture on its side, trying to tell which comics he was holding. He was a big Green Lantern fan, I remembered but from the picture I couldn't tell if those were what he had. He might have been clutching Archies or Richie Rich's, favorites of mine as well.

"Don't call 911, I got stuff all over the place," Ray snapped, sounding out of breath. "Just give me a hand with Michael, help me get him down the stairs."

Ray and I got on either side, looped our arms around his shoulders, and got him downstairs. In the street, no cabs would stop. They'd come close, have a look, and then veer away. "You guys go wait in the vestibule, I'll handle this," I told Ray. Michael's head lolled around like a little baby's. He had no time for words now. The abuse he'd heaped on Ray hadn't helped at all. The first cabbie that stopped took one look at Ray and Michael staggering towards him and even as I held the door open, yelled, "No way!" and took off. Michael and Ray retreated to the vestibule and I tried again. When this one stopped I climbed in directly behind the driver and explained that we had to wait. "Have you ever considered inviting Scientology into your life, may I ask?" I said, obliging him to turn towards me, away from the direction from which Ray and Michael were approaching. Once they were in, I scrambled out and off to Lenox Hill they went.

I flew back upstairs to Ray's apartment and rifled through his kitchen for the dope he said he had hidden. Nothing. I walked the four blocks home to my own walkup and lay on my bed, trying to salvage what torpor remained of the dope which all the excitement had now nearly wasted.

I'd stopped off for a fresh pack of Winstons and now lay on top of my covers, chain smoking and thinking. I thought about how someday this whole thing with dope would end. Who knew when but I was sure it would. Then when I'd look back, it would be like acne; terrible while it was happening but not so bad afterwards. I guess most things are like that. I thought about those pictures on that guy's desk where I'd called Roberta and how someday, instead of this, I'd have pictures of my own, documented proof I was doing what I was supposed to. There seemed no help for it; that was what I was bred for and why I became a lawyer. I'd have the wife, the kids, the school plays, the supermarket on Saturday and afterwards, unless the babysitter copped out, an evening at the theater.

It occurred to me I'd need a hobby and I catalogued the usual ones healthy males seemed to gravitate towards; golf, tennis, hunting, fishing, boating, hang gliding. The way I understood it, you chose one and stuck with it, you didn't go gallivanting from one to another. Duckhunting, I decided, would be most appropriate for me. You wore a hat, you carried a gun, you hung out in swamps with a dog and when you were done, even if when younger you'd never traipsed through Mekong bayous stalking NVA, you still had muddy boots and a bunch of dead ducks to prove you were a man.

I smoked half the pack, then got on the phone. My old friend Ernest, from Queens like me, picked up on the second ring. "So, what are you doing tonight?" I asked once he'd stopped laughing over my story. Ray was from Queens too.

"A bunch of us are going to eat at Fiesta de la Paloma's."

"Girls too?"

"Some, sure."

"Shit, I hate eating Mex, though."

"So, stay home."

"What about the chairs, are they comfortable? I don't think I know this place."

There *were* girls, four if I remember, with dark curly hair and coarse features, and about seven guys, everyone seated at an oval table that wobbled until the busboy came, knelt at our feet and secured the leg with matches. I was still stoned but it was fading and to keep it alive a little longer, I smoked every minute. The warmer the sangria in the pitcher got, the more like spit it tasted.

The walls were adorned with autographed photos of celebrities. I could make out the usual array of first-tier entertainers who, in the past, had presumably enjoyed the gracious hospitality of Fiesta's host and owner, Bruce Orthwein. There were as well a sizable number of second-raters and has-beens whose portraits were also on display.

I wondered whether your face on the wall mandated a free meal. It was hard to guess and I was willing to concede this was one of those things where experience provided the answer; maybe someday, should I become sufficiently exalted myself, my portrait too would adorn one of the walls of Fiesta De La Paloma and then I would know.

Across the room, over by the wall, in front of the unlighted fireplace, a contingent of Fondas was dining. There was Henry, grey and fragile but still with that puzzled, sincere look in his eyes. There was his wife, Shirley, a slim brunette in her thirties, wearing a yellow pantsuit and those glasses that go from dark to light depending on conditions. There was Jane, and Tom Hayden who, when it came to acting, I was sure, could have taught them all a thing or two. And there was Peter, also wearing glasses, with a woman who may have been his wife and a youngish blonde girl who may have been their kid. When I first recognized the Fonda Family I felt really special, as if I was famous too or soon would be or was at least unique; their magic seemed to permeate the room and imbue everyone with something they wouldn't have had otherwise, but as the meal went on the feeling faded and I found myself looking for signs that in spite of their good fortune, they were unhappy too.

"What do you do?" the girl next to me asked and I answered, "Lawyer," in a tone designed to encourage her to shut up. Noting the surfeit of hair on her bare arm, I tried to gauge how hairy her other aspects were; did she have hair tumbling down from her navel to her groin; did she have pubic hair sprouting from the insides of her upper thighs? The fact she didn't have a moustache made me think the answer to both questions was Not Likely. I couldn't ask so I asked her instead whether she'd ever wondered how it was that on every TV show and movie ever made there was just one standard sound to indicate a ricochet, thinking maybe if she was interested in that I could use it as a lead-in to talk about what had happened earlier but she didn't care to pursue it. She was a commercial artist, was all I knew about her. All of them at the table were and because they worked at home, they had their whole lives, it seemed to me, to do with as they pleased. They were all friends of Ernest, a commercial illustrator. The only one I wanted to talk to, a courtroom artist with long slender hairless arms I could imagine licking, was seated at the other end of the table, listening patiently to Ernest, who was loud and drunk. When he got drunk he talked about money, how much he had, how much he made and how, someday soon, he was really going to rake it in. Sober, though, he was fun.

The Fondas left before we did, which was too bad because I'd have liked to have seen the kind of cars they traveled in. It slipped my mind to notice whether they had been presented with a bill. Once they'd cleared off our dinner plates, I ordered a flan for dessert, then had another, then announced that I had to go. Nobody even looked up. I said it again, louder this time, addressing myself to Ernest. Some people looked up then, but I wondered whether they were looking to see what Ernest thought.

"We're all going to the Raccoon Lodge," he announced, pushing his chair back, giving himself room to speak; sometimes I hated him. "When we're finished here. Don't you want to come?"

"I have to meet someone," I lied, then went around to his end of the table and gave him a twenty before he could ask. "Here, this should cover me."

Outside it was gorgeous, one of the first nights of spring. I envisioned dozens of nights like this, one after the other, stretching endlessly through the months ahead, and it terrified me that I was without a girl.

Sullivan Street was all backed up so I walked to Houston and caught a cab to Canal Street, giving the driver the address of the club where the week before I'd met that girl who wouldn't come to the phone now. It was a club like lots of clubs where if they didn't like your looks, they didn't let you in. I knew with those ten people I'd eaten with we'd have been left standing out on the sidewalk all night.

When I got there they wouldn't let me in but no one else was getting in either, since they hadn't opened yet. Twenty other guys with the same idea as me milled around in the street, all of us thinking we were so smart for arriving early, and now look at us. A photographer I'd known since college came walking up the street. "They're not open yet," I told him.

"They open at eleven," he replied. "Come on, we'll go smoke this joint."

"Shit, I hate smoking pot."

"We all have to do things we don't like, sometimes," he said with a conceited smile.

"I'll just go for the walk," I said and we headed up the street. He lit his joint, drew on it, then offered it to me.

"No thanks," I held up my hand as if to ward it away. Then for good measure I waved my hand in front of my nose as if the smell bothered me. I was thinking whether or not to tell him what had happened earlier but before I could even decide, it took hold of me and came pouring out; the gun—how petite; the noise—how loud; the blood—how rich and thick, and when I was done he looked at me like he didn't know what to think. In the awkward silence of his stare, I realized I had told him all this in the same tone of voice I might appropriately have used to announce I'd been nominated for an Oscar or been signed to a record deal.

He might not have known what to think but in my head what I wanted him to think was crystal clear; I wanted him to be amazed and yet, at the same time, to think that such an event wasn't *that* unusual in the life I led. I wanted him to think I was cool and had an exciting life. I wanted him to think I was the sort who could witness outrageous things and take them in stride.

Instead he just kept looking at me. I guess the problem was I wanted him to do all kinds of thinking he simply wasn't prepared to, given the hour and the joint and, most of all, me, and when I realized this, I just walked away. "I'm going back, I'll see you inside," I said and left him there. All along I'd been worried anyway that the club would open while I was down the street and the guys in charge of the door wouldn't let me in as quickly as if they knew how faithfully I'd been waiting.

When I got back, they were letting people in but choosing them really slowly. I stood off to one side of the entrance while this maestro on a sort of loading platform decided who could enter. Then my friend with the joint came up on the other side of the door and as soon as the doorman saw him he lifted up the rope and whisked him through. Bad as it was to see that, I was too embarrassed to call out his name in the hope he could get me in too. Which he could have, I realized right then, he had a bunch of his photographs hanging in the place and, in fact, the night I'd met that girl there it had been a party to celebrate his pictures. All I'd had to do was stay by him and I'd have been in too.

I waited outside almost half an hour and by the time I got in not only wasn't I stoned anymore but I was six inches tall. I gulped two rum-and-cokes, then set out to look for the girl. There were two floors which meant I had to keep running up and down the stairs. Of course, she wasn't there. I don't know what I would have said anyway. She must have been pretty smart though; smart enough to turn me down, smart enough not to show up that night at the club where we might meet. If she was really brainy, of course, she never set foot in there again.

Wendell Mayo

La Lengua Serpentina

Educate yourself to silence.
—Daumier, Fellini's *8 1/2*

WHEN SUDDENLY Antonia discovered, as one only discovers when dreams are remembered in a waking stupor, that she no longer dreamed in lovely forms—of the urn; the saucer; the upturned shallow bowl, like a breast; the deep, pendulous shape of the penis—but only sounds, gibberish, the racket of remembered events, she went and found her mother, who was cooking lentils, an older woman, for Antonia was nearly forty herself.

"Mama," she said, "I no longer see things in my dreams."

"You are lucky, child," she replied, for Antonia's mother still called her child. "You are lucky you still dream at all. Count your blessings. I've stopped dreaming."

So Antonia made a dish of couscous, pale yellow, and sprinkled it with bits of green and red peppers, mint, and carrot. She dabbed her spoon in the colorful, fragrant heap of couscous, but did not eat; at last, she put a spoonful of tahini on top of the couscous, then pushed the dish from her and went to her room at the top of the stairs. There, in the middle of the day, she dozed as she often did, feeling a sadness for her mother, but not knowing the source of the sadness. She closed her eyes and heard the slapping of the little pellets in the hem of the curtain against the window sill, and under her eyelids made colors and shapes from the light trapped in her eyes: blue and purple and green clouds. Then, with the weak light in the room coming through the thicket of veins in her eyelids, she made red clouds of all shapes—and these, all these clouds of all shapes, became the nearest substitute for the shapes and colors she remembered had been in her dreams as a younger woman.

But when she at last dropped off, her sleep was dark and dreamless, and through the terrible exactness of perfect darkness she heard only the sound of her brother's laughter in the back yard, her brother who had moved away from home to college, then from college to Vietnam, and died there. Then in her dream made of only sounds, she remembered thinking that her window was open and that the curtain was slapping the sill, that she may be hearing him laughing in reality through the open window. Then she remembered he was dead, even as she slept she remembered this, and when she awoke she remembered only two things: that she had heard him laughing and that he was dead. And there was one thing more, not a memory, but a feeling about the sound of his laughter, something distinct that stayed with her, but she could not take the sound from the place inside her and make it with her mouth;

and she could not make the sound by thinking it in her brain; and she could not use the feeling of the sound to bring her brother's face back to her; and she could not know the time and place the sound had occurred because the sound had no time or place, nothing, and it wouldn't come into her mind or mouth or eyes.

In the morning, Antonia watched her mother's hand tremble in the light coming from the window over the sink in the kitchen. She wanted to tell her mother about the sound in her dream, but she hadn't the words or the pieces of words she knew were there to describe it. So she left her mother standing at the window, a cigarette in one hand, its glowing tip quivering in the light.

At the bakery where she worked, a block from her mother's house in Montauk, Antonia worked dough with her hands, feeling its cool, floured surfaces in her palms. She slapped the dough on the table, pausing a moment as a tinny refrain from the radio on the shelf above her died out. She switched the radio off and continued to work the dough with her hands, listening for the thump of the dough on the table and feeling the thump in her hands. She tried to hold the sound of the dough on the table in her hands as long as she could, but knew they would be calling for the dough soon; they would bake it and sell it; she knew that no matter how many times she tried to make the improbable nexus of feeling and sound in her hands she would need to give it away.

Later, after work, she took her bicycle and rode it to a small city park, Kirk Park, near Montauk Pond. She rode along a narrow grassy path with wild roses leaning in at all sides. The path led to a small dock connected to a covered pavilion. She set the bicycle on the grayed floor beams of the pavilion and saw two empty wine glasses and a bottle of red wine, half-full, setting in the center of the floor. She looked all around but saw no one, and she shuddered a moment, feeling isolated, seeing only the little waves rolling over the pond with the wind, over themselves, making translucent shadows in their shallow crests and valleys. She looked for other people across the pond, other docks and jetties poking into the water, yet, remarkably, she was entirely alone.

She stood in the pavilion a long time looking at the wine glasses and the half-empty bottle of wine. Then she knelt on the planks near them and tipped one glass on its side, and in her perfect solitude, while looking at the two curvaceous shapes, their stems, and the bottle near them, placed just so, a sound came from her dream, a bit of sound broken out from all the others she'd heard in her brother's laughter.

"*Ka*," she whispered.

When she first made the sound it seemed hollow, simple, empty, and in no way referred to the bottle and glasses she saw on the floor of the pavilion. She thought of making the sound again, but she shuddered at the idea of others hearing it. Even though she was so alone, she feared she may let the sound slip from her lips later at work, or recognize it in a string of sounds made by another person, so it would be part of something else. As hollow as it was, the sound seemed precious to her. So she let the idea of repeating the sound slip away, left the bottle and glasses on the floor of the pavilion, and bicycled home, keeping the bit of sound all to herself.

Antonia nudged the edge of a small slip of white paper, upon which her mother had written that she would be spending the night in the City, the West Village, with a friend. Antonia poked at the little note until it moved into the center of the kitchen table, then she rotated it with a finger so the corners did not quite align themselves with the corners of the table. Seeing the note in this attitude, she suddenly wanted to say something to her mother. Her wants often exceeded her knowledge of what was possible. She even wanted her mother's friend to be possible, a sculptor from the Village she didn't particularly like, an impossible man with black paint under his nails and tiny white spots of paint all over his hands. She didn't like him because he was too quiet and spoke in whispers, and only about his work, which seemed strange and disconnected to her: here a bicycle handle, a surfboard, a piece of petrified dung; the rest of the time he was inside himself. . . . But she wanted the impossible man to be possible even though she was sure he would never care to listen to her mother's indecipherable sorrow. Antonia wanted only what she knew was not possible.

So seeing her mother's note, the bit of white paper, just out of kilter with the larger, flat white surface of the Formica table, and thinking about the impossible man, another fragment from the laughter she remembered her dead brother make in her dream came to her.

"*La*."

And she was silent, inside herself the rest of the evening, not saying anything, keeping her new sound close to her in perfect silence. She did not speak, even under her breath, even for the sake of herself or the wallpaper or the sofa, and after a time of this silence she began to know that she was entirely inside herself, and knew that she spited the wallpaper and the sofa with her silence, and she enjoyed this, enjoyed keeping everything away from even the inanimate things around her. Then she thought, hiding her new sounds all the while, and forming her thoughts instead from pure feeling and nothing else, *Who can be more silent than this?*

Later, in her bedroom, in her house alone, without her mother or the impossible man from the City, she tried to dream a dream other than the one of her brother laughing in the backyard, but she couldn't. Nothing came to her and she slept like a dead woman.

The next morning, she felt numb while she worked at the bakery, kneading, rolling, and cutting the dough into raw doughnuts. She closed her eyes each time she cut the doughnut shapes out; she had cut the shapes before this way, and she knew only that she had shaped the dough with her hands before cutting it and couldn't bear the act of cutting something she'd felt so intimately with her hands.

After work, she again bicycled to the little city park and dock and pavilion. As she walked out along the dock, she noticed that the wine glasses and bottle were gone, and in their place set three mallard ducks, two with the bright green and red markings of the male, and a smaller, brownish duck, the female. Antonia paused and wondered if she might approach them without scaring them away, then seeing that they were unaware of her, she watched them from the dock, recalling again as she watched the ducks the sound of her brother's laughter in the dream she could only feel, and another bit of sound suddenly broke out from the memory of the feeling of her brother's laughter in her dream.

"*Roo*," she whispered at the ducks.

That night, she came home and found her mother alone, sleeping at the table in the kitchen, her cheek resting on the hard surface. An empty wine glass set near the note her mother had written to her the day before. The glass had a pinkish ring in the bottom where the wine had evaporated and a bit of lipstick smudged just below the lip. Antonia pushed a finger gently at the base of the wine glass, moved it near her mother's cheek, and left the kitchen. She paced the house quietly. For a short time she believed with all her heart that she had managed it—a revelry of silence, beyond all that could ever hurt her again, the long-forgotten impressions of grief and loneliness, her secret sounds hers, no one's but hers. She sat awhile in a chair by the picture window with her eyes closed, with no other need but to keep the silence all there to herself . . . and her mother?

She went back to the kitchen where her mother continued to sleep and leaned close to her ear.

"*Ka*," she whispered, but her mother did not move. "*Ka . . . La . . . Roo . . .*" she said softly and waited, wanting some sign of stirring, the tiniest flinch in the most delicate lines of muscle in her mother's eyelids, but none came.

Her mother did not stir. The house did not stir. Nor did the things in the house she had spited with her silence. But neither did the sadness inside her in the same perplexing way. She went to her room upstairs, where the curtains rustled against the sill, the night air against her skin. Alone, before falling asleep, she practiced the serpentine tongue again, clear and wordless, perfect and simple, a language without bounds, the purest song she knew and could sing to no one.

Steven
Barthelme

The Job

I

HIS HAPPINESS LASTED only a moment. Until the telegram came, a foreign-born boy with a pad brought it. He signed. The boy left. He put the telegram on the table, the table in the center of his room in the center of Texas.

Who would send me a telegram? he thought. From Chicago? What an odd thing to do.

He looked at the envelope on the round, white formica table. The sheer beauty of the telegram took his breath away. He fell down, gasping.

He fell asleep on the rug. In his dream Jesus came to him in white flowing robes as in photos of the Resurrection. In the dream Jesus left a white telegram in a white envelope and told a parable. In the parable a man with a hat came into a city of bareheaded people. The stranger was subject to suspicion. The townspeople were confused. Eventually, they put the man to death, ate him, built a temple, worshipped the hat. Jesus left, through the roof. He ran to the telegram and tore it open. HAVE A HEART, it said.

He woke up, on the rug, feeling suddenly alert. I feel like a cat feels, he thought. I slept like a cat.

He looked east and west, out the windows, and saw rain. He looked at the telegram at the center of Texas. Picked up the yellow envelope. Opened it.

> NUDE WOMAN IN YOUR AREA GIVEN TO JUMPING IN WINDOWS NAKED. WHILE NOT INTERESTED IN MEANINGLESS BEHAVIOR, ABILITY TO SAVE WORLD UNDERMINED BY UNTIDINESS MEANINGLESS BEHAVIOR. THEREFORE PREPARED TO REWARD HANDSOMELY IF FIND WOMAN AND SATISFACTORILY DETERMINE PURPOSE MEANINGLESS BEHAVIOR. WHO DOES SHE WORK FOR? WILL CONTACT SEPT ONE. DO NOT ATTEMPT CONTACT. BENEVOLENT.

A tough assignment, he thought. Three weeks.

Fortunately, he already knew her, if only to say hello to. She had leapt in the previous April, quite a jump, two floors from street level. She was, of course, beautiful. Dark hair, dark eyes, a spectacular tan. He cursed himself for having sex with her instead of asking what she meant. An opportunity for serious communication and all he had thought of was fellatio. Bah!

He went to the kitchen and pulled out a drawer, took a handful of sugar and ate it. Then he fixed a glass of ice water and returned to the table. Go, he thought.

He went to the laundromat, driving through rain. Hiding in a dryer, he watched the patrons come and go. He watched the women, looking for her, the way she kept her head down just a little. His neck began to hurt. By three AM the laundromat, bright and empty, felt like a chapel, and it occurred to him. A nude woman doesn't wash clothes often. Of course. He thought about this until about seven, when new patrons with more dirt began arriving. He felt stiff. It took two or three hours to get out of the dryer. He got his Out of Order sign.

He left the laundromat and drove to the grocery store. Supermarket. He parked his red '63 Chevy in the single space left by forty-seven silver cars built in the years after. They looked curiously alike, and told something about America.

He loitered around the avocados. Examined carrots. Lolled in front of the orange juice. Attended carefully to what seemed an extraordinary number of cracker boxes. Debated about dinner. There was no sign of her.

In the supermarket he saw one hundred viciously beautiful housewives, most nearly naked. The abundance made him giddy. He saw two representative examples of every possible type and kind of breast, there being one hundred types in all. He got one hundred small slips of paper with names, addresses, and husband schedules. Absence tables.

Ten minutes, twelve minutes—these women are out of their skulls! he thought. Out for liquor; Gardening; Hardware store: nails—they must not realize how fragile I am. How can they be so sure?

Luckily he caught himself. This is where I went wrong the last time, he thought. If only I could concentrate like everybody else.

He drove home and went to sleep. When his father knocked at the door the following afternoon, he woke up.

"Pop!" he cried.

He threw his arms around the short, stout older man whom he had not seen since he was six. There was so much to talk about.

"You— How—"

"Parole," his father said, rearranging the furniture. "That's what they said; I figure they just reconsidered. They have our best interests at heart."

His father an XYY carrier who had lived in the minimum security facility at Fort Worth for twenty-seven years, for having children. His father was guilty as sin. Nine boys had been introduced into evidence.

"I'm glad you're here, Pop. I need your advice."

"Everywhere fathers are gardening," the old man said. "I get to give advice. Okay. I was always good at that." He settled on the couch. "Nice couch. You build it?"

He nodded.

"Get me the pliers," his father said, leaning over the end of the couch.

"I don't have any pliers." He was lying to his father again.

"Huh?"

"There're no pliers."

"What's the matter with you, boy?" his father said. "No pliers? How you ever expect to fix anything?" His father straightened up and thought about the foolishness of youth. Shook his bald head. "Well, you need some advice? You can't have any money, but I'll give you every last bit of advice I ever owned." He recognized his father's favorite joke.

"I've got this job, Pop."

"Well hot damn!"

"No, wait. It's not a real job." He explained his job, the girl, the windows.

"Seems like you've got a problem, son. You a homo?"

He shook his head. "I'm getting paid, Pop. And, nowadays, the word is gay."

"What?"

"Homos."

"Oh," his father said. "You kinda lose track, in the big house."

"Slammer. Joint."

His father thought for a minute. "Well, rent another apartment," he said. "Leave the windows open." That oughta do it, the old man thought. "Wonder why she does a damn fool thing like that?"

He watched his father eyeing a silver Alfa Romeo GTV parked down by the sidewalk.

"Probly just trying to make it interesting," his father said. "Probly not satisfied with what beauty there is in this world. Trying to add beauty. Damn women, they know things took me sixty years to figure out." He got up. "Got to see your mother, sell the house, go to Mexico, learn to swim, print some pictures, and get our ass outa that damn Pan-Am. You know what they were trading that for last week? Four!" he said. "I got in at twenty. Shit!"

His father left, stole a car.

He researched the subject. Women. Why hadn't it occurred to him before? He could spend his whole life in the grocery store.

He read eleven books about women. They all said the same thing. He read four magazines about women. They said nothing at all. But the pictures were terrific. He learned things anyway.

He discovered that the world of women, in terms of iconography, is more interesting than the world of men. Something he had suspected. Virginity, eyeliner. There are, of course, compensations.

He discovered that women had discovered that they were not just like everybody else, something he had yet to discover. He discovered that the differences between all people at all times are always exaggerated for the private benefit of the person exaggerating. It's no way to live, he thought.

I had a thought about the Condition, he thought. Damn. I ought to get paid for that.

All that thinking made him nauseous. He went into the kitchen for a handful of sugar. He was going at it badly. Almost two weeks and he hadn't found her. He should try something else.

So he rented an apartment, left the windows open, and the girl leapt in. Her name was Mimi. She was nude, her breasts pointed, he staggered in the glare.

"Wait!" he said.

"I want to talk," he said.

She fell over laughing, kicked the TV trays, then said, tears in her dark eyes, "Oh, you'll talk to me and then you'll just go and talk to someone else," and several other things she had always wanted to say.

She pressed lightly against him, knocking him over backwards. Why can't I ever concentrate? he thought, trying to focus his eyes. It was hot. The rug was scratchy. Excess polyester.

"Well?" she said.

"Oh, uh . . . Want some tequila?" He got up and went to the medicine chest for some Valium and some monoamine oxidase inhibitor. Also some Phenobarbitol. He brought the tequila. She took it in the traditional way, salt first, lime after. Mano a mano.

He thought about the way in which one thing is said to follow another thing. He thought of Zeno, the paradoxes. He began.

"Why do you jump through windows without clothes ready for bed when we don't expect it, when we expect the breeze and an occasional bug but not you, and even if you, not you nude, without any clothes; no halters, headdresses, no skirts, half-slips, chemises, camisoles, peignoirs, nylons, hose, stockings, shoes, nightgowns, negligees, blouses, shirtwaists, empires, evening gowns, sundresses, shifts. None of that stuff. Why do you do it? This is not the kind of strangeness we expect, that we're accustomed to. What's your motivation? It wasn't in the catalogue. What's the meaning of this? What are you trying to prove? Is it a hostile act? What are we to think?" he said. "Forgive my curiosity."

"Your question is foolish," she said.

"Well," he said.

"Your question lacks charm."

"Yes."

"Here is a list of people from all walks of life who would have despised your question had they lived," she said, giving him the list.

"Thank you."

"It's a seedy little question."

"It's not really my question," he said.

She left a note on the table. He found it in the morning. The note said: "Things are made more beautiful not by what we think but by what we do."

Well, that old son of a bitch, he thought.

II

He thought about what he was going to do with the $10,000 which he assumed was the handsome sum mentioned in the telegram. He could not think of anything. He fell asleep waiting for the first of September.

In his dream he was in a hardware store he had frequented as a child. The hardware store was barren. He took a pistol and then a dime at gunpoint. He walked down the sidewalk to the drugstore. He stuck the gun in his belt and walked around looking for something to steal. There were a lot of pink things in the drugstore. He couldn't find anything he wanted. He left and walked back to the hardware store. Put the gun and the dime on the counter. He woke up.

Instead of a second telegram, there were four armed bishops at the door. Three Print Bishops and the Bishop of Broadcast. They were leaning in every direction in the doorway. Their crossed cartridge belts flapped against their thin chests. They had the look of men and women of such discriminating taste that they did not like anything. They were starving to death.

"We want an explanation," the first bishop said. She seemed to be the leader. "But first give us something to eat." She was wearing a brown dress. Her eyes, ears, wrists, throat and upper arms were bare.

He went to the kitchen, to the drawer, and poured out four plates of sugar and four glasses of water, brought them back and set them before the bishops. They ate.

"What is this?" she said.

"That's sugar, sugar," he said.

They stepped toward their rifles, where they had thrown them on the rug. He stepped back.

"We do not expect jokes," the lead bishop said, pulling burrs from her hair. "We expect answers."

He nodded, as submissively as he could.

"We are here for a purpose. We picked you because you seemed equal to the task. Because you lived at the center of Texas. Deep in the heart. You were stable. We felt you could do it." She took an envelope out of her pocket.

"I did it," he said.

The other bishops belched and looked at the floor. They looked familiar, brown hair and mustaches, bleached Pancho Villas staring at the carpet.

"We have your check," she said. "It's government money." She held the envelope high. "If your work has been satisfactory."

"The girl about whom you inquired— Well, she's on your side. She sees herself as working for everyone. She thinks she is adding to the store of beauty in the world by the most direct route possible. She is using her imagination, then acting. Doing what she can. Trying to stay alive. She intends continuing until the television people arrive. Then she intends trying something else. She may well live out her days trying one thing and another." He said.

The four armed bishops grumbled together in a corner. The lead bishop said, "Where do you get off?" The other bishops drifted back to stare at him.

"I told you how we feel about jokes," she said.

Maybe I put it badly, he thought.

"We will give you another chance," she said. "If you don't come across, we are going to slit your throat with these rifles." They waved the rifles in the air.

Pop, he thought, what do I do now?

The telephone rang. He answered it and stood leaning over the receiver for twenty minutes, nodding, then returned to the center of the room, to the guests.

"Well," she said.

"Well," he said, "the girl who leaps in windows, the one you asked about, is a member of the last great ethnic group, the middle class. She has suffered through a long life of oppression, from those not middle class and from those not women. All those hamburgers, sniggers, expectations, trips, schools, CD players, curling irons, cosmetics. She was not loved in the way she wanted to be loved. She was not respected in the way she wanted. She had green eyes when she wanted blue. It drove her crazy. Damaged her psyche. So that these naked leaps are in some way a perversion of her natural drive to . . . uh . . . to . . . "

She handed him the envelope. They picked up their rifles and left, without saying goodbye. It was a check for $10,000. It was obviously worthless. It was crawling with bacteria. He felt ashamed and encouraged. They would never get her.

Aaron
Balkan

Something that Hasn't Happened Yet

AS FAR BACK as you can remember, it was just dinner. Not two hours ago. Adam's mother cooked a full meal for the two of them, and while they ate they talked about their days. Adam told his mother that in school they were learning about Manifest Destiny and that the pioneers killed millions of buffalo until they were almost extinct and then they came back. And Adam's mother told Adam how her boss treats her worse than anyone and one of these days she's really going to get him and call his wife right up and tell the woman he's a goddamn infidel and that she's married to a bastard. And after they talked about their days, they both decided they had had average days. For a while, she stared at him. After dinner, Adam took in the dishes and brought his mother her cigarettes and her blanket while she watched TV, and she thanked him for taking care of things. Then Adam put the dinner table back and joined his mother on the couch and they were going to watch TV together. Not two hours ago.

Then, just like that, everything changes but it goes on. The TV's still on. For Chrissakes it's the same movie that was on. And Adam is there and he's still holding the cordless phone, waiting for it to ring again. When it does, it sounds the same as the last time—not a ring, but an beep, weightless and delicately electronic, barely even audible. But when it comes alive in Adam's hand, it's somehow different, because it's enough to put him at complete attention. And it's enough to raise him out of his seat, just enough that he may be standing up. As he bows his head ever so slightly, and clenches his teeth ever so much, and then, almost as if he were to take a real, deep breath, he answers.

"I knew it Adam, I knew it!"

"Mom! Where are you?"

"I knew it Adam. What? Are you just sitting there?"

"Mom, Mom, where are you? Why won't you tell me where you are?"

"You know damn well where I am Adam. Damn well you know everything."

Some static begins to come into the phone because Adam's mother is calling from her car. She's had that thing in her car for years and never once touched it. Never once a call. Now all of the sudden she's calling on the thing every five minutes.

"I can't hear you good, Mom. I don't know where you are and I can't hear good on that phone. Why can't you come home?" Adam begins to cry into the phone.

"If those were real cries I wouldn't be driving around this goddamn city. What if I never came home Adam? What if I just left? What then Adam? You wouldn't know if I was dead or alive and then they'd be real cries Adam. They'd be real cries and I'd never hear them. All my life. All my life Adam. How would I ever know when those prissy little whimpers became real cries?"

"Mom, please—what do you want me to do? I don't know what I'm supposed to do. I don't understand what you—"

"You know damn well what to do Adam. Damn well you know everything. You knew enough to drive me to this. You knew enough to make me do it Adam. You just don't know how to love me. You won't let me come home Adam, because you don't love me, and this is what happens when you don't love someone Adam. If I die Adam, it's because this is what happens."

Adam is balling now and the static is beginning to come into the phone again.

"I can't do this much longer Adam. I don't know how much longer I can do this." She stops for a few seconds and waits for the static to pass. "If I'm not sure you're going to love me, I don't know how I could ever come home."

Then she hangs up, and if nothing seems changed it's because there's only so much that can be changed and it can't be much. Adam's still there and he's still holding the phone, but for a moment—not more than a second—he forgets everything, and remembers instead what he learned that day in school. About the buffalo. It's yet only a moment, and not long enough for anything to be changed in it, but in it, he remembers, once, there were so many buffalo in the plains that you could ride through whole groups of them, for hundreds of miles even, and never once leave the same herd. And he remembers they were so dense, you could literally walk accross their backs—from horizon to horizon—and never once touch the ground. And the way they moved—shaking the earth and sounding thunder—and then the sound was missing. And he tries to remember what could have happened to such a great and total sound, but he can only imagine himself instead. Walking for hundreds of miles but only seeing bodies on the land. And so he closes his eyes and tries to hear harder—the sound of the earth not shaking and there is no thunder—but he can only see himself. Walking across their dead bodies, left skinned and rotting on the land.

Then the moment is over, and Adam leaps up from the couch and runs upstairs to his mother's bedroom. In her bedroom, the drawers are pulled out of all the dressers and there are clothes strewn everywhere. The objects on her night stand are knocked over and jewelry is out of its boxes. Everything on the floor and the mess was there before. Adam could hear it from downstairs while it was happening and, the moment his mother ran out, he rushed up there to sort through it all. Even then, he knew exactly what to look for, and he scoured the room, looking in the drawers and under the bed and in the night stand and even the bathroom. Even in the goddamn shower. But he didn't know where to look then and, after a while, he began to think she could've had it with her all along. In her purse maybe, or maybe she had it in her car. Or maybe she had it with her at the dinner table. For all Adam knew, she could've had it in the pocket of her robe and she could've had it with her all along.

And Adam doesn't know where to look now anymore than before, but that doesn't stop him from looking again. This time, he pulls the drawers all the way out and looks behind them. He looks in parts of the closet where he hadn't looked before, or where he'd forgotten he looked, or where he simply thought he may have missed something. This is what he does: he looks under the bed in ways he thinks to be closer. Better. More scrupulous. He looks in honest ways and pleases himself with the way he looks. Like a detective. Like an archeologist. He stands atop the bed and scans the room, looking at the placement of everything, and where there could possibly be something he may have missed.

Of course, because he's only a child, he doesn't think to check the window. The only thing you can see out the window anyway is a garage for the tenants, and an empty lot beyond that, and beyond that a shopping mall with a parking lot surrounding. And in this parking lot, in no such view of the light on in the bedroom, or the boy standing on the bed, or the way both have cast a shadow of his silhouette against the bedroom wall, a woman sits in her car waiting. Waiting while everything could be changing for good reason. While there is still good work to be done. While there are lights in the parking lot that stay on all night, and trees that stop moving in the fleeting wind, and for the first time in her life when she could live for something that hasn't happened yet.

Deena Metzger

Inside a House One is Truly Alone

For Nancy Aronie

IT'S ONLY INSIDE a house that one is truly alone. . . . Inside the house, though, one is so alone that one can sometimes lose oneself. And so I have lived for ten years as I now realize. Alone. But this has enabled me to write books that have made me and others understand what I am as a writer. . . . One does not find solitude, one creates it. Solitude creates itself. Alone. I created it here because I decided that I should be alone, that I would be alone to write books.

Marguerite Duras writing about Neauphle-de-Chateau[1]

The familiar. The handle of the teapot fits into the palm of my hand and my fingers home into the three depressions and lift. My teapot. I bought it six months ago after the other one sprung a leak because I'd let it burn dry on the stove one time too many. None of the other teapots I ever had sang. This teapot sings one note—A. Even here, three thousand miles away from my house and my kitchen, this teapot sings the same note. Am I home or am I not home?

It is as difficult to find the rhythm which will become the template for the story as it is to make a satisfying creation from the odd chairs and plates and fabrics one has gathered over the years. It won't help to throw everything away and begin again. If one does that, her house will look like a window in a furniture store. As it is, it looks like my house, as if furnished by a an eccentric writer or gathered together at a fire sale.

Crow atop the telephone pole raises his wings three times as if he is going to fly away, as if he is shrugging his shoulders, as if he adjusting his suspenders, as if he is shedding the golden light on his black feathers which occasionally flashes red depending on the angle. Somehow Crow has managed to make that sawed-off pine trunk his perch. The task is to be that comfortable in a sentence.

Now I'm happy in this house. In this house where Nancy was once living my life, where she once made tea, where she was winding her long thin fingers around the handle of the tea pot grateful for the song. A singing teakettle, she thought, when she bought it. I know because that is what I thought when I bought mine.

The first sentence determines everything. You can only go so far on that sentence and no further. If you go further than the sentence can stretch you have to bring in welding tools. Everyone will see the suture; it can't be avoided. If you have to go further, get yourself a sentence that can go the distance. Crow swoops low across the yard and up the hill. The wind has come up and holds him up even though he's close to the ground. No one expects him here. Mouse will think he's a shadow or a black plastic bag escaped from the garbage.

The familiar implies everything known and by its negative space everything unknown. The known and the unknown. I think we're safe.

When writing, everything is so familiar and so unfamiliar at the same time. These are one's words. My teapot. My chair. My cup. And yet they are surprising, they have never been uttered before in this sequence and so they are entirely new since creation is not a thing in itself but is association, an admixture, at its best, a melange. This and that. Before and after. Never before. But also here and not there. Time and space. This place.

I sat inside as the ferry made its way from the mainland to the island. Cold though it was, I could have gone to the open deck, but I didn't want to see the way across. I wanted to arrive there in the forty minutes as if transported. Then we went out of the boats open maw in a dark file, one car behind the other, turning left and then right and then right again and then I was to follow the road without a name for miles until I came to the tri-via where I was to turn left and go .6 of a mile and make a left at the Writer's Workshop sign into the common drive and then the first right. "The small lights will be on," she said. The house won't be locked. "No key," Nancy had said.

"There's no key to my house either," I answered.

"Wood stove. Can you handle a wood stove?"

"A wood stove heats my house," I said.

"It's only a cabin," she murmured. Had she made a mistake, was I someone other than she had imagined? Would I need more? Doors on the open shelves for example. What about the mice? How would I feel about the mice?

She didn't mention the mice. "My house is only a cabin," I assured her. "A little white cottage is how I describe it. No dishwasher. To get ice cubes you have to go outside to the laundry room."

"No dishwasher," she said.

"No dishwasher," I confirmed.

"I don't think you'll have trouble finding it. Pretend you're coming home."

I sat at the tri-via a long time trying to read the instructions she had sent to be certain I was at the right place and then I went on and saw the white picket fence on the right, the small hand painted sign on the left, like the one on the chain link fence at the entrance to my land and the road going up across from it, the white phantom bicycles pedaled by ghostly riders, a gilt telephone under the pine tree, a quadruple sarcophagus with a plastic top which could only be the promised hot tub, and the cabin to my right. My car came to rest just next to the painted typewriter invisible in the dark. The door was closed with a stone which I moved out of the way with my foot, familiar with such gestures from relocating the brick that props open the door to my bedroom, and I went across the threshold entering into the kitchen as we do from the patio into my house. Only here the stove was directly to my right and my hand found the teapot immediately as if it were already singing. On the counter between the stove and the sink was a wide shallow dark blue and white mottled metal bowl with a striped stone in it like a small island in the wind tossed night sea. When I bought metal dishes for my house in the Tonto National Forest, the cabin in the trees which was more of a house than the cottage, I found a deep salad bowl but I had never found this one. There was a note beside the bowl. It said, "Light all the candles at once." Pale pink candles, not quite pink. Not quite salmon. Paler than flamingo, more fiery than rose quartz. Not quite amber. Sandstone from the western desert. Or carbonatite of plutonic origin. Presence of hematite and flame.

You have to understand that I only met Nancy once and we never spoke one to one in person except during the writing workshop I had been leading the previous August when I asked her to rewrite a piece from the point of view of the other. Impossible, she insisted. By which she meant, 'I won't.' But, she did. So splendidly, that I was startled and in as much as she ran from the room the moment the workshop was over, I determined to write a note to her expressing surprise and delight at the task accomplished and the manifestation of an other in the room like a crystal growing before our eyes, both transparent and adamantine.

The room has minerals in it but is not mineral itself. On the other counter between the kitchen—which is so narrow passageway that a large man would have to turn sideways to pass through to the door—and the living room are collections of stones, one heart shaped, several candlesticks and a vase of small white orchids. "I asked a friend to bring white orchids to the house to greet you," she told me later on the telephone when I told her about the mice eating out of the cat's dish.

"Are you sure?" she asked. "We had thought it was a large animal scratching at the floor from its burrow under the house."

"Mice," I said. "Several of them. I'll get a Have a Heart trap. I'm used to them. I take them to the park several miles away from my house, I'll take them a similar distance. And to the same place, so they won't miss each other."

Small lights arch over the slate faced fireplace down to the Tiffany lamps by the windows opening to the wintering vegetable garden and compost heap speckled with egg shells. The cat, Baby, climbs this wall to indicate that she wants into the house. Scratch scratch on the screen. There are the conga drums which I usually store by the side of my desk and the basket of tambourines, rattles, whistles, bells which I have standing in the triangle between the wall and the chaise angling into the living room. Her couch is covered with layers of floral and striated brocades in the same tones of golden pink and rosy amber of the candles. It isn't upholstered in these fabrics, they are thrown over the couch the way one might cover a divan in the desert when one knows she will intermittently pick up her tents and wander, Desert colors. Pale lichen greens, like the little striped whiptail lizard scurrying atop late afternoon sandstone cliffs. But abundant, elaborate, curvaceous. When you live in the desert as I do, but in a house, in what was once and will become a desert again in less than a year if the irrigation were to fail, you tend to bring blues and greens into the house, water colors, cobalt and turquoise. It's a survival strategy. Pale green oriental carpet on her kitchen floor a mate to the one in the living room. China, I guess as the country of origin. In my kitchen, if she were in my house, she would walking across the wine and blue carpet. Afghanistan. Persia. Still, only mad women put fine carpets in their kitchens.

"Maybe it will feel familiar," she had said on the telephone. She had thought of everything, had left maps, names and telephone numbers of friends, directions to wine shops—down Island only—and good restaurants, a guest book which was really a journal to sign—but she had not prepared me for this. For the shock of the familiar from which I would want to run immediately into the simplicity of the unknown.

And there on the coffee table before the couch and the fireplace is a book, *Writer's Houses*. It is a gift to her from two students who had found her house and the writing workshop a sanctuary. They had found themselves in her presence. They had found their voices here. A magician. She hadn't told me she was also a magician though they identified her as one in their inscription.

If I were to quote them to her, she would laugh. I can hear the laughter. It would remain in the air long after the bell of laughter had been sounded. Like a smoke? No. Like a ripple? Better. Like a mirage. You heard it even if it wasn't there. It was a feature of her landscape. It drew me to her even before I heard it.

A writing exercise: Begin to write a familiar scene, an incident in which you were involved with others. A stranger intrudes into this moment. A stranger with a certain magnetism. You are drawn out of what you know toward the unknown. The stranger is irresistible. Soon you are in the vortex of the stranger. The familiar, those you know are left behind. Something new develops. The writer is compelled toward the stranger exactly as the character—yourself as character—is drawn toward the stranger. Writer and protagonist suffer the same jeopardy. Divisions between then and now, history and fiction dissolve.

The book on the coffee table. Yes, it is the very book from which the opening quotation of this story derives. The preface was written by Marguerite Duras whose house is also featured. Marguerite Duras. When I answered a questionnaire from Pen America, I wrote: Marguerite Duras, she is the one I would nominate for the Nobel Prize. Because of the beauty of every line and because she wrote, "I don't drag the millstone of totalitarian, i.e., inflexible thought around with me. That's one plague I've managed to avoid."

Did she win the . . . ?

Forget it.

That exquisite moment when a woman who is living alone takes a beautiful glass from the cupboard and sets it down in exactly the right place between the stones, the lace doily that belonged to her grandmother's sister and the candlestick and then slowly turns the screw into the cork, winding down in the center of the soft yielding material until the metal arms raise like the prosthesis of angels and then she presses down on the wings, damn the angels, and slowly extracts the stopper, pop, wipes off the lead sediment at the lip and pours the first liquid notes of wine. The woman has learned to be alone.

The coffee table is covered with a white linen open work embroidered cloth from Central Europe. I trace the delicate floral patterns with my fingers. How often I have done this since I was a child opening my mother's linen closet when she was away and tracing the patterns of the cloths she had brought with her from Europe or bought whenever she came across similar cloths in a shop but when I asked her about Poland, she said, "They were murderers. Don't bring me anything from there. Don't go to Vilna on my account."

We didn't have a visa for Vilna which was in the Soviet Union then and who knows where it is now but we went to the Polish border near Chelm and looked across the wide river to the Soviet union and I ignored the sign that said: TAKING PHOTOGRAPHS IS STRICTLY FORBIDDEN and tried to take a photograph from a camera held in my pocket, wanting only the light on the water down river, not the land, not the military installations but a siren went off across the water at least a half mile away and so I ceased and desisted.

There is a larger version of the tablecloth hanging over her closet door. It would never have occurred to me to hang the cloth there or to drape the smaller version over a table permanently. After I use my grandmother's cloths, both the large one and the smaller one I put them back in a box. They are my mother's treasures. They were my mother's treasures. I just washed the cloth and put it away after using it on the Passover table the Monday before the Wednesday when I arrived on the Island. It was a difficult and beautiful Passover in which we spoke about what it means to pass out of the narrow place. How much I missed my mother who died last December. I had to make the meal and host the community and *prave* the seder. I had been doing it for years but this time my mother wasn't there to remind of what we needed to remember.

"Did you hear the story about the oranges and the seder table?" Nancy asked me on the telephone.

"My aunt who is quite audacious asked an uncle who was reading the Haggadah when women would be equals in the ritual. 'When there are oranges on the Seder plate,' " he said.

As it turns out, Nancy added, "sliced oranges look very beautiful on the Seder plate next to the spring greens and the paschal egg."

"I always put oranges in the *tsimas*," I said, "oranges, carrots, yams, apricots. Cardamom and cinnamon, red pepper and saffron from Spain. Homage to the sun, to the light in the desert, to the last moment before the red sea parts."

My grandmother's cloth is a doorway in Nancy's house. I want to fill the Italian pitcher I bought on the Riviera which is standing on a shelf above cookbooks and advice from Andrew Weil with orange juice or ice tea tinkling with ice cubes and scented with lemon slices and rose water.

It is not until the second day, when I kneel down to lay towels and silver foil against the window to protect the floor from the driving rain, that I see the small figure of a young girl, kneeling, like I am kneeling, on the grass. Carved of smooth gray stone, the girl, her eyes lowered modestly, stares nevertheless quite happily into the house. We are almost eye to eye.

I have come to a juncture. I do not know if I can go back, if I can make a turn or if I must proceed down this relentless path. The same young girl kneels with similar contentment in my own garden among the ivy and succulents which form a ground cover. My friend carved the sculpture. She carved only one. She carved it at a time in her life when she had been brought to her knees. It looks like innocence but it exudes brokenness This sculpture cannot be in two places at once. I am either here or there. I do not think I can be in both places at once.

I hear a voice in my head: "Under certain cases, physics may permit it." Nancy's husband is a physicist. A physicist manqué but enough of a physicist, I calculate, to read my novel *The Other Hand* and tell me if I got the physics and the astronomy right.

The phone rings and I listen to a woman leaving a message. She wants to know the dates of the summer workshop. Will she feel safe? Will the other women be kind? Will there be an opportunity to finally write a story she has been afraid to write? She has been waiting all her life for this moment. She has decided to take the plunge.

I scramble to my feet. Where did I put my calendar? I don't remember agreeing to teach in the summer. It has happened again, has it? I promise myself that I will take the entire summer off so that I can begin the novel that is demanding language and form, and it seems I have reneged on my promise to myself, unable once again to refuse the woman I have never met. The caller hangs up. I will find my calendar later and call her back with the dates.

Nancy calls in to pick up her messages. The woman has disappeared in the playback version, she is only a voice now. Nancy doesn't notice. As she listens to the electronically simulated voice, she writes the woman's name on a list, she inserts her telephone number alongside, she gives her a number on a sheet of paper under the date of that particular workshop, number three, July. There are enough applicants; Nancy will do the workshop. She will care for the woman. She will make her feel safe. My summer remains inviolable.

You understand that the woman who is writing this story never had sisters. That is obvious, isn't it? She has not been inured to the shock of the apparition of her shadow, albeit taller or thinner or stooped or older or younger. She thought she was alone in the world. That is why she came here. To deepen her loneliness. This is a return. Twenty years ago she traveled to Cape Cod in the winter, spoke almost to no one, photographed her own shadow. Wrote poems about women she knew. If she had been asked then and if she had had words, she might have said she was a cocoon. She was not in the cocoon, she was the cocoon. It was winter and the salt spray from the ocean froze in mid air before it reached her cheeks so that it bit into her, so that it scratched red lines on her face. She would have said . . . . She would not have said anything. If you had asked her, she would have turned aside as if to wrap herself even more fully around the frozen core that would come to nothing if it thawed.

For the first few days, she skated over the surface of the house as if she was afraid that the ice would break and she would drown. But skated the way she imagined a champion would skate so smoothly that she would not leave a mark. She made an inner alliance with snow to protect its pristine nature. She barely moved. After she drank the glass of wine, she returned the bottle to the place where Nancy stored her own bottles, she washed the glass and returned it to the shelf, she smoothed the antimacassar to erase the imprint of the bottle, her glass, the side of her palm. The cat came in and out, the door blew open and was shut, the wind entered and settled down. Otherwise, you would not know the house was occupied. She lived in it as a ghost.

She spied on Nancy from every vantage point. She sat in her chair. She ate only what she thought Nancy would eat. She sat at Nancy's desk and read Nancy's journals. She made a few changes, corrected some oversights. She read Nancy's books making notes in the margins in pencil as Nancy did. She put on Nancy's jacket and rolled up the sleeves. She scurried into Nancy's bed, arranging all the pillows on two sides so that she slept in the narrow channel remaining. She turned out the lights at the first sign of dark and remained burrowed in feathers until the first dawn light that turned the Tiffany lamps amber with an natural glow they would never carry otherwise. And found herself longer then from lying straight perhaps between such narrow constraints of one body and another, reduced to bone by the furrow she had plowed for herself.

Forgive me, I meant *I*. It was suddenly easier to talk about myself as a she, as someone I was observing, as the woman. I was lost and so looked for myself in sentences. And in doing so, lost myself even more.

Here I am. I am the moth asleep in the daytime that will fall down into dust or burn herself to death in the glow of these Tiffany lamps. I have never been attracted to Tiffany lamps but my dead friend Barbara adored them, adored art nouveau. That such a formidable intellect could be entranced by art deco, pre Raphaelite decor, sentimentality fascinated me, fascinated all of us. She adored Woolworth's, little Tokyo, paper lanterns, dragons, and shells that opened in water sending up paper blossoms. I don't know whether I learned to like what she liked, or whether her exuberance entranced me and I would have followed her anywhere for the elegance of her story telling and because of the way words no one else spoke flowered on her tongue as if the vocabulary itself was the bouquet she was offering. I was never certain if it was the word or the event that was marvelous for the word may have been ordinary but transformed by her sense of wonder. "The air is so soft," she had said just before she learned she was dying and I remember those five words as if they were uttered on her death bed.

Barbara, like myself, was an only child. So we became sisters and tried to learn the entire vocabulary of siblings in thirty short years. Nancy, I can see, has sisters and some of the photographs include the mother as if she is also one of the sisters. Three women in a hot tub, laughing at the naked sister who is taking the photograph. Their melon breasts bobbing on the water in rhythm to their delight. A photograph both ordinary and incomprehensible to one whose relationship to her mother was shaped by the fact that their were no siblings, no one to help break down hierarchy, role. My mother was always my mother even when I had to mother her and I was always her daughter advised to take a jacket or a sweater when I went out. I bundle deeper into Nancy's plaid jacket which has a mandarin collar and fastens with black frogs. I roll up the sleeves twice until they rest on my wrists. It is warm inside Nancy's clothes. It is as if I am inside her body.

I am staring again out the window at the kneeling girl when I notice that rain has leaked through the window onto the floor and as I bend down to wipe it up with the towel which I hadn't placed carefully enough to absorb all the water, the porcelain flapper with a short skirt and red bow perky on her black hair falls down as I inadvertently jostle the table she was perched upon and breaks her neck. Super glue does the job as it had once before. But now I know that I have to remove her and all the other unfamiliar objects from the room.

It takes a long time. First I have to map each room sketching in the furniture and the objects upon it in exactly the way they are displayed and then I go to the market to get boxes and newspapers and carefully wrap everything that doesn't belong to me or didn't ever belong to me or isn't a variation on what I own and put them carefully into the boxes, everything carefully labeled so they can be restored with ease before Nancy returns. At first I think of removing the family pictures, particularly those of Nancy and her two younger brothers when one of them calls on the telephone and I realize it is her son and as I have sons and my current husband is not much older than they and Nancy's husband the cosmic juggler, she calls him, looks like an older brother even though he's a father, I decide to keep them but carefully labeling each face with post-its on which I've written the names that belong to me, Marc, Greg, Michael. Michael as cosmic juggler. It works. I cut the yellow post-its into triangles and write their names in block letters and place the paper on their chins so that they each appear to sport little yellow Van Dykes. I place other names on the lips of the melon breasts—Barbara, Naomi, Hella. Hella having been twenty years older than me qualifies as the mother though she wasn't maternal but then the image of a mother splashing nakedly in a hot tub with her two daughters doesn't strike me as maternal either. Barbara and Hella didn't know each other but as they are both dead, they may know each other now. Hella was a psychic and a fine photographer and Barbara was fascinated by photography and clairvoyance, so they have much to bind them together over there where, of course, none of these interests matter much at all.

Soon the house is ready. The bathroom was easy. She has the same green towels, and similar tile; I am not disposed to tearing down the walls. I have put my toothbrush and my toothpaste and my toiletries on the sink and they look like they could be hers. She has a picture of stars which coordinates with the stars floating in the lucite handle of my toothbrush. The living room was equally easy. I only removed a few books, mostly cookbooks as she is more of a vegetarian than I am though it would be my preference. She has more time to cook, I realize because she only works in the summer when I am off writing and she has nine months to muse while her husband works half the week in Boston just as Michael spends half the week at UCLA. Her husband, the cosmic juggler camps out at his mother's house while Michael camps out in his car between shifts and so it seems exactly the same. Only I'm working those three days, taking care of those desperate and hopeful women without voices while she's stroking Baby or running down the road to the water in her Nikes or meeting friends for lunch. When her husband comes home, it's like a honey moon or a pre-marital affair. I've been married to Michael for as long as her marriage has been in a state of renewal.

Baby is the problem. She doesn't resemble Owl or Isis. I cannot pretend she is a wolf. I lock her out. She is happy outside for a while. She climbs up the wall to be let in. "Hunt," I order her. Isis has been known to bring in mice. Baby's eyes glare like sapphires in the dark. I think of Isis's yellow agate eyes. Cat's eyes. Now Baby's yowling outside, wild and angry enough to wake the neighbors. The screen is being shredded. The calls could draw blood. I let her in. She has a lizard in her mouth. It's a start.

I bring the other drums, recorders, rattles from the bedroom into the living room and lean my drum against them, remove, shake out and replace my grandmother's cloth on the coffee table. Return Margaret Duras and add my copy of *Practicalities* to the pile. Wendell Berry, good. Thomas Berry, good.

The kitchen is a little more difficult. Not the dishes on the open shelves. I know them but I have to throw out all the jams and jellies because I don't eat them and bring down the hot sauces and peppers from the upper open shelves which she can reach easily but for which I need a chair. The same collection of Celestial Seasonings and I add my box of Bigelow Darjeeling Blend to the batch. Then there is the problem of the open shelves. They are exactly the same as the open shelves in my house, unfinished pine shelves and frames against white walls, exactly as the open shelves in my house *were*. *Were* until the earthquake came and wrecked everything and we had to rebuild and I put doors on the shelves. Why doesn't she remember?

I remember the pink floral cloth Nancy has tacked over these shelves though it surprises me that such memories remain. My mother and I had gone to the garment district in New York the day that WWII ended and suddenly all the windows opened on every one of the thirty floors or more of every building and jubilant people were unfurling bolts of cloth and throwing fabric samples on to the street so that we were walking ankle deep in them. My mother saw the opportunity immediately and took shopping bags from the sack she always carried and we filled them with paisleys, plaids, brocades, stripes, checks, linens, ginghams, piques, laces, appliqués, trying to take only what we loved. My mother was undone that we couldn't take them all home but it would take trucks and dozens of street cleaners to clean them up eventually. I had found the pink squares with the green leaves and white blossoms which now cover Nancy's open shelves. It's mate, in autumn colors of burnished apricot, forest green and tan which I also found on the street on Broadway near 32nd street, is on the table near the hot tub.

In the bedroom, I rummage through her drawers and remove the kinds of underwear and bras I don't wear anymore because Michael has different tastes than the cosmic juggler. The jewelry is really easy. She hangs her earrings on the wall just like I do and we wear the same Native American beaded earrings and necklaces, the same mid-eastern filigree work, the same faux ethnic pieces. I don't know what she has taken with her, but she had left my things behind. The bed is a problem. I sleep in a regular sized bed, this is king-sized. She's tall, remember, and I'm short. That's how I am telling us apart. And the sheets are brown striped—I wouldn't have brown in my house and I wouldn't have stripes or plaid on my bed. I rifle through her disorderly closet—quite like mine—and find a blue and turquoise Balinese cloth with block prints of lizards large enough to cover everything up. The disguise is sufficient.

Her study. A piece of cake. Her television is on a shelf behind a cloth. As close as putting it the closet which is what I do. Her music, my music. Keith Jarrett, Edith Piaf, Louis Armstrong, Billie Holiday. It is very blue; I like it. Now I dawdle. I put on one tape after another as I carefully arrange her books in alphabetical order according to author and subject—fiction, American, author or fiction, British, 19th century, author, or philosophy, American, contemporary, or feminism, American, contemporary. We both have too many books of the sort I label "New Age" and I hide them at the most inaccessible end of the shelves. We're not going to read these a second time. I take all the books she has of mine, that is those I have written, and arrange them on my desk next to my computer which I had plug into the round master switch surge protector under the desk. This is the only moment that I feel envy because I know that the surge protector is industrial strength and will protect her computer and fax machine against any catastrophes.

She has left me chocolates from the manufacturers down the street. Chillmark chocolates. I don't like chocolates with nuts in them. I like the kind with syrup or cream. Her first mistake. I put them in the freezer and carefully brush the ravenous and exultant ants on to a newspaper dated from before my stay and set them outside.

The phone rings. "I miss you. I love you so much. When can we meet?" There is no indication on Nancy's phone that she is out of town. The woman is anguished. She hasn't heard from her in so long. How did her lecture go? How was her stay in Boston? Isn't she home by now? Who is taking care of Baby?

I come close to picking up the receiver—our voices are similar—and making a date with the woman for lunch the following week. But I don't go to lunch. Nancy goes to lunch. Or takes lunch, as they say in Hollywood where, accordingly, I wouldn't ever take a lunch even if I were starving. I was born in Brooklyn. I listen to Nancy on tape while I organize the irregular piles of tapes of her workshops and public presentations and order them in the ways I would have liked to order my own but never did. Our voices are warm, husky, kind, with a bit of Jewish in them though we have both married men who aren't Semites at all. But finally I don't pick up the phone. I want to spare Nancy the ordeal of lunch with someone who wants so much from her and baits the trap with enthusiasm.

This is the truth. I have come to love Nancy. In the way I might have loved a younger sister when I couldn't love myself. In the way, I would like to protect a young sister from everything that has mattered to me and tortured me—needs, obligations, responsibilities, duties. I lie down on the day bed, on the mohair blanket I bought in Canada when I was engaged to Reed, who became my first husband and the father of my children. I still have it though it has thinned considerably and keep it in the cedar lined drawer of the armoire I bought after Reed and I were divorced and I had to move to a house in the suburbs so the boys could bike around, take buses and invite their friends home to swim in the pool and smoke dope. If they were going to smoke dope, and there was nothing I could imagine could be done to prevent it, they might as well smoke it at home, I reasoned, where I might be able to supervise them somewhat. One of my other delusions.

I want to spare Nancy in the way I wanted to spare my children. But that is only a half truth. I am also grateful that we are doing the same work in the world. She is doing the writing workshops. She is helping the poor broken bird women find their own nightingale voices. She is creating circles for them. She is worrying when they cancel appointments. She is concerned when they cry as if they will never stop crying. She holds them in her long, lovely arms when then they reel with memory and despair. And now she has written a book about all of this. *Wish You Were Here. I Finally Am.* Probably something like *Writing For Your Life.* The women will begin to call her from all over the country, even from Los Angeles. And this will set me free. "Wish *you* were here. *I* finally am." I write this in her guest book.

Lying back on the pillows I have covered with the familiar pillowcases I found in her linen closet, I read through the drafts of her book, following the first thoughts as they change, mature, going along with her in the familiar heartbreaking process of finding a voice, one's own voice, identifying a self that can be trusted. Sometimes there are pages missing; I go into her computer. Get lost among drafts and journal entries, letters, bills, brochures. Then I return to her book. It is a fine book. Earnest. Present. Honest. She doesn't descend fully into the void but she does descend. She faces the shadow and she emerges triumphant. She thinks the shadow can be vanquished as long as it is faced. Well, she is, I remind myself, younger than I am. I remember this belief. By the time she learns differently, she will be old enough to bear it. I am amused by how young she seems. More sister than mother to these boys. More girlfriend than wife. More daughter than mother to her own mother. It's because she's tall, I tell myself bewildered once again that somehow just before my mother's death, I became a crone despite my young husband and what some people call an indomitable spirit. At some point, I realized I had to take care of things.

Nancy, for example. Even as I am coming to hope she will be taking care of things for me. "You are my teacher, you are ahead of me," she told me on the phone. "I want to learn from you."

I thought nothing then of this kind and respectful phrase. One which momentarily pleased me, maybe it flattered me. But now in Nancy's house as I set about ordering our joint souls I think about it deeply and feel, as I have so many times in the last few years, the necessity to respond, to be responsible, to act with thoughtfulness and loving care in the interest of the other. Yes, she could easily be my younger sister if she were not six feet tall. Maybe this is not the barrier I have been making it. My mother always commented that her younger sister, Doris, had been tall and it was true that my cousin Lowell is six feet tall which is considered tall in my family though my son, Greg, is almost as tall himself. My grandmother was said to scrutinize young women walking through the streets of Vilna until she found an attractive short woman she could point out to my mother, "Look Bella, she doesn't look so bad at all."

If not for the matter of shelves and the necessity to try out rental cars to be certain that I can see over the steering wheel, I wouldn't think about the matter of shortness and tallness. Greg once brought a girlfriend to the house and afterwards asked me what I thought of her and when I was neutral he asked me about her height which I hadn't paid any attention to assuming, as I stood next to her, that we were the same height. "She is 6 feet tall," Greg was simultaneously exasperated and amused. As amused as he had been when he had first spurted up to his own 5'10 and had liked to pick me up and carry me from one side of the room to the other.

One's appearance is not neutral for a writer. This house, for example, is Nancy or is me, which I can't be sure. It is not a neutral territory. It is a cocoon from which only this butterfly not that butterfly will emerge. What happened in the secret darkness, what spells were cast, what formulae unfolded, under the influence of what brew, won't be known until one of us emerges fully formed without much, if any, memory of the time we had been cooking.

This is a known mystery even if the telling of it is prosaic. Marguerite Duras, for example.

"For fifteen years I've had a uniform—the M.D. uniform. It apparently created a 'Duras look', which was taken over by a fashion designer last year: black cardigan, straight skirt, polo-neck sweater and short boots in winter. I said I didn't care about clothes, but that's wrong. A uniform is an attempt to reconcile form and content, to match . . . what you think you are with what you want to suggest. You find this match without really looking for it. And once it's found it's permanent. And eventually it comes to define you. This is what's happened to me, and it's a help. I'm very short.

"I didn't need to dress up, because I was a writer."[2]

One doesn't need to dress up. No. But one needs to wear something. Not only for warmth, decency or to protect the furniture, but for the sake of self, in the same way that one needs to wear a house on one's back, the way everyone is a snail at heart.

Short and tall are states of mind. They have more to do with daring and subterfuge. People expect me to be tall and Michael dreamed I was "a giantess with two singing daughters" the night before he met me. And sometimes I think of the sibyl, shriveled up to the size of a pea in the pod of the great god Apollo who nursed from her oracular breast.

So here we are. There is a circle of small stones outside the window of the study and I see that I have more to do than I planned. There is the matter of the pansies. Nancy had hoped to leave a pot of pansies by the entrance to the house and I want to leave some for her. And then the bird feeder is empty and I see no bird seed around. I have a fifty pound sack at home but didn't bring any with me. The mice have gotten into the dry cat food. Baby can't open cans by herself.

I get up and get in the car and drive to the garden supply shop where I buy one or more of every possible color of pansy, burgundy, purple velvet, black, golden eye, white, etc. and 20 pounds of bird seed that will feed every type of bird. I plant the flowers in a clay pot and place it by the sign announcing the Chillmark Writing Workshop. I have mixed an absorbent into the soil so it will hold water for a long time. I carefully fill all the feeders and sprinkle seeds everywhere on the ground as I would at home and leave the sack outside leaning against a far tree. I take out the garbage and dig it into the compost pile. I empty the hot tub and when it dries I sweep the sand that has accumulated at the bottom out, then I replace the cover careful to adjust the bungie cords so that it won't blow away in a storm.

It has stopped raining. I sit outside in one of the garden chairs which I have wiped dry with a kitchen cloth, the blue striped cloth I bought at Holds Everything in Woodland Hills. Yes, I would like to read but the light is blazing in the bare tree and it looks like the Burning Bush and I am overwhelmed with love for Nancy and the gift she has given to me. This is paradise. It is exactly the way I imagine paradise.

I get up fitfully and go through the house again. My computer is open to my journal on her desk. I have written some last notes in her guest book. The files I brought with me carefully arranged in alphabetical order according to the proper categories in her file drawers. The orchids are still gleaming in a cobalt blue vase like the one Michael bought for me after he dropped one of mine onto the tiles behind the fireplace where it shattered in a thousand blue splinters, ice on clay.

Everything is perfect—the books, the clothes, the dishes, the bowls, the glasses, the papers, the blankets, the wine bottles, the hearts, the heart shaped rock. Everything is aligned. I have chosen my chair opposite the wood stove and lay a few books next to it, some are hers, some are mine. I sit in it and nestle the pillows to my shape. Anyone would know I had sat there taking in the warmth of the fire just as anyone would know how my fingers fit the indentations of our tea pot.

"The wood stove is broken," Nancy had said and then the physicist and cosmic juggler instructed me in making a fire from above. "Lay the fire," he said "and then go into the store house at the back end of the hot tub and get the large can of kerosene and pour a cup of kerosene over the wood and drop in a few matches. Don't worry," he said, "it won't flare like gasoline will. But be careful to take the turquoise container, not the blue one which has gasoline in it."

I carry the ten gallon jug into the house staggering more than a little and take all the wood he has carefully cut to size and stacked and lay a fire as I like to do, arranging the wood carefully, at just the right angles, so that it looks like a star about to blaze. I have made fires for years and only once did a fire fail to take at the first attempt and that was because, I later learned, the wood had not dried for a year as it must. I pour the amber fluid carefully so that it soaks into the wood and then with another loving glance around the room, stand on my tip toes to press my lips to Nancy's lips as she smiles down at me from the almost life-size blow up of a photograph so that the moment is almost erotic, almost real, self reaching out to self, despise the coldness of the glass between us.

"Thank you," I whisper, "thank you." And strike the match. The paper flares and then the wood, soon to turn to coals but now golden flames edged with blue. The colors I love.

I let the car warm up and then turn on the radio as I back up on to the dirt road, like the dirt road to my house and hear a news report from California. Early fires not so unexpected because of the recent droughts are moving once again through Malibu and up into Topanga canyon threatening the Community House where people who have fled their houses have gathered with their animals in the early morning. The houses above the Community House are in danger and everyone and all animals are being evacuated from the canyon. I understand there is no hope of stopping the fire storm before it reaches my house. I drive past the fire house thinking that if I keep going I can make the afternoon ferry to the Cape where this time I will keep my eyes open as I go across. Checking the rear view mirror, I see I am alone on the road. Alone behind me and alone before me. I see my eyes in the mirror. You could say I have emerged from the house like a wraith, like a translucent moth, like a curl of smoke free at last.

For fifteen years I threw my manuscripts away as soon as the books came out. If I ask myself why, I think it was to wipe out the crime, to make it seem less important in my own eyes. . . . I used to keep bits of sewing material and left-overs from the kitchen, but not manuscripts. So for all those years I burned them.

"the deed used to be done in the fireplace in the living room at Neauphle. It was total destruction."[3]

---

1 Preface to *Writer's Houses*, Francesca Premali-Droulers and Erica Lionord, Vendome Press, 1995

2 "The M.D. Uniform," *Practicalities*, Marguerite Duras, Grove Weidenfeld, 1987, p.65

3 "House and Home, *Practicalities*, Marguerite Duras, Grove Weidenfeld, 1987, p. 54

Michael Guista

The Wrestler

IF STANDING NEXT TO another boy at the urinal, I stared straight ahead at the wall; if getting undressed in a public locker to change clothes for swimming I eyed objects and not people: the lockers, their locks, the peeling paint on the walls, the buzzing fluorescent tubes. I didn't even look at my own and when I bathed at night I didn't dare touch it but hoped that soaking it in the water would get it clean enough without the use of my hands. At the same time I was considered manly: I was taller than anyone else my age and had early whiskers and was good at athletics—and this is what eventually made high school the most difficult time of my life, for I possessed a contradiction of assets I was to learn about the same way someone is struck dumb by epiphany, all starting with P.E.

I was playing pre-season football in the summer, practicing twice a day, morning and afternoon, sweating and punching and push-uping and manning the ball in general, and was quite good at it all, really. I played right guard (the smart, quick one) and linebacker on defense, but (and maybe this was part of the problem) it was all too easy for me, the exercise, the hitting, the keeping-my-mind-busyness that athletics provide, and I was all set to start both ways the first game and be moved to Varsity my sophomore year. "First draft Nebraska, when he's to college. Yup. First draft, the lucky bastard." That's what the coach used to say about me when Nebraska was really hot, but I didn't shower after practice, never would, refused to; instead I would sneak out of the locker room during a dirty joke or the hazing of a freshman, some time when I was least likely to be spotted, though of course I had to shower eventually and that has made me what I am today. I am a wrestler.

On that morning there were about forty of us standing around our lockers, the room smelling of sweat and mentholatum and farts and bad breath and unsuccessful cologne, locker doors slamming and towels cracking on concrete walls and butts, jokes like "Hey, what color's your cum, Gonzales?" hanging in the air like cigarette smoke. I saw all those dicks dangling like cords loosened from their mothers, giant thumbs swaying back and forth, balls hanging low and huge like fallen, overgrown walnuts, and it hit me like a ball peen: I was little, a baby, boyish not mannish, and I hid my small penis in disgust. I hid it behind my towel, my locker door, my hands, my knees, my shoulder pads and jersey, and it was in that moment, that dazzling, cracked, stained-glass moment, I realized I was different and would never be a man, no matter what I did, in comparison to the others, and worse yet, their manhood disgusted me, sticking out the way it did, purposeless and hateful, like dirty socks.

I also knew they'd be coming after me soon, demanding to know why I wasn't like them, mocking me, but this surprised me then and has never stopped: I didn't want to be like them because they were ugly. They were ugly walking down the halls, their Levis looking bleached around the buttons from the constant pressure of dicks against denim; they were ugly sitting in their cars at lunch time, their bulges like angry fists trying to sneak their way out; they were ugly at weddings and at funerals and in backseats at drive-ins; and they were ugly in repose in the locker room after workout, dicks and balls slumped across benches. Suddenly all I could see was penises; it was as though a lifetime avoiding them was catching up with me all at once, as though penises were bursting over the dam's walls and slapping me in the face like flopping beached fish; I was drowning in them.

Everywhere I went, I was comparing myself to the others, the men, the real men. I longed for the lost innocence of the holy water and the sign of the cross of my childhood, the priest dressed up in whites and purples and passionate, hot reds with us black-and-white altar boys at his side, our bodies tucked away and hidden beneath thick cotton below the bloodstained Jesus on the cross in His loin cloth. But there it was before me wherever I looked, the evidence, to be a man is to have a dick, the bigger, the better. Guys aren't pretty, anyway; so what if the ugliest asset they have is also their measure of worth?

For rarely is a penis nicely shaped, and then, when one is, it's usually small like Michelangelo's David's, or like a little angel's penis (soft focus is best); and regular- and large-sized penises usually have too much meat in one place or another, so that they end up looking sickly, out of control, like genetic mistakes, tumors, cucumbers with mottled veins. There were the stumps, too, short stubby penises going on for four or five inches evenly paced then, whack, squared off; it was as though they'd been sheared off in a paper cutter. And the long, skinny ones, like those economy garden hoses you buy when you can't afford to do your yard first rate; and the ones bent too far to one side like crooked tree limbs, or too far up as though always slightly excited to erection, and there were the straightaway shafts leading to a little toadstool-button head. And of course studying penises this way also led me to study the penises' partners in crime—huevos, Easter eggs, testicles, balls, some little and heavily lined and hard looking; some big as tangerines, soft and saggy like dirty pillows, all tangled in black or too-dark blond hair, even red hair, which always seemed so out of place, so female, so criss-crossed undecided and made up. They added up, the whanger and the chestnuts, the sausage and the meatballs, no matter how you put it, they ended up, the whole package, ugly, as I've said; but ugly is what I wanted, because men were ugly and I wanted to be a man whatever the cost.

For a while I took what refuge I could in learning to cuss better. I hadn't been much of a cusser, not at all, since I had been raised to be so religious; why say something as trite as "god damn" if those mere words could cast you into eternal Hell and didn't do any good anyway? So cussing didn't sound right when it came from my mouth; it sounded unnatural, like I didn't mean it, like I was new at it (I was), like I was too self-conscious (I was), a thinker instead of a doer. I had to learn to spit the words out, to seem really angry, a man on top, a powerhouse, and to say "shit, what the fuck's going on, goddamnit" casually, as though overtaken by the words, overcome, as though they'd spilled out of the guts right onto the goddamn page. I had to look like I didn't even know what I was saying, what I'd just said. And I had to make more grammar mistakes, too, get all those good sentence construction skills out of my head so I wouldn't seem so damn feminine and pristine like my pretty little dick.

All this learning took some heavy practice, especially since I also worried all the time about who was looking at my crotch, who had heard the rumor in P.E. class that I didn't have a manly penis and was now checking me out to see if that was the truth, who now suddenly was looking at my pants to see if I bulged around the 501 buttons, who watched me from behind when I bent over to see if there was any sign of force against my pants' inseams.

Then there was swimming, smack dab in the middle of fall, so the cold alone made everything shrink. Not only would I have to change in the locker room, but I also would have to exhibit myself to everyone, right there on the pool's concrete deck and worse yet on diving boards, everyone staring at me, wearing what amounted to thick, tight underwear; that's what swimsuits are and everyone knows it. The loose look wasn't in at all, and if I'd chosen baggy shorts it would have been obvious to everyone who saw me in the showers as to why. Why couldn't men's bathing suits come puffed up like girls' bras, I wanted to know; why couldn't I wear padded underwear that would make my pants swell like a rain-soaked root trying to push its way up? Though now I guess somebody's finally marketed stuffed underwear for guys (actually I know for a fact, I've seen them; ah, too late), back then I had to imagine ways to stuff my underwear. But after the imagining came doing it, as I wasn't just a thinker anymore, I told myself, but a doer, too; so I'd get some socks and tie them up in knotty balls and jam them into my underwear, but then I had the problem that a jammed-up sock doesn't look like a penis and balls, the shape's all wrong, so someone might look at my crotch and know that it wasn't a penis and balls in there but a jammed-up sock, so I went to work on shape. One sock I'd fold in two so it was about six inches long (I wear a size twelve, that tale about foot size and penis size is crap, I want you to know); then I'd stuff it with another sock to give it some mass; then I'd staple another rolled- up sock to the penis prosthesis. I knew to be totally realistic I'd need to staple two rolled up socks, but one ball is usually bigger than the other anyway and once the socks got jammed together in my underwear and then compacted by my pants I had a nice enough bulge to fool anyone, at least anyone I didn't shower with in P.E. And the socks worked pretty well, at least I felt so; I walked more relaxed, even swaggered, since I was no longer paranoid that everyone was looking at my pants and laughing at me behind my back, even if the socks did begin to stink of sweat eventually. Who cares if a guy smells like sweat, anyway? The props were making me feel so much better about myself I decided to stuff my swimsuit, too, though using staples in such a tight package as Speedos seemed risky. I had to attach the socks together and attach them to the suit somehow, so one night when my mom had gone to bed early I sneaked into a cabinet and got out a thread and needle and sewed in socks the same color as the suit.

I felt better in the pool, too, most days, and I had everything packed nice and carefully in my locker so that I could race my swimsuit on in ten seconds flat behind a towel and no one would see its secret ingredients. Then one day we all had to experience the high dive as some sort of macho rite of passage. I was scared, I don't know why, maybe because the only time I'd ever tried the high dive was when I was young and I had belly flopped, stinging my torso against the glassy water. There were about four or five of us in line at a time and the rest just sat on the pool's deck watching and laughing; still everything would have been okay that day if only I'd realigned before I got on the high dive, but I was nervous and in a hurry to get the dive over with and sure enough, the worst thing possible happened; while I was up there bouncing up and down (the coach said we had to bounce three times on the board before jumping in, for "confidence building"), the socks came unstitched. As I was diving down, they flew off without me in a rolled-up ball attached to a tube. It was like I'd lost my parachute while skydiving; it was sailing just above me unattached, and at first everyone didn't know what to think, then there was a big laugh, then just quiet. No one said a damn thing to me. No one made fun of me or looked at me after that and even when I took a shower no one looked and they left me alone.

Then a couple of days later I saw them in my locker, hanging from a jock hook, the socks that had left my body. The secret was out, all across the little high school by then, I figured, Goddamnit, the word was out, but there was still school left; I couldn't just leave high school altogether. But something snapped in me and I started cussing with enthusiasm, and I didn't think about it, just went on goddamning-motherfucking-slutting around without giving a second's notice. And I didn't care about men anymore—well, that's not true. I didn't care if they made fun of me because I hated the buttfuckers anyway. So I went out for sports again and became a wrestler.

I no longer cared what people saw or didn't see, even in the tight wrestler uniforms with the suspender-like shoulder belts that pulled up on the crotch. I became an engineer of wrestling, studying diligently the mechanics of anatomical leverage, the collar-and-elbow tie-up and the square stance and staggered stance, the single-leg, double-leg, duck-under, and snapdown, the cross-angle pick and the high-crotch and the near arm-chop and inside-angle pick, the navy ride and the tight-waist ride and the chicken-wing ride, the take downs and the breakdowns and the other rides and the pinning combinations. I lifted weights every day, upper body one day then lower body the next, abdominals every day, and I went on steroids which made my testicles shrivel but who cares anymore, I asked myself, and shrugged my shoulders because I won my matches and had a fucking good time winning.

What I'd do, you see, was so simple; I'd get the guy's elbow, usually the left one, and hold onto it with one hand and grab his collar bone with my other and I'd penetrate, take one long step between the guy's legs, all the time pulling hard on his elbow, and then I'd move my arm from his collar bone right down into his crotch and drop down on my hips and throw the guy down to his side. Hell, he couldn't move, you see—he didn't dare; I'd kill him and he knew it—and then I'd take my other arm, my free one, and move it up the V of his legs, his knees bent hard, my weight crushing him, my left hand spider-like up his leg and then to his crotch, and then I'd squeeze the balls and penis all at once, imagining I was the jaws of life going backwards, not opening up a hole but closing in on something, you know what, and I'd squeeze—usually the guy'd start screaming, the ugly wuss, and I'd squeeze harder—my spider-fingers becoming a vise, except vises press evenly and though that's what I'd start to do I'd change, gripping his animal wound one finger at a time, then hard with the thumb.

That's how it was and still is to this day: I imagine the crotch all working together is a pimple I want to pop, a testosterone-gone-crazy bump I want to wipe off this guy's body; then it's like an explosion or an implosion—I can't tell the difference anymore—and usually the ref calls it off and I look at the poor guy on the mat, prone and hunched, and let my body kind of float above his for a few seconds like ether in a room full of matches, and I win, I win every time, and it all kind of numbs me like ice, like saltpeter, like success.

Miriam Sagan

Sister Margaret

THE MORTUARY was following me up. I didn't mind. I had liked the mortician, a pleasant Italian from a traditional family, a man not much older than I. He'd been genuinely courteous when I went in to pay by credit card, charging the cremation of my only husband to Visa, where I'd be forced to see the reason for the bill one last time on my monthly statement.

So when Sister Margaret, a nun and resident grief counselor called, I did not resist, but made an appointment to see her. Sister Margaret was wearing the kind of clothes nuns have been wearing since they were dehabited in the seventies, skirts and thick shoes, blouses with clashing pins.

"Do you sense your husband, feel him around you?" Sister Margaret asked.

"Not really," I have to say.

"Try to feel his love," she urges me.

"I don't really believe in an afterlife," I tell her.

"But your husband sounds like he was so spiritual . . . and you're a poet!"

I shake my head. I'm tired of being a widow in New Age Santa Fe where virtual strangers demand to know where Robert has gone, as if I were Madame Blavatsky.

"Whatever the forces of the universe are, I'm sure they function perfectly well without my belief," I tell Sister Margaret.

"Are you sleeping?" she asks.

"Not well. I have anxiety attacks in the middle of the night."

"Try to feel Robert's love around you when you wake up."

I nod. Robert was a swell guy, but somehow I suspect that wherever he is he has another girlfriend or something. I'm not sure he quote loves unquote me in quite such a tangible way.

"Are you eating?"

"Better," I say. Sister Margaret is a grief counselor, well-trained, she knows our issues, we bereaved, our snacks, our vices.

"Some people start drinking."

I shake my head. Sister Margaret does not seem like the person to tell I have been smoking an extremely high grade quality of sensemilla, golden buds that fill the lungs with euphoric smoke.

" And sex," says Sister Margaret. A nun has just said the word sex to me, a Jewish person. This is what it means to be a widow—anything can happen.

"Sex," I say.

"Some women can't go without sex," says Sister Margaret.

"I have a boyfriend," I say.

"Sex can be a drug," says Sister Margaret.

Thank God for that. I don't tell Sister Margaret that I have never gone for more than two and a half months without getting laid since I was sixteen years old and I don't intend to start now. I don't tell her that I have recently had the most mind blowing sex of my speckled career, brought on by a London blitz style conjunction of sex and death. Or by fourteen years of monogamy broken by the appearance of an old lover.

"A woman once sat in this office and told me she had to get remarried immediately so she could have sex."

"Oh."

"But I told her—just masturbate," Sister Margaret smiles at me beatifically.

"Oh," I say.

"How is your interest in things in general?"

Sister Margaret continues the intake. After a few more questions she studies a grief graph on her desk and informs me "you are just at the start of your grief process. Try to feel your husband around you."

"But Sister Margaret," I protest, "I want to let him go." I don't tell her about my dreams, unfortunately reminiscent of an Esalen encounter group, where I tell the man I loved: I can't be monogamous with you anymore, I have to date other people.

After a bit more chitchat, I thank Sister Margaret and get up to go. She embraces me, the purposive but impersonal hug of a nun or professional. Back out in the parking lot I feel dazed. What just happened? I seem set on some unusual stages of grief course, grieving through sex and drugs. Then suddenly I am aware of gravity, that universal law. For the first time I understand its true purpose—to keep me stuck to the earth, crossing the asphalt, instead of flying directly up into the blue New Mexico sky once and for all.

Nicole
Louise
Reid

Blue Cathedral

I FOUND AMELIE last week. I'd been walking the beach, trying not to step on sand fleas that wriggled underneath my toes. The rental house had been noisy, everyone clamoring for sunscreen and sunglasses. My mom was taping the beach umbrella to the deck railing and hollering for more tape. The ocean was frenzied like our house, and I sat in the sand to calm.

There she was, sliding backwards down the middle piling of the pier; this blue, wet, wrapped thing plunging her head into the waves that knocked against her post. She looked like a lizard, every inch of her soft to wrap around the piling. She was a cold chameleon faded to the water that had climbed her blue swimsuit. Her hair and shoulders were wet; she'd just come from the waves, and was going right back in. She dunked her head under and stayed there for what seemed ten minutes.

Her toes were counting the seconds she'd been under. I left my shorts and sunglasses on the sand, waded, and then swam out to the middle of the pier. Then I took a deep breath and sank under. I crawled out to her post, slowing as I neared her. I blew bubbles from my puffed-out cheeks, and stared into her upside-down eyes. She was startled, but still. I pulled her in, taking her arms from the post, then unhooking her ankles. I drew her through the ocean into me.

Amelie cannot swim. That's why she hung with her face in the water and everything else ready to yank herself up. Amelie is deaf and a wave in her ears is one of the only things she can hear.

We did not speak under the water. I took her from the pier and we glided over waves to the sandbar. We knitted our fingers together and floated on our backs for so long I became seasick and almost blind from the white reflection of sun off water. But Amelie traced letters into my palm and we spoke like this. The words were so disjointed that I thought I misread them at first.

"B-L-U-E," she put in my hand. "C-A-T-H-E-D-R-A-L."

I was still. I closed my eyes. I thought. I was slow. Yes, blue cathedral.

"T-H-E O-C-E-A-N," I answered. That was the water passing in and out of my ears. That was the wash over coral and crabs' backs. That was a wave tipping my ear up and out and then plunging it back in. I could hear what was beneath me. I knew exactly how deep the water was, where the sandbar ended, and what lay between the floor and my back—just from the pressure and passing of waves in my ears. The feel of water pooling under my chin and then falling away with the lift of a wave was like sunlight and air through the blue rose windows at Chartres. Blue cathedral.

With my words in her skin, she popped up to sit. But water moved beneath and her legs fell; she stood. Over my shoulder, I shook my head and closed my eyes again. She lay to the top, and took back my hands.

"A-M-E-L-I-E."

"M-A-G-G-Y," I wrote. I was hers.

We both go to the Outer Banks in August. I go because my family has for the last eighteen years—since I was six years old. Amelie goes to hear. My family has taken well to Amelie. Relationships are casual in our group; every year since we were in high school, each of the kids has come back to the shore with a new girlfriend, a new fiancé. Each is welcome and remembered. Each finds a bed. So when I came up the deck-way with Amelie last week, no one gave us a second look—except for Anna, my older sister, who is always looking. Amelie became a resident of the rental—as fully welcome there as if I had driven both of us down from Philadelphia.

"Maggy, is Amelie staying for dinner?" my father asks even though she's been with us for a week. He is pulling pasta boxes from the kitchen cabinet. The rental's kitchen is tiny. The oven smells of char when warming up, and all of the silverware is spotted. But it has no walls from the big room, and I like to see my Dad cooking again; it's been years since I lived at home.

Amelie's back is to the kitchen so he asks me. I put my hand over the ace stacks in the middle of our Solitaire match and mime a ravenous spooning of something from bowl to mouth, then raise my eyebrows to tell her that this is a question. I can't make my fingers work the few signs she's taught me every night this week—not in front of my parents, Anna, Daniel and his girlfriend Karen, and the family who rents with us each summer.

Amelie smiles and nods once.

"Yes, Dad," I call to him.

Daniel looks up from the ubiquitous *USA Today*. Everyone reads *USA Today* at the beach—at least the silly colored graphs on each section.

Just before my dad's late dinners, this glass room glows yellow with extra reading lamps. Shouts from nearby decks echo in the air and the early night winds rattle the windows. There are always books—no *USA Today*, the night is for serious reading—always card games, always puzzles, and always someone's feet back and forth making rounds throughout the main level looking for a shopping list or stamps for post-cards. Someone writes long letters while bent too low to the table. Someone rocks side to side in front of the small stereo, trying to decide what to play next. And someone goes out to the deck to smell the salt and feel it stick to skin—the sliding glass door grinding open and shut in its sandy track, and each time more air on us. We all hear walkers returning up the deck, even Amelie who feels their first footsteps shake to her lap.

Sheila and Owen, the parents of the family that rents with us, brush their feet just outside the sliding door, and slip back into their rubber flip-flops to come in. Amelie and I pick up our cards and go back to turning them by threes. But from the far corner of the open combination living- and dining-room, Anna's eyes are up from her lines of Akhmatova. She watches the air between Amelie and me, and waits for words. The house becomes so quiet with Amelie in it, like to speak would be rude. Or maybe they are all doing what I do. I try to squeeze my ears shut, to pin them closed so that all I can hear is the heat of my breath and the push of blood. I'm sure Anna is trying on deafness.

Amelie plays her last card well before I get to the bottom of my hand again. She looks at me with skinny, curled lips: her little laugh. We sort through the cards, count mine to see how close I was to finishing (not very), and then pack them up in their boxes. Amelie slides her sandal off of her foot and holds it up to me, now *her* eyebrows up for a question.

"How long until dinner, Dad?" I ask to make sure we have time.

"Oh, at least thirty minutes." He is slicing eggplants, and still needs to sweat them.

"We'll be back by then. Does anyone want to come with us?" I hope not, but this is the expected line of anyone taking a walk, and I have to ask. I step into my shoes by the door.

Karen pokes Daniel's shoulder. "Wanna?" she asks. They unfold from their layers on sofa and floor.

"We'll catch up with you, okay?" Daniel stretches to his feet.

Amelie takes my hand and we walk the long deck and stairs down to the beach. She studies the rental from below to make sure we'll know it later if the sun is gone completely. With one step, my shoe is full of sand. I take both off and set them on the landing from our deck. Amelie does the same. We rush to the water that's already cool for the night. I slip a toe under the muddy sand, and let the next wave wash it out. We walk towards our pier, feeling a magnetic draw neither one of us questions.

Daniel and Karen are twenty feet back. I watch him to see what an older brother knows about women. I doubt there is much he could teach me. There is no hand I haven't already put on Amelie's neck, no look she hasn't already given back to me. So Amelie and I lead, stay ahead all the while.

There is a spot we found in the night last week where wind split a dune to cut a path. At the top was a level place set in among reeds and sea oats to keep us in the hollow of moonlight reflecting water. There, Amelie taught me her alphabet. The letters had fallen from her tall hand against the sky into my eyes. But the transition from sight to sound and knowing were so beyond me. Amelie's letters were like piano scales that I hadn't practiced. I was sight-reading exercises at my lesson, and Amelie, next to me on the bench, knew all of the sharps and naturals before I chose which note to play, which letter to form. My hand was slow. Deciding where to put each finger was thick thought sliding from brain into hand. And sometimes no thought came at all. Sometimes my skin was too thick and stiff, and nothing in shapes meant voice to me. I simply couldn't get from language to movement; my hand sat dumb in the sky. Finally, Amelie took it down. She traced circles and squares into my palm—things she knew I could see. She closed my eyes and put loose words in my hand and put her hollow ear to my chest.

She can do this. She can string words together that mean nothing, then everything. Amelie's words are whole words. Her thoughts are whole. Each one says as much as it can. Nothing is broken, half meant, half understood. I can give her ten fickle words that will never near the worth of her two. And each of hers stays with my head in the water, on the sand, on walks with Amelie for peppermint clam shells, playing Solitaire with her. There is a list somewhere in my brain of everything she has said to me—a short list, a full list.

We see our spot and are careful not to look its way so that Daniel or Karen may see and claim it. Needing it to be ours tonight, I turn around to begin the walk back.

Daniel is reluctant. "So soon? Yeah, I guess it's about time." He bends down for a peppermint clam shell. That's what he and I have called the pink-and-white spiraled ones since our first summer here. He brushes sand from it and tucks the smooth thing into Karen's shorts pocket. On the walk back I watch for peppermint clam shells, but Daniel must have found them all first.

Dinner is almost ready. Amelie grabs my elbow on the deck. She stops me and makes me smell. Garlic nibbles the edge of my nostrils, and I stand still to let it in.

"O-W," she writes into my back. "M-M-M."

I turn to her; our eyes shake with giggles.

Dinner is as good as the smell, and we all stuff ourselves. I sit across from Amelie so she can read my lips. Anna sits at the end of the table, staring at the still air between us. The table is too quiet. I pretend to cough into my napkin and say, "Talk. Everyone talk." Amelie just laughs and shakes her head.

With that, the table erupts into its old summer vacation discussions on politics, news, money, and the literary merit of the Tom Clancy novels Owen reads each year for, as he says, a much-needed break from teaching Keats and Shelley. Anna clears the table with the other family's kids—Blake, Wendy, and her husband Tim. Amelie and I load the dishwasher and scrub the spaghetti pot and bread pans. Karen and Daniel plan the next day's dinner. Amelie wants to wash, so I take the rinsed plates to the machine.

Once done, she turns to me, grabs my hand, and writes, "T-O-W-E-L."

We go shoeless this time, but I pick up one of the towels my mom has folded and set near the sliding glass door. We hurry down the beach to our spot just before our pier. No one has taken it. It's ours. This blind part of the beach is secluded: no people, no house lights on, no views to the street behind. She lays the towel over the sand, and smoothes it for us. We sit. Moonlight pools around her head like a tiny, round ocean. Amelie pulls off her shirt and then mine. She raises her hips to slide out of her shorts. I do the same. Her blue bathing suit is the color of the sky and she seems to fade when she stands—all but arms and legs, and her red hair. She holds there a moment, her long toes curling into the sand beneath the towel. Then she pushes her straps from her shoulders, down her arms; she pulls the whole thing down from her round hips to her place at my feet. She is slow, unstooped to me. The moon backlights her every curve and the ocean behind me is on her so that she is stained glass and I see through her. The ripples of each wave groove her body and I run my hand up her thigh to feel the way flesh becomes glass.

She pulls me up and then sits where I've been. I peel down my own bathing suit and stand for her. We do this; we reciprocate. I stand between white moon and inky water to show her what I have seen. Amelie has to be naked to speak to me, and I have to be naked to hear her hands. She needs the night on my skin to be in her language, and my fingers only work for her. We lie on our backs, our thighs up and tangled into each other's. She takes my right hand to speak. I take her left to answer.

"L-E-T-T-E-R-S?" Amelie asks.

"Y-E-S." I will try.

She straightens her arm and holds it into the sky. Her fist is tight, ready like a gymnast waiting to mount her beam. Then her fingers begin moving through the signs for letters. They are fluid, white in the moonlight against the dark ocean sky. They are slow shooting stars, changing as slowly as melting ice cream. Her left hand passes through the letters five times without stopping. I pull her arm down to rest, and then kiss her cheek five silent times. Inside our ring of dune grasses, set inside our own puddle of ocean and moon, I shut my ears to everything else. I hear like Amelie, just the wind tumbling into and out of my ears. If it has come across the water, the air stings my face and beats my lips. If it has moved up the beach, it is dry and tickles. But if the wind has come across Amelie's naked blue skin to mine, it is soft and holds to me. Hers is slow air and I hear it whispering against my body.

Amelie and I lie under our own sky, and I under her starry hand, for hours. Finally, her arm gives out and we pull to each other—tiny gusts passing up to our ears through the tunnel of our stomachs and breasts nested into one another.

She traces her name into the lines around my lips. She passes her fingertip over my eyebrows, smoothes them with her nose, and then writes on my cheek, "A-L-W-A-Y-S L-I-S-T-E-N." I close the air pockets between us, rub myself closer into her.

When the wind whips around our ears and the tide moves the rimming grasses, I pull her up to sit. The air is heavier now, our cathedral ceiling falling. She reaches for her blue suit, but I take it from her. I dress her and kiss every place that will be covered. Amelie lies back smiling. Her toes grip the reeds lining our bed. And now rain. Tiny droplets dot our clothing, our faces.

We walk back to the rental no faster than we came, our wet hands clasped but talking to each other, and our eyes down looking for peppermint clam shells. We've been gone so long that few deck lights remain. At each one, we stop. Amelie looks up to the deck, places the picture over the one of ours in her head and then moves on until the tracings match.

Our cottage is dark, each bedroom door shut. Even my father is asleep—not slumped over in the front room's rocking chair like every other night, but in my parents' room. Karen and Daniel are already in their bed in our basement room. On her first night here, Amelie and I pulled our mattress to the floor so that we would hear the waves crash forty feet down the shore. I didn't feel the surf on any of the other nights, but tonight, each one shakes my spine. The little door to this room presses in and out with gusts of wind. The one window that is above our heads rattles with each raindrop. The storm has come closer.

Amelie stands at the window. She presses her left hand to the glass and hears every crack of thunder before I can feel it in me. She watches the same blue-black sky whose moon has lit our bodies just minutes ago, mix in purples and pinks. The night seems cut open under water: heavy streams dye the sky and then wash away until another rush of blood.

"Amelie," I whisper so that Daniel and Karen won't wake. But the quiet of her back hits me, and I go to her at the tiny, shaking window. "C-O-M-," I start, but then rub out her back to erase the word. She is listening, and the times when she can are limited. I can't pull her from that. I set a flattened fist into her back, leave it there for her to hear me.

She reaches her arms back like she had them around the pier's post when I first saw her. Her skin presses to mine, conducts the sound, lets me hear the force of the thunder, the spark of the lightning. Each raindrop outside trembles against my skin like it has fallen there itself.

"L-I-S-T-E-N-I-N-G," I write in the gully between her breasts, feeling each letter through her as if my hand were between my own.

We stay there through the worst of the storm and then go back to bed. Amelie wraps herself around me, and we sleep with whispers of raindrops and wind between us.

Before breakfast, Amelie and I check our night spot in the dunes. The rain has torn its wall apart, and the reeds lie in a heap on the beach. Our hands are still against each other; no words. We walk back towards the rental, not even looking for peppermint clam shells. But the storm has missed one. I pick it up, rinse the moist sand from it in the sleepy ocean waves, and tuck it, without a sound, into Amelie's pocket—just like Daniel did. Amelie slips her fingers into her pocket and holds the pink-and-white spiraled shell there against her skin to listen to it.

We were the first up this morning, and the empty front room is tempting, so we hurry back to claim a new spot. On the deck landing, we shower the rain-tamped sand from between our toes, and dry our feet at the glass door. Owen has just returned from his *USA Today* and doughnuts run. He takes two glazed and heads off for his first morning nap. Amelie and I each pull a rainbow section of paper and a doughnut, and then curl feet to feet on the blue and white sofa. We puzzle over our obligatory bottom-of-the-page graphs, lick the sugar from our fingers, and sleep. Each of us hears the spent waves that come after a storm lap at our sides, the movement of the sun climbing up through the water, and the early morning walkers rinsing their peppermint clam shells in the pools around their feet. We sleep with still hands—toes in toes, bent knees against bent knees—while the house shakes loose from its quiet night. Amelie and I wake with Anna's eyes back on the air between us, and Karen and Daniel kneading tonight's pizza dough. Owen is napping again. My mother slices tomatoes for lunch, and my dad is just about to give up on a jigsaw puzzle of Monet's Haystacks.

"Ay yi yi! This is too hard, and my fingers are too big." He throws up his arms.

My mom giggles and then stops suddenly to check for all of her fingertips.

"You just started." Daniel throws more flour over the fat ball of dough on the counter. He punches his fist into its center and starts working it with both palms.

"That puzzle's hard anyway," says Karen, "there's too much sky."

I look to Amelie, my eyes asking if there could ever be *too much sky*. Her toes curl up into the arches of my feet and push; she stretches from naps like a cat. I think we'll make cheese soufflé for dinner tomorrow. She takes my hand and writes, "L-O-V-E C-A-T-H-E-D-R-A-L."

Robert Olen Butler

The American Couple

MY SISTER AND I dressed up like ducks and our sign said DON'T DUCK A DEAL and so I ended up in Puerto Vallarta, Mexico, with my husband. This was the deal my sister and I made after the show. She would take the money that went along with the special vacation package that turned out to be behind curtain number two, and I would take my husband to Puerto Vallarta. If we'd had a chance to make the deal just before ours, I would have won a car. I could see a very slight bulge just to the left of center in curtain number three, and sure enough, when they opened it to show the couple dressed like killer bees what they'd passed over, there was a Ford Escort which was pulled up just a little bit too far. They do that sometimes. I noticed it. The killer bees did not notice it and they won the goat behind curtain number one, a goat which nibbled the hem of the electric blue dress on the beautiful blond model holding the goat's leash. Everyone laughed except the couple dressed like bees, and my sister and I laughed too, though when I leaned over to my sister and told her that I had known where the car was, she slapped her forehead in distress and stopped laughing. I am very observant. This is a good thing, I think, though in Vietnam, where I was born and raised, it is not thought to be a good trait in a woman, unless she keeps it to herself.

My husband is of two minds on this matter. Sometimes I will notice something that will help him in his business. He is a very fine businessman. He is a very big success in America, just as he was when he was in Vietnam, even though he had to start over again from the beginning in this country. In Vietnam he made much money in the export of duck feathers. This is what inspired my costume on "Let's Make a Deal." Duck feathers were the fourth largest export business in The Republic of South Vietnam and they make very soft pillows and very warm blankets. Once a man who my husband trusted came to the office and said that he was dealing only with my husband, but I observed a duck feather in the cuff of his trouser and that duck was not one of ours. My husband was very proud of my observations on that day, but I know I make him nervous because he thinks there is a great deal that I can see and know about him at all times.

It's true that I know quite a few things from what my eyes tell me. It's true that I was happy to have a chance to bring him to Puerto Vallarta and that I myself struck the deal with my sister that made this possible. We flew in over the mountains and he was sleeping beside me and I watched out the window. The mountains were covered in a lush green that looked like velour and it was very much like Vietnam. There was a river running over the mountain, a brown river, as brown as a Mexican child, and our plane followed it until I could see the city out ahead of us strung along the sea. It was very beautiful coming in and I nudged my husband, hoping he would wake and bring his face near to mine and watch with me. But he became instantly concerned with finding his shoes, which he always slips off when he sleeps, and by the time he felt like nothing was lost and he was not being caught off guard by anything, we were too low for romance and all I could see outside were ragged fields and a neighborhood of poor houses, tin and wood, also like Vietnam, like the places all around Saigon, which is the city I am from.

The airport was pretty ragged, too. All the strips of land in between the runways were overgrown and the airport building was long and low and it looked mostly like cinder block, which they tried to hide by giving big sections of the outside walls a different texture, a certain roughness, but it reminded me of crepe paper and they painted these parts in bright colors, red and yellow and lime green. It just all seemed pretty cheap, and I could see my husband's eye for business picking up on that right away, along with all the weeds. He'd been to the slick American places—Las Vegas and Miami Beach and Lake Tahoe—and he knew what the customer expected. In the taxicab he was snorting at the potholes in the road—the cab had to slow almost to a stop several times—and at the occasional piles of stony rubble and at all the weedy fields. This whole corridor to the fancy hotels should be done up right, he was thinking. And he wasn't all that happy about doing this trip anyway, I knew. He was sorry to be away from his work, even for a week, and he didn't like my sister being his benefactor. Especially not since she and I dressed up like ducks.

I didn't like that either, really. I must admit I love the game shows. I love American television in general. The soap operas. You'd think I would've had enough of daily disaster, but the soaps remind me that somewhere somebody knows what life can really be. It makes me enjoy even more all of this wonderful lightness before my eyes in America. And I particularly like one of the soap operas with an older woman character. This actress has been around for years and even though the shows are taped, she always seems to me on the edge of disaster. The actress personally. She is saying her lines and I can sense some light go out in her brain and you can see her eyes slide just ever so briefly off camera. She's looking for the prompt cards, you see. She's forgotten her lines. And this must be happening to her all the time, for these moments to be left on the tape, even if they are subtle and maybe I'm the only viewer in the country, other than perhaps another professional actor, to notice. There's always this real-life drama going on. I like her very much. This woman has guts, continuing to act without a memory.

Sometimes she gets the other actor in the scene positioned just right and her gaze lifts over the actor's shoulder and you can see the faint scanning of her eyes as she reads. It is very subtle, this movement, but I can see it, and at those moments I feel very good for her. She can see what there is to say. But I also feel good for her, a little thrilled even, like watching an ice skater doing a leap, when her character suddenly becomes chatty and slightly unfocused and it's because she is cut off from the prompt cards and she's improvising around until she can find her way back to the script. This is what's good about America. There is always some improvisation, something new, and when things get strained, you don't fall back on tradition but you make up something new.

Still, if I could have been part of all that without dressing up like a duck, that would have been better. I wish I could have won Mexico by answering questions or solving puzzles or guessing prices. Something like that. I'm very good at all those things. Just last week I did several things that no one else could do—I identified Jeremy Brett as playing both Sherlock Holmes on public television and Freddy in the movie "My Fair Lady" and I read the phrase "Desperation Tactics" even without any vowels and I knew that a Kitchen Aid dishwasher and a year's supply of Toast 'Ems cost between $650 and $700. But you have to try out for these shows and they stay away from people who have an accent. I put the words of English together as well as most Americans, but you can hear my foreignness in my pronunciation.

And only once did I get as far as the tryout anyway. I finally had sense enough to turn my name around and leave out the middle two. I turned Trần Nam Thanh Gabrielle into Gabrielle Tran. My parents had given me a French name because they had always admired the French, for their food and for their riding club in Saigon, mostly. But arranging my name like Gabrielle Tran won me a tryout—I guess the producers thought I might be like Nancy Kwan, the actress who I enjoy on the old movies and who can speak English very clearly when she wants to.

I was very good at doing what they asked when exciting things happened in the game. You'd think that they'd have long ago gotten used to asking for this. But the man with the headphones and a clipboard seemed almost shy when he got around to it. Like we were on a date and he was asking for something sexual and a little strange. There were three of us trying out at once, three women, and he said, "When something very good happens, could you . . ." And he stammered around for a bit and then said, "Could you show it physically. That is, could you kind of, you know, bounce up and down. Jiggle around." So we all laughed at this, but then we did it and I did it very well. He even stopped us and put his hand on my shoulder and said to the others, "Yes. Like this. Watch Mrs. Tran."

I was very good, you see. And it was natural to me. I was having fun. But then when they started talking to us, asking our names and where we lived and such, I could see the little squinting that went on when I spoke. They asked questions and I got them right and I bounced up and down, but I knew I wasn't going to make it. And I think I probably talked a little too much, as well. I even kidded the host—I won't mention his name—about the kiss he gave his hostess during a break. They had both disappeared while the director walked around setting cameras, and when they returned, they did it without looking at each other at all and the host's TV makeup was smudged around his lips. It's not as if I said this on the air, but instantly I could tell that it wasn't the thing to do.

My husband told me that it was all I should have expected. In America he is in the food service business. Not restaurants. He thinks that's like being a trained elephant in a circus, running a Vietnamese restaurant in America with paper lanterns and china soup bowls and all of that. He thinks it's just putting on your foreignness and playing a part. Instead, he makes food for institutions that need meals—like hospitals, schools, airplanes, banquet facilities. He is a very good businessman. He appreciates America very much for being the sort of place where a man like him could succeed. But he has no use for the things I like about America. He said that I should have known the game shows would never take a woman who has my face or my voice.

But in a way I proved him wrong. The proof was that he and I were going up in the elevator at the five-star Fiesta Vallarta Hotel in beautiful Puerto Vallarta where we would spend an exciting four days and three nights. The crowd at "Let's Make a Deal" knew the value of this. They let out a long sigh of envy. I know they'd been asked to make this sound, just like the winners had been asked to jump up and down. And it's true that I'd seen shows when the crowds made long sighs over an electric coffee maker or a lava lamp and they didn't even laugh at themselves afterwards. They were playing this wonderful game in this wonderful world where these things can make people happy. When your coffee drips through a filter in the morning and it tastes so good, you sigh. Or you turn off the lights, all but your lava lamp, and these wondrous shapes rise beside your bed and you turn to your husband and say, Look how beautiful. And you say, I won that. We got that for free. Well, the trip was really worth a sigh, and I won that.

So my husband and I went up to the tenth floor and we entered our room and the glass doors in the far wall were open and the filmy white curtains were fluttering and we stepped through them, out onto the balcony, and there was a wonderful view, the sharp ocean horizon, Banderas bay a jade green out far, and to the left was the curve of the shore, the hotels all nestled there and also the distant city with its red-tiled roofs and palms and the mountains rising behind, thick with trees. It was very nice. I had seen but I did not look at the band of brown water, maybe seventy-five meters wide, stretching along the beach. I supposed it was the tide-drifted water from the mountain river I'd seen coming in, water full of mud and leaves from the jungle. Sort of romantic, if you think about it, jungle water hugging our shore. But of course my husband's eyes went straight for this stain on the bay and he didn't see any romance in it. He just shook his head.

"Look," I said and I pointed to half a dozen pelicans flying past at our tenth-floor level, very close, their necks curled back and their wonderful flappy lower jaws somehow tucked in. We could see their eyes and I said, "Look, Vinh," and they wheeled around for me and passed by again.

We live in Louisiana, in New Orleans. Pelicans are the state bird, but we never see pelicans in Louisiana. Here were six of them almost at arm's length. But Vinh only nodded and he leaned on the rail of the balcony, his arms stiff, and I wanted to put my hand on his shoulder. I see many things, and I knew that somewhere inside, part of him was unhappy that the businessman could not stop running his mind. How do I know this? Because this sigh he made was not just in exasperation that these businessmen had not done better in Puerto Vallarta. A neater airport, better roads, a nicer corridor of elegance to get us to the hotels, a beach with perfect white sand and green water. What were those things to my husband that they should make him sigh? Even though I knew that these were the thoughts on the surface of his mind. He even said, as his elbows stayed locked, "They should do better with this place."

I nearly reminded him that this was free. But I did not want to give him more reason to diminish what I had done. I said nothing, and I almost raised my hand to put it on his shoulder, but my husband is old-fashioned, really. He would rather touch me first. So I simply nodded at his words. They were true. And we both looked down at the pool, shimmering with sunlight, and the sun was hot on our faces and we were soon floating there on red, white and green Fiesta Vallarta inner tubes, and all about the pool were hibiscus with their yellow flowers and elephant ear plants and philodendron and bougainvillea and my husband paddled near to me and said, "The pool is very good. They take care of it very good. The water is clean and not too much chlorine." He paddled away and I felt like he had just embraced me. He is a good man. He was telling me that I had done all right, that he was going to try to enjoy this vacation, even that he was a little bit sorry he had been brooding so far. This is his way. It is a good thing that he is married to an observant woman.

I looked around the pool and three other couples caught my eye. All of them were American. I could see that from their faces and the way they held themselves, loose but every once in awhile like somebody told them to stand up straight. And more than that. Somehow I knew that they were all game show winners. They didn't know this about each other yet, but I did. And it didn't surprise me, really. For a long time, an exciting four days and three nights at the five-star Fiesta Vallarta Hotel in beautiful Puerto Vallarta was a prize on just about all of the game shows. I had already imagined a hotel constantly full of game show winners, and so when I saw these three couples around the pool I knew at once what they were. Not to mention the fact that each couple had at least one person, usually the wife, with a very animated face, and one woman who actually jiggled up and down in excitement when her husband unexpectedly brought her a drink from the pool bar.

They didn't yet know about each other what I already knew about them. They were scattered about and I floated near them in turn and I played a little game for myself, trying to figure out which type of show each had been on. One woman was wearing a black two piece suit and she still had on jewelry, a pair of hammered silver and turquoise earrings and a heavy matching necklace and even the bra of her suit was held together by a metal brooch. She was maybe fifty and hoping to look in her thirties and her hair was bleached a blond so shiny and light that in the glint of the sun it seemed almost the color of her hammered silver. She seemed easy for me to place on one of the puzzle-solving shows, not just because she was working a crossword puzzle in a tightly folded newspaper but because of the smugness of her smile as she did it and the fact that she was doing it in ink.

The next was a young couple, and this was the woman who jiggled up and down about the drink and she flashed blinding smiles all over the pool. But when she lay back on her lounge chair and I floated past the wrinkled bottoms of her feet, I knew they'd logged many hundreds of miles in shopping malls and I figured she was from one of the price-guessing shows.

I paddled around to the other side of the pool, which was quite big, and I passed an American man playing with great patience with a little Mexican girl wearing water wings. The child's father was standing a few meters away in the water and the little girl would swim from her father to the American and back again with great glee. The American was very loud and very gentle in his encouraging the girl and the father was pleased but a little nervous, as well. The American was bald with a big laugh and a big blond mustache and he was wearing dog tags. His hair was too shaggy for a current military man and he was perhaps in his early forties, and I knew from his age and the dog tags that he was a Vietnam veteran, one of those who was either unable or reluctant to forget where he had been. But it was his wife who I realized was the game-show woman. She was sitting on her lounge chair and she was reading a book and I know she was the veteran's wife because of the looks she gave him now and then as he grew particularly loud. His voice bellowed, "Swim, little darling, swim over there to your daddy now," and the wife lowered her book and her head angled slightly to the side and there was something around her eyes and her mouth that was very hard to read. Like she loved this man and was distressed by him in such equal parts that there was only something very small and placid that she could ever show about him. Or maybe even feel.

I looked toward Vinh and he was still floating on his inner tube, though his stomach was not visible, as if he was slowly sinking through the hole. I wondered if this was comfortable for him, if I should go over and try to help him adjust himself on the tube. If I just let him float and slowly sink, he might finally decide to slip into the water and feel refreshed and then comfortably readjust himself and he would like this place even more. But he might sink farther until he felt stuck and it would irritate him and make his business mind reawaken and criticize these people for offering inner tubes instead of inflatable mattresses and this would be the final little irritation that prevented him from having a moment's real enjoyment for the rest of the trip. It could go either way. So I watched his tube slowly turning and he was very still and I looked back to the wife with the book and I decided she'd appeared on a question-answering show.

As it turned out, however, I was wrong about two of the three. The one with the jewelry turned out to be from the pricing game and the young one who jiggled was a puzzle expert. I know this because after awhile the three women, each in her own time, ended up in the hot tub at the side of the pool. As each arrived, there were little hello-to-a- stranger nods and I didn't want to miss any of their talk so I pulled myself from the pool and plucked the bodice of my one-piece up into place—I am happy to be very slim but I am small-chested—and I approached the hot tub. A beautiful dark-skinned Mexican woman was ahead of me going up the steps of the hot tub. She was wearing a skimpy two piece suit and was in the process of making it skimpier, twirling and tucking the cloth of the panties of it into the separation of her own very lovely bottom so that it was now like a string bikini and the eyes of the three American women rose and then whirled like the steam from the water. The Mexican settled into the water and the three others moved just a little bit closer to each other in the shared put-down they'd felt from the flamboyant sexiness of this woman.

They hardly gave me a glance as I eased into the hot water in the space between them and the Mexican, who had thrown her head back and closed her eyes as if the most handsome lover in the world had asked her if he could kiss her throat. The Americans could hardly say what they had on their minds, for fear that this woman spoke English, but at least her presence broke the ice between them.

The bouncy one that I had pegged as a shopper spoke first. She looked at the other two and said, "Well, y'all look like you're from the same side of the border as this little old girl."

I looked at the Mexican woman and she did not move; she kept receiving the kisses of Valentino's ghost or whoever and I myself felt downright invisible. This wasn't a bad feeling, but I did glance out into the pool and at moments like these, a sense of Vinh's no-nonsense business eye was something of a comfort to me. He could always see through anything, it seemed to me, and I could imagine myself standing beside him on a hill above it all.

This all happened in a brief moment and when I looked back to the others, they were chuckling at the remark, though the woman with the veteran for a husband was covering up the laugh with her hand, like she was a little guilty about it. The woman wearing the jewelry said, "You don't sound like you're too far over the border. Texas?"

"Louisiana," the bouncy one said, and I sank lower into the hot tub, some sort of reflex. Then she said, "Not New Orleans, either. I'm from up north where the real southerners are."

The one with the jewelry said, "So you don't do Mardi Gras?"

"No way, honey. That's for the people with no shame whatsoever." And her eyes moved to the Mexican woman and the eyes of the other two followed, though the woman from the question-answering show was the last one over and the first one to look away again. When she did, she saw me and it seemed to be with a little shock, like she hadn't noticed me before. Maybe she hadn't. Or since I was submerged now to my chin, maybe it looked like I was just this disembodied head floating on the surface of the hot tub. I smiled at her like she was the red light on the camera.

"I bet you're from California," Northern Louisiana said to the woman with the jewelry.

"Minnesota," said the other. "Not Minneapolis either. I'm from up north where the real northerners are."

Everybody laughed and I wanted to sink a little deeper, but I'd run out of submergible parts. I thought about getting out of the tub, but I still wanted to hear them discover the game-show connection, and fortunately that happened very quickly. Northern Louisiana asked Minnesota what it was that brought her to Mexico, no doubt anxious to let these women know that she was a winner on a show. But Minnesota got the first chance. She declared that she won on "The Price is Right" and Northern Louisiana jiggled up and down in excitement and proclaimed her own triumph on "Wheel of Fortune." I pouted briefly at getting these two wrong, and the third woman finally spoke and said she'd won on "Tic, Tac, Dough" and then I nearly drowned in the hot tub because they all three began to jump up and down in the excitement of this revelation and the waves of hot water rushed over my face splashing up my nose and into my mouth and eyes.

I was happy that no one noticed. I rose up and gasped quietly to myself while the others talked all at once. The Mexican woman was looking at me, but I nodded to her that I was all right and after a slow, contemptuous look at the three Americans, she closed her eyes and put her head back once more, though this time she turned slightly to one side as if to ask her lover to kiss a new spot, just under her ear. I was ready to get out of the tub, away from all the excitement, but I lingered for a time watching this woman, so comfortable in her body, so relaxed with matters that touched on sex.

A little later Vinh and I were walking along the beach. It was the Mexican woman who stayed in my mind, not the game show winners. I knew I was seeing them too flatly. They were complicated human beings, like all of us, in spite of how hard they worked at making their surfaces simple. But they bored me right now. I thought about the Mexican woman and I wished I could take Vinh's hand. Perhaps this was foolish of me, to have this hesitation. I am a smart woman, a modern woman. Vinh has never said a word to me that would discourage me from doing something like taking his hand as we walked on the beach. But there are forces in me that are very strong. Just as strong as the forces that make the two women from Northern Louisiana and Minnesota speak and dress and act the way they do. They have no control of those things. I doubt if they could change any of those things even if they were conscious of them and wanted to. I spent the first twenty years of my life living in a country and a culture that expected certain attitudes from women and men and you can't just put all that aside because your mind says, Why not? Nobody's mind is that strong. You have to wait. Things have to change from the inside.

Like Vinh. He walked beside me on the beach and the waves rustled near us, running up now and then and licking our feet, and there was bright sun and a blue sky overhead while across the bay, the mountains had disappeared into a dark gray sky and there were leaps of lightning over there and the contrast between this sunny beach and that storm-dark mountain was very romantic. But Vinh could not see these things. He was brooding again, thinking about Delta Airlines or the Superdome or the Hilton Hotels, thinking about five-hundred chicken dinners or a thousand Swedish meatballs. A man strapped into a harness beneath a parachute was rising from the beach just ahead of us, a cable running out to a speedboat in the bay going taut and dragging him into the air, and I stopped to watch it rise and Vinh realized what I did and he too stopped, following my eyes into the air but not really seeing anything, because he said, "Can you remind me to call Nicholson when we get back? They've got some big engineering conference coming in."

"Okay," I said, still watching the man on the parachute getting smaller and smaller in the blue sky and I thought that this was something I might like to do. To get up there above all of this and just float around.

"You'll remember?" Vinh asked because I had answered without looking at him. It wasn't in irritation that he said this. It was just that I was important to him in this way. He depended on me. I have a very good memory.

I lowered my eyes and he was looking at me with a face that seemed eager, almost like a child. Sometimes he seemed to really enjoy the work he did. I was glad for that. I said, "I'll remember. You know I'm like an elephant."

My Vinh smiled at this. I have said this same thing to him many times and it always makes him smile. And that always makes me smile, that this should amuse him so. I smiled and then a young Mexican girl appeared at Vinh's side and she had lizards on both shoulders and on the top of her head, large lizards.

"You take picture of you and iguana?" she asked. "Very cheap."

Vinh looked at her and stepped back, startled, I think, at these large green creatures crouching on the girl. "No, gracias," he said.

"Like in the movies," the girl said.

"Where's your camera?" Vinh said, and the girl shrugged and looked toward me. I was carrying a bag large enough, I suppose, to hold a camera. Vinh said to her, "You should have a camera. If you want to make money, you get a camera and shoot the picture yourself. Comprende?"

I don't think the girl comprended. But even if she did, making an investment in a camera to improve her business probably was worthless advice. I said to Vinh, "She never has that much money at one time, to be able to buy a camera."

Vinh nodded and sighed. "She'll never get anywhere."

By now I'm sure the girl thought we were both a little cracked, so she drifted away. I came to Vinh's side and we walked on. "Iguanas," he muttered.

I said, "Do you know why iguanas?"

He shook his head no.

I said, "Because Puerto Vallarta is a very romantic place, and it has to do with iguanas."

Sometimes I will surprise my husband with a piece of information, and though it usually has something to do with the parts of American culture he has little patience for, his natural curiosity gets the better of him. This was one of those times. He looked at me sideways, not exactly turning his head to me; he was trying to say that he wasn't really interested in this but I'd better tell anyway. In these situations I don't say anything immediately. I choose to ignore this look of his. I make him ask for it.

The culture I grew up in does give a woman certain subtle ways of maintaining her dignity.

"There's a reason?" he finally asked.

"A reason?" I said, as if I'd already forgotten about it.

"Yes," he said firmly. "A reason for the iguanas on the beach."

"Oh, yes," I said, and I waited.

Vinh stopped walking abruptly. I took a few more steps, as if I didn't notice. "Gabrielle," he called after me, and I stopped and turned and looked surprised not to find him beside me. I returned at once, being the good wife that I am. When I got to him, he settled himself so as not to seem too eager to hear whatever this was that I knew. He even used the casual form of my name, though he said it with the French pronunciation and I don't think he has ever learned that in English he could have a little joke on me with it. "Gaby, why is it that they think tourists want to have their pictures taken with iguanas?"

"It's nothing really. It's just a foolish thing."

"Gabrielle," he said in the voice I was waiting for. My husband is very attractive at this sort of moment. Someone else might get angry or imperious or dismissive or whiney. But Vinh turns gently urgent, like he is a child with a little pain that his momma has to make better. "Please tell me," he said.

So I told him about Liz and Dick. Elizabeth Taylor in "National Velvet" is a wonderfully beautiful girl. Even later, in "Cleopatra," she is very beautiful. You might think that a Vietnamese would not appreciate that kind of full bosomed beauty. But people often admire qualities that are quite different from their own. And Richard Burton of that same time is equally attractive, say in "Look Back in Anger" or "The Bramble Bush." His voice, particularly, can thrill a woman. He, too, was in "Cleopatra" and that, of course, is when the story I told Vinh really began. Liz and Dick—Cleopatra and Antony—fell in love, and since they were both married to other people and that was in 1962, there was a big uproar. Then the next year Richard Burton came to Puerto Vallarta to make a film. (I didn't tell Vinh the name of the film at this point so that I could hold back the big answer to his question and keep his attention. He was still wondering about the iguanas.) Elizabeth Taylor followed him to this place and they rented two houses with a bridge between them, over a cobbled street, and the world was watching that bridge very closely for months. By now Vinh was getting a little impatient, I knew. Just impatient enough—I always could sense when I was about to lose his attention. So I told him that the name of the movie was "The Night of the Iguana" and there were Puerto Vallarta iguanas featured in it and that's why the little girl had her business.

Vinh was disappointed at the payoff of this story. I knew he would be. He almost always was. His brow wrinkled up and he pursed his lips and I wasn't upset at his reaction. I liked it very much that he continued to insist that I finish these little stories even though his deep practical self almost always ended up finding them trivial or foolish or simply incomprehensible. He still always asked me to go on. He insisted. And I don't exactly understand it, but I took it as a kind of faithfulness to me.

"Iguanas," he muttered and I heard the word again late that afternoon, across the lobby lounge in the Fiesta Vallarta Hotel. Vinh and I had a handful of drink coupons, an unexpected extra benefit from curtain number two, and we'd come down to the lounge in the open air end of the lobby facing the sea. The three American game show couples were already there, and I could feel Vinh tense up because they were loud and they were having a frivolous good time and I knew that what pleasure Vinh hoped might be squeezed out of this trip had to do with being quiet and peaceful.

Northern Louisiana and her husband were at the bar and they were both facing into the lounge, their elbows thrown back behind them onto the counter. The husband was young and so blond his hair and mustache seemed almost white, made even more pale by the deep tan of his skin. I was thinking his work kept him out in the Louisiana sun, but Minnesota and her husband were sitting in overstuffed chairs at a little table nearby and he was at least thirty years older than Mr. Northern Louisiana and his hair, though thinned out quite a bit, was just about the same bleached white color and his skin, though more leathery, was just as tan. I couldn't see him sweating under a Minnesota sun, so I figured maybe they both went to the same franchise of tanning salons that turned all their clients out like this.

The Tic-Tac-Dough woman was at an adjoining table and she was smiling and speaking to the others and it was from her that I heard the word "iguana." She was probably telling them the same story I'd told Vinh, since her specialty (I'd been right about her) was question answering and this was a set of those countless facts that clung to her mind. I have a similar static-cling mind and as I watched her, her husband crossed my sight carrying two drinks from the bar. He handed one down to her and turned to sit and his T-shirt had a map of Vietnam and the words I'VE BEEN AND I'M PROUD. This didn't surprise me because I'd felt certain I'd read the sign of the dog tags correctly. The veteran sank into the overstuffed chair and as he was trying to arrange himself he glanced our way. Vinh was tugging at my elbow. He wanted to leave, I'm sure, but I kept my attention on the veteran whose eyes widened slightly at us and then slid away as Minnesota laughed loud and said to his wife, "Eileen, honey, nobody today would even give them a second thought. What's a little adultery anymore?"

Vinh had my elbow in a strong grip now, but I leaned near to him and said, "We've got free drinks coming and I need one right now."

Vinh whispered, "I'd rather pay in a quieter place."

I answered, "There is no such place." This was a little gamble. I didn't want to turn him more strongly against the vacation, but I did want to sit and watch these people. It was like television, like the games and the soaps were mixed together.

Vinh sighed and nodded to me that it was all right, that as long as he was stuck in this whole thing, he really couldn't do anything but go along with me. So I took him to a table not next to the three couples but not far from them either. Vinh turned his chair at a right angle to all the other people and he faced the line of bougainvillea at the end of the lounge and the sea beyond. I listened carefully for awhile.

Minnesota went on about how acceptable adultery had become and I watched her husband and he seemed to be trying to figure something out about the ice in his drink and I suppose he was used to this kind of talk and she finally grabbed his arm and said that present company was of course excluded. And then Northern Louisiana told a story about how one of the game shows she tried out for turned her down because she wouldn't let the host kiss her on the lips and this had come out in a discussion with the director of the show who was prepping the contestants and he said that the host always kissed the women contestants on the lips. Not her, she'd told him, and that's for damn sure, honey, they didn't do that where she came from. And then the question- and-answer woman, whose name apparently was Eileen, said that she wished she'd gotten on "Jeopardy"; that was the show she really wanted to get on, and it didn't have anything to do with not wanting to kiss somebody. If something like that had prevented her, it wouldn't have been so disappointing.

And somewhere along the way, as I was sipping the drink that the waiter brought and feeling invisible, I realized that the veteran was glancing now and then in my direction. I wondered if he'd learned enough about us over there to recognize a Vietnamese when he saw one. I knew he was thinking about it, wondering if Vinh and I were from Vietnam. And after a time I began to worry just a little bit what his attitude might be. The very visible veterans I'd encountered were unpredictable. They seemed to be one extreme or the other about us. We were fascinating and long-suffering and unreal or we were sly and dangerous and unreal. I kept my own eyes on his wife, who was certainly pitched to a lower key than the other two women and whose sense of disappointment about the show she had appeared on intrigued me. I would have expected her to feel only proud of winning at whatever she did. Though maybe this expectation is my own little prejudice showing through. Why shouldn't this American woman have the same sort of disappointment of dignity that I myself felt. She interested me. She felt disappointed and she hadn't even had to dress up as a duck.

To overcome a slight lull in the conversation Northern Louisiana declared how wonderful a coincidence it was that they should all meet, all Americans and all game show winners. At this, the veteran turned to me and said, "Are you from America, too?"

This took me by surprise. When I first saw the movie "The Invisible Man" with Claude Rains, it got me to thinking about what it would be like to be invisible. And the scary part was always getting yourself into a place where you shouldn't be and then suddenly becoming visible again. Well, that's how I felt at that moment. The man had a loud voice and the attention of all these people suddenly swung around to me. And to Vinh, as well. Before I answered, I looked at him, to see if he wished to speak for us. He glanced over to the veteran but he returned to the sea and I faced the group and I tried very hard to make my pronunciation just right and I said, "Yes, we're from America. I won this trip on 'Let's Make a Deal.'"

Everyone laughed very loud and I was certain that it was friendly laughter, all of it, laughter at this sudden extension of the coincidence, no laughter at me, no one imagining me dressed up like a duck, no one thinking how absurd for this Asian woman to be a game-show winner. Minnesota cried over the laughter, "Four winners. What a hoot."

The Vietnam vet seemed particularly pleased. I could tell, though, that there was still a question in his mind about our home country, but his hunch about us was getting stronger. All of this was in his face, the way he finished laughing before the others and began to squint at us with a little smile. At least I could read him enough to know he wasn't a Vietnamese-as-the-enemy type of veteran. I looked at the faces of the others as the laughter faded and they were all friendly, and I mean no disrespect or arrogance when I say this, but I felt a little bit proud of them, like they were children who behaved really well when you didn't expect it.

The veteran said, "May I ask where you're from?"

I understood what he meant, but I chose not to show it all at once. "New Orleans," I said. Perhaps not to betray my little game with the veteran I did not look at him directly when I answered. I glanced across all the other faces and the young woman from Northern Louisiana could not hide a little jolt of distaste over this. Even that pleased me, somehow. These were human beings and they had to have their own narrowness, their own prejudices. This woman showed it to me not because I was an Asian claiming game-show equality with her but because I was from New Orleans.

"I mean originally," the veteran said, and he added, "You don't mind me asking?"

I was turning back to the man and ready to smile at him and say I didn't mind at all and let him wait a few more moments before I confirmed his hunch, but before I could say a word, I was surprised to hear Vinh's voice, not hostile or angry but still very firm, say, "We are from the Republic of Vietnam originally. Now we are American citizens and so are our children and so will be our children's children."

For him to take over and answer the question would not surprise me. But the elaboration of it, talking about our children and our children's children (though in Vietnamese culture the unborn and even the unconceived children are already thought to be part of the family), this is what surprised me. He was looking directly at the veteran and the veteran was looking directly at him, and maybe Vinh thought he was drawing a line, like the man does, the male animals do, here's the line of my territory—look at it and don't get too close. But maybe not. Because when the veteran suddenly smiled broadly and jumped up and strode the few steps over to us and bent and insisted on a handshake from my husband, Vinh gave his hand without hesitation and he was very intently looking into the face of this American, as if he was a man who needed a thousand baked chicken dinners and hadn't decided who to buy them from.

The veteran said, "I'm Frank Davies and this is my wife Eileen." He checked back over his shoulder and his wife was looking a little confused, not knowing whether to continue to talk with the other Americans or to come over to us, as her husband was motioning for her to do. Then the pinch of confusion was gone and the face I saw at the pool returned, the placid face exactly in between exasperation and affection. "Come on, honey," Frank Davies said, and the couple at the bar turned to get the bartender's attention and the woman from Minnesota said something to her husband and Eileen Davies rose and came over and shook our hands and she and her husband sat down with us.

I saw no discomfort on Vinh's face at all of this. I could tell if he was really wishing to make a quick escape and he wasn't. This interested me greatly. He turned slightly toward these two people but not all the way. He was still angled more toward the balcony and the bougainvillea and the sea than he was toward the veteran and his wife, but he clearly accepted their being with us. He did not look away from them, and there was not a single little glance to me as if to say, Look what you've led me into now. He was apparently content.

Frank Davies said, "I was in Vietnam, as you can see," and he thumped himself on his chest. Vinh and I both dutifully read his tee shirt once more.

Eileen's hand came out now and fell lightly on her husband's as it returned from his chest and landed on the arm of the chair. The gesture seemed to be a reminder not to say certain things that he had said many times before. When he felt her hand, Frank looked at his wife and he began, "My wife . . ." But he paused, again measuring his words. I expected him to tell us that his wife didn't like him talking too much about all of that, but apparently even this was something he'd agreed not to say, for he finished the sentence: ". . . she's the winner in the family."

This was a reference to her game show victory, but when Frank heard himself say this, you could see his face flinch as he unexpectedly interpreted his own words in another way. He could not resist: "I wish I'd been part of a winner for you folks."

Eileen smiled faintly and I looked at Vinh and he thought for a moment and then he squared around in his chair, leaving the sea. "What are you drinking?" he asked.

"Coca Cola," Frank proclaimed. "I've given up the hard stuff."

"And you?" Vinh smiled over to Eileen, and she looked at me before she answered. Her eyes searched my face for a moment and it seemed she was trying to see if it was okay with me for her to answer him, if there was some sort of hidden protocol from our culture that she needed to observe in requesting a drink from my husband.

I felt so sure that this was what was going on that I was about to remind her that we were from New Orleans, but before I could speak, she looked back to Vinh and said, "White wine."

Vinh called over the waiter and ordered the drinks and Frank caught the waiter by the sleeve before he went to get them and said, "Coca Cola from a bottle. Not a can, por favor."

The waiter nodded at him as if he understood this request and Vinh said, "You've given up cans, too?" When Vinh was in his sharpest business mood he could probe people like this, and it was not always with a friendly intent. But Frank laughed loud and he said that he sure as hell was. Vinh smiled and nodded, and this may be surprising, but I was having trouble reading his mood. I make so many presumptions about people from the things I observe, and I'm usually right. But I've been around Vinh long enough to observe when he has made his feelings invisible to me, and this was one of those times.

So the drinks came and we talked, Vinh and me and this proud-to-be Vietnam veteran and his wife, Eileen. We asked where Frank served and it turned out that he was a helicopter mechanic in Qui Nhon. He told us a story about how he'd had trouble with a "butter bar" because Frank was going up on his own time as a door gunner and he was supposed to be just a mechanic. When I got a chance I asked what a butter bar was and he said a second looey and that was not much help. It had to be some kind of Army man, perhaps a rank. But as his words flowed on, I was sitting there thinking about Frank Davies going into the place where the Army men eat their meals and there was an incident at one of the tables, Frank was arguing with a bar of butter and they came to blows and Frank squeezed the bar and it was oozing through his fingers and all the men were sighing like a game show audience, but Frank was in big trouble.

Then Eileen was at my elbow. She'd moved her chair closer to mine and she leaned near and she said in a low voice, "The men do go on about the war, don't they?"

This snapped me out of my little fantasy and I looked over to Frank and he had turned his attentions strictly on my husband, and Vinh was listening to him, leaning slightly forward and listening as if with great interest. He spoke to Frank and I didn't catch the words, but Frank nodded vigorously and said more and I turned to Eileen and replied, "My husband doesn't often talk about all of that."

"Was he a soldier?" Eileen asked.

"Yes," I said, "a very good one. He was a major in the airborne. But later, about a year before the end of the war, he was reassigned to Saigon City Hall where he worked in a special program to develop business in the city. They were trying until the very end to make the economy work, to make people want to defend their way of life. Everyone respected my husband."

Eileen looked over to her husband and pursed her lips. "Frank was a good soldier too. He wanted to do so much. He really felt like he was responsible for everyone."

I looked at Frank and his hands were before him, gesturing, shaping some point. He was talking about helicopter engines. I said, "He has so much energy."

Eileen sighed softly, in both appreciation and exasperation, it seemed. "I just wish I could get him to focus it where it's needed."

I wondered where that might be, but I did not ask. Perhaps I should have. Perhaps Eileen had something she needed to talk about and she was waiting for me to ask. But I did not. I have no trouble intruding on people's lives by reading the things that they show. But I have trouble asking my way in. So I sipped my own glass of white wine and Eileen and I watched the men talking for a while longer and then she leaned forward and touched her husband on the arm and said it was time to go.

Frank turned to her and looked at his watch and said she was right. He rose and shook our hands—his hand taking mine was large and hard but surprisingly gentle—and Eileen thanked each of us and said she hoped we could speak again soon and they moved off. I watched them carefully. Frank led the way with an air almost of determination, like weaving between these tables and overstuffed chairs took the skills of an experienced tracker. Eileen followed two paces behind. Passing by, Frank bumped one of the chairs and kept on moving and Eileen paused to straighten it.

When he was clear of the lounge area, Frank stopped and turned and waited for his wife, but when she drew near him, he was looking out over our heads, back out to the sea and she spoke a word to turn him and they walked off. They were side-by-side now, but they did not hold hands, though American couples often do.

Vinh and I remained in the bar for only a brief time. In the elevator, we were alone, but as the doors were closing, a young couple got into the car with us. She had one of those hairdos that looked like she'd slept standing on her head, full of wild waves and wrinkles. The man had a very thick neck and they were both wearing bathrobes. But their hair was not wet and they did not smell of suntan lotion, so I knew they'd spent the day in bed. Newlyweds. And I knew at once that they, too, were from a game. When they entered, the wife's robe fell open at the top and showed a lot of bare cleavage, and the husband clamped it shut and looked at me and said, "She's like that." "So are you," she said, slapping at his hand. "My little show-off," he said and he tried to kiss her on the cheek. She turned her face in mock anger and then kissed him and I looked to the front of the car. "The Newlywed Game." Unquestionably.

And I thought about Frank and Eileen, leaving the lounge. How they had moved away with a space between them and he had not taken her hand and she did not take his, for whatever reason. As Vinh and I lay beside each other that night in the dark, well before Vinh's breathing was due to turn soft and regular with sleep, I said, "What do you think of them?"

From the few moments of silence that followed I knew that he understood who I was talking about, even though he finally said, "Who's that?" If he really didn't know, then he would have asked that question immediately. Instead, he'd been trying to think what to say, or perhaps trying to understand for himself why he'd been as receptive as he had to the couple. So now he either knew the reason and didn't want to tell me or he was as puzzled as me; I didn't know which.

"Frank and Eileen Davies," I said.

"Oh, them," he said, and then there was silence again.

I waited for awhile and decided not to let him off the hook. "Well?"

"What's that?" He forced a slur into his voice. But I knew he wasn't really sleeping.

"You seemed to be very friendly with Frank."

"Was I friendly exactly?"

"You ordered him a drink."

"I couldn't avoid that. There they were."

"When the two of you were speaking, you leaned forward for his words. You don't do that to just anyone."

Vinh thrashed about with his covers. "I hate it when you do that," he said.

Two could play his little game. I let a few moments pass and then said, "What's that?"

"You know what I'm talking about. When you start telling me what my little gestures and looks mean. *I* don't even know."

I could hear music from somewhere. Very faint. I couldn't control the sigh that billowed up from my chest. It was very clear, the sound of my sigh in the dark room, but I wasn't sure that Vinh had noticed. I wished that he had. I wished that he had my own little gifts so he could tell me why it was that I made that sound right then.

Then he said, softly enough that I could hear the music behind his words. "I'm not being critical."

I didn't answer. I turned my face toward the sliding doors. I'd left one of them open and the curtain moved a little in a breeze and the music was out there, out in the bay. There was a horn and there were guitars and a violin. "I don't know," Vinh said.

"You don't know what?" I asked, and I truly didn't.

"I don't know what it is about that man."

I found I didn't care, for the moment. I rose and moved to the windows and listened to the music. It was a looping kind of melody, a mariachi waltz. I brushed the curtain aside and stepped out onto the balcony and far out in the dark bay was a triangle of colored lights, red and blue, and it was moving slowly and I looked harder and could see the boat, its decks flashing faintly, color wheels whirling there and I could imagine the couples waltzing, the sweat still on them from the fast songs and now they were holding each other close and gliding across the deck, their skin flushed with colored light.

"What is it?" Vinh's voice came to me faintly, as if it was he who was far across the bay. I could even hear the rasp of the maracas now. And then the maracas faded, and then the strings, and the horn, and I watched until the boat disappeared down the shore. When I slipped back into bed, Vinh was asleep.

The next morning I left Vinh snoring faintly in the bed. It was pretty early. I wanted him to have at least the pleasure of sleeping late on this vacation that I'd given him, so I put on my bathing suit and eased the room door shut behind me and I went down to the pool. The lounge chairs were all upended and the Mexican boys with their white trousers rolled almost to their knees were mopping up, and one of them was skimming the surface of the water with a thin screen at the end of a pole. I stood there not wanting to go back upstairs. The morning sun felt very nice—a soft kiss on my forehead that wouldn't stop—and finally one of the boys saw me and he bowed and put one of the chairs on its legs and motioned me over. I thanked him and stretched out there and I looked back up the facade of the hotel and tried to figure out which was our balcony. But I caught myself at this. Did I hope to see Vinh's face looking down at me? This hope made me angry at myself for some reason. So I closed my eyes and thought of the cruise boat on the bay last night and the anger just sharpened. This surprised me and I wished I could step outside of myself and look back. Maybe I could see something that would give me a clue about what I was feeling. But all I could see was the fall of dim light-shapes in my closed eyes and then a woman said, "Can I sit beside you?"

I opened my eyes and found Eileen Davies. "Of course," I said and I got up and helped her put a lounge chair beside mine. I sat back down and watched her take off her robe and she had a one-piece suit on, a little frumpy, though her figure was pretty good in the way that Americans like their women. That was my first impression, but as she folded her robe very carefully and put it inside the large canvas bag at her feet, I could see that her bottom was probably a little too large and the pocks that the TV ads call "unsightly cellulite" were beginning to appear on the backs of her thighs. All of this was, no doubt, a development in the last few years. When her man was in Vietnam, I was sure that her figure was very fine indeed.

She was beside me now and she smiled over at me and said, "We're the early ones."

"Yes," I said. "It's a habit I can't break."

"I like the mornings," she said. "You can feel sometimes that you're all alone in the world." After a moment Eileen seemed to hear how that sounded and her hand fluttered out toward me as if to grab back any inference I might have made. "Just for a little while," she said. "I wouldn't want to feel like that for more than maybe an hour or so."

"An hour's about right," I said.

"I love my husband." Eileen did not need to declare this to further explain the alone-in-the-world remark. I figured it must've come from the same place that made her give him that look I'd seen a couple of times.

For myself, I could have replied in a number of ways. I could have just stayed silent or I could have made some little nod or uh-huh or something. But instead I said, "I love my husband too."

My saying this didn't seem to strike Eileen as odd, though it certainly struck me that way. She just nodded and laid her head back and pulled her sunglasses down from her forehead. I lay back too, but if we were going to grow quiet and sleepy side by side here in the sun, I didn't want to leave off speaking on such a strange note. So I tried to make small talk. "Have you ever been down here before?"

"No. Have you?"

"No." This still wasn't enough and I tried to figure out how to say more about never being here.

But for some reason I'd lost control of all my social skills and the silence persisted and before I could think of some new track of small talk, Eileen said, "The Love Boat stopped here."

I should have known what she was talking about. As I said, I love American television. But at first I thought she was talking in a metaphor or something. "What's that?"

"The television show," she said. "'The Love Boat'. It always stopped in Puerto Vallarta."

I laughed. "Of course it did."

"Do you believe in romance, Gabrielle?"

I turned my head and looked at her. I hadn't thought about the subject, really, and yet I felt like I would say something. I actually wondered what would come out of my mouth, like I was sitting in a chair behind me and eavesdropping. This was getting a little strange. "Romance?" I said. "I'm not sure. Not in the easy ways, I don't. Not for anybody over the age of twenty."

"The easy ways." Eileen repeated this phrase thoughtfully and I turned it over in my mind, too. The Love Boat, for instance. And a lot of the other things I could easily get weepy over on television. Reach out and touch someone. I always choked up at the telephone company ads. Pick up the phone and two people could love each other no matter what might've happened between them. The easy ways. I knew it wasn't easy for Eileen and Frank.

"Never in the easy ways," she said and her voice was firm, like the thought was her own now.

But of course, it was easy to say it was never easy. I kept my mouth shut about that, though. And Eileen said, "Puerto Vallarta is a very romantic place, you know."

"Yes?"

"They made a movie here."

"'The Night of the Iguana,'" I said. "I know all about it."

"It wasn't easy for them."

"Liz and Dick?"

"Liz and Dick. It wasn't easy for them," Eileen said and she lifted her sunglasses and turned her head and looked me in the eyes.

"You're right," I said.

"The ruins of the movie set are still there. Near Mismaloya Beach." Eileen sat up straight. "Why don't we go down there."

"Just you and me?" I asked, not sure what I wanted to do about that.

Eileen lifted her eyebrows and pinched her mouth tightly shut. She didn't say anything right away. Finally she let her face relax and put her sunglasses back down. "We can try to take them."

"Is that what we want?"

She lay back down and thought this over and I was struck by how odd it was that we were treating the two men as if they were somehow the same. This was something that I really didn't see at all. It was why I'd asked Vinh in the dark last night about his impressions of Frank. I'm not the kind of woman who thinks that men are men, all alike in certain basic ways.

Eileen said, "Sure it's what we want, isn't it? They're our husbands. Wouldn't it be nice to go poke around that place with the men in our life?"

"Sure," I said, though I wasn't convinced. But we let it drop at that. Eileen said no more and we both just soaked up the Mexican sun for a while. A long while. I'd even fallen asleep, because I was suddenly startled by a great red and yellow bird passing before me. I blinked and it was gone and I was twisted on my side on the lounge chair; I'd moved into my natural sleeping position and I sat up and looked in the direction of the great bird and it was one of the parasailors, lifting higher and higher on his tether and veering out to sea. I looked at my watch and nearly two hours had passed.

As if she read my thoughts, Eileen said, "You were sleeping pretty hard."

My head felt oversized, the contents not really fitting inside my skull, threatening to squeeze out my ears. I turned to look at Eileen. The back of her chair was angled up and she was sitting with a straw hat shading her face and she was holding a copy of People magazine before her. She said, "You missed an interesting sight."

"What was that?"

"Our two husbands apparently found each other in the lobby. They walked by about half an hour ago and waved at me and they went on down to the beach."

I rubbed at my temples and tried to take this in. Vietnamese people are funny in a few ways. Sometimes they can be very indirect. (Maybe that's the Chinese influence in our culture, though we'd rather think that such an influence does not exist.) But at other times, Vietnamese can be very blunt. This is true. Americans have their own contradictions. All peoples do. Sometimes indirect and sometimes blunt is maybe a little less disturbing to everyone concerned than sometimes tolerant and sometimes intolerant, though I'm not trying to be critical of my new country.

Anyway, my Vietnamese bluntness suddenly made me stop rubbing my temples and lean near to Eileen and say, "Tell me. Do you understand why our husbands seem to be hitting it off so well together? What does Frank say about Vinh?"

Eileen kind of jiggled her head like she was trying to unclog her ears. And her voice got pinched and even a little whiney. "My husband never had anything against Vietnamese people. He hated the Vietcong, of course, but he knew that there was a difference between them and the others."

"Of course," I said firmly, like I knew this all along. And maybe I did. That wasn't really what I was getting at, I decided, though I couldn't quite say what was.

"And how about your husband," Eileen said and her voice was brittle. "What does he say about Frank?"

I leaned closer and smiled my warmest smile. "Like your husband. He knows how to see the individual."

There was no reason for this bit of empty rhetoric to soothe Eileen's hurt feelings and make things right between us again, but that's just what it did. She and I had done a pretty lousy job of understanding any of this, but at least we were smiling at each other again and she said, "Do you want to find them now? Maybe we can get them in a cab and take them away to the movie set."

"Sure," I said and we gathered up our things and walked along the pool and past the hot tub—the rest of the game show people had not made their appearance yet, much to my relief—and we went down some stone stairs and stepped onto the beach.

Immediately the vendors in white clothes and straw hats surrounded us. They were selling white clothes and straw hats, and somewhere jostled in the crowd I saw the girl with the iguana on her shoulder. Eileen and I no-graciased our way into the clear and we looked around. The men weren't in our immediate view and we both seemed to become distracted by the water at the same moment. Without a word to each other we trudged through the sucking sands and down to the water's edge.

Down here beside it, the bay seemed enormous. I wondered if the music I'd heard last night would have been more powerful here, too; I wondered what if Vinh and I had been in this spot when the boat passed. Would he have done more than ask what it was? Would he have taken me in his arms and waltzed me over the sand? But that's a vision of romance the easy way, I thought; I should remember the soaps, where everything is hard. There's another contradiction, on the television that I watch. Can we believe both these things? The Love Boat docks and everyone finds what they're looking for; and the next day's installment of "As the World Turns" always brings more disaster.

"I see them," Eileen said.

She was right. The two men were walking along the shore far down to our left. They were walking side by side, heading away from us, and my husband had his hands clasped behind his back, a thing he does when he paces around during business meetings. He was wearing his tan Bermuda shorts and his one purchase for our trip, a rough-weave red cotton shirt from Pakistan. Frank Davies was dressed all in black—I didn't realize until I saw him that they made Bermuda shorts in black—and he was moving his arms, gesturing. We couldn't hear a word, but we saw his hands rise up above his shoulders and flare open and fall.

"I know that story," Eileen said with a sigh. "An ammunition dump has just exploded in Qui Nhon."

"I hope no one was hurt."

"My husband was quite a hero in the aftermath, is the way I understand it." Eileen turned to me. "Listen, Gabrielle, I'm sorry if I seemed upset a little earlier."

"Upset?"

"When you asked about how our husbands were getting on."

I wish I'd been blunt right then and pressed for the two of us to figure out the men in our life a little better. But I can't imagine that we would have made any sense at that point. We certainly wouldn't have been able to anticipate what happened later on. But for whatever reason, I didn't push it. I just said, "That's okay, Eileen. No problem." And we made off down the beach in pursuit of our husbands.

We caught up with them when they turned around and continued their walking discussion back in our direction. Eileen called out Frank's name and both men looked up at us with a start. At just that moment some young Mexican men shouted at us and motioned us a little farther along the beach. We all followed the Mexicans' gaze high into the air and saw a parasail swinging off the bay and over the beach, and one of the young men blew a whistle and the man hanging beneath the sail reached up and grabbed the rope above and to the right of his head and he pulled. The sail began to veer to the left, angling toward the beach before us and it was coming down fast. I heard Frank's voice say, "You were airborne, that right?" Vinh grunted in affirmation but I did not look at the two men. I kept my eyes on the parachute, the great red and yellow scoop, tight with air, carrying a man down from the sky. I could do that, I thought.

The whistle blew again and the man let go of the rope and he was coming down fast, and the young men on the ground rushed forward, reached upward, and the parasailor landed with a little run and his chute crumpled behind him.

"Hey guys," Eileen was saying. "Guys."

I thought for a moment that she was talking to the Mexicans, that she wanted to go up into the air. But I looked and she had pulled the attention of our husbands to her and she said, "Gabrielle and I want to do something. All of us together."

"That's good," Frank said.

Vinh just looked at me with a faint rebuke in his eyes. He hated to be taken off guard like this. I should have talked to him privately first. I understand his feelings, I suppose. An airborne ranger is always prepared. A successful businessman, too. But I just blew his little grimace a kiss and he forced a chuckle to show his good nature. I didn't much care, to tell the truth. I couldn't keep my eyes from slipping back to the Mexicans and their parachute. I knew I would feel disappointed to see anyone get onto that chute right now. It was meant for me. I was just a few moments away from soaring high over the bay, over the whole city, far above all of this.

"Don't you agree, Gabrielle?" Eileen's voice dragged me back to her. She was looking at me meaningfully, like it was time for me to nail this thing down.

"Of course," I declared, not knowing exactly what she had said but sure from the way she was looking at me that this was the right response. She waited, wanting more, and I said to the men, "Let's go. I really want to."

Vinh said, "Is this the place you were telling me about? The iguana thing?"

"Sure," I said. "It'll be fun."

Now I could see Vinh turn up the heat in his eyes. Who were Liz and Dick to him, after all? Only a product of what he had big trouble tolerating in America. I knew I was supposed to persuade him now. He was persuadable about these little interests of mine, but he always made me work for his approval. Well, I didn't feel like it at the moment. That was for certain. All I knew was that the great red and yellow parachute was lying slack on the beach and I wanted to excite it, wanted it to fill up full of this warm morning air and carry me into the sky.

So without a word I stepped past Frank and Eileen and Vinh, and I asked the young Mexican man holding the harness how much and he told me and I paid it and I turned around and the man put me in the harness, and all of this was so unexpected and it was done so quickly that nobody could react. Frank and Eileen and Vinh just stood there in a row and gawked at me and finally, just before I took off, Vinh choked out a "Gabrielle what are you doing?" and Eileen suddenly smiled and cried something that wasn't quite a word, like hurrah or something. And the Mexican was telling me about the whistle and about the rope up there over my right ear and the boat was moving and the tether went taut and there were hands on me briefly, helping me rise, and then there were no hands and I was soaring into the air.

I did not look back. The boat headed straight out into the bay for a time and I looked down at the water and it was calm, it looked as stiff as vinyl, like I'd bounce off it if I fell. But it was very fine being up here. I was very aware of being alone. Off to my right about a hundred meters was a little pack of pelicans heading back toward the beach. They were returning but I was still on the way out. The wind whistled faintly in my ears and it struck me that this was not the ravishing physical experience I expected it to be. My feet dangled down, but there was no heaviness in them, like the ride at the carnivals where you sit in a chair and they swing you around. My feet just dangled like I was a child in a tall chair. I was not frightened. The harness held me tight and I gripped the ropes and I looked down at the sea, the green wake of the boat ripping apart the great brown stain from the mountains.

And the boat turned now and headed along the coast and my parachute brought me around and I was as high as the highest hotel, but I pondered the long stretch of Puerto Vallarta along the beach as calmly as if it was a mural on a wall. I was flying but I was very quiet inside. This was more like a certain kind of dream, where you can fly and everything is peaceful. Or it was like I'd left my body, the way some people on the Donahue show had done when everyone thought they were dead. I was separated from my body.

And now I looked back over my shoulder and found the beach and the three tiny figures there, still standing in a row, still gawking, probably. So I turned around and let go of the rope and let my hands dangle like my feet and I felt the air flowing against my face and I drifted there, thinking yes, I've just died and it's all very nice and I won't have to worry about anything on the planet earth anymore.

And this feeling lasted for however long it was that I was in the air. It was probably no more than ten minutes, but it seemed much longer, which struck me as odd later, because I enjoyed the experience, I truly did, and usually that makes time go fast. But I floated along and the boat turned and headed back the opposite way and I swung around, too, in a long curve, very graceful, like a gesture I might make with my hand if I was a big movie star. And I was nearer to the shore on the return trip. I was only a little ways out over the sea and I could look to my right and see the hotel pools passing, the bodies all laid out in the sun.

Then I found myself moving nearer to the shore and nearer still, and I was over the beach. I looked ahead and saw the boat curving out to sea, but it must have slowed because I was starting to come down. That's when I heard the whistle. I looked ahead and I could see the beach where I'd taken off. It was not far away. The whistle blew again, insistent, and I felt a little knot cinch in my stomach. I had something to do now. The rope over my right shoulder. I reached up and grabbed it just as I was supposed to. I pulled it.

It didn't move. It was a heavy rope. Hard to pull. The knot inside me cinched tighter and I pulled as hard as I could. The rope gave a bit, but not nearly as much as it was supposed to. Pull it down by your ear, I remembered the man say. I pulled harder and it budged a bit further and my muscles clamped up in my fist and down my arm and under my arm and down my side all the way to my hip.

I was coming down, down, and I was curving a little, but I could see already I was in trouble. The curve wasn't sharp enough to bring me into the path to the waiting men and the three faces of Frank and Eileen and Vinh, which I could see very clearly for one moment. Their eyes were wide and their jaws were dropping and my arm and side were trembling now and shot full of flames and I didn't know if I could even hold the rope down at all for much longer. The Mexicans were running up the beach and I saw a line of coconut trees at the back of a hotel and I was heading straight for them, I was at about the fourth floor level and falling fast, like an elevator out of control, the third floor and the trees were dipping like they were afraid of me but they couldn't run, and I fell past the second floor.

I lifted my other arm and grabbed the rope with both hands and I pulled as hard as I could and I closed my eyes and the rope gave some more and I felt myself veer away and a man's voice rushed from beneath me and it said, "Caramba!" and then my feet hit the sand hard and I flexed at the knees and came up standing but I was instantly moving forward again, dragged along the sand and then there were hands on me, many hands, and I was upright again.

But I was laughing. My eyes were open and I was laughing, though I wished I was back in the sky, especially since everyone was rushing over to me like I'd just fainted or something. Eileen cried, "Are you all right?" as she approached and I looked and I saw Vinh running beside her. His face was sweet. His lower lip was pushed up like he was pouting, like he was a little boy and pouting at some very bad news. Then Frank came from around the other side of Eileen and he was running fast and was the first one to get to me.

"You're one gutsy lady," he said. "Airborne all the way." And he brushed the Mexican boy aside who was taking off my harness and Frank's big hands went flick, flick, and I was free. He took me by the arm and turned me toward Vinh who finally arrived, puffing.

"I'm fine," I said firmly to them all. "Don't make a fuss."

Vinh pulled up before me and he said, low, "Are you sure you're okay?"

"Yes," I said in a voice as low as his but as sharp as I could make it.

He looked into my eyes and nodded and then he shook his head, "I suppose the only thing to do after an adventure on a parachute is to go to a movie set."

Eileen's face snapped toward Vinh and she said, "Great idea."

I wasn't sure what I thought of the way this all came about. Did he think I went up on a parachute to force his hand on this? Like I was a child threatening to do myself harm if I didn't get my way? It wasn't true, if that's what he thought. At that moment I would've traded the whole trip to Mismaloya for one more flight over the sea. But, of course, that wasn't possible.

Frank said, "Outstanding," and I figured I would at least get a chance to watch these two men together a little more closely.

So Eileen and I went back to our rooms and changed from our bathing suits, both of us reappearing in the hallway almost simultaneously and in record time, for we did not want the men to have a chance to change their minds. We met them in the lobby and we all stepped out the front doors of the hotel together to a chorus of "Hey taxi" from half a dozen men in sandals and jeans. Vinh stepped a little in front of Frank and motioned for the first man in line and I drew near to the two men because they interested me very much.

"Dodgers," Frank snorted and I'm sure Vinh did not know what he was talking about, but when the taxi rolled up in front of us and the driver sprung out he was wearing a Los Angeles Dodgers baseball cap. I knew the cap from television. Many of the actors on television series wear baseball caps and this one was very popular, though I liked the bright red color and the tangle of letters on the cap of the St. Louis Cardinals the best.

The driver saw me looking at his cap, I think, and he did a surprising thing. He tipped it to me, and he opened the back door. He was a man about the same age as Vinh and me, perhaps forty—I could see it around his eyes and in the smudge of gray in his hair—but there was a bounce to him that was very young.

Vinh said, "Why don't you sit in the front, Frank."

"Hey there, major, you outrank this soldier by quite a lot. You should take the favored place."

"I always rode in the back seat as a major," Vinh said, and there was just a little sharpness in it. But then he added, "Besides, you've got the longer legs by quite a lot."

Frank laughed and so did Vinh. Then Frank turned to us and said, "You watch out for that man back there."

I wanted to hear more of this. Was Frank kidding my husband over some stories they had shared about women? I looked at Vinh and his face was blank and then the taxi driver said, "You are Americans?" and the conversation moved on.

Vinh motioned first Eileen and then me into the back seat and he climbed in last. Frank was talking to the cab driver as he circled the car and I felt Vinh pressed against me in the crowded back seat. I never thought of my husband as being the kind of man you had to watch out for as a couple of women in the back seat of a car. I was sure it was just a typical male joke, a natural frame of reference for Army men. Vinh had never given me any reason to doubt him. I had always watched those parts of the soap operas about adultery with some detachment. He had always been with me whenever he wasn't working. He wasn't the kind of man to go out on his own. He was a very conservative man. His work was his mistress, I knew, and that was hard enough for me, I guess. But it was odd how my mind kept working at this silly joke Frank made. All the silence between Vinh and me, all the formality, all the waiting for him to take my hand: would it be better for him if I was someone else? If he was with someone else? Elizabeth Taylor had a husband and he was a singer. Richard Burton had a wife, too, though she was less famous. I listened again to the voices bumping around in the taxi.

"Mismaloya Beach?" the driver said, turning his head alarmingly far around, almost a hundred and eighty degrees. He looked at Eileen, who I suppose had just told him where we were going. Then he looked at me and I was afraid he would force his head still further, a hundred and ninety, two hundred degrees, two hundred and ten until he could see Vinh sitting to my right. But I guess I should have been more worried about the car than about the man's neck snapping. He was rolling down the long drive from the hotel and not watching at all. He said, "You know that you are going to a very special place?"

"We know," Vinh said firmly.

"You know about Liz and Dick?" the cabbie said.

"*We know*," Vinh said and I could hear in his voice how little my husband wanted to sit through this story again.

"It all put this town on the map, you know. I was just a teenage delinquent hanging around the beaches all day and trying not to work hard like I do now. We loved it when all the world started looking at our Vallarta." By now, the man's eyes were back on his driving and he turned onto the main road we'd taken in from the airport.

In making the turn, he stopped speaking for a moment and Frank said, "Hell, it must have been nice to be a teenager just goofing around the beaches. Living in a place like this. When I was a teenager, all I cared about was turning myself into a goddamn soldier some day. That's *another* kind of teenage dumb."

I was a little startled at how far Frank had to reach to pull the conversation around to his military experience. I wondered if he was doing this for Vinh's benefit, having picked up, too, on how my husband hated all the talk about Burton and Taylor. Vinh said, "When I was a teenager the beaches and the war were all in the same picture."

He said this like he'd topped Frank. He could get wound up about the war, I knew. I'd heard him with our Vietnamese friends. But was this the kind of thing he and Frank had been doing together? Is this what I'd missed? Just the two of them jerking the conversation around to top each other? Or was this a little instinctive game that would keep our cab driver quiet and us two women out of the conversation?

I didn't know. But our driver wasn't picking up on any hints. "The airline, they tried to start it. This was some sleepy godforsaken place when I was a little guy, you know. Then Mexicana Airlines started landing a DC-3 on a dirt strip where the center of town is today."

Frank turned himself half around in his seat. "You ever fly in a DC-3, Vinh?"

"Sure. They were using some DC-3's as troop transports when I was a recruit."

There was only the slightest of pauses after this, like Frank was just taking a little breath before he spoke an answer, but Eileen had wonderful reflexes—probably the key to her success on the buzzer of her game show—and before Frank could open his mouth she said to the driver, "We know the basic Burton and Taylor story but tell us something about it we might not know."

Frank rolled his shoulders and turned to the front and I felt Vinh shift a little bit away from me, and the driver said, "Have you seen the house they stayed in?"

"No," Eileen said. "Can we?"

"Sure," the driver said, and to their credit, the men did not protest. "It's in Gringo Gulch. That's where all the rich people came when they found out about us. Leonard Bernstein, you know that man with the orchestra?"

"Yes," Eileen said. "You know about him?"

"Sí, Señora. I like good music. I lived in your country three years, in Los Angeles. That's how I speak English like you. I listened to the radio all the time and I liked the good music." The driver raised his hand like a conductor and sang, "Da da da dum," the opening to Beethoven's Fifth Symphony, the Daily Double Audio Clue only last week on "Jeopardy." "But don't worry," the driver added quickly. "I'm just a regular Joe. I liked the bad music too in Los Angeles."

"Who else lives in Gringo Gulch?" Eileen asked, afraid, I suspect, that if our driver strayed too far, the men would reclaim the conversation. Not that I would have minded that, really. I wanted to hear them connecting to each other, though it was even very interesting to me just observing this shared silence between them. They were both looking out windows and I'm sure each man was conscious of the other.

The driver said, "There was some Lord and Lady from England. The Queen even came in her yacht and visited them. And also living in Puerto Vallarta is a very important American I bet you don't know." The cabbie paused for a moment, like we were supposed to guess.

"I bet it ain't Westmoreland," Frank said.

"Any clue?" Eileen said.

The cabbie made an exaggerated nod. "I will tell you his name and it will still be hard for you. Milton Gunzburg."

Frank hooted at this. "The famous Milton Gunzburg is living in Puerto Vallarta? Hell, you remember him, don't you, Vinh? He's the guy who landed his chopper in the middle of Tu Do Street, got him about four bargirls, and took off again for Vung Tau and some Air Cav R&R."

Vinh grunted, Frank laughed, and the driver said, "That must be another Milton Gunzburg."

Eileen leaned forward. "Don't you pay any attention to him, Senor," and she dug her knuckle into Frank's shoulder. He flicked at her hand but without any anger, just a casual little flick like a mosquito had buzzed him.

I started feeling disloyal to Eileen. I'd been happy just to sit back and watch all this, but she needed some help. So I asked the driver, "Who is this Milton Gunzburg of Puerto Vallarta?"

The driver turned his face way around to look at Eileen and me. "The inventor of 3-D movies."

I pointed to the street in front of the driver, just to remind him that this was all in 3-D, too. He took my hint and looked to the front just in time to curve around a slow moving pick-up truck full of collapsed and bundled cardboard boxes. He didn't even flinch. "This was a very important invention," he said. "My favorite movie is 'The House of Wax'. You know that movie?"

"Yes," I said, "but I've never seen it in 3-D."

"When I lived in L.A., I saw it there in a theater. Also 'Spacehunter: Adventures in the Forbidden Zone.' These are my favorites in 3-D. I hope Peter Strauss someday will move to Puerto Vallarta. He starred in 'Spacehunter'. I would like to drive him wherever he wants to go. He is my favorite actor. Did you see him in 'Rich Man, Poor Man'? It was a wonderful thing from American television. Even without 3-D. But Peter Strauss is much better in 3-D."

Vinh's voice was suddenly in my ear, pitched low. "Do we have to go by the house? Isn't the movie set enough?"

I glanced at him and he was looking at me with his head a little bit dipped, as if he had glasses on and was peeking over them. This was the position he assumed when he was asking something that he knew he shouldn't.

"It's okay," Eileen said, putting her hand on my arm. "Let's skip it."

I glowered at Vinh and he shrugged. "No, no," he said. "I'm sorry. It's just that we should have plenty of sunlight for the trip to the movie set."

"It's barely noon," I said, not letting him wriggle away.

"Noon," Frank said. "There's a place to eat at this beach, isn't there?"

"Good food at the beach," the driver said. "They sell whole fish roasted on a stick."

"Oh man," Frank said like he'd just heard about a plane crash.

Eileen leaned forward and said to the driver, "You can skip the Burton-Taylor house."

"No, don't do that, driver," Vinh said.

"I'm Esteban," the driver said.

"You guys hate your C-rations as much as we hated ours?" This was Frank broadcasting from another part of the world.

"You can call me Esteban."

"I don't mean to drag you around," Eileen said, leaning a little bit across me to address Vinh.

"It was rude of me to try to overrule your wishes." Vinh spoke with a combination of gentleness and firmness that I have always admired in him.

"It's very close now," Esteban said.

I wanted this for myself too. I made my voice firm for the driver. "Fine. Drive us past."

"Of course we hated our C-rations," Vinh said.

"It figures," Frank said.

"But not as much as we'd hate a fish on a stick," Vinh said and I wished I had the privilege of digging my knuckle into his arm even if it was to provoke only a casual flick in response.

Frank laughed. "Roger that."

I was sorry I was sitting in the center in the back seat. I wanted to just put my head out the window and watch the street go by like there was nobody else around. But as it was, I looked across Eileen and watched the shaggy fields and the men talked some more about Army food and we passed a low, white-washed arena with big cut-out signs on top, the silhouettes of bulls. A place for bullfights, I supposed. And then there were palm and coconut trees and then a run of shops and I just kept my mind out the window as Esteban had finally let himself be shut up by the husbands.

Then we took a curve and there was a statue of a seahorse and we were running along the beach and we passed an artist on the street with his work propped up on display, and the paintings were of tigers and Jesus Christ and Elvis Presley on black velvet and I hoped Vinh didn't see this, but it all made me smile. Am I somehow perverse this way? Not that I would buy a black velvet Elvis Presley, much less hang it on a wall in my home. But there is something that makes me smile about it. I have seen Elvis Presley many times as they sell his face and his voice on late-night television, The King, The One and Only, The Idol of Millions, The Loved and the Mourned, just a phone call and a credit card number away. Why does this make me feel comfortable? Even safe?

The car was on a cobbled street now and we were jiggling and rattling about and the men's voices were cracking and they stopped speaking. And soon we turned into a narrow lane and Esteban said, "Up ahead is where the lovers lived in 1963."

We bounced along and there was a stone wall on one side and an undetached run of houses on the right and Esteban said, "It is where you see the bridge over the street."

A stone pedestrian bridge rose from a roof covered in rose bushes and arched over the cobblestones and landed on the second floor of the house across the way. Esteban stopped the car. "Would you like to get out and take pictures?"

I felt Eileen turn my way, though it was probably Vinh that she looked at. "No," she said. "This is fine."

"There were really two houses," Esteban said. "The one on the left was Elizabeth Taylor's and the one on the right was Richard Burton's, and the whole world watched that bridge for months to see them go back and forth."

I'm sure that Eileen and I were quite a sight to further irritate our husbands—we both leaned forward and strained to look at the two houses. The bridge was tan and had a waist-high rail with a row of little pot-bellied balusters. I learned that word, balusters, somewhere—I don't remember where—and if it ever appears on a quiz show, I will probably be the only one to get it right. Why do I go off on this little detail now? Because my mind snagged on it even then, even though I obviously was very interested in the houses before me. And why was I distracted by that detail? Sometimes I can read myself pretty well. It was because the bridge between the two houses made me feel bad. It seemed so empty. It arched there against the blue sky and it cried out for some lover to come across and take his woman in his arms. But it was empty. The rose bushes, which were full of blooms, nodded faintly in a breeze and the bridge stayed empty.

"You like to buy this house?" Esteban said. "It is for sale. Richard Burton bought it for Liz Taylor as a birthday present many years ago and do you know how much he paid?"

"What year?" This was Vinh, whose sense of business was suddenly stimulated.

"I don't know. Maybe 1964. Sometime about then."

"Seventy-five thousand," Vinh said without a pause and all I could see was that empty bridge. The man who crept over it at night so that the world would not notice, he was dead.

"Very close, Señor. Sixty thousand dollars American."

Vinh leaned forward next to me and I sat back. He said, "And what are they asking for the house now?"

"One million."

"Ha!" Vinh declared, and I'm not sure what business conclusion this represented. But when Esteban said that the house had been for sale for nearly five years, and no one had bought it yet, Vinh nodded like he wasn't surprised.

It was now that a little voice chirped into the car. We all turned our heads and a young girl was at the back window, right next to Vinh, and she had a basket slung over her shoulder. She lifted a yellow flower that was really very beautiful, with large blossoms and a white center. "You buy?" she said. "Copa de oro."

Esteban turned around in his seat. "'Copa de oro', you know what that is?"

"A cup of gold," Eileen said.

"Right, Señora. From the movie."

"Yes," Eileen said, "Richard Burton buys it for Sue Lyon at the beginning of 'The Night of the Iguana.'"

I was impressed. This was a detail that I myself had forgotten. I wanted to reach across Vinh and take the flower. I almost did. I had told my arm to rise and move through my husband's space and pluck this beautiful flower from the little girl's hand. I remembered the scene now. Burton, the defrocked and alcoholic priest who could not restrain his desire for the women who reminded him he was alive, buys this flower, the cup of gold, for the sexy young girl on the bus tour that breaks down here in Puerto Vallarta. Even this ravaged and failed man knew that a woman would love a flower such as this, the copa de oro. I was prepared now to lift my arm, to take action, even as Esteban said, "Would you like to buy a flower?"

But Vinh and Frank in chorus said, "No," and Frank said, "We've got this movie set to get to," and there was nothing more to be done.

Esteban stuck his head out the window and said something to the girl—there was clearly some connection between them, at least a working arrangement for when he brought tourists to this spot. I'm sure Vinh noticed it and I figured he felt smug about it, so as the taxi began to move, I leaned near him and said, "I loved that flower."

I don't say something like this very often, so it must have had a sharp effect, because Vinh turned his face to me and he looked very sad for a moment. It was clearly sadness, to my eye. His mouth sagged and his eyes softened, and I wondered what he would do. But we were going faster now and I turned away to look at the bridge growing larger and then we passed beneath it, the shadow rushing over the car, and Vinh did not say, Wait, let's go back and get a flower. He did not even say, Oh I'm sorry, Gabrielle; perhaps another time. He said nothing at all, though he may have continued to wear his sad face. I don't know. I didn't look at him.

The taxi was climbing in the hills now, the roads twisting and turning. At first beneath us there were the stacked shacks of the poor people, with the baked red mission tile roofs, and then we were among the villas, the immaculate high walls and the stippled stucco, and then we were rising even above the rich and I watched the ocean and it was very beautiful, very romantic, and I liked being near Vinh, even if he was hardened against all of this.

The roads were very bad, even here, and we had to slow almost to a stop for the big potholes, again and again, but all along the ride there were new hotels going up. We could not go more than half a mile without seeing another hotel with the men barebacked and languorous on the open floors, just the frames of the rooms constructed and the ocean visible through them, and the men were carrying a bucket or smoothing a wall with a trowel or just standing around, happy to be in the shade of a room with its walls open to the sea.

Finally I saw a landmark that the guide books had told me about, three huge rocks hunched into the water not far offshore and one of them had a great arch through it, like a pair of hip boots standing out there with no man in them. Mismaloya was nearby. Then we passed a large hotel, a finished hotel, and we descended a little hill and the road that cut down to the beach ran along a concrete wall that contained the site of still another hotel under construction and the road was rutted and scruffy and instinctively I said to Vinh, "They're still building." It was an apology for the weeds and the ruts and the dog peeing against the wall and then we stopped at the back edge of the beach.

"Here you are," Esteban said and he sprung from the cab and circled the car, opening our doors and even before we could step out, the vendors were swarming around and Esteban was talking to them, waving them away, but not too far. The vendors in white clothes were draped in rugs and silver jewelry and a man was motioning us to a stack of inner tubes for rent. A dog drifted by with skin sores and I concentrated on the beach, the waves coming up, but to our left was another little river running down from the mountains, and the surf at this beach, too, was smeared with brown.

I looked around and thought that this had been a big mistake, that I would lose face, as the Chinese say, with Vinh. Of course he was right. This place was not ready for the kind of pleasures that even I had come to expect. Not that if it had all been perfectly beautiful—immaculate—that Vinh would have thought any better of it. Then it would have been just like television, slick and irritating to him in a different way. And as I thought these things, a ruckus of men's voices started behind me. I turned and Vinh was holding his hand out as if to brush Frank away. In Vinh's other hand was his wallet and he said, "I'll handle this one."

Frank said, "I'm not a Spec-Five anymore, Major. I make good money."

"I'm sure you do," Vinh said. "But it was I who suggested coming down here."

"We can split it."

Meanwhile Esteban was smiling at them both and smiling at me and smiling at Eileen and in between he was shooting little glances at the vendors, holding them off until he could finally get his own money and leave.

"I'll tell you what," Vinh said. "I'll pay this time and you pay for the cab going back."

Frank flipped Vinh a sort of funny half-salute. "Roger that. You pay the man and I'll secure the beach." At this he turned, and while Vinh was making change, Frank took Eileen by the arm and they moved past me, Eileen hopping a few steps to take her shoes off as she walked.

Vinh joined me and he held my elbow to guide me through the uneven footing of the sands and Esteban called after us, "It's to your left. You must wade across the mouth of the river and then follow the sea wall to the old dock."

Vinh turned his face to me. "Did you get that?"

"I'll find it," I said.

We all four of us stopped at the water's edge for a moment and the vendors were orbiting us. Frank and Vinh sort of pulled together near the water and kept their faces out to sea and they flipped their elbows when the silver plate Indian masks and the VIVA MEXICO throw rugs and the iguana head tee shirts came too close. I myself was tempted by the tee shirts. Why not? They had a large green iguana head, and they made me smile. But then I wondered when Liz and Dick disappeared from the tee shirts. How many years had it been that the lovers had stopped being an inspiration to the world. I mean "inspiration" in the same way that the late-night television ads would say that Elvis Presley, forever captured on three cassettes or two CDs, is an inspiration. But it was a little sad to me, how things that seem so important can come to an end. Even before Richard Burton was dead, there was no love between these two lovers who had crept over the bridge to each other in Gringo Gulch.

I watched Frank lean near my husband and say, "I wish everybody would just back off." This was spoken in a lowered voice, as if he was trying not to let someone hear who might be offended. This was a surprise, coming from Frank, and it made me wonder who he was talking about. The vendors? They hardly spoke English and their feelings wouldn't be hurt by this anyway. He wasn't talking about Eileen and me because it would be "they," not "everybody."

I looked at Vinh to see if he was puzzled, but he didn't seem to be. He nodded. It must have been a continuation of some earlier conversation. I suddenly wanted very badly to know what it was all about. I'd been distracted for this whole trip, I realized. These two men had what Sam Donaldson on the news would call their own agenda. I stepped nearer, hoping for more words. Señora, silver. Silver, Señora, real silver. I flapped my elbows at this sound and Vinh said something I couldn't catch, casting the words out to sea, and Frank nodded and then Vinh said, "If only one could find a clear betrayer."

"The marchers," Frank said.

"Too many of them. It's like hating a whole race. And if we were winning, no one would have listened to them."

I'd come too near. Frank glanced over his shoulder and he smiled and nudged Vinh and said, "It's time to pull out, Major."

Vinh turned, too, and he said, very deliberately, being a good husband, "This is nice here, Gabrielle. The sun feels good. I'm ready for a walk and some cinema history."

"What's our heading?" Frank said.

Eileen was beside me now and she motioned off to our left, across the narrow river mouth and past a long line of food stands near the shore and down to the end of the beach and then, beyond, along a low seawall running beneath a little hill thick with trees. And in the distance, just before the shore turned, I could see a tall pole in the center of a broken concrete dock and just behind it were two levels of terrace, broad stone walls.

"I see it," Frank said. "Shall the men walk point?"

"Of course," I said, and I heard myself sounding a little bit sharp, though I had not meant it that way. I just wanted them in front of me. I wanted to watch them.

So the two men went ahead and we all took our shoes off and waded across the river, the rocks smooth underfoot and the water rich and thick with its mountain stew and I tried to stay close to them. We waded around a little gaggle of boys casting nets in the rushing water and Vinh went on about who to blame. "I tried to make it Mr. Thiệu. He was such a grasping fool. But we didn't lose the war because our gold was in some Swiss bank." Frank stumbled a bit and Vinh's hand went out fast to catch his elbow.

"I'm okay," Frank said, snatching his arm away, and then without a pause, "I still think it's the goddamn marchers. They hated our guts."

We came up out of the water and our calves were pasted with leaves. And there was a wonderful smell that I'd smelled when we first got out of the taxi but which only now did I really notice—wood fires, food cooking on wood fires. There were maybe a dozen food stands, permanent looking ones with frames of timber and tin roofs. A boy came down from one of them with a handful of long pointed sticks each skewering a whole fish.

Frank was walking on the inside and he recoiled from the boy. "No gracias, kid," and he was very emphatic, obviously bothered by these fish. And they were a pretty grim sight, if you weren't used to such things. There were four fish bobbing there in a row and they all looked rather startled to be dead and cooked and stuck and ready to be eaten. And the roasting over the fire made them look crusty, a little like the lepers on the streets of Saigon.

We moved on and Eileen said, "Aren't you hungry, honey? For something else maybe?"

"Not anymore," Frank said.

Vinh looked at him with a smile that I've seen him use on a particularly stupid customer. "You don't like to see dead fish?"

"Just a slab of their meat on a plate is the only way."

"You never fished as a boy?"

"I was a landlocked kid. Too busy building tree houses and stock piling dirt-clod hand grenades."

"A boy who does not fish or hunt misses the real life and death," Vinh said and I could hear what I took to be the little male thing going on again between them.

"Who said anything about hunting?" Frank said. "I could hunt."

"The animals you killed had eyes to stare at you too, didn't they?"

"I never killed anything slippery. And I always did it with a gun. What's all this worm on a hook shit? What's fishing to a born grunt?"

"Grunt?"

"Grunt. An infantryman. You guys didn't call them that?"

"I heard the word. But I thought you were a mechanic."

It surprised me that Vinh was starting to be hard on Frank. The things that had passed between them that had made them these little vacation-spot buddies so far—was that over now? Had I missed it all? Then it occurred to me that maybe I was myself the reason for Vinh pulling back from Frank. He had not wanted to say anything to me about Frank last night when I asked him. There was something about the man—that was all Vinh would say. Maybe it was just me. He didn't want to show *me* what it was that he and Frank had together.

But Frank didn't seem to pick up on Vinh's mood. He replied quite calmly, not at all defensive, just explanatory, "Anybody who carried a rifle and shot it in anger was a grunt to us. And I did that plenty."

Vinh wouldn't let it drop. "Why were you so anxious to fight, Frank?"

Eileen was probably listening to all of this, too. And it surely bothered her for what were probably some pretty complex reasons. As it was, I had totally forgotten her, I'd become so wrapped up in the men. But now she seemed not to want to hear any more. She said to me, loud, riding over the men's conversation, "It's exciting to be going to this movie set, isn't it? When was the last time you saw the 'Night of the Iguana'?"

As soon as I heard her voice, my face snapped over to her and I grew flushed with shame. I was very sorry that I'd been ignoring her—I'd contrived this trip with her; it was supposed to be mostly for the two of us; we were the ones to enjoy it.

I told her when I'd last seen the film and Eileen and I lagged a little behind as Vinh and Frank talked on, only a background mumble to me as my mouth and part of my brain did their duty to Eileen. But I was still conscious of the men, the red shirt and the black. And I watched the backs of their legs. They both had really fine, solid calves that clenched and fell, clenched and fell as they walked in the sand.

And we waded another little stream and then climbed some boulders by a beach bar and we went single file down a rocky path, Eileen's voice going on about other Taylor and Burton movies that I loved—"Cleopatra" and "The Comedians" and "The Sandpiper" and even "Who's Afraid of Virginia Woolf?," which I think was really the beginning of the end for Liz and Dick, even though they stayed married for eight years after that. But I was hardly hearing any of this; I was responding over my shoulder and watching the men, Frank out front walking the stones of the path as if they could be booby-trapped and Vinh following carefully, very quiet, placing his feet, it seemed to me, only where Frank had put his.

And then the path ended and we went even more carefully along the seawall, pretty narrow really, with a shore of boulders just below us on our right and the sharp incline of the weedy bank going up into the trees to our left. Even Eileen stopped talking as we teetered along. The early afternoon sun was very hot and the sky and water were so bright they hurt my eyes. So when I wanted to glance away from Vinh's heels, which I was carefully following, I would look up the slope into the thick trees. It all felt familiar, up the hill. I don't know why, but it reminded me of Vietnam, even though I was really a city girl. My parents would take me for vacations to Nha Trang and even a few times to Qui Nhon, where we had some relatives and where Frank served, though I hadn't said anything about this to him. But both Nha Trang and Qui Nhon are on the South China Sea, and there must have been some place like this, with the sea so bright and the trees up a slope so thick. Some really special little moment that I had as a girl that got buried too deep to remember specifically, but which cleared my eyes and opened me up now to the shine of the water on Banderas Bay off the Pacific Ocean in Puerto Vallarta and to the thick looming of the trees up here near the set to "The Night of the Iguana."

Then we passed a cut in the trees, a groove down the hill, a place where the water runs off and I could see a brick building up there, crumbling in the woods. But we passed it by and Frank led us farther until we arrived beneath the pole at the dock, rising up maybe forty feet, and it puzzled me what it once was supposed to do. Maybe it was some sort of crane or something to unload supplies. But it kind of gave me the shivers, standing up there so stiff and alone. The dock itself jutted out over the sea here, but its surface was gone; it was just the frame gaping out over the water and I turned around and there were two levels of balconies built into the hillside, field-stone walls all jagged and irregular.

They had seemed so imposing from the beach, but up close it was clear that they were just facades, illusions, for as walls they contained nothing but the hillside, and as balconies, they didn't connect to anything at all. Frank had climbed the broad stone steps beside them and he had run into a dead end. I could even see it from where I was standing. The steps went nowhere, just ending in the weeds and the trunks of the slope trees. "Just a real fine collection of small animal turds up here," Frank declared. Then he glanced down to Eileen at the foot of the stairs and said, "Sorry, Honey, at least I didn't say 'shit.'"

Before I had a chance to react to what would have been a slightly surprising prudishness in Eileen, she said, "That's right, Sweetie. At least you didn't say 'shit.'" And all of a sudden my surprise shifted to this almost tender private joke between them. I was glad for that, but it did take me by surprise.

Frank came down the steps and I looked to Vinh. He was sitting on a pile of stones in the shade and he was watching the sea. I thought to go sit beside him, but Frank passed Eileen by—I was surprised again, expecting the little thing that had happened between them to surely end in an embrace of some sort, or at least a touch, a glancing kiss, something. But Frank went past her with his attention already on my husband, and before I could act, it was Frank sitting next to him. This was still all right by me. I wanted to just get close and stay quiet and hope that they would eventually get back in their private mood with each other.

There were more stones piled nearby and I sat down and Eileen came and sat next to me and I was afraid she'd start talking, but she didn't. We all looked out to sea, looked at the big rocks hulking out there and the jagged line of mountains far across at the other side of the bay. Finally Frank said, "This isn't so bad. I figured there'd be people all over us out here selling Liz and Dick stuff."

"Don't you believe in free enterprise?" Vinh said, and I listened for the sound of combat in his voice again. But it wasn't there, exactly. I knew he didn't like all the swarm of vendors either, in spite of his being a businessman. He had too strong a sense of decorum.

Frank kept his face out to sea and he shrugged. "Sure I do. But sometimes it just gets so goddamn silly."

Vinh laughed, and it was a deep, appreciative laugh. I couldn't believe my good luck. All these two men had to do was sit down in the shade for a couple of moments and the first things out of their mouth let me find the thing I was looking for. "You've got it there, Frank," Vinh said. And I understood that however foolish Frank could appear hanging on so hard to the Vietnam veteran part of himself, however embarrassing it might sometimes be for Eileen, he certainly hadn't given in to the light and lively and less filling and soft as a cloud and reach out and touch someone culture that America had to offer. All the things that I had a sweet tooth for, my husband couldn't stand, not this man who'd been through a war and survived, the man who'd made his way in a strange land. And here was another man as uncomfortable with all that as he was. Sure these two could be buddies for a week. I fancy myself an observant woman, and there it was at last for me to see, as I sat on a crumbling boat dock at the foot of the set of one of my favorite movies.

Well, that was a relief, I thought. I even turned to Eileen and said, "There's got to be more to the place than this."

"Of course. Through the trees you can see buildings up there on top of the hill." Eileen turned her attention to her husband. "Honey, get us up to the top."

"The stairs lead nowhere."

Then I remembered the water runoff we'd passed. "I saw a place to go up," I said.

Frank and Vinh slapped their knees in acceptance and we all got up and I walked point this time, leading everyone back along the seawall to the cut in the trees and that groove coming down. "We can go up here," I said.

Vinh stepped in front of me and looked up the hill and said, "Okay. If you have to do this."

"There'll be no T-shirts at the top," I said. "I bet I can promise that."

Frank laughed and it looked like he was going to make a move past Vinh to lead the way, but Vinh started up the path too quickly, getting out in front and Frank hustled to follow. I looked at Eileen and we both watched the men jockeying like this for position, and then she rolled her eyes at me. We both offered the other the opportunity to go next—I wasn't all that anxious to be near them, now that I thought I understood. But Eileen finally insisted the hardest, and I went up the rut before her, the hillside squeezing at my hamstrings. I climbed with my face down for awhile and the water runoff widened, turned into something more like a path, and there were even a few flat stones along the way, like the cast and crew had used this same way up the hill.

I finally raised my eyes and the two men were about thirty meters ahead, moving pretty fast, Frank still behind. I stopped and watched them and I don't know why I noticed it, but they were remarkably quiet. They were traipsing up among dead leaves and twigs and such and yet I didn't hear them at all. There must have been something in the way they were moving that made me sensitive to this, because somehow I knew it was on their minds, as well. They were a little hunched and alert and they moved without any wasted motion, not even bobbing up and down. Then they reached the top of the rise and stopped and Frank came even with Vinh. I followed the turn of their heads and off to their left I could see a small, one-story brick structure without a front wall. They cocked their heads and looked into the gaping concrete rooms.

I put my head down and strained at my tight legs and went on up, conscious now of how much noise I was making, crunching leaves and scraping on the flat stones. I'd always wondered what it was like when Vinh was with his company out patrolling or whatever they did in the jungles. I felt suddenly like I knew. When I got to the top of this rise, I was surprised to find the men gone. The path continued on ahead, through a little open meadow and then began to climb again. I could see along it far enough to know the men hadn't gone that way.

I flexed my legs to try to stretch out my muscles and I looked around. The two men were nowhere to be seen. The two side-by-side concrete rooms gaped open to me and I glanced down the path and Eileen was struggling up, making a last effort, and then she was beside me. "Where are they?" she asked.

"I don't know."

"Frank?" Eileen's voice quavered into the still, hot air and there was no reply. There was just the sound of the distant surf, coming from over the hill ahead of us, and the buzz of some insect whisking past and then away.

I was curious about this little building. It was too basic to be anything used in the movie and then as I approached, I noticed an inner wall of tiles and the stubs of old shower heads. This was in the left-hand room, and I stepped into the room to the right as Eileen called out Frank's name again. The walls here were covered with graffiti, the profuse linking of names from floor to ceiling. Ramon and Maria, Ed and Mary, Sigmund and Katherine, on and on, a swarm of lovers touching letters, stuck by arrows, bound in by ragged marker-pen hearts. I saw a flash of color out of the corner of my eye. It was through the back window, beyond a row of low bushes. A red shirt slipping past in the trees, and I looked closer just in time to see the black shirt following.

"They're out in the back," I said to Eileen.

"Frank," she called again.

"Yes, Eileen?"

"Where are you?"

"Here I am." The voice was coming around a corner of the little building now and I looked again at all the names, running my eyes quickly around and around the wall packed with true love, and I wondered how many of these couples were still in love right this moment.

"Vinh and I were exploring out back."

"You having fun, Sweetie?" Eileen said, and there was no ridicule or irritation in her voice. It was like she was indulging an active child.

I stepped out of the lovers' room and I thought it was a shame that the front wall was broken down and the place smelled of mildew and stone dust.

Frank did not answer Eileen's little motherly question. Instead he turned to my husband and said, "You keep pretty good noise discipline there, Vinh."

"Perhaps you drowned out my mistakes."

"You weren't hearing any sounds out of this troop either," Frank said and his voice rasped a bit from Vinh's sharpness.

"Can't we go on?" Eileen said, pretty sharp herself now. "This isn't really part of the set."

Both men looked to the path tracking up and over the hill and I could feel the tension between them. Frank turned first and moved off pretty fast, and I was surprised to see Vinh follow just as fast.

Eileen cried out, "Wait for us," and this did slow Frank down and pull him into an upright position. He glanced over his shoulder and Vinh was coming up on him and it didn't seem fair to me for him to pass Frank while he was just paying attention to his wife.

So I called, "Vinh!" and my husband slowed and even stopped and turned to wait for us. Frank stopped as well, just beyond him. Eileen and I looked at each other and I didn't know exactly what was in her mind, but she was obviously noticing the same odd thing going on between the men that I was. She and I took our sweet time about getting ourselves together and strolling up the path and the men were waiting, so I let myself look around.

Things were still pretty wildly overgrown, but we could see some full buildings off to our right, set on higher ground that looked back into the bay. This was the main set, I think, the hotel run by Ava Gardner in the movie.

"Isn't that the place?" I said to Eileen, nodding to buildings.

"Maybe so. Maybe."

We looked around for a path going off in that direction but the only one we found didn't go twenty meters before it was overgrown and then just disappeared into a really nasty thicket.

"I don't see a way over there," I said to Eileen, and she was not where I expected her to be. I found her up the hill, at the crest, and she was looking off in the distance and she had her hands folded before her with the wind blowing her hair back and she looked very nice there, very contented. Like a bookplate I once had, a girl standing against a breeze on a hill. Books make you dream, I think it said, just over the place where I wrote my name, This book belongs to Trần Nam Thanh Gabrielle. I miss bookplates. You can't hold a TV show in your hand and put your bookplate inside the cover where a girl stands on a hill dreaming of a wonderful future, just like in this wonderful book.

I glanced at the men and they were shuffling their feet and sniffing the air. I climbed up beside Eileen and the view was very nice; the bay was broad and very blue; the shore over on this side was deserted, a long curve of lacey surf. Very nice. I looked at the path and it wound down the ragged hill to a crumbling two-story brick building, though this one still had its front wall. And closer to the beach was the concrete frame of a foundation, all the walls gone from this one.

"We going over the hill?" Frank said.

It was all lovely but very lonely, too, up here. There was nothing of the movie to recognize, really. No sense of Richard Burton and Elizabeth Taylor ever being here. No ghosts here at all, it seemed. Just wreckage and weeds and silence. I turned my face to the wind coming in from the ocean and I stripped off a scarf that I'd used to tie up my hair and the wind blew my hair behind me, a nice feeling, I guess, though I wouldn't kid myself or anyone else that it had any intensity, this feeling. The wind in your hair is really a thrill only for a girl who hasn't met a man yet.

I don't mean that as cynical as it sounds. I just felt a little letdown, I guess. There was a pretty snapshot up here, but no romance. That may sound odd from the woman who found romance in the muddy water spoiling the bay, but this was the mood that had suddenly come over me. I was weary of this vacation. And the men wanted nothing more than to charge over the hill. Frank was waiting for an answer and Eileen apparently wasn't going to give him one. I looked at her and her eyes were closed and I hoped that she was feeling more than I was.

"Over the hill," I said, and Frank flashed past and then Vinh, who gave me a quick glance as he went by. I knew all my husband's gestures, the subtle language of his face, all of that; I knew these things with such certainty and accuracy that it never surprised me when he sometimes seemed uncomfortable around me. But this glance of his as he went over the hill had something to it that I had not seen before and that

I did not understand. Like the startled and yet fully comprehending look he might have if he and I had been standing on the edge of a cliff and the ground had just given way and he was hanging out there in the air about to drop straight down and he and I both knew there was nothing to be done about it.

If all this sounds a little odd, well that's the way it was. I was feeling a little odd, and I sat down. I went to the edge of the hill in a bald spot in the weeds and I sat down and I tucked my legs up to my chest and I looked for a few moments at the breakers all along the shore, but I soon turned my eyes back to the men. They were winding down the path and they were moving, I knew, like they were on some patrol in some real hot battle area in Vietnam. They were just gliding, keeping low, and they were halfway down the hill, heading toward the brick building.

All of a sudden Frank pulled up and raised his hand in the air like he'd heard something. Vinh must have been watching the path at that moment because he ran right into Frank and nearly knocked him over. They were suddenly standing chest to chest and talking fast, both of them, and waving their arms.

I leaned forward and I grunted in frustration, loud enough for Eileen to get alarmed. "Are you going to be sick?" she said.

"No," I said and I guess she was still looking out to sea, dreaming about whatever it was that made her close her eyes to the breeze. I wondered just for a moment if she was thinking of Frank as he once was, or maybe somebody else altogether. But there was no shifting of my attention, really. The men were arguing and I was out of earshot and that made me angry. A Vietnamese woman never curses, especially aloud and especially in the presence of some other person, but I came very close at that moment.

I wanted to get near the action but I knew I couldn't just run down there. It would stop the words for sure. I wanted this thing to follow its own course. Then I determined to use all of my powers of observation and figure it out. And I did pretty well, I think. I started by keeping in mind the way they'd been going down the hill. Low, silently, like they were on patrol in the war. It had something to do with all that, I figured.

The men had begun to take turns talking and it was Vinh's turn at the moment. I watched his hands. It's hard to ruffle Vinh, but when he does get worked up, he has very expressive hands. His right hand flipped with its palm upturned at Frank—like, This is what you did—and then Vinh pointed up the path they'd followed. He quickly traced the path down the side of the hill—This was the way they came, down this obvious path—and then he turned back to Frank and raised both his hands and slowly brought them together and then flared them out, talking all the while, and it was like I could hear him. You led us down this path and it's the obvious place for the VC to put booby traps; I was watching the path and not you because you put us in danger by doing the obvious thing.

Meanwhile Frank had his arms folded over his chest and when Vinh finished his point, Frank opened his arms and tilted his head like he was being indulgent with a bright child. Frank made a sweeping gesture to indicate the low weeds all along the path down the hill—That area is no more safe than the other, I could sense him saying; at least you can see what there is on the path better than in the weeds. Then he turned and pointed at the two-story brick building—This was our objective; it's there that we have to be the most watchful. And Frank ended by motioning off to the trees that were tall and thick just behind the building—That's where they are; the enemy's out there in the trees.

Some of this maybe I figured out a little later from what happened, but I was pretty sure right away that this was basically what the argument was about. Who was right? I don't know. Vinh had an answer for Frank, but he crossed his arms on his chest, so I couldn't figure it out. Frank answered that, and he stuck his fists on his hips and I had lost any feeling for the conversation and I whispered "Damn," very softly.

The two men kept talking and finally they loosened up a little bit. They dropped their hands and they jangled around and Frank even laughed, a friendly, rearing-back kind of laugh. Vinh nodded and nodded again and he looked around.

I have to admit I was disappointed. It struck me as odd even at the time. It wasn't just that I had missed the argument, had only been able to guess at it, though that was certainly part of my disappointment. I'm pretty observant and I felt I'd gotten the pieces right that I'd figured out from the gestures, but there was something else going on, something even beneath the words they were speaking. I needed to hear those words, needed to turn my talent on the words themselves, looking deeper. Then Frank even cuffed Vinh on the shoulder. I said it louder: "Damn." Now they were friends again. I'd missed it all and there didn't even seem to be any hard feelings that I'd be able to observe later. Foolish men. They didn't even know how to hold a grudge.

They were gesturing. I leaned forward. Frank indicated Vinh and pointed off to the trees. He touched his own chest and swept his arm toward the sea. Then Vinh pointed at the brick building and they nodded. I didn't figure this out very quickly. It even puzzled me when they both stooped down and studied the path and separated, picking things up off the dirt and stuffing them into their pockets. This was very strange. Then Vinh stood up briefly with one of the things from the ground in his hand. He held it up and it looked like a stone, a rather large stone, and Frank came up behind him and looked too and shook his head no. He held something up and it must have been another stone, smaller. Vinh nodded and dropped the large stone and they both kept looking. But when Frank's back was turned, I saw Vinh return and pick up the big one.

I was beginning to understand. They finally had enough stones in their pockets and they approached each other once more and spoke briefly and then they stood back to back, Vinh facing the trees and Frank facing the hillside and the sea. It was like in all the old movies where two men are going to fight a duel. I wondered for a moment if that's what they were going to do, if they'd just go ten paces, turn, and throw rocks at each other.

But they had something else in mind. At some signal between them they began to walk away from each other, but they just kept walking. Frank went over the edge of the hill and disappeared. Vinh kept going until he splashed through a narrow stream and came up to the edge of the woods. I understood now that this was some kind of little war game. They were going to stalk each other or something. Maybe try to capture and control the brick building. When this hit me, I suddenly grew aware of Vinh's red shirt, how it would stand out among the trees. But, as it sometimes happens between husbands and wives, Vinh seemed to have the thought just as I did. Or maybe I sent it to him. I don't know. But he stopped at the trees and looked back, looked briefly for Frank, and when the man was not in sight, Vinh took off his red shirt and rolled it up and put it under his arm.

My husband's chest and arms are quite strong, really, and I tilted my head at seeing them suddenly like this, across a field, against those trees, the breeze coming off the bay, and I felt a little wriggle of something in me, a snakey little romantic feeling that started in my chest and then, as Vinh moved into the woods and the dark skin of his broad back faded into the shadows, the feeling slithered out of my chest and down inside me real fast and I looked out to the sea and closed my eyes.

Here I was in this little pose and if someone was watching me who knew what to look for in people, she would wonder if I was thinking of Vinh as he once was, or maybe someone else altogether. The answer was that I was thinking of neither of these. As soon as I closed my eyes I was aware only of myself; I stepped out of myself and saw me, and that was all that was in my mind. The romance was gone right away. I'm sometimes too observant for my own damn good. It should've been Vinh as he once was who I was thinking about. That would have been nice, that moment.

But instead, I remembered Eileen sitting in this same way nearby, and I opened my eyes. The hillside and the brick building and the woods were deserted. I glanced over to Eileen and she was lying on her back, her forearm over her face. She seemed to be asleep.

I looked back down the hill and that feeling of being let down that I'd had earlier came back. The whole scene in front of me kind of blurred. Even all the things that my mind knew were beautiful seemed flat all of a sudden, like a postcard you'd buy in a hurry at the airport.

But I did wonder where the men were. So I looked harder. Frank had claimed the shore and the hillside, and I figured it would be easier to spot him at this point. The slope went down and then rolled over a crest and into another slope I couldn't see, and beyond, there was the meadow with the naked foundation in the center. Farther on was another crest and another invisible slope, this one dropping down to the shore and the sea. I figured Frank was on one of the far slopes and I waited for a few moments and he was staying out of sight and so I peered into the woods where Vinh had gone.

It seemed like a pretty silly game to me. I wasn't sure what they were doing. They weren't exactly stalking each other, or they probably would've both gone into the woods. But maybe they were stalking. Frank had to defend his earlier actions out here in the open, going down the path and all. Maybe he was the force that had taken the beach—like those first Marines coming ashore in Đà Nẵng or something. And Vinh was the other side—would he actually play the part of the Vietcong, who he hated? Perhaps. Perhaps if this American had given him no choice, he would play the Vietnamese no matter what the politics. I didn't know. And I guess it's important to realize that I didn't know what Vinh would do in this situation. The man in the woods was hidden from me, too.

Then I saw Frank. His black shirt and shorts would have been good camouflage in the shade of the trees, but against the meadow he was very clearly visible. He was moving in that low glide of his and he crouched behind the stone foundation. He peeked up and looked in the direction of the brick building, which was maybe a hundred and fifty meters across the meadow and up a roll of the hill. I didn't know what he was waiting for, if the point was to go take the building. Vinh was nowhere in sight, and I didn't know what Vinh was waiting for either.

The truth be told, my husband was in the airborne, but I think he was mostly back at the base camp giving orders and organizing supplies and looking after paperwork. He is a businessman, always has been and I guess he always will be. And Frank said himself he was a helicopter mechanic. These men weren't fighters, in spite of their nearness to a war.

I scanned the tree line and then I saw Vinh. He was sliding around a tree, and it struck me that I was watching this old movie. These men were crouching and hiding and sneaking around like all the old movie actors in all the old war and spy and detective movies ever made, all those wonderful old unreal movies that made my hours after midnight so peaceful. Vinh was a heavy sleeper and I had good hearing and so I could watch these films in my bed. I would pull the sheet up to my nose and lie there on my Posturepedic mattress and I was in the United States of America in an era of peace and prosperity in spite of the deficits and I could hear the wind outside as a Louisiana summer storm blew in and I was safe and I was cozy and I was watching a whole world of men with steel pots or fedoras on their heads and they were in the middle of big trouble, but boy, could they sneak around and glide around and they were never going to get hurt by anything, you knew that for sure.

Vinh slipped out of the woods and I realized Frank didn't see him because the brick building was between the two of them. Vinh stood by the little stream and he looked up to the top of the second floor of the building and sighted from there down to his feet on the bank of the stream. Then he laid his rolled red shirt next to a rock and he crouched low and stepped over the flowing water.

I looked at Frank and he was moving. He was going around the far side of the foundation in his low crouch and he was heading, I guessed, for the building. Meanwhile, Vinh was edging his way around the near end, his neck craned hard to his left so he could catch early sight of Frank if he should suddenly appear. But Frank was circling wide now to approach from the other direction, and so the men were still unaware of each other.

Vinh made it to the side staircase that led to the upper floor. He climbed it quickly but he slowed abruptly and ducked down as he neared the top. Then he peeked over to make sure that Frank wasn't already there, and when he saw that the place was deserted, I swear I could see his body actually ripple in delight. He scrambled up on top of the building, went to the back edge so he could view his red shirt by the stream, and he dug into his pocket and placed some of his stones beside him.

Frank was highstepping down a slope and he disappeared as soon as I saw this. I waited, and then a few moments later, his head popped up at the crest of the hill at the far side of the brick building. The head disappeared again and then popped up once more.

"Aren't they lovely?" This was Eileen's voice. Needless to say, the sentiment surprised me. I turned to her and she was still on her back but she had moved her forearm off her eyes. She was looking up into the sky. I followed her gaze. There were some high, white clouds.

"That one is the head of a pony," she said. The head of a pony. Do I sound like that sometimes? I bet I do. Eileen and I probably respond to the same things. Not even the head of a *horse*. She saw a sweet little pony. Of course. A lonesome little pony and the little girl makes a long distance phone call to the pony and it isn't lonesome anymore. If they filmed that and put it on between the soaps, I'd weep at that one too. The little pony shaking its forelock in delight as someone holds the phone up to its ear. I'm a sucker for any of that. But at this moment the pony struck me as pretty uninspired. Dumb, even, seeing a pony in the cloud and getting dreamy-voiced over it.

But I said, "It sure does" as sincerely as I could and I turned to see Frank spank across the grass and throw himself—out of my sight now—against the far wall of the building. Vinh raised his head and looked over his shoulder. He had probably heard the impact. I waited and I expected to see Frank ease his way around the corner and come along the front wall. But he was apparently suspicious of the front, because I waited and waited and so did Vinh, though he eventually turned his face back to his shirt at the stream.

Finally I saw Frank. Vinh tipped me off by suddenly lowering his head. A moment later I saw Frank slip up and press himself against a tree at the back of the building. He was looking toward the woods now, and I wondered if he saw the shirt. Even as I thought this, Frank did a double take. A real double take, a little bit like the cartoon characters, though Frank's eyes didn't bug out. His face extended forward and he looked at the red color, and connections were going off in his head.

He looked all around and he studied the tree line carefully and then he dug into his pocket and armed himself with a rock—I could imagine him whispering to himself, Lock and load, troop. And Vinh was all this time sneaking little glances over the edge of the roof, his rock already in his hand. I wondered if it was the big rock that Frank had made him throw down. I figured it wasn't, however. Not at this point. Vinh even held the stone up briefly, perhaps to see if it was the roundest one, the one he could throw most accurately, and it didn't look from this distance like the big one. I was glad. I was sure if he used the big one that Frank would get very angry.

Frank was slung low and creeping up to the stream, eyeing the red shirt very carefully. He stopped just across the stream and he looked at it and he cocked his head and finally he even straightened up. I don't know what he was thinking. So it was Vinh's shirt. Did he expect that to help him find the man? Obviously Vinh wasn't in the shirt. But I think Frank was very pleased with himself for finding it. It seemed meaningful to him. Then Vinh's stone hit him right on the point of his left shoulder.

Frank spun around and I could hear his curse even from this distance. Vinh immediately jumped up and raised his arms in the air in victory. Frank rubbed his shoulder and then he darted away, behind a tree, and then to another and then he ran to the near side of the building and pulled up and pressed himself against the wall. Vinh was clearly agitated. He thought he had already won. He flapped his arms in exasperation and I could see Frank was ready for more war. He had a stone in his hand as if to throw it. He looked up above him and dashed to the foot of the steps and again pressed back against the wall. Vinh called out something that I could not hear. Probably Frank's name. Probably telling him that the little game was over.

But Frank was creeping up the steps and obviously wasn't answering my husband, and finally Vinh dug in his pocket for more stones and moved into the center of the roof. He figured that Frank was on the way up. This time Vinh looked very carefully at the contents of his pocket and I knew even before he held it up that he had the big stone.

I stood up, afraid for them both. But there was nothing I could do, of course. Frank figured he was just wounded, since Vinh had only hit him in the shoulder. Vinh figured the war was over and was really angry when it turned out that it wasn't. I wanted to call out to them, but I could find no words. This was a distant event, farther from me even than the Hollywood studio-set wars I watched from under the covers. It was as far from me as my husband was far from me; as far as that secret, silent part of him that was so difficult a thing between us.

Frank stopped just before his head was ready to show itself to Vinh. My husband was now poised in the center of the roof with the big rock in his right hand and cocked back over his shoulder, ready to throw. Frank waited and I could feel him mustering his strength, focusing on one leap into the open, his own rocks flying. Just like in the movies. But for a moment I wondered if Vinh would kill him. If Vinh would fire at the first sight of the man's head and he would hit him in the temple with the big rock and that would be the end. I could not draw a breath. "How lovely," Eileen sighed.

Then Frank clambered up the final few steps, very slowly, it seemed to me, although his legs and arms were obviously straining to make this a lightning strike. Hold, hold, I cried in my mind to Vinh's arm. Don't aim at the head.

Frank's first stone or two flew wildly past Vinh and Vinh did wait, he waited and set himself and he threw the large stone and it hit Frank in the pit of the stomach. I knew this because Frank doubled over and then there was a moment of suspension. Frank's knees bent and he put one hand on the surface of the roof so he didn't fall over, and Vinh stayed in the crouch he'd assumed after the throw. The two men were suddenly frozen there, like props left over from the movie.

"How truly lovely," Eileen said.

Then Frank lifted his face a little and I guess he saw the stone that Vinh had used. It must have been lying there before him. He looked up at Vinh and I think he said something, probably some angry name, and then he lunged forward and Vinh tried to sidestep him but only got partly out of the way and Frank glanced off him, scooping wide with his arms, but Vinh was turning away and slipped Frank's grasp, although he did fall backwards, even as Frank spun and hurtled on and also fell on the rooftop.

I hoped that that was the end of it, but both men bounced to their feet very quickly and there seemed to be no question of what to do now. They rushed at each other immediately and Vinh, being smaller, got under Frank's grasp and he butted Frank in his stomach with his head. Frank fell backwards and Vinh fell on top of him and they rolled over immediately, first Frank on top and then Vinh, and arms were flailing and legs and the two men were fighting hard.

"A great white duck," Eileen said. "I had one just like it when I was a child."

I looked into the sky and sure enough, there was a white cloud passing overhead that looked like a duck. You could see its bill and its long neck and even its wings.

I sat down and chose curtain number three—the sea. I glanced at the men, still rolling around on the roof, and I chose the sea. The sea was bright and flat and it crumpled along the shore and I just watched that for now. How silly it had been for me to think I'd understood them. They neither of them could stomach the feel-good culture. But that was hardly all of the feeling between them. They had shared something once, something important—rage, fear, the urge to violence, just causes, life and death. They'd both felt those things in service of the same war. And neither of them wanted to let go of all that. But even finding *this* connection between them didn't really explain everything.

Don't ask me what did. I watched mostly the sea for the next few minutes and when I finally peeked back in the direction of the brick building. I saw them sitting about ten feet apart, their backs to each other, their legs spread and their arms lolling in exhaustion. Frank was facing the woods and my husband was facing the sea. He seemed to be looking very intently out to sea. Just like I was.

We took separate cabs, the two couples, back to the beautiful Fiesta Vallarta Hotel. Vinh had come up the hill first and he was a mess. He had forgotten his red shirt, but he wouldn't have been comfortable wearing it over all the abrasions anyway. Eileen screamed when she saw him. "It's all right," I told her. "They're both all right." I didn't say any more. I just went with Vinh along the path and left Eileen on the hilltop ready to kill Frank, I think. She was already assuming the worst.

I didn't say anything to Vinh as we walked back to the beach or rode in the taxicab or crossed our hotel lobby and entered the elevator or even when we first stepped into the room. Nor did he say anything to me. When our door clicked shut and we were out of the eye of the public, I turned to him, but he averted his face and dipped his head and I knew he could say nothing about this anyway. Still, I yearned to know what it was that he felt, what he may have learned.

He said, "I'm going to wash up."

"Do you need some help?"

"No," he said. "Thank you."

I nodded and he stepped into the bathroom and closed the door.

I crossed the room and the curtains ruffled before the open balcony doors. It was getting on to late afternoon now and the light looked very nice on the floor beneath the curtains and so I opened them. The sunlight was suddenly thrown against the wall and the shadow of a potted plant on the balcony was pressed there, too, like it was trying to sneak in without anyone noticing. A silly impression, a hangover from the scene I'd witnessed at Mismaloya. I sat on the end of the bed and looked at the wall. The light was really very nice. A pale, buttery yellow, and the plant dipped and rose there, the broad, shapely leaves of a croton.

I'm not sure why all this was occupying my mind. Maybe because of Vinh's silence. Maybe it was the weariness that had come over me again. All this fresh air, hilltops and beaches—I wasn't used to it. It made me want to sleep. I thought to lie down on the bed, but I heard the water running in the bathroom and I waited. I sat on the end of the bed and I waited, and the shadow of the croton crept across the wall and then at last the bathroom door opened and Vinh stepped out.

He was dressed in gray slacks and sneakers and one of the short sleeved dress shirts that he usually wears to work in the hot Louisiana summers. His hair was wet and combed down neatly and the battle showed on his face only in a dull red abrasion the size of a silver dollar on his cheek. He looked at me for a moment and I strained to see some clue there of something, anything. His mouth was relaxed but unsmiling. His eyes were steady on me and all I could sense was that whatever he had felt this afternoon was not yet put aside. Then he moved to me and stood over me where I sat on the bed. I felt I should stand up before him; perhaps he would take me in his arms. I was about to do that, but before I could, his hand came out and brushed a lock of hair off my face.

That was all. Was he trying to say that since he was cleaned up now, I should pull myself together as well? I didn't know. Then I thought there was something nice about his hand, but before I could identify it, he took the hand back and said, "I'm going out."

I nodded and he turned and he was across the room and out the door quickly, closing it behind him with the softest of clicks. I lay back on the bed and looked at the ceiling and I wished it was a sky full of clouds, full of ponies and ducks, and I put my forearm over my eyes. But the thinking did not stop. Where was he going? I had lived with my husband for nearly twenty years, and I should have been able to guess where he was going after the events of this day. At first I thought he was going to Frank's room to make things up with him. But that didn't feel right. Perhaps tomorrow, running into them as if by accident in the lobby. That would be the time to shake hands. My husband would not seek the man out at this moment.

Then the thought struck me that from all of this purging of the war, he was now free to do something special. There was tenderness in his hand when it scolded my stray lock of hair. I thought that perhaps Vinh was going down to get into a taxi and go to Liz and Dick's bridge and buy me a copa de oro, a cup of gold. He had denied me a flower earlier and all of a sudden he realized it; he had even denied me that flower in chorus with the man who he went on to fight to some resolution on this day. I tried to imagine Vinh coming through the door and bringing the flower and putting it into my hair, the very hair that he had arranged before he left.

But this was the thought of a woman who could weep over television commercials. I realized that very quickly, lying there alone on the bed in the Fiesta Vallarta Hotel. And then I thought that Vinh would never return. He had walked out of this room and he had decided never to come back to me. He had put his passport and his ticket into the pocket of his gray slacks and he had walked out forever.

This I believed for perhaps ten minutes, and they were the worst ten minutes of my life in America. I suddenly knew that it was I who had withdrawn from Vinh. I had embraced this culture with such intensity that it isolated me from him, made it impossible for him to find a way to touch me anymore. Even Frank, this poor American living in the past, knew enough to pull away from the excesses of the empty-headed culture around him. That must have been terrible for Vinh, that even this man who he would fight was more accessible than his own wife. I was, for about ten minutes, as black and still as the water that ran beneath the river shacks of Saigon. My skin felt like it could be wiped away with the slightest touch, like the skin of the leper beggars who did not even have a river shack. Could I not remember these things?

But then something in me said, Wait. It's not just me. Vinh, too, has been distracted by the American culture. He is a seller of Swedish meatballs and cocktail franks, after all. He wears his dark gray suit and he studies his spreadsheets and he flies here and there carrying a leather briefcase with all the other Americans and he makes much money from food that people eat with toothpicks. But in Vietnam, in the war, there was passion. And there is a passion still inside him. He did fight with this man today.

I lay there for a few minutes more and I don't know what it was, exactly, that moved me to think about stepping onto the balcony. The sunlight on the wall had darkened into peach and I stood up and faced the breeze from the bay. It was lovely out there, with the sun nearing the horizon. A tight little family of pelicans drifted past and I moved through the sliding doors and leaned on the balustrade. I watched the pelicans wheel off to their right and head out to sea.

But my eyes stayed with the shore and a parasail rising there. I sent my body out to float with the sailor. I didn't need to be on the parachute myself; I could stand here and let myself separate from my body, from all the strangeness that had come upon me, that made up my life, and I could glide in the long angle of this sun and feel at peace. And so I watched the parasail swing around and head this way. The chute was red and yellow and it was as high as my balcony now and I closed my eyes briefly, remembering the green wake of the boat far below me, and I rode over those waves smoother than any ship.

I opened my eyes and the parasailor was drawing almost even with my hotel, right at my eye level, and I of course expected to see the dangling bare legs of someone in a bathing suit. But these legs were clothed in long gray slacks. And my eyes went instantly to the face and it was Vinh. He was holding the ropes and at first I wondered if he was being an airborne soldier again. But it was very much different from that. I had failed to understand his face when he was standing before me, but this much I could tell now as he glided past me strapped to a parachute. He was looking down with the calmest of pleasures. The angle of his head, lolled to the side like I was scratching his neck up under his ear like I used to; the loose hold of his hands on the ropes with one elbow even tucked comfortably into his side; the slight boyish kick in his legs; all this told me he was enjoying himself. He was high above Puerto Vallarta and the sea and he was happy now.

And finally he was eye to eye with me. The boat went on down the coast, into the glare of the sun, but then it swung around and when Vinh came past once more he turned his face to the Fiesta Vallarta Hotel and he saw me on the balcony and he smiled. I could see the smile very clearly, and when I waved at him, he raised his hand and threw me a kiss. He drifted past and I looked out to the setting sun. Just like in the movies. A beautiful sunset at the end of this very strange day. Night was coming on and my husband was about to return to earth. And so was I.

Contributors' Notes

HENRY ALCALAY lives in New York City. He has published articles and short fiction and is at work on a novel.

STEVEN BARTHELME has published essays, poems and stories in the *New York Times, Los Angeles Times, Elle Décor, Southern Review, North American Review, Epoch, Boulevard, Denver Quarterly, Yale Review, Pushcart* and elsewhere. A collection called *And He Tells the Little Horse the Whole Story* was issued by the Johns Hopkins University Press. He teaches at the University of Southern Mississippi.

AARON BALKAN wrote "Something that Hasn't Happened Yet" in May, 1997. He currently lives in New York City.

MARK BLICKLEY is a widely published short-story writer, essayist, and playwright currently anthologized in *The Best Men's Stage Monologues* of 1998. "The World's Greatest Saxophone Player" grew out of a frightening realization that as the century slides to a close, his life-long belief in Art as Religion can no longer sustain him.

JODI BLOOM lives and works in Washington, D. C. where she and her husband own a graphic design and Mac consulting firm. Her fiction has been published in *Happy, Gargoyle, Membrane, Spelunker Flophouse, The Sulphur River Literary Review, The Washington Review, Wordwrights*, and other literary journals. "TripleX," like most of her stories, came about when a character's voice began to chatter away in the author's head, in this case giving articulation to her own fascination with the potential for morality within segments of society that we traditionally view as entirely immoral.

ALLIE BULLOCK-KAGAMASTER created "Swamp Princess" through a series of workshops, first as a three-page thriller, subsequently blown into a screenplay to flesh the characters out—several revisions later—into short story form. The premise determines that our deepest thicket of fears can keep us from true passion or deliver us into adventurous love—giving up a jungle for a swamp. She completed her first novel, *The Avenue*, about a little girl madly in love with her parents who are breaking up circa early 60s Manhattan suburbs. Currently, she is at work on a second "ghostly" biographical novel titled *Fred Bullock's Granddaughter* about a generational tie twixt her British grandfather, born in the nineteeth century, known as Northcliffe's Crown Prince Reporter, celebrated for beating the world on the Titanic recovery story, the Wright Brothers' prototype, and the Lindburgh kidnapping. She is also preparing a non-fiction children's picture book about movie monsters titled *They're Killing My Monster.* In addition, she is working on a political love story based on her poetry collection, *The Kiss of Poland.*

FREDERICK BUSCH, Edgar Fairchild Professor of Literature at Colgate University, has published twenty-three books, including thirteen novels and six collections of stories. His works include *Closing Arguments, Sometimes I Live in the Country, Harry and Catherine, Girls,* a novel based on his widely anthologized story, "Ralph the Duck," and *The Night Inspector.* His awards include the PEN/Malamud Award and the National Jewish Book Award, and Mr. Busch has held Guggenheim, Woodrow Wilson, NEA, and James Merrill Fellowships.

ROBERT OLEN BUTLER has published nine novels and two volumes of short fiction, one of which, *A Good Scent from a Strange Mountain,* won the 1993 Pulitzer Prize for Fiction. His most recent novel is *Mr. Spaceman.* His stories have appeared widely in such publications as *The New Yorker, Esquire, The Paris Review,* and *Harper's* and have been included in four annual editions *The Best American Short Stories* and six annual editions of *New Stories from the South.* A recipient of both a Guggenheim Fellowship in fiction and a National Endowment for the Arts grant, he also won the Richard and Hinda Rosenthal Foundation Award from the American Academy of Arts and Letters. He teaches creative writing at McNeese State University in Lake Charles, Louisiana, where he lives with his wife, the novelist and playwright Elizabeth Dewberry.

ALAN CHEUSE is the author, among other works of fiction, of the novels *The Light Possessed* and *The Grandmothers' Club.* His latest book is *Lost and Old Rivers,* a collection of stories. Cheuse lives in Washington, D.C., serves as book commentator for National Public Radio's evening news-magazine "All Things Considered," and teaches in the writing program at George Mason University.

JANICE DAUGHARTY was born in Echols county, Georgia, where she has lived for fifty years. Second in a family of seven children, she graduated from Echols County High School, and several years later attended Valdosta State University as an English major. She has two daughters, a son, and three granddaughters. She began writing fiction in 1982, and has had stories published in various literary journals.

MAGGIE DAWSON is a student of physical anthropology at the University of California, Santa Cruz. Her interests include studying primate evolution, dancing, playing dress-up, green growing things, The Forest, and reveling in the opposability of her thumb.

HARRIET DOERR was born in Pasadena, California in 1910. She attended Smith College in 1927, but received her B. A. from Stanford university in 1977, where she was accepted into the creative Writing Program. Her first novel, *Stones for Ibarra,* won the 1985 National Book Award for First Fiction, the Bay Area Book Reviewers Award, the Godal Medal of the Commonwealth Club of California, and the American Academy of Arts and Letters Harold D. Vursell Award. Her second novel, *Consider this Señora,* was a national bestseller.

MARK DONNELLY appears in *The Best Men's Stage Monologues of 1998.* He was commissioned by Ensemble Studio Theatre in Manhattan to write a play on physicist Richard Feynman for the Alfred P. Sloan Science and Technology Project. His poetry has recently appeared in *Minimus* and in *Columbia Publications* anthologies. The life and death of his close friend Larry Pardue served as the inspiration for "Old Blue."

STUART DYBEK is the author of two collections of stories: *The Coast of Chicago* and *Childhood and Other Neighborhoods* and a collection of poems, *Brass Knuckles.* His work has been published in numerous magazines including *The New Yorker, Atlantic, Harper's, Paris Review, Antaeus, Poetry, TriQuarterly, Ploughshares, The New York Times,* and other publications. His work has also been translated into several languages, and is frequently anthologized. His awards include a Guggenheim Fellowship and two fellowships from the NEA. He has also received four O. Henry Prizes.

LUCINDA EBERSOLE is the author of a novel, *Death in Equality.* She has edited six books including *Mondo Barbie,* and *Women, Creativity and the Arts.* She is an editor at *Gargoyle* magazine and owns Atticus Books & Music in Alexandria, Virginia.

DEBORAH EISENBERG's most recent collection of short fiction is *All Around Atlantis.* She lives in New York city and teaches at the University of Virginia.

EDWARD FALCO's work has appeared in the *Atlantic,* the *Georgia Review, TriQuarterly,* the *Virginia Quarterly Review* and many other places including *Best American Short Stories, 1995.*

MAVIS GALLANT was born in Montreal and worked as a journalist at *The Standard* before giving up newspaper work and moving to Europe to devote herself to fiction. After extensive travel, she settled in Paris, where she still resides.

ANNIE LA GANGA — At the time of publication, there was no available biographical information on this writer.

MICHAEL GUISTA has published in *American Short Fiction, Quarterly West, Prairie Schooner, The North American Review* and other journals. He is currently working on a non-fiction book *Looking for God* and a novel *A Little Death.* He won a fiction fellowship for 1996-1997 from the California Arts Council.

AD HUDLER has had stories and essays published in *Mississippi Review*, *Mid-American Review* and *The Christian Science Monitor*. "Por Favor" was published in the *Wisconsin Review*. A Colorado native, he lives in Macon, Georgia, with his wife, Carol, and their eight-year-old daughter, Haley Joy. On writing "Por Favor," he says: "I have never been a waiter, I've never been Hispanic, but one day Rosa just barreled into my head and wanted to talk, so I sat down and wrote her story. It took me two hours. I still don't know who she is — but I like her very much. I hope to meet her some day."

KYLE JARRARD is an editor at the *International Herald Tribune* in Paris. His first novel, "Over There," was published by Baskerville in 1997, and his second novel, *Down in There*, will be published by Steerforth in 2000. His short stories and poems have appeared in various magazines, including the *North American Review, Mississippi Review, Frank, Eclectica, Rain City Review, Pharos, Descant, New Orleans Review* and *American Way.*

VICTORIA LANCELOTTA was born and raised in Baltimore, Maryland, before driving south a few years back and winding up in Hattiesburg, Mississippi. Her fiction has appeared in *Glimmer Train*, *The Threepenny Review*, the *Mississippi Review Web*, and other magazines. She has been a resident of the MacDowell Colony and the Djerassi Resident Artists' Program and a visiting scholar at the 1997 Breadloaf Writers' Conference. She is the fiction editor of the *Georgetown Review.*

MIKE MAGGIO is a poet and fiction writer currently living in Virginia. His work has appeared in *Synaesthetic, Apalachee Quarterly, Live Poets, Gypsy* and many others. He is the author of two collections of poetry, *Oranges From Palestine* (Mardi Gras Press, 1996) and *Your Secret is Safe With Me* (Black Bear Publications, 1988). The concept for "Letters From Inside" came while he was living in Saudi Arabia during the Gulf War. During this time, information was tightly controlled, and daily life was a surreal tableau of constantly conflicting stimuli.

WENDELL MAYO is author of four books of fiction: a story collection, *Centaur of the North* (Arte Público Press, 1996; 2nd edition, 1999), winner of the Aztlán Prize and finalist in the Violet Crown Book Awards and the Associated Writing Programs Award Series in Short Fiction; a novel-in-stories, *In Lithuanian Wood* (White Pine Press, 1999); *B. Horror and Other Stories* (Livingston Press, 1999); and Paukštis Giesmininkas (English: Songbird), translated by Diana Alionienė, for publication in Lithuania by Ceklis Press (forthcoming). His short stories have appeared widely in over seventy magazines and anthologies, including the *Yale Review*, *Harvard Review*, *Missouri Review*, *Indiana Review*, and *Prairie Schooner*. He has been awarded lectureships seven times by the Ministry of Education of the former-Soviet Republic of Lithuania. He is recipient of a 2000-2001 National Endowment for the Arts Fellowship and teaches at creative writing at Bowling Green State University.

JULIE A. MCCRACKEN's stories have appeared in a number of small magazines, including *Other Voices*; *The New Delta Review*; *Passager* (University of Baltimore); in the 1993 and 1994 annual *Side Show*; *Sidewalks; The Lynx Eye,* which nominated a story for The Pushcart Prize; *The Dickinson Review* (1997); *Earth's Daughters* (1999), and *The Onset Review* (1999). A story was performed at the Zebra Crossing Theater in Chicago, and non-fiction pieces have appeared in *The Chicago Reader*, a weekly newspaper.

DEENA METZGER is a writer and healer. Her most recent books include: a novel, *What Dinah Thought* and two books of poetry, *Looking For the Faces of God*, and *A Sabbath Among the Ruins*. She teaches writing in Los Angeles and at workshops around the country. She has two sons, is married to writer/healer Michael Ortiz Hill and lives at the end of the road with Michael and the wolves, Isis and Akasha.

JOAN MÖBIUS lives in the California high desert with her husband and her horse. Möbius is her real name.

DENNIS MUST is editor-founder of *Flying Horse*, an alternative literary journal. His plays have been performed Off-Off Broadway, and he has published work in *Writers' Forum, Salt Hill Journal, Sun Dog-The Southeast Review, Rosebud, Southern Indiana Review, Red Rock Review, Sou'wester, RE:AL, Blue Moon Review, CrossConnect,* and many other literary journals and anthologies. A collection of his stories, *Banjo Grease* (Creative Arts), will be published in spring of 2000. He resides in Massachusetts with his wife and two teenage daughters.

RICHARD PEABODY is the founding editor of *Gargoyle* magazine, co-editor of the Mondo Series (*Mondo Barbie, Mondo Elvis*, et al.), and the editor of *A Different Beat: Writings by Women of the Beat Generation*. His most recent book of poems is *Mood Vertigo*. His most recent book of stories is *Open Joints on Bridge*. He lives in Arlington, VA with his wife Margaret Grosh.

GARY JOHN PERCESEPE is a former fiction editor at the *Antioch Review*. A native New Yorker, he was a student of T. Coraghessan Boyle (back when he was just Tom) in high school, and has studied with William H. Gass and Mary Grimm. The author of four books in philosophy, he has a novel in progress as well as a new book on postmodern theory, *Beyond Suspicion*. His fiction, essays, and poems have appeared in the *Mississippi Review Web Edition*, *Enterzone*, and other places. He teaches at Wittenberg University and has a bird named Romeo and a cat named That Baby.

PETER PRYOR is the former managing editor, editor and editor-at-large of the entertainment newspaper *Daily Variety*. He lives, writes poetry and fiction, edits books and flies sailplanes in Southern California.

Nicole Louise Reid has won awards for her fiction and poetry from the F. Scott Fitzgerald Literary Conference, *Antiem Review*, *Georgetown Review* and George Mason University's Creative Writing program where she is completing her M. F. A. Her work has appeared in *Green Hills Literary Lantern*, *South Dakota Review*, *The Baltimore Review* and *Isle*. She is currently working on her first collection of short stories, as well as editing an anthology of stories about redheads.

Robert Reid has published short stories, essays and plays in *Confrontation: The Literary Journal of Long Island University*, *Poems and Plays*, *International Third World Studies Journal and Review*, *American Culture and Literature* (Published by Hacettepe University in Ankara, Turkey), *The Prague Revue*, *the Annual Czech Language Anthology of the Jama Cultural Foundation* (Prague, Czech Republic), *Fiction and Drama: The Literary Journal of The National Cheng Kung University* (Taiwan), *Anyone is Possible* (Red Hen Press), i.e. magazine, *The Acorn*, *Breakfast All Day* (Dieppe, France) and *The CLA Journal*.

John Rybicki has had poems and stories appear in *The North American Review*, *Quarterly West*, *Northwest Review*, *The Quarterly*, *Yankee*, and others. His first book of poems, *Traveling at High Speeds*, is out on New Issues Press, foreword by Rick Bass. He lives in Richland, Michigan, swings a hammer, and teaches Creative Writing to buy the time to write. He currently lives in Delton, Michigan.

Miriam Sagan is predominantly a poet. Her poetry books include *The Art of Love: New and Selected Poems* (La Alameda) and *True Body* (Parallax Press). Her most recent book is *Dirty Laundry: 100 Days in a Zen Monastery* (La Alameda, 1997) a joint diary written with her late husband Robert Winson. Editor of New Mexico *Poetry Renaissance* (Red Crane, with Sharon Niederman) and *Another Desert: Jewish Poetry of New Mexico* (forthcoming, Sherman Asher, with Joan Logghe). She teaches writing in Santa Fe and nationally.

Greg Sanders lives and works in New York City. His short stories have appeared in various magazines, including *The Mississippi Review*, *WV*, and *Timeout Net Books*.

Hart Schulz teaches and has been teaching writing for sixteen years, primarily at California State University Northridge. Hart was born in Berlin and came to America in 1960. He is currently working on a collection of thematically related stories called "Driving Home Alone." His most recent publication of fiction is in *ONTHEBUS*, a piece of experimental fiction called "Eucalyptus." He has a book of poetry, *Wesly* (Anacapa Press, 1984).

Lore Segal's novels include *Other People's Houses* and *Her First American*. Among her books for children are *Tell Me a Mitzi*, *The Story of Mrs. Lovewright and Purrless her Cat* and translations from the Grimms and the Bible.

FLOYD SKLOOT is the author of three novels, *Pilgrim's Harbor* (1992), *Summer Blue* (1994) and *The Open Door* (1997), as well as a collection of essays about the illness experience, *The Night-Side* (1996) and a collection of poetry, *Music Appreciation* (1994). Skloot's work has appeared in *The Atlantic Monthly, Harper's, Poetry, The American Scholar, Virginia Quarterly Review, Hudson Review, Salmagundi, New England Review, Shenandoah, Sewanee Review, Southern Review*, and was included in *The Best American Essays of 1993.* He was born in Brooklyn, N. Y., in 1947 and lives in Amity, Oregon, with his wife, Beverly Hallberg, in a small round house Beverly built herself in the middle of twenty hilly acres of woods. He has been disabled since 1988.

DAVID STARKEY in an assistant professor of English at North Central College and has published several collections of poetry with small presses; the most recent is *Open Mike Night at the Cabaret Voltaire* (Kings Estate, 1996). He is also editor of *Teaching Writing Creatively* (Boynton/Cook-Heinemann) and co-editor of *Smokestacks and Skyscrapers: An Anthology of Chicago Literature* (Loyola). His fiction has appeared in *The American Literary Review, BlackWater Review, Illinois Review, Rhino, Rio Grande Review*, and other publications.

TOBIAS WOLFF's books include the memoirs *This Boy's Life* and *In Pharoah's Army*; the short novel *The Barracks Thief*; and three collections of stories, *In the Garden of the North American Martyrs, Back in the World*, and most recently, *The Night in Question.* He has also edited several anthologies, among them *Best American Short Stories 1994, A Doctor's Visit: The Sort Stories of Anton Chekov*, and *The Vintage Book of Contemporary American Short Stories.* His work had been translated widely and has received numerous awards, including the PEN/Faulkner Award, *The Los Angeles Times* Book Award, and the Rea Award for the Short Story. He teaches at Stanford University.